ZEN
and xenophobia

JON DOWNES
what happened after the song of Panne

Typeset by Jonathan Downes,
Cover and Layout by SPiderKaT for CFZ Communications
Using Microsoft Word 2000, Microsoft Publisher 2000, Adobe Photoshop CS.

First published in Great Britain by CFZ Press

CFZ Press
Myrtle Cottage
Woolsery
Bideford
North Devon
EX39 5QR

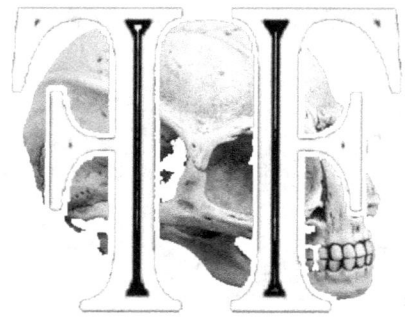

© CFZ MMXVIII

ISBN: 978-1-909488-56-4

For Steve Rider, Kev Rowland and Charlie

"We can't do anything to change the world until capitalism crumbles. In the meantime we should all go shopping to console ourselves."

Banksy

"We had no lessons to do, and we were thus free to attend to any adventures which came along. Adventures are the real business of life. The rest is only in-betweenness—what Albert's uncle calls padding. He is an author."

Oswald Bastable

Pan
O goat-foot God of Arcady!
This modern world is gray and old,
And what remains to us of thee?....
Then blow some trumpet loud and free,
And give thine oaten pipe away,
Ah, leave the hills of Arcady !
This modern world hath need of thee!

Oscar Wilde (1854–1900)

I am not a hero, I never wanted to be a hero, and I have never had any intention of being a hero. I don't like heroes and the inevitable posturing that accompanies them. All I want to do is to be left alone to get on with what remains of my life in peace and quiet. So why don't you all fuck off?

Jonathan Downes, c. 2016

Διόνυσος
Diónysos

Plea In Mitigation

About twenty years ago, when the vast majority of my disposable income came from writing bollocks about unidentified flying objects for the plethora of UFO magazines in the UK that sprung up as a result of the huge popularity of the *X-Files*, I received a rather tawdry novel from a publisher whom I thought really should have known better. It was written by somebody who had quite a reputation within the UFO field, and was prefaced with a tagline claiming that, or at least *hinting* that, the events in the book were true, but by presenting them as fiction he had managed to circumvent the Official Secrets Act, yadda yadda yadda. I didn't believe it then, and I don't believe it now. And I'm certainly not going to do the same thing.

Some of the stuff in this book is perfectly true, and you might be surprised to find out how much. But I ain't telling. Other bits are just shit that I made up!

The annoying thing about real life is that there are never any convenient beginnings or ends. In the opening chapter to the magnificent *The Otterbury Incident* by C. Day Lewis (1948), the main protagonist and narrator bemoans the fact that he doesn't know where to start the story, musing that he could have gone back to the beginning of the Second World War, (the book is set a year or two before it was written) and he even makes a case for it going back as far as the time of the Romans, until he finds a compromise that satisfies him.

Cecil Day Lewis was Poet Laureate from 1968 until his death in 1972, whereas my poetry is mostly doggerel of the "'There was once a girl from Nantucket..." variety, and I would never presume to be anything like as good a writer as Lewis was. But in a funny sort of way, I have the same problem. Because real life doesn't work the way it does in books, and beginnings, middles and ends are not only not very clearly delineated, but - basically - it could be argued that everything is 'middles'.

Three years ago, I wrote a book called *The Song of Panne*, which told the story of how my dear, long suffering wife Corinna and I ended up having a hairy humanoid forest Godling (to steal Kipling's nomenclature) living in the airing cupboard in what used to be my father's dressing room. You can take it as fiction if you like, or you can believe every word I say. Believe it or not, it truly doesn't matter to me one way or another. This book continues the story roughly from where it left off, although the vast majority of it tells the story of a few days in the Autumn of 2015, and explains some of the things left hanging in the first book. I would like to think that you can read this book as a standalone volume, although - as an impecunious author with wife, family, animals and forest Godling to support - I could always do with the cash if you would like to buy the previous book.

Although some of the characters in the book are real (whatever that means), in order to protect my kneecaps, it is probably better if you assume that everybody here except for me and Corinna is completely made up.

Because of the aforementioned complexity of life, the universe, and everything, I decided to pepper the original volume with footnotes (including a footnote to explain what a footnote is[*]), mostly because it amused me (and because I like footnotes). I have done the same in this volume, for much the same reasons. You can read them if you like, or ignore them, depending on your point of view.

I would warn you that if you are of a nervous disposition, or easily offended, you will find parts of this book both offensive and upsetting. There is sex, violence, drug abuse, occultism, pornography, firearms, politics, religion, and not a little sociology. But there is also love, kindness, faith, and redemption.

All I would say before bidding you farewell is *Caveat Lector*. And I'm not providing a footnote for that, because if you don't know what that means then you probably shouldn't be reading this book.

Hare bol.
Jon Downes,
May Day 2018

---

[*] I was tempted to do it again, but decided that would be too silly.

Διόνυσος
Diónysos

I

In February or early March 2011, I was sitting in my office having just had my breakfast. I was contemplating my electricity bill with some distaste when a bloke who then worked for me burst in through the front door. I never liked him very much, and he was only a few points above being completely useless, but he had been landed on me, and there was no way that I could get rid of him without being more unkind than I wanted to be.

"Have you heard the news?" He wheezed excitedly, self importance oozing from every yeasty pore. I did my best to ignore him and pored even harder at my electricity bill hoping that he would get the hint and go away.

But he didn't.

"This is real people power" he guffed on.

"It was all arranged on Facebook and 4Chan * you know"...

---

* No matter how much I enjoy footnotes, I think that to explain Facebook to you, gentle reader, is probably superfluous as five months ago (as I write this in may 2018) it had 2.2billion monthly users. 4Chan, however, is a little more arcane. It is an English-language imageboard website upon which users generally post anonymously, with the most recent posts appearing above the rest. 4chan is split into various boards with their own specific content and guidelines. The site has been linked to Internet subcultures and activism groups, most notably Anonymous, the alt-right and Project Chanology.The site's "Random" board, also known as "/b/", was the first board to be created, and is the one that receives the most traffic. As its name suggests, the Random board has minimal rules on posted content. Gawker once jokingly claimed that "reading /b/ will melt your brain".

I couldn't ignore him any further without being completely offensive, and it was too early in the morning for me to be that without real provocation. So I grunted non-committedly as he yabbered on about the 'Arab Spring' (I hate the way that even insurrections and financial disasters [*] have to have cute little trade names these days) and how it was bringing "real democracy" to the region after years of oppression. He was clearly imagining something like a series of Liberal Democrat coffee mornings across Syria, rather than a return to medieval brigandry, and a wave of crucifixions, disembowellings and beheadings.

He burbled on in this way, each sentence ever more fatuous than the last, until I truly couldn't bear it any more. I wanted to scream at the bloody man. Hadn't the lessons of Iraq been learned? Once the old military regimes were gone it left the door open for ever more batshit insane theocracies to take their place. But no, the fact that the revolutions had been partly organised on Facebook and 4Chan made everything alright, and there would now be a whole swathe of the world where people could giggle about the fact that Longcat was so long [**].

Unlike some of our verbal altercations which ended in verbal violence on my behalf, (and on one memorable occasion by my throwing a half empty gin bottle at his head) this one ended peacefully. The telephone rang, and I answered it, and my quondam employee wandered back outside still muttering to himself about democracy, as I tried my best to argue with the accounts department of the Electricity Board.

However, just because I found my then employee's fatuous bullshit too much to take before I had actually finished my breakfast, I had actually always been interested in the rise of the online hacktivists, particularly those who operated under the banner of 'Anonymous'. It was a movement with which I had a lot of sympathy.

One of my favourite fictional books for the past forty years has been *ISMO,* written in 1963 by the late Sir John Verney[***]. It concerns a revolutionary anarchist group, mostly consisting of young people, and in the words of an un-named Internet pundit, who by his own admission found the book both irritating and confusing:

---

[*] *quod vide* "The Credit Crunch"

[**] Longcat is one of the most recognized cats on the Internet. He is known for his epic length, spawning photoshops and even an entire mythology around his magnitude. The original photo of Longcat, whose name is Shiroi (白い ー "white" in Japanese), first appeared on Futaba channel (2chan) sometime between 2004 and 2005 by a man from Japan. On 2chan, she was referred to as "nobiiru"[2][3], which means "stretch." Variations of this included "nobiiru-tan," which was attributed to 2chan's /27/ board as early as February 2nd, 2006.

[***] Sir John Verney, Bt (1913-1993), British author and illustrator. Amongst other things, his eldest daughter joined a cult and ran away to a place called Xtul. Coincidence? No such thing probably.

"What is the mysterious new movement called ismo? A challenge to established forms of government? A change in the human heart? An elaborate piece of fooling? Or all of those at once? Started more or less as a joke by a party of students in a Florence cafe, ismo has spread silently and with amazing speed round the world— as if it was what the idealistic young had been waiting for. And not only the young". *

So when a very similar thing started to happen on the Internet, which was nothing more than a gleam in the eye of various science fiction writers when Verney invented ismo over half a century ago, I was immediately interested. Anonymous had exactly the same mixture of idealism and tomfoolery, and like ismo it was equally at home with fatuous practical jokes as it was with meddling with international politics.

The group's involvement with the events of the 'Arab Spring' began in January 2011, when Anons took a number of actions known initially as Operation Tunisia. A hacktivist called Tflow (a London schoolboy called Mustafa Al-Bassam) created a script that Tunisians could use to protect their web browsers from government surveillance, while fellow future LulzSec member Hector Xavier Monsegur (alias "Sabu") and others allegedly hijacked servers from a London web-hosting company to launch a DDoS attack on Tunisian government websites, taking them offline. According to various sources Sabu (who, by the way, was later to become a turncoat as an FBI informer) also used a Tunisian volunteer's computer to hack the website of Prime Minister Mohamed Ghannouchi, replacing it with a message from Anonymous. Anons also helped Tunisian dissidents share videos online about the uprising, and it is undeniable that much of what we in the West know about the uprisings themselves is due to the machinations of some idealistic young people in the UK, Ireland and the USA operating out of their bedrooms. **

In Operation Egypt, Anons collaborated with the activist group Telecomix to help dissidents access government-censored websites. Sabu and Topiary went on to participate in attacks on government websites in Bahrain, Egypt, Libya, Jordan, and Zimbabwe. And like a house of cards, a whole slew of regimes in the Middle East, which - only a few short months or years before - one would have imagined to have been impregnable, started to fall.

---

* I can't actually find where I got this quote in the first place, and it doesn't really matter, except for the fact that it annoys my more OCD tendencies. But I didn't make it up, honest.

** The most entertaining account of all this is in Parmy Olsen's book *We Are Anonymous: Inside the Hacker World of LulzSec, Anonymous, and the Global Cyber Insurgency* (Little Brown, 2012), but I would also recommend Gabriella Coleman's *Hacker, Hoaxer, Whistleblower, Spy: The Many Faces of Anonymous* (Verso, 2014) which is a better piece of academia although not as funny)

A lot has been written about Anonymous and the hacktivists who operate under its umbrella, but one thing that I never have understood is when commentators wonder why governments, especially the British and Americans, have cracked down so violently on those cyber insurgents that they have managed to arrest.

I would have thought that it was perfectly obvious. Anonymous is a guerrilla organisation by every definition of the term, and governments are terrified by guerrillas. Small urban guerrilla groups like the Red Brigade [*], the Angry Brigade [**], and the Symbionese Liberation Army [***] can carry on for years evading all efforts to detect them and, as the Americans found with the Viet Cong [****] in Vietnam, and the British found with the IRA [*****] in Ireland, a guerrilla army is almost impossible to defeat.

And Anonymous were only the first online cyber anarchists The powers that be wanted to make sure that they were the last. But, as usually happens when governments try to achieve something in haste, they usually fail, because the events of the spring of 2011 were only the beginning.

---

* The Red Brigades (Italian: Brigate Rosse) often abbreviated BR) was a left-wing terrorist organization, based in Italy, responsible for numerous violent incidents, including assassinations, kidnapping and robberies during the so-called "Years of Lead". Formed in 1970, the organization sought to create a "revolutionary" state through armed struggle, and to remove Italy from the North Atlantic Treaty Organization. The Red Brigades attained notoriety in the 1970s and early 1980s with their violent attempts to destabilise Italy by acts of sabotage, bank robberies, kidnappings and murders.

** The Angry Brigade was a left-wing revolutionary group responsible for a series of bomb attacks in England between 1970 and 1972. The Angry Brigade decided to launch a bombing campaign with small bombs – in order to maximise media exposure to their demands while keeping collateral damage to a minimum. The campaign started in August 1970 and continued for a year until arrests took place the following summer. Targets included banks, embassies, the Miss World event in 1970 (or rather a BBC Outside Broadcast vehicle earmarked for use in the BBC's coverage) and the homes of Conservative MPs. In total, police attributed 25 bombings to the Angry Brigade. The bombings mostly caused property damage; one person was slightly injured.

*** The United Federated Forces of the Symbionese Liberation Army (SLA) was an American left-wing revolutionary and domestic terrorist organization active between 1973 and 1975 that considered itself a vanguard army. The group committed bank robberies, two murders, and other acts of violence.

**** The Việt Cộng also known as the National Liberation Front, was a mass political organization in South Vietnam and Cambodia with its own army – the People's Liberation Armed Forces of South Vietnam (PLAF) – that fought against the United States and South Vietnamese governments during the Vietnam War, eventually emerging on the winning side. It had both guerrilla and regular army units, as well as a network of cadres who organized peasants in the territory it controlled.

***** The Irish Republican Army (IRA) is any of several paramilitary movements in Ireland in the 20th and 21st centuries dedicated to Irish republicanism, the belief that all of Ireland should be an independent republic. It was also characterised by the belief that political violence was necessary to achieve that goal. The first known use of the term "Irish Republican Army" occurred in the Fenian raids on many British landmarks, towns, and forts in the late 1700s and 1860s. The original Irish Republican Army formed in 1917 from those Irish Volunteers who did not enlist in the British Army during World War I, members of the Irish Citizen Army and others.

II

The killings began on Midsummer's Eve.* This is arguably the most sacred night of the year, one of the four Fire Festivals of Pagan and Neopagan belief, which was very early on co-opted into the pantheon of the Christian Calendar as the feast day of that most pagan of early Christian martyrs, St John the Baptist **.

I didn't know anything about it. Whereas it has become our custom to celebrate Bealtaine on or about May Eve, when our friend Andy the druid comes and performs the old Celtic ritual of the Bealtaine fire *** and I make a huge cauldron of Mexican red beans and rice, which have no magickal significance at all to the day, but are one of the things that I enjoy cooking and even more enjoy eating, and as many of our extended family come and sit in the garden and drink wine or tea, and munch on whatever is available, we don't really celebrate Midsummer. This is partly because

* Midsummer, is the period of time cantered upon the summer solstice, and more specifically the northern European celebrations that accompany the actual solstice or take place on a day between June 19 and June 25 and the preceding evening. The exact dates vary between different cultures. In late 14th-century England, John Mirk of Lilleshall Abbey, Shropshire, gives the following description: "At first, men and women came to church with candles and other lights and prayed all night long. In the process of time, however, men left such devotion and used songs and dances and fell into lechery and gluttony turning the good, holy devotion into sin." The church fathers decided to put a stop to these practices and ordained that people should fast on the evening before, and thus turned waking into fasting.

** John the Baptist was a Jewish itinerant preacher in the early first century AD. John is revered as a major religious figure in Christianity, Islam, the Bahá'í Faith, and Mandaeism. He is called a prophet by all of these traditions, and is honored as a saint in many Christian traditions. John used baptism as the central symbol or sacrament of his messianic movement. Most scholars agree that John baptized Jesus and ome scholars believe Jesus was a follower or disciple of John. According to the New Testament, John anticipated a messianic figure greater than himself.

John rebuked Herod for marrying Herodias, the ex-wife of his brother (named here as Philip). Herodias demands his execution, but Herod, who 'liked to listen' to John, is reluctant to do so because he fears him, knowing he is a 'righteous and holy man'. Herod's daughter Salome dances before Herod, who is pleased and offers her anything she asks for in return. When the girl asks her mother what she should request, she is told to demand the head of John the Baptist. Reluctantly, Herod orders the beheading of John, and his head is delivered to her, at her request, on a plate.

*** Beltane is mentioned in some of the earliest Irish literature, and it is associated with important events in Irish mythology. It marked the beginning of summer and was when cattle were driven out to the summer pastures. Rituals were performed to protect the cattle, crops and people, and to encourage growth. Special bonfires were kindled, and their flames, smoke and ashes were deemed to have protective powers. The people and their cattle would walk around the bonfire or between two bonfires, and sometimes leap over the flames or embers. All household fires would be doused and then re-lit from the Beltane bonfire. These gatherings would be accompanied by a feast, and some of the food and drink would be offered to the aos sí. Doors, windows, byres and the cattle themselves would be decorated with yellow May flowers, perhaps because they evoked fire.

I first heard about them in the song 'Ride a White Swan' by T Rex (1920) and always wanted to see one. So, when we first met Andy socially, I asked him if he would do one for me. We found it so spiritually satisfying, that he has done one ever since.

they are in the habit of going off to a Pagan festival that weekend, and many of my friends are at Glastonbury, or preparing to go there. We mark the two winter festivals, Yule and Samhain, again with little workings from Andy and appropriate feasting. But on Midsummer's Eve this year we were at home, about our own business.

As far as I was concerned, that business was recording in my home studio with my old friend Mike Davis, which was probably a good thing, as it turned out, because otherwise I would not have had an alibi. And unfortunately, I was eventually to need one.

Down the coast about thirty miles into Cornwall, is a small seaside resort town, and on the outskirts of that small seaside resort town is (or rather, was) a small and badly run zoo. At least it advertised itself as a zoo, but it was really just a tacky child's adventure playground with a few unhappy looking animals in badly designed and rickety cages dotted about the grounds. I had been visiting it on and off for about thirty years, and had been mildly friendly with the previous owners. When I had first been there it had some really cool little exhibits, but by the time I went there with my soon to be ex-girlfriend Sallie and her family, about fifteen years back, it was obviously on its last legs, and I was not at all surprised to hear that it was for sale.

A couple of years passed, Sallie and I split up, Corinna and I met (the two events were completely unrelated) and we eventually got married and moved to my old family home on the outskirts of the little North Devon village of Woolfardisworthy. When we heard that an old friend of mine and his mildly bimboesque paramour were planning to buy the aforementioned little zoo, which was by this stage very much on its last legs, we invested a large sum of money in the project, which (as it turned out) was one of the more stupid things that we could have done, and in the event did do.

It only took a couple of years for us to realise that we had not only sunk all our available capital into something that was never going to make a profit, but that our ideas of what should constitute a properly run zoo, and even more importantly what a zoo was actually *for* were completely different, and so we withdrew, leaving the vast majority of our money tied up in the project. We heard very little from our erstwhile friends and colleagues after that, although I suspect, but cannot prove that a lot of the unpleasantness that happened when we were stalked and trolled across the Internet by one or more malicious people hiding behind facile pseudonyms, was somehow related to them.

So, when our two erstwhile partners, and the person that I strongly suspect was our long term Internet Nemesis, were found dead, face down in a pool of ammonia with metal crossbow bolts through the back of their heads, I was a fairly obvious suspect.

Luckily for me at that time, not only did I have an unimpeachable alibi, as explained above, but the plods had *not* done their homework, and it was a long time before they were to come knocking at my door, and by the time they did, the plot had thickened to the consistency of B&Q readymix cement.

But I am running ahead of myself. The story is complicated enough without me doing that.

It took a week or so for us to get to hear of the events at the zoo, because I am the first to admit that I have become a semi recluse in my late middle age, and whereas I used to be an avid reader of the daily news, I now figure that if it is important enough for me to have to know about it, then someone will tell me sooner or later, and so it was in this case.

"Did you hear? Someone shot that shitbag Simon and his girlfriend!" came the Facebook message a few days later from someone who should really remain nameless, because such callousness, though understandable, is not really a character trait to be encouraged. I made some enquiries, and found that it was true.

But it turned out that the story was far more complicated than that, because the triple murder was actually the culmination of a whole string of peculiar things that had happened at the zoo, and which we as shareholders, albeit reluctant ones, should really have been told about. But we weren't, and although I like to think that if we had been aware of what had been happening over the previous year or so, that we might have averted what happened. But we probably wouldn't have, and if I am truly honest about it, I think that if we *had* been still involved, we might have ended up dead as well.

The zoo property was surrounded on three sides by fairly old deciduous woodland, which one can see is part of a long strip of woodlands, deciduous and manmade that runs along much of North Devon and North Cornwall, and which although not completely contiguous, is never more than a mile or so from the next patch of forest. And for a year coming up to the fatal events of Midsummer 2015, while I had been struggling to find out the truth behind another series of strange events in some woodland near me, some very strange things had been happening there.

It wasn't, however, until I looked at Google Earth about ten minutes ago, as I was preparing to sit down and write this narrative that I found out that to all intents and purposes the woodlands surrounding the quondam zoo, and the woodlands where I, but nobody much else, knew that The Children of the Three * were about their arcane business, were the same.

Suddenly everything began to make a bit more sense, if anything about the affair could be said to make any sense at all.

Householders in the little hamlet which surrounded the zoo had found that although nothing had ever been *taken*, their houses showed unmistakeable signs of having been broken into. There property had been moved around [**], and there were occasionally the wet prints of bare human feet. These depredations had even started to happen at the zoo, and although I am reasonably reliably informed that once again nothing was stolen, various small animals were moved from their enclosures and out into other ones, and - peculiarly - badly cared for tanks and cages had been cleaned and repaired.

And, weirdest of all, although I cannot confirm this, because the security videos have long since been taken by the police as evidence, the badly maintained VHS surveillance system (it was typical of Simon and Debs that they would have an array of obsolete and barely functioning security equipment) gave a few tantalising glimpses of the intruders. They were human, and they appeared to have been rolling in earth. But they were also young, female, tattooed, and naked.

III

As adults in the 21st Century we tend to equate the idea of nakedness with a sexual agenda, when it is, of course not necessarily anything of the sort. We are born naked, many of us sleep naked, we perform our ablutions naked, and many peoples who are described as "primitive" because they have not invented weapons of mass destruction, iPhones or electric toasters, spend their entire lives naked, or practically so.

And, of course there is the grand tradition of ritual nudity. The devotees of many strains of neopaganism carry out some or all of their rituals skyclad, believing that nudity is the great leveller, and for them to perform in the skins given to us by the Gods, means that we are closer to them as we do so. It has been said that Gerald

---

* See *The Song of Panne* for more details.

** When I first heard aout this I was irresistibly reminded of The Manson Family who carried out burglary missions they called "creepy-crawling" where They would break into random homes at night while the residents slept, rearrange their furniture, and steal items. People who have read *The Song of Panne* will remember that The Manson Family and some of its members turn up in that narrative as well. If you want to know who the Manson Family were/are look it up. I have already explained who John the Baptist was. Do you expect me to do *all* the work for you?

Gardner, the founder of modern neopaganism took the idea of ritual nudity from a sect of Jain monks whom he had encountered whilst a British Colonial Service officer in India. However, it has also been argued that Gardner just made stuff up according to his own proclivities, and that the ancient New Forest coven run by Old Dorothy Clutterbuck, into which he claimed to have been inducted in the 1940s, almost certainly did not exist, and that Mrs Clutterbuck was actually a pillar of the community and head of the local Conservative Women's Group.

I have written at length about this stuff elsewhere, and this is neither the time nor the place to discuss the rather murky origins of modern neopaganism, because it has very little to do with the narrative of what I am trying to tell you about. But I have what can be described as a grasshopper mind that bounces from one subject to another with very little rhyme or reason, and so I make no real apologies for disappearing off down intellectual and conceptual rabbit holes every little while.

In the 1930s a writer called Margaret Murray wrote a brace of books suggesting that there were remnants of an ancient witch cult scattered across Europe. Amazingly one of her intellectual followers was my late Mother, probably the least likely person to be interested in witchcraft of any shape, form, or hue, that one could ever think of. Murray, whose ideas were often pooh pooed by more mainstream academics, believed that this pan-European Cult, which worshipped the Graeco Roman Goddess Diana, hence Murray's appellation for it - Dianic - was the original European religion and that echoes of this cult and its beliefs were found right across European culture. Over twenty years later she published another book which expanded wildly on the

---

* Gerald Brosseau Gardner (1884 – 1964), also known by the craft name Scire, was an English Wiccan, as well as an author and an amateur anthropologist and archaeologist. He was instrumental in bringing the Contemporary Pagan religion of Wicca to public attention, writing some of its definitive religious texts and founding the tradition of Gardnerian Wicca.

Born into an upper-middle-class family in Blundellsands, Lancashire, Gardner spent much of his childhood abroad in Madeira. In 1900, he moved to colonial Ceylon, and then in 1911 to Malaya, where he worked as a civil servant, independently developing an interest in the native peoples and writing papers and a book about their magical practices. After his retirement in 1936, he travelled to Cyprus, penning the novel A Goddess Arrives before returning to England. Settling down near the New Forest, he joined an occult group, the Rosicrucian Order Crotona Fellowship, through which he claimed to have encountered the New Forest coven into which he was initiated in 1939. Believing the coven to be a survival of the pre-Christian Witch-Cult discussed in the works of Margaret Murray, he decided to revive the faith, supplementing the coven's rituals with ideas borrowed from Freemasonry, ceremonial magic and the writings of Aleister Crowley to form the Gardnerian tradition of Wicca.

Moving to London in 1945, following the repeal of the Witchcraft Act of 1736 he became intent on propagating this religion, attracting media attention and writing about it in *High Magic's Aid* (1949), *Witchcraft Today* (1954) and *The Meaning of Witchcraft* (1959). Founding a Wiccan group known as the Bricket Wood coven, he introduced a string of High Priestesses into the religion, including Doreen Valiente, Lois Bourne, Patricia Crowther and Eleanor Bone, through which the Gardnerian community spread throughout Britain and subsequently into Australia and the United States in the late 1950s and early 1960s. Involved for a time with Cecil Williamson, Gardner also became director of the Museum of Magic and Witchcraft on the Isle of Man, which he ran until his death.

theory, taking in an influence from Sir James Frazer's *The Golden Bough,* an anthropological book that made the claim that societies all over the world sacrificed their kings to the deities of nature. In her book, she claimed that this practice had continued into medieval England, and that, for instance, the death of William II was really a ritual sacrifice. She also claimed that a number of important figures who died violent deaths, such as Archbishop Thomas Becket, were killed as a replacement for the king. No academic took the book seriously, and it was ignored by many of her supporters. My Mother certainly believed in this theory, and when Diana, the namesake of this ancient Goddess died on the last day of Summer two decades after the year in which two sevens clashed, she was not the only one to feel that Murray had somehow been vindicated.

It is certain that much of Murray's theorising found itself into Gerald Gardner's nascent neopaganism, and it is also certain that because of her writings many people believed that there had been ritual magics going on across Europe for centuries. Whether or not this tradition of magickal practise involved ritual nudity depends partially at least on whether or not you believe that Gerald Gardner was a a dirty old man with a taste for both alfresco nudity and flagellation.

So there are all sorts of reasons why people of all ages take their clothes off in company, and despite what the moral watchdogs of our increasingly neopuritan society would like to have us believe, quite a lot of them have very little to do with sex. But why were there naked girls covered in mud skulking around the environs of a fourth-rate Westcountry tourist attraction which masqueraded as a zoo, purely to make the proprietors feel less embarrassed about what they were doing? And did these naked girls covered in mud have anything to do with the untimely and rather grotesque deaths of said proprietors?

I finally came to England to live in 1971 after a babyhood spent in Nigeria and a childhood spent in Hong Kong. I still remember my first day in the country vividly. After a long journey across Europe we took the ferry for England with a sigh of relief, and although my grounding in Biggles[*] books had prepared me for a feeling of glorious patriotic fervour at the sight of the white cliffs of Dover it was a rough crossing, I had over-eaten at lunchtime and at the first sight of my glorious motherland I was copiously and messily sick in my mother's second best hat. As we

---

[*] James Bigglesworth, nicknamed "Biggles", is a fictional pilot and adventurer, the title character and hero of the Biggles series of adventure books, written for young readers by W. E. Johns (1893–1968). Biggles made his first appearance in the story The White Fokker, published in the first issue of Popular Flying magazine and again as part of the first collection of Biggles stories, The Camels Are Coming (both 1932). Johns continued to write "Biggles books" until his death in 1968, the series eventually spanning nearly a hundred volumes – including novels and short story collections – most of the latter with a common setting and time.

---

disembarked at Dover a seagull shat messily in my brother's eye, and it was two smelly, disgruntled and cross children who were ushered onto the train that was to take us from Dover to London.

At the time, I was obsessed with the Second World War. The cessation of hostilities had been less than three decades before, and in the same way that so many of the children of my contemporaries seem obsessed by *The Beatles* - an ensemble who played their last notes as a group well before they were born, I and my contemporaries were obsessed by the War. It was, after all, the defining event of our lives, even though it had been over for fourteen years before I was born. Our parents had fought in - or at least lived through - the war, there were still a surprisingly large number of derelict bomb sites, and as late as 1974 Japanese soldiers who refused to believe that the war was finally over, emerged from the jungles of The Philippines in unbowed triumph.

As our train trundled and ambled through the verdant Kent countryside I gazed rapturously out of the window. Gone was the smell of vomit, and I forgot that my little brother, still snivelling, stank of seagull shit. I could see Oast Houses, I could see hop fields. These were the fields over which The Battle of Britain (as immortalised for me by the eponymous 1969 movie) * had been fought. I was finally in England, and I would soon see the land, for which we had fought the Hun, not once, but twice in my Grandparents' lifetimes. As the dusk began to gather round, I picked up a newspaper that had been left on the seat of our carriage by a previous passenger.

I leafed through it idly, but my attention was transfixed by one particular story. The headline read "Little Miss Starkers," and told the story of how several motorists driving home late at night along one lonely stretch of road near Sevenoaks had been startled to see the figure of a young teenage girl - completely naked - emerge from a

---

* *Battle of Britain* is a 1969 British Second World War film directed by Guy Hamilton, and produced by Harry Saltzman and S. Benjamin Fisz. The film documented the events of the Battle of Britain. The film drew many respected British actors to accept roles as key figures of the battle, including Sir Laurence Olivier as Hugh Dowding and Trevor Howard as Keith Park. It also starred Michael Caine, Christopher Plummer and Robert Shaw as Squadron Leaders. The script by James Kennaway and Wilfred Greatorex was based on the book *The Narrow Margin* by Derek Wood and Derek Dempster.

The film endeavoured to be an accurate account of the Battle of Britain, when in the summer and autumn of 1940 the British RAF inflicted a strategic defeat on the Luftwaffe and so ensured the cancellation of Operation Sea Lion – Adolf Hitler's plan to invade Britain. The film is notable for its spectacular flying sequences, in contrast with the unsatisfactory model work seen in *Angels One Five* (1952) and on a far grander scale than had been seen on film before; these made the film's production very expensive. It was shown in Hong Kong (where I lived at the time) in mid-1970 and I became completely obsessed with it for several years: one of the earliest of the series of cultural obsessions which have defined much of my life.

pond by the side of the road and cross the road slowly in front of them paying no attention to the oncoming traffic. One report even described the girl's breasts as being draped in waterweed from the lake. All the witnesses (five in all - I believe - although you must remember that it is over forty years since I read the story) described how she had disappeared into the undergrowth on the opposite side of the road.

The journalist who had written the story was quick to blame these sightings on drugged skinny-dipping hippies, but I was transfixed. Not only did I find the story almost unbelievably sexually arousing, it was also redolent of my spiritual mentor, Doctor Cornelius's * quest for the "Old Narnians". Perhaps "Little Miss Starkers" was a dryad of some sort - a water spirit, a living embodiment of the healing stream. It was a stunning image for an eleven year old with an overactive imagination. When said eleven year old was also within twelve months of the onset of puberty, it gave him a fixation with alfresco sexual encounters that would take him another decade to experience for himself, but that is another story. However, I can truly say that the five minutes that it took me to read that poorly written newspaper story changed my life and set me on the trail of wild men, and unearthly humanoids amongst England's green and pleasant land.

And over the next half century or so, like Doctor Cornelius, I spent a lifetime searching for the world of mythology that I was convinced lay just below the surface of England's green and pleasant gentility, and like Doctor Cornelius, I occasionally got fleeting glimpses of this nether netherland, but never enough to do more than tantalise and disappoint. But then, as some of you know, last year everything changed.

IV

What is fiction? Well this is, sort of. Some of it I am making up as I go along, but most of it I'm not. Am I going to reveal which is which? No, of course I'm not.

in the first episode of the short lived TV show *Constantine*, ** the eponymous protagonist says that he is not a 'master' of the dark arts, rather a dabbler. I could say

---

* Doctor Cornelius was the mentor, advisor and teacher of the young prince Caspian X in the second of the Chronicles of Narnia books. As a person of half-dwarfish, half-human blood posing as a human, he was one of the few people in the Telmarine-ruled society of Narnia under King Miraz that knew of the history of the Old Narnians, and introduced Caspian to them. The idea that "civilised" people are afraid of nature, and shun the wild woods and waters is a cultural meme that has dominated my life.

** Constantine is an American television series developed by Daniel Cerone and David S. Goyer for NBC, featuring the DC Comics character John Constantine, a British exorcist and occult detective who actively hunts supernatural entities. The series aired from October 24, 2014 to February 13, 2015, over 13 episodes.

much the same about me, although I will be the first to admit that my adventures on the left hand path were very small and trivial, and that my only real reason for embarking on that spiritually insalubrious journey, was so that I could sleep with New Age women. I will also admit that I succeeded in my aim on a number of occasions, and that I quit once and for all when I realised that the closer that one got to the dark side, the more fucked up your life became, and that no amount of louche sexual adventures was worth the inevitable end of the journey - somewhere that I truly didn't want to go.

So I quit. I went cold turkey, and on the last night of the Millenium, which began with a battle between Athelstan, King of the Saxons and the invading Danish brigands, just a few miles up the road from where I then lived, a friend of mine gave me the biggest helping hand that I have ever been given. Despite all the commemorative TV shows, and the firework displays a year before, the first year of the 21st Century was actually 2001, a horrific year in which the fall of the Twin Towers of the World Trade Centre ushered in a new era of global Realpolitik, and England's Green and Pleasant Land was shrouded in the disgusting smog caused by the funeral pyres of most of the ungulates that had lived therein. Some of us knew that it was going to be a horrible year, ushering in what was probably going to be a horrible decade, and quite possibly a horrible century, and I for one didn't want to be involved in anything more horrible than I had to.

But I was on a path that I couldn't get off without help. Not drug addiction or alcoholism; I had been there, done that and bought the fucking t shirt, but the horrible game of footsie that I had been playing with the powers of the dark side ever since I first started studying things like the grotesque Owlman of Mawnan. The Owlman? What the fuck is that? I hear you ask in the aural equivalent of my mind's eye. It's a strange feathered birdman, something like Max Ernst's Loplop from *Une Semaine de Bonte* * which is seen occasionally by teenage girls in the environs of a churchyard just outside Falmouth in southern Cornwall. If you want to know any more then read the book. I wrote it and could do with the money.

You can also read books that I wrote about the equally grotesque chupacabras of

---

* Loplop is the name of a birdlike character featured in prints, collages and paintings by artist Max Ernst. Loplop was an alter ego which Ernst developed and functioned as a familiar animal. Loplop first appeared in Ernst's collage novels La Femme *100 Têtes* and *Une Semaine de Bonté* in the role of a narrator and commentator. *Une semaine de bonté* ("A Week of Kindness") is a comic and artist's book by Max Ernst, first published in 1934. It comprises 182 images created by cutting up and re-organizing illustrations from Victorian encyclopaedias' and novels arranged to present a dark, surreal world.

I write about Ernst and his many and multifarious links to the mythos of the Cornish Owlman in my 1997 book *The Owlman and Others* which has been republished a few times since andis, certainly, both my best known and best selling book.

Puerto Rico, and about vampires in the Mexican desert [*], but I don't want to try and portray myself as some weirdo demon hunting Van Helsing type. I never did, because I never was, and truly I never wanted to be. All I ever wanted to be was a minor academic writing as scholarly papers as he was able, upon subjects that interested him. And since January 1st 2001 that is all I have ever been. Well most of the time, anyway.

On the last night of the previous thousand years I was with an old friend and quondam lover of mine and her boyfriend in a cold, grey city in Northern England. I have never be fond of what is known euphemistically as 'The Festive Season', and in the years between my first wife leaving me, and my second wife marrying me, I always did my best not to be alone during that horrible slow week between the anniversary of the birth of Our Lord and the beginning of the new year, and that year my friends in Yorkshire had been kind enough to open their home to me. It had not been the most successful of visits. The night before Christmas Eve I took an overdose of Methadone after a bottle of Jack Daniels in a vain attempt to leave this world behind, and despite the fact that the whole sorry episode had ended with me being copiously sick everywhere, everybody involved had been badly shaken. Then twenty four hours later I came down with the worst headcold that I have ever had.

Then on New Year's Eve, my hosts, especially my quondam lover (I am not going to say ex-lover, because our friendship lasted a decade and a half, whereas our sexual relationship only lasted a weekend) who was the second most powerful magician that I have ever met, and I took part in a magickal ritual designed to cut my ties with my past. Entirely. And cut they were.

If you watch things like that on television it is all about chanting, and ritual nakedness, and blood sacrifices and athames and swords of strange design. Well all those things took place, but it was much quieter, much more prosaic, and far less dramatic than it would have been if it had been portrayed on the small screen. These days the athames and swords of strange design probably come from eBay, but in those days they came from a market stall in Halifax market, run by a wizened little man who went under the name of 'Freaky Freddy', and who looked more than a little like Mr The Toad in the Zippy the Pinhead cartoons by Bill Griffith [**]. The blood sacrifice was mine, and the blood came from a single cut from one of the

---

[*] *Only Fools and Goatsuckers* (2000) and *The Island of Paradise* (2007). I am prouder of the latter, but will be quite happy if you buy both, because I always need the money.

[**] William Henry Jackson "Bill" Griffith (born January 20, 1944) is an American cartoonist who signs his work Bill Griffith and Griffy. He is best known for his daily comic strip Zippy the Pinhead. The popular catchphrase "Are we having fun yet?" is credited to Griffith.

aforementioned athames on the palm of my hand. And as far as the ritual nudity is concerned, it all looks very sexy in a Kenneth Anger movie. It used to look even more titillating when the News of the Screws * used to run one of their regular exposes on the "innocent looking primary school teacher has shocking secret life in wifeswapping coven" stories.

But when the celebrants involved are all middle aged and elderly people, about half of whom I had never met before, mostly overweight and with the well-bred British reserve which normally precludes even speaking to someone to whom one has not been introduced, let alone getting one's kit off in front of them, trust me, there is nothing sexy about it.

The ritual took many hours and cut many of the ties to things that had been making me unhappy for years, including some of the less conventional and/or socially acceptable relationships I had with my own parents, my ex wife, and various other people, including my recently ex-girlfriend who had been fucking up my wellbeing for some time, and who had finally left me with the intention of becoming a nun, because she said that my involvement with the occult was "having truck with The Devil" (her words not mine).

[...here I should like to say that I know very little about Satanism, I have never practised it, and to the best of my knowledge I do not know anyone who does. When in 2001, some Exeter Satanists came to our annual conference, and started to hand out leaflets I had them thrown out...]

The events of New Year's Eve 2000, were also the beginning of the end for my involvement with organised religion, but that is an entirely different story, although it is one that I suspect that I shall return to at some point in this narrative. But in a very real sense that ritual shaped my life as it was to become in the new Millenium, and although of the only two people involved whom I knew, one is dead and I haven't seen the other since a year or two after we concluded the ritual, put our clothes on and got on with our lives, I owe all the people involved an enormous debt which is never likely to be fully repaid.

For not only had I finally cut the emotional ties with some people and memories that were dragging me down into an emotional abyss, but the psychic ties with some of

* The *News of the World* was a national red top newspaper published in the United Kingdom from 1843 to 2011. It was at one time the highest-selling English-language newspaper in the world, and at closure still had one of the highest English-language circulations. Its fondness for sex scandals gained it the nickname News of the Screws. It had a reputation for exposing national or local celebrities' drug use, sexual peccadilloes, or criminal acts, setting up insiders and journalists in disguise to provide either video or photographic evidence, and phone hacking in ongoing police investigations. Should I tell you what an athame is? And who Kenneth Anger might be? No, I don't think I shall.

the "things" (as Ivan T Sanderson [*] would no doubt have described them, which I had 'investigated' during the previous half decade, and which had attached themselves to me, sucking away at my Odilic life force [**] and my psychic energy, and turning me into something that I had never intended, and never wanted to be.

I was free at last. But the freedom came at a price.

There is an old Spanish proverb that goes something like: "Take what you want, and pay for it says God" [***]. I took what I wanted, and then I paid for it. I was free of the pain, the disgust and the horror of the previous few years, but now - fifteen years later - I can hardly walk and I am in continuous pain. So yes, I am free, but at quite a heavy cost.

And now, events have conspired to manoeuvre me into a situation where it all might have been for nothing!

V

As the summer progressed things rapidly began to get strange. I do my best to be a recluse these days; I don't like people, I don't like humanity and I much prefer to spend my days in my little house with my extended family. But I *do* hear things, and during the weeks following mid-summer all sorts of disturbing reports began to filter in.

North Devon is a peculiar place at the best of times, which is probably one of the reasons that I like it here. It is nowhere near as peculiar as it was when I was a boy, probably because of the gradual gentrification of the area, and the fact that many of the old families have either died out or moved away.

The nexus of the sea-change in the infrastructure of the area can probably be traced

---

* Ivan Terence Sanderson (January 30, 1911 – February 19, 1973) was a biologist and writer born in Edinburgh, Scotland, who became a naturalized citizen of the United States. Sanderson is remembered for his nature writing and his interest in cryptozoology and paranormal subjects. He also wrote fiction under the name Terence Roberts.

** A hypothetical energy first propounded in 1850 by Baron Karl von Reichenbach, and written about quite widely in The Rising of the Moon, a book I wrote in 1999 with Nigel Wright; but which makes far less sense to me now than it did when I was taking more recreational drugs. Unfortunately it also ripped off much of the plot of Forbidden Planet (1956), which I didn't realise at the time. I think our theory is basically correct but needs polishing by someone prepared to put in the energy. That someone is not me.

*** I got this proverb from a story by Agatha Christie, but it also apparently appears in *Zorba the Greek* by Nikos Kazantzakis (1946), which is a book I have never read. And I am still noy explaining Kenneth Anger, but you can watch *Scorpio Rising* on YouTube; the best use of a Philm Spector song in a film ever.

back to the Foot and Mouth epidemic of 2001 * which dealt a holocaust-like blow to the heart and soul of the area.

The vast majority of hoofed livestock were crudely and often inhumanely slaughtered, and their bodies pitched onto makeshift funeral pyres which covered the landscape with a pall of fatty smoke.

This proved too much, emotionally and financially for many farming families, who just gave up, and the social and economic framework of the area changed overnight.

For a few years – around about the time I came back here to live - North Devon appeared disturbingly normal, but in the mid summer of 2015 all of that began to change.

Like so many other places in the country. There have been reports of shadowy big cats stalking the highways and byways of the region, although even these have begun to tail off in recent years. However in the past few months not only have the big cats begun to return, but people driving along the wilder stretches of the A39 as it drives across Bursdon Moor, and past the dank, dark green forestry plantations, reported seeing an enormous bird of prey silhouetted black against the sky. It was only ever seen at dawn or dusk, but if the reports are to be believed, is enormously bigger then any natural denizen of the area. And that is even considering that this is where I, and others, saw a massive white tailed sea eagle in the late 1970's.

But this isn't all.

People driving through the spider web of interlocking lanes which criss-cross the forest between Welcome, Hartland and Woolsery at night were beginning to see other disturbing things.

Such as a gigantic human shape which they would see out of the corner of their eyes and which melted away into the thick forest of trees by the side of the road.

Such as a gigantic black dog with red glowing eyes which padded implacably along

---

* Foot-and-mouth disease or hoof-and-mouth disease (*Aphthae epizooticae*) is an infectious and sometimes fatal viral disease that affects cloven-hoofed animals, including domestic and wild bovids. The virus causes a high fever for approximately two to six days, followed by blisters inside the mouth and on the feet that may rupture and cause lameness. The epidemic of foot-and-mouth disease in the United Kingdom in the spring and summer of 2001 was caused by the "Type O pan Asia' strain of the disease. This episode resulted in more than 2,000 cases of the disease in farms throughout the British countryside. Around ten million sheep and cattle were killed in an eventually successful attempt to halt the disease.

on some mysterious mission of its own. [*]

Such as the repeated sightings of a small band of slight figures seen running along the decilitre lanes, eliminated only by the light of a flaming torch in the grip of the leader.

Things were definitely getting stranger then usual.

Then came another murder. Six or seven years ago when I was making a film about mystery cat sightings in the region [**]. I heard repeated rumours that one of the local farmers had actually shot one of the big cats. When I heard his name, this didn't surprise me. I'd been at school with him and he was a vicious little bastard then. The fact that he seemed to have matured into a sadistic and completely unpleasant human being was no surprise either.

He was active in most of the local blood sports, both legal and illegal, and was widely suspected of both beating his wife, and brutalising his children.

The night he died, apparently his screams for mercy could be heard by his tenants living in the outline cottages of the farm. But he was so roundly disliked, and, by this time people were so spooked by the strange things that had been happening, that nobody was prepared to venture out into the pitch dark of a North Devon night in order to go to his aid. The next day his battered corpse was found face down in a pool of ammonia with a steel crossbow bolt protruding from the front of his skull.

He was so unpopular in the area that nobody was particularly surprised by his murder. There were so many suspects that it was widely believed that the local police would have an impossible job knowing where to start, but it was the manner of his murder that was so entirely surprising.

---

[*] A black dog is a spectral or demonic entity found primarily in the folklore of the British Isles. The black dog is essentially a nocturnal apparition, some of them shapeshifters, and are often said to be associated with the Devil or described as a ghost or hellhound. Its appearance was regarded as a portent of death. It is generally supposed to be larger than a normal dog and often has large glowing eyes. They were quite commonly reported in Devon util the mid 20th Century, the most familiar of these - culturally - being the Hound of the Baskervilles, featured in the eponymous novel by Conan Doyle (1902). 'Black Dog' is also a euphemism for Clinical Depression. Is this stuff all relevant? Some of it, yes, other bits are red herrings. Red herrings and black dogs in the same footnote. We could also bring in Winston Churchill and Led Zeppelin. Golly.

[**] I finished editing *Emily and the Big Cats*, but it was never mastered or completed. This is mainly because there were several people in it with whom I was no longer associated for some reason or another, and I had omitted to get any of them to sign release forms. So - sadly - it can never come out for these, and other legal reasons. One day I may get someone to leak it for free onto You Tube, but not for a while, and not until I have an unimpeachable alibi.

Not only had death by crossbow not been part of the favoured *modus operandi* of North Devon thuggery for about 500 years, but the murderers had left a trail of muddy bare footprints belonging to at least three small figures, lead out of his house, across the farm yard, out the gate, and into the forest.

VI

But I didn't know any of this, or not much anyway. I never set out to be a recluse, but I seem to have become one by default. I have to be dragged kicking and screaming to leave the garden, let alone the village, and whilst I have my wife, and Graham, my mate who lives in my spare room, a circle of friends that I see regularly, and various children who come for guitar lessons, and of course the members of my household who do not live with me, like my various secretaries, (none of whom seem to last very long) Carl the naturalist, and Coby the gardener, I have very little to do with the outside world. And it is an existence that suits Corinna and me pretty well. My friends are also very protective of me, and so I didn't hear about either murder until some time after I probably should have done, because the people who are in contact with me, both on and offline wanted to make sure that I wasn't unnecessarily upset by them.

What I don't think any of them took on board was that I had disliked all the victims intensely, and that I had personal grievances against all of them, and every reason for wanting to do them harm. Except, of course, that I didn't. But you only have my word for that.

I love the summer months in my garden. My Great Grandfather went bankrupt, allegedly because he drank away the family fortune, and in 1909 he took his wife and three youngish children to Canada.

The family seat, Hunston Manor in Sussex, was sold, and he was never to see England again. They took with them some ancient roses from the Manor gardens, and when he died and my Great Grandmother remarried and brought the children back to Sussex, they brought the roses with them. The middle child was my maternal Grandmother who became a Land Girl when the first world war broke out, and then scandalised the rest of the family by becoming involved with a dashing young Royal Flying Corps pilot who was from a family still best known for being travelling fair folk, and the result in April 1922 was my mother.

As my Grandmother was the first of the three children to get married (her brother Tim was one of the officers in the ill advised Siberian Expedition to aid the White Russian army in their abortive attempt to overthrow the relatively new Communist administration, and was terribly wounded, only recovering by a fluke, and her younger sister was still at school) she took the roses which remained in her garden for the rest of her life. When she died in 1975 the roses came to my parents, and eventually to me.

Unfortunately, the weather has changed dramatically in the last forty years since my parents first took over custody of the family roses, and the windy, waterlogged garden of the 21st Century is not conducive to rose cultivation or so it seems. However, some of them, especially those in the circular bed around the top lawn, seem to be flourishing despite it all, and I love watching the bees and butterflies flitting around them in the short periods of hot summer sun that we still get now and again.

I have always been a great lover of butterflies, and whilst, when I was a boy, this meant catching and killing them, and exhibiting them in neat rows in a home-made cabinet which fell apart even before the specimens did, nowadays it means not removing food plants, and providing the best possible habitat for these delicate but fascinating little creatures. It always amazes me that pristine looking red admirals that we get in the early Spring may well have migrated hundreds of miles to get here, and I always do my best to ensure that the have the best possible reception.

I have two aviaries, one that until recently contained a pugnacious cock Reeves' pheasant and some rescued pigeons, and the other which is presently empty apart from three ex-battery chickens, but which I usually keep for whatever rescue birds come along. At the time we had a 4m run containing a rescued hedgehog which was too tame to release, and a pond containing various goldfish, a colony of palmate newts and some frogs, and various common toads and slow-worms (for those of you not aware of these, they are neither slow or worms, but actually a legless lizard) and a plethora of resident birds including three or four pairs of blackbirds, a pair of robins, a largeish flock of blue tits and at least one pair of wrens which breed here annually. There are also wood pigeons, collared doves, thrushes, greenfinches, and occasionally more exotic visitors like nuthatches and bullfinches, and despite the fact that we have a number of cats and two neurotic dogs, the vast majority of these birds survive the year to return and breed again the following one.

I have always intended to optimise my garden for wildlife, and I am reasonably pleased with how well we have done. I suspect that this was why Panne made itself at

---

* The Siberian Intervention or Siberian Expedition of 1918–1922 was the dispatch of troops of the Entente powers to the Russian Maritime Provinces as part of a larger effort by the western powers and Japan to support White Russian forces against the Bolshevik Red Army during the Russian Civil War. The Imperial Japanese Army continued to occupy Siberia even after other Allied forces withdrew in 1920.

---

home so readily. One would occasionally see it flitting between the hazel trees which divide the older part of the garden with the newer bit, or sometimes sitting cross legged by the pond, staring into the water as if it was trying to scry the long distant future.

This was in the hot weather. In cold weather it was often to be found indoors playing with, teasing, or snuggled up with the cats and dogs, or engaged in furious sqwawking arguments with the autocratic crow x rook that was rescued from a garden in Torrington last spring, and which now rules the roost over all the other animals and people in the house from a huge metal cage in the kitchen.

It has taken me the best part of a year to get used to the fact that just because Panne is basically humanoid in structure, that it is not even slightly human. Once upon a time there was a little girl who - as a result of an apotheosis that I can hardly understand - became Panne. But now it is about as unhuman as it is possible to be. Neither is it female just because it once was. Panne is a God, and as far as I can understand, Gods do not reproduce sexually, so they have no need of gender. Which is why I endeavour to use the gender neutral personal pronoun 'it', even though it sounds oddly cold and impersonal when being used to describe a being of whom I am very fond, and who seems to be very fond of us.

When we brought Panne home in the Autumn of 2014, it was battered, weak and wounded, and while Corinna and I treated its injuries, I took the opportunity (wearing my biologist hat, and with my beloved wife as a chaperone, although one was truly not necessary and I very much doubt whether Panne would have understood the concept) to examine its poor battered little body.

I have been a rule of thumb zoologist for much of my adult life. I have dissected, or assisted in the dissection of all sorts of creatures from a woodlouse to a dolphin, and I have even been an observer at a human autopsy. And I have never seen anything like Panne before, and I very much doubt whether I ever shall do again.

Panne was superficially like a pre-pubescent girl, about four feet in height and covered with a coat of russet hair. It had big, yellow eyes with the vertical pupils of a goat, and small (but as I have mentioned before, surprisingly cute) curled horns on its forehead. Panne's face was a mixture of human and caprine traits, and it had black cloven hooves at the end of its legs, which again were partly human and partly reminiscent of the little barking deer that I would glimpse occasionally on the hillsides where I used to play as a child in Hong Kong. Just above its buttocks Panne had a small tail with a tufted end. Unlike the horns, which I knew from personal experience, had a practical application, I have never seen Panne use or even acknowledge the fact that it has a tail, but as a basic biologist I always believe that everything has a function, even if that function is not an obvious one. So I am assuming that I haven't yet worked out what that function is.

Panne has no nipples or sign of mammary glands, which again makes sense when one takes into consideration that Gods not only do not reproduce sexually, they do not suckle babies. And no. Whilst Panne has the organs for excretion of both solids and liquids roughly where they would be on a human being, which is not surprising considering the enormous appetite it has on occasion, there are no signs of anything that could even be construed as sexual or reproductive organs.

But Panne is an affectionate little thing, and quite often - especially on cold nights - has been known to crawl, uninvited but always welcomed, into bed with us and the dogs, and usually sleeps at the bottom, curled up with Archie by our feet.

So while the dark forces were gathering around us, I spent much of the summer with my little natural and supernatural family, watching the roses and the butterflies, breeding tropical fish, making music and trying to write deathless prose, and vaguely working out how I was going to pay the next electricity bill.

VII

When I was a boy in Hong Kong, and a pupil at Peak School on Plunkett's Road, my favourite lesson was - not unsurprisingly - Nature. This was a vague precursor to Secondary School science lessons and covered rudimentary Chemistry, Physics and Biology, all wrapped up in a sort of post-Paley Natural Theology. One of the first things that was drummed into us was that there are three classifications of things:

1. Live
2. Dead
3. Never alive

---

* William Paley (July 1743 – 25 May 1805) was an English clergyman, Christian apologist, philosopher, and utilitarian. He is best known for his natural theology exposition of the teleological argument for the existence of God in his work Natural Theology or Evidences of the Existence and Attributes of the Deity, which made use of the watchmaker analogy. The words most closely linked to Natural Theology are actually by Shakespeare from *As You Like It:*

"Sweet are the **uses** of adversity; Which, like the toad, ugly and venomous, Wears yet a precious jewel in his head; And this our life, exempt from public haunt, Finds tongues in trees, books in the running brooks, Sermons in stones, and good in everything".

However, my perambulations through the omniverse over the half-century that has passed since then, has led me to theorise that there are several other classifications, probably none of which Paley and his ilk would actually balk at. For men of his time believed in spirits, and believed in daemons, and so the first two categories that I would add would be:

4. Immortal

5. Undead

And possibly even:

6. Spirit

Because, whilst I am quite prepared to believe that deities may be immortal, I am also quite prepared to believe that there are other, intangible beings that are capable of being destroyed, even though this would seem to go against the first law of thermodynamics. Because the first law of thermodynamics is a version of the law of conservation of energy, adapted for thermodynamic systems. The law of conservation of energy states that the total energy of an isolated system is constant; energy can be transformed from one form to another, but cannot be created or destroyed. The first law is often formulated by stating that the change in the internal energy of a closed system is equal to the amount of heat supplied to the system, minus the amount of work done by the system on its surroundings. Equivalently, perpetual motion machines of the first kind are impossible.

I've never really approved of the word 'impossible'. I've seen too many things which most people would describe as such in my life to believe in it as a concept, but on the other hand I don't believe in hocus pocus and mumbo jumbo either. I live in a massively haunted house, for example, and it is a matter of record that I have encountered at least two things that most people would refer to as impossible monsters *. I truly believe that all of these things are governed by laws of science which we don't understand yet.

Unfortunately, although I do my best to live an ostrich-like existence and ignore events on the world stage which don't actually impact upon my life, during the summer of 2015 life was getting increasingly weird, and, across the world, events were beginning to get out of hand. My old friend Richard Freeman remarked to me a couple of years ago that: "it feels like we are in 1939". But it has got considerably worse since then. Huge swathes of the Middle East were under the control of disgusting medieval brigands who have reintroduced burnings, mutilation, slavery and crucifixion as acts of war. The major powers had been pussyfooting, and

---

* A bigfoot-like entity in Bolam Woods, Northumberland in January 2003, and a lake monster in County Kerry, Ireland, in September 2009. I have also seen the so-called 'Beast of Bodmin' in May 1997, but that is undoubtedly a flesh and blood creature, and by no stretch of the imagination is a 'monster'.

posturing, around each other in a way that we haven't seen since the height of the Cold War. Russian military air craft have invaded British air space, and when the Russians took military action in Syria their leader claimed that it was Russia rather than the West who was the guardian of true Christian values.

> "Euro-Atlantic (the West) states have rejected their own roots, including the Christian roots which form the basis of Western civilization. In these countries, the moral basis and any traditional identity are being denied - national, religious, cultural and even gender identities are being denied or relativized.
>
> The excesses and exaggerations of political correctness in these countries leads to serious consideration for the legitimization of parties that promote even the propaganda of paedophilia. People in many European states are actually ashamed of their religious affiliation and are indeed frightened to speak about them. Meanwhile, Christian holidays and celebrations are abolished or "neutrally" renamed as if one were ashamed of those Christian holidays. With this method one hides away the deeper moral nature of those celebrations.
>
> Without the moral values that are rooted in Christianity and other world religions, without the rules and moral values which have been formed and developed over millennia, people will inevitably lose their human dignity and become brutes. We think it is right and natural to defend and preserve these moral Christian values."

My favourite book is *Stranger in a Strange Land* by the late Robert Heinlein, which is an allegory about the human condition. At the beginning of each section he includes quotes and news stories from the world press at the same time as the events had taken place. I briefly considered doing the same thing in this one, but I found the whole experience to be far too depressing and even frightening. Truly, during the summer of 2015 the world that we knew was changing so fast as to become almost unrecognisable and it became impossible for anyone to ignore the coming apocalypse.

Only, they *did* ignore it.

Whether that was because people were completely blinded by their Gadarene rush towards an inevitable precipice, whether they were too distracted by the horrors around them, or – more likely – by the bedazzlements of their increasingly absurd consumerist and capitalist lifestyle, or whether the Western nations truly live in a permanent state of denial, I don't know. I *do* know, however, that I spent the summer pottering in my garden or writing barbarous hexameters [**] in the badly converted potato shed in which I spend most of my life. Certainly nobody paid much attention

---

* http://everydayforlifecanada.blogspot.com/2017/01/why-this-about-christian-roots-from.html

** Tennyson, *Translations of Homer: Hexameters and Pentameters*. But like so much else, I got the phrase from Kipling, more specifically from *Stalky and Co.*

and people continued to overeat, overspend and overindulge like there was no tomorrow, which there quite possibly wouldn't be.

Looking back at it all, it seems absurd that more people didn't pick up on the patterns behind it all. I am a self–professed Fortean for goodness sake. One of the mainstays of my intellectual existence is the synergistic interconnectedness of all things, but while I am quite good at divining patterns in out of place animals, or anomalous phenomena, I completely failed to do likewise with the events happening all around me. In my defence, however, neither did anyone else.

With hindsight it seems unbelievable that nobody apart from the most clinically paranoid * even began to claim that there was a method behind all these horrific events which could not be coincidental.

VIII

ut then events, on a local scale at least, became impossible to ignore. One of the things that really began to worry me more than anything else was Danny Miles. I hadn't heard from him for over six months, since his shamefaced apology for the events at Christmas which had seen my friend Martin's house burglarised, and Martin himself held at knifepoint **. But since then nothing at all.

I have known Danny for many years, well over three decades in fact, and there have been many times during that period when I haven't heard from him for years on end. And there have been even more times when I have heard from him, when I truly wish that I hadn't. But this time was completely different. Danny had become mixed up with a very dangerous crew, and by default had got me mixed up with them as well. And, what makes things worse, is that the previous winter I had rescued (for rescued read kidnapped) the youngest and most fragile of the aforesaid dangerous crew who had been living under my protection ever since. And in those intervening months life in my own peculiar little demesne had been relatively quiet and peaceful. But I was under no illusion that it would stay that way. So, for a change, Danny Miles' absence was a cause for concern rather than for celebration, if for no other reason that if I didn't know what Danny was up to, I would have no idea what *Xtul* were up to in their

---

* Such as me

** Again you should probably check out *The Song of Panne* but I feel remarkably guilty whenever I write this, 'cos I don't want to come over like some breadhead continually trying to part my readers from the contents of their bank accounts, because I am not. Honestly. I just have a story to tell, and this multi-volume series of books seems to be the best way of doing it.

redoubt in the deep woods.

And they were obviously up to something. Even a fat butterfly enthusiast writing about cryptozoology, rock and roll, and the parlous state of British moths in a disused potato shed tacked on to the edge of a tumbledown cottage on the outskirts of a village that nobody much had heard of, in rural North Devon could see that. Because things were continuing to happen. Disturbing things.

In early August three different arson attacks took place. One on an abattoir, one on a butcher and one on the house of one of the marksmen who had been employed to cull badgers in north Somerset the previous year.

Now I am a vegetarian and an advocate for animal rights, and I had campaigned vigorously (and continue to campaign) against the cruel, expensive and totally pointless badger cull [*]. But I have never gone to the lengths of setting fire to people's houses. But somebody certainly was, and it appeared that whoever it was, was the same group of people responsible for the deaths of the farmer, and the management team at the zoo, news of both of which had finally trickled into my secluded retreat in the potato shed.

Witnesses at each of the crime scenes had reported seeing the most unlikely group of perpetrators that one could imagine; three or four young women, naked, plastered in mud and brandishing weapons as they slid away from the crime scene and ran into the night. And in all three of the crime scenes lines were found scrawled in chalk, from a poem by Dryden [**].

It seemed unlikely that there could be two groups of heavily armed young people in the same area, so I supposed that somehow these killer girls, and the renegades out in the deep woods were somehow connected. But there was no way that I could actually prove this, and I had nothing more than my innate paranoia to go on. But all the accounts that I had ever heard of the genius level children who were doing God knows what with their computers and their Elephant God out in the middle of nowhere, was that they were conventionally, even modestly, dressed. And somehow these wanton killers didn't seem to fit in with the *modus operandi* of Mr Loxdonta and

---

[*] The powers that be, against all scientific evidence, insist that badgers are the main vector of Bovine Tuberculosis, and have put a price on the heads of these mostly innocent mustelids, purely because governments need to be seen to be doing *something* in order to allow them to keep on spending taxpayer's money.

[**] John Dryden (9 August 1631 – 12 May 1700) was an English poet, literary critic, translator, and playwright who was made England's first Poet Laureate in 1668. He is seen as dominating the literary life of Restoration England to such a point that the period came to be known in literary circles as the Age of Dryden. Walter Scott called him "Glorious John".

his followers.

Everything that I knew about the so-called Children of the Three, led me to suppose that they were enemies of the entire human race, rather than celebrants of it, and these naked female hashassins[*] were more reminiscent of some peculiar aspect of the 17th Century cult of the Noble Savage. In English, the phrase Noble Savage first appeared in Dryden's play, *The Conquest of Granada* (1672): "I am as free as nature first made man, / Ere the base laws of servitude began, / When wild in woods the noble savage ran."

And these were the words were found scrawled in chalk at each crime scene.

The term "Noble Savage" only began to be widely used in the last half of the nineteenth century and then as a term of disparagement. In French the term had been the "Good Savage" (or good "Wild man"), and, in French (and even in eighteenth-century English), the word "savage" did not necessarily have the connotations of cruelty we now associate with it, but meant "wild" as in a wild flower.

But these girls were both savage *and* cruel and, despite the lofty sentiments expressed by Dryden, showed no sign of anything even approaching nobility. But they did seem to be some strange celebration of their humanness which put them in a diametrically opposing position to the Children of the Three, whose position *vis a vis* the future of their own species seemed to be one that would make Zoltan Istvan [**] at his most radical seem like a cultural shrinking violet.

But they had the be connected. Logic dictated that two such radical groups of young revolutionaries could not be in such close proximity of each other without there being some connection. And if so, what was it?

---

* Order of Assassins or simply Assassins (Arabic: أساسين‎asāsīn, Persian: حشاشين‎Hashâshīn) is the common name used to refer to an Islamic sect formally known as the Nizari Ismailis. Based on texts from Alamut, their grand master Hassan-i Sabbah tended to call his disciples Asāsīyūn (أساسيون‎)meaning "people who are faithful to the foundation [of the faith]"), but some foreign travelers[who?] misunderstood the name as deriving from the term hashish.[citation needed]

Often described as a secret order led by a mysterious "Old Man of the Mountain", the Nizari Ismailis formed in the late 11th century after a split within Ismailism – a branch of Shia Islam.

** Zoltan Istvan Gyurko, professionally known as Zoltan Istvan (born March 30, 1973), is an American transhuman-ist, journalist, entrepreneur, and Libertarian futurist.

Formerly a reporter for the National Geographic Channel, Istvan now writes futurist, transhumanist, libertarian and secular themed articles for major media, including Vice's Motherboard, Wired, The Huffington Post, TechCrunch and Newsweek. Istvan regularly appears on television and video channels discussing futurist topics. He is one of the world's most influential transhumanists and believes transhumanism will grow into a mainstream social movement in the next decade. Istvan is the author of The Transhumanist Wager, a philosophical science fiction novel.

I have spent so much of my life on the track of illogical, and fundamentally absurd animals and men, that I am actually feeling quite angry with myself for thinking so conservatively. But I suppose that means that at heart I am far more conservative, and less of a freethinker than I thought that I was, and that is something that I find more disturbing than I probably should do.

But I wanted to set my mind at rest, but in order to do that I needed to speak to Danny Miles, and in order to speak to Danny Miles on my own terms I would have to get hold of him, and this was something that I had no idea how to do. So I would have to just wait and see what happened, and this was something that I have never liked doing. But on this occasion it looked like I didn't really have any option.

IX

Although I have always had my suspicions about Gerald Gardner [*], I have been interested in Witchcraft for many years. My Grandmother was, allegedly, a traditional hedge witch whose practises predated the rise of neopaganism by many years. Two of my cousins follow the craft, and I have always read widely on the subject.

However, over the same period of time, I began to slowly fall out with Mother Church, and whilst I still consider myself to be a Christian, if I may mix my religious metaphors, I am a hedge Christian, rather than an active member of any Christian coven.

The biggest series of events to provoke my schism from organised Christianity happened about fifteen years ago when I was dating a devoutly Christian woman called Lydia. It was to cut my emotional bonds with her, as well as many other things, by the way, that the magickal ritual I told you about earlier in this narrative took place on Millenium Eve. With hindsight what happened to us was inevitable not ill fated, as she came from a family so dysfunctional as to make mine seem ordinary, and they were not just dysfunctional but they were God Botherers [**] to the nth degree. I was bad news to them all, and to her ex-husband who was the 'elder' of the peculiar church to which the rest of her family subscribed, and to the members of the Roman Catholic

---

* See note on page 17

** I have always wondered whether these are people who bother God, as well as bothering the rest of us on the subject

church to which Lydia herself belonged. Whether this was, as they all proclaimed loudly, bellowing platitudes from the pulpit at me, because I was divorced (which made me a sinner) and a journalist specialising in Fortean stories (which made me an idolater) and someone who had made a small art movie, and written two fairly eminent books featuring naked witches and moonlight rituals (which made me a blasphemer) or whether (as I suspected) that they were afraid that Lydia (who had a sizeable private income) would stop financing their activities if she had ended up marrying me, I don't know, although I have my suspicions.

It all ended rather nastily, with sermons about me being preached from the pulpit, and poor Lydia being forced to scourge herself (honestly, I couldn't make this shit up) to make amends for her sins of fornication, and I believe that the local priest was brought round to do something approaching an exorcism of the flat in which she lived to cleanse it of the evil spirits that I had brought into it whilst visiting her on and off for about ten months. Her family did all sorts of hocus pocus with holy water, and I had a series of threatening telephone calls late at night which continued until I referred the whole matter to the police.

The whole business disturbed me mightily. Lydia's father was a retired Church of England vicar who had - allegedly at least - sexually abused Lydia and her sister while they were growing up. However, they were all still living together, and he had never been brought to book for his actions. Her sister was a massively ugly woman like a malevolent toad who manipulated everyone around her with breathtaking skill, and only turned against me when it turned out that I was one of the few people she was unable to manipulate. Both her daughters were serious druggies, and the father of her grandson was at the time in Oxford Prison for drug related offences. The whole family lived in different flats making up a huge and rather spooky Victorian house on the outskirts of Dawlish Warren, and their various flats (especially those of the two daughters and their various boyfriends) acted as a hub for the local criminal fraternity.

With hindsight I should have run a mile as soon as I met this trainwreck-like family, but that is the annoying thing about hindsight. At the time I just found myself getting sucked in slowly and inexorably, only to be expelled violently when it became obvious to them that I wasn't going to fall for their searing bullshit. But it was the attitude of Lydia's priestly advisors that sealed it for me. How could anyone claiming to worship the gentle Christ of the New Testament, Gentle Jesus Meek and Mild, force a mentally ill woman to scourge herself with a miniature cat o'nine tails, until she drew blood, for the imaginary crime of sleeping with someone who was divorced?

As soon as her family found out that I had friends who were followers of the craft, and even worse, as soon as they found that I had taken Lydia to meet the notorious Tony 'Doc' Shiels, that was it. One Friday lunchtime I was sitting at my makeshift desk by the front window of my little house in Exeter, writing as usual, when a sinister looking shrew-like little man came shuffling up to my door. He introduced himself to me as Father Bailey, the Ecumenical Psychologist, and explained that he had been sent to visit me by those who were concerned that I was in truck with The Devil. This was the sort of thing that I could have probably sold a story about to one of the newspapers, so I probably should have invited him in and allowed him to interview me. But I'd truly had enough by this time, and I brusquely told him to go and fuck himself, and slammed the door in his face.

The next time (the last time) I saw Lydia was later that afternoon. She was with her sister. I could hardly recognise her as my friend and lover of the past ten months. She walked stiffly, and spoke with a strange mechanical voice. It was the second time that day that I was told that I was in truck with The Devil, and that Father Bailey had explained things so clearly to her that she now realised how I had possessed her feminine soul with my diabolical urges, and that she would now have to spend the rest of her life in a religious retreat for women who had fallen from Grace, if she was to stop her eternal soul from going to Hell for all time. Her sister crossed herself and hissed at me, and the two women turned on their heels and shuffled away. I never saw either of them again.

About two years later at the 2002 Weird Weekend, which was held at Exeter University I met Sally, the elder of Lydia's daughters, again. She had always been the nicer of the two, and I was genuinely glad to see her. Our eyes met and she ran across the room towards me and gave me a huge hug. Diffidently I asked about her mother. The news was more bizarre than even I could have imagined. Apparently Sally's Father, the elder of their particular cult, had died suddenly. Her Grandfather had taken over the role as elder (I truly don't know whether this should have a capital E or not, and as I have nothing but contempt for these people, I will not dignify them with it) and had almost immediately been arrested for some sexual impropriety or other. Sally couldn't tell me what, because by that time she had been banished from both the family and the Church for the sin of having insisted that her little girl have Rubella inoculations.

What she could tell me, however, was that Lydia had gone from bad to worse. Sally's sister Martha had given birth to a baby girl, and almost immediately died of an overdose. Lydia had named the baby girl Dorcas, and was rearing the baby herself, despite being in and out of the local mental institution, most recently for having smeared messages, allegedly from Satan, on the walls of a public lavatory in her own faeces. I gave Sally a hug, told her my telephone number (which she has never used) and left, sending up a silent prayer to my particular pantheon of deities apologising that I had never got further involved with that insane family, and walked out of their lives forever.

X

I had turned to the Church of Rome, away from the Anglican faith in which I had been brought up, because the Church of England seemed to be becoming ever more peculiar and irrelevant. I remember back when I was about nineteen and - believe it or not - on the local Parochial Church Council being asked about starting up a church youth group in an attempt to make the church more "relevant" to young people. I said then that replacing the old hymns with trite poppy tunes, and dumbed down sermons, would irritate more people than it impressed, and that if the Church continued to implement change for change's sake it would end up like an ecclesiastical version of the Liberal Party.

I was ignored, and - as I predicted - people (including me) left in droves, and most never came back. I found more gravitas amongst the left footers, but it was getting impossible to ignore the moral inconsistencies, and - as I have already explained - a series of events in my private life led to me leaving that path for good about fifteen years ago. Over the years I tried dipping my foot back into the Church of England millpond when it was politically (with a small p) or socially expedient, but on each occasion I found that I couldn't stomach the soaring bullshit which came along with it, and that I couldn't in all conscience continue with something which seemed to have the political and moral gravitas of an episode of *Eastenders*.* So, about seven years ago, I left for good, and I doubt whether I shall ever go back.

I still consider myself a practising Christian, but these days I carry out my devotions by myself, and in private. I am sorry to have ranted on about my relationship with Christianity, but it is really rather important when one considers what happens next in the narrative that I am attempting to impart in my typically muddleheaded fashion.

"Thou shalt have no other Gods before me" said the Lord dictating the

---

* As I know that some of my readers live outside the UK, I should probably explain that EastEnders is a British soap opera created by Julia Smith and Tony Holland which has been broadcast on BBC One since 1985. Set in Albert Square in the East End of London in the fictional Borough of Walford, the programme follows the stories of local residents and their families as they go about their daily lives. Initially there were two 30-minute episodes per week but since 2001 episodes have been broadcast every weekday apart from Wednesdays.

When I was a nurse, I vaguely watched it in order to have something to talk about the next day with my fellow toilers in the NHS vineyard, but have not bothered to look anywhere in its vicinity for nearly thirty years.

commandments to Moses. Later in the King James version of the Bible it reads: 'When the LORD made a covenant with the Israelites, he commanded them: "Do not worship any other gods or bow down to them, serve them or sacrifice to them.' (2 Kings 17:35)

I can cite a dozen different references, but I shan't. Everywhere the Lord of Hosts says that his followers are forbidden to worship any other god BEFORE him. Nowhere does it say that there are no other Gods (with small or upper case g). In fact it implies that there are, but that they should not be worshipped. That is fine by me, because I have what is unquestionably a God living in the airing cupboard in what used to be my father's dressing room, and although I am very fond of it, and on cold winter nights it even snuggles up with the dogs at the bottom of Corinna's and my marital bed, I have no intention of worshipping it. Indeed the matter has never entered my head.

But why do I say it is a God? C. Scott Littleton's *Gods, Goddesses, and Mythology* defined a deity as:

> "...a being with powers greater than those of ordinary humans, but who interacts with humans, positively or negatively, in ways that carry humans to new levels of consciousness beyond the grounded preoccupations of ordinary life".

Panne is a delightful little thing, but it certainly ticks all those boxes, and by that definition, I have a burgeoning amount of evidence (although I will admit freely that I have been doing my best to ignore it) to suppose that there are at least two other deities living out in the woods between Meddon and Hartland. And it seems that these deities may not be as pleasant company as is Panne, and probably (unlike Panne) do not like being scratched behind the ears whilst they guzzle chocolate.

This year's Weird Weekend went really rather well, and I had settled down to my customary period of doing nothing for a few weeks.

However, this year something had changed. For various reasons with which I shall not bore you stuff got in the way and I was not able to take my customary month of September holiday, and even though it was my secretary's day off I therefore was actually awake, sober and in the office, when Danny Miles broke his silence of nine months and actually deigned to contact me at last.

XI

*I*nauspicious is a word used to describe what happens when the omens of the day, or for those of you who do not believe in such things, those little things in life which hint what life has in store for us, hint that the things that are about to happen are not necessarily going to be that good. It is the opposite of Auspicious which is a word which dates back to Ancient Rome.

The augur was a priest and official in the classical world, especially ancient Rome and Etruria. His main role was the practice of augury, interpreting the will of the gods by studying the flight of birds: whether they are flying in groups or alone, what noises they make as they fly, direction of flight and what kind of birds they are. This was known as "taking the auspices." The ceremony and function of the augur was central to any major undertaking in Roman society—public or private—including matters of war, commerce, and religion, and the words 'inauspicious' and 'auspicious' derive from that.

In great works of literature, and even in the less great, the protagonists have often said that so and so was either an auspicious or an inauspicious day. But - not for the first time - I have found myself in the position of deciding that the Queen's English is somewhat inadequate for my needs, and so I am forced into having to invent a neologism.

As I write this, it is just before eleven on a Sunday night at the beginning of winter in the year of our Lord 2015, coincidentally a year after my slightly embarrassing and rather more painful adventures at Miss Britannia's cottage, and I am trying to sit down and write deathless prose whilst a pair of half grown kittens (Squeaky and Dotty) play catch as catch can around my feet, two tortoises (Nero and Calpurnia) noisily copulate in the four foot vivarium on the floor, the sofa is inhabited by a teenage girl with bright blue hair and a large fat dog with impressive jowls, (the girl is Deanie and the dog is Prudence), and my elderly Mother-in-Law is sat in a Victorian nursing chair watching a Harry Potter movie on TV.

Corinna and I are both writing, a jet-black cat called Lilith is staring into the front of a large vivarium holding a magnificent Mexican black kingsnake named after the Crown Prince of Jollilinki* in a quasi racist joke (a black prince turns into a black

---

* Leading character in several of the Dr Dolittle stories by Hugh Lofting. Often cited as being a racist plot device, those who condemn him conveniently ignore that he is portrayed as being brave, loyal and intelligent. And although the plot originally portrayed him as an African prince who wished that he could be white so that he could marry the white princess, the *real* moral of that particular story, is that people should never try to change themselves to fit a fictional ideal. But, of course, the PC brigade never see things like that

king, after all, unless he is Edward of Woodstock*) and in front of the gas fire which will heat the room until I can afford to have the chimney fixed is a hairy heap consisting of a large orange cat named after a Frank Zappa song,** a badly behaved and somewhat neurotic Jack Russell terrier ***, and a naked, hairy forest Godling, who appears to be invisible to at least half of the humans in the room. In the last year I have never been able to make up my mind whether Mother can actually see Panne, but she has reached the age where she is surprised at very little, and would presumably be unlikely to discuss the matter if she did.

I had actually planned to spend a quiet evening drinking my daemons away, and catching up on writing this narrative, but the wings and sparrows of outrageous fortune (as Horace Coker once put it****) took a hand, and Deanie (who is one of my ever growing band of adopted nieflets) ended up coming to spend the night, hence precluding my plans for inebriation, and explaining the DVD that Mother and Deanie are watching whilst the rest of us ignore it to a greater or lesser extent.

---

* Edward of Woodstock, known as the Black Prince (15 June 1330 – 8 June 1376), was the eldest son of Edward III, King of England, and Philippa of Hainault and participated in the early years of the Hundred Years War. He died before his father and so never became king. His son, Richard II, would succeed to the throne instead. Edward was created Duke of Cornwall in 1337. He was guardian of the kingdom in his father's absence in 1338, 1340, and 1342. He was created Prince of Wales in 1343 and knighted by his father at La Hogne in 1346.

In 1346 Edward commanded the vanguard at the Battle of Crécy, his father intentionally leaving him to win the battle. He was named the Black Prince after the battle of Crécy, at which he was possibly accoutred in black armour.

** *Cheepnis* is a song by Frank Zappa and The Mothers, which is a tribute to B-movies. The song sings about the special effects in early horror movies, including a monster, named "Frunobulax", a very large poodle dog. The poodle is a recurring theme in other Zappa songs and is an illustration of what he referred to as the "conceptual continuity" of his body of work. *Cheepnis* is from the album *Roxy & Elsewhere*.

When I originally wanted an orange kitten, Corinna told me that I could only have one if I gave it a sensible name. So I thought long and hard before naming him Captain Frunobulax the Magnificent. Corinna then named him 'Peanut', and he has two names, although nobody calls him anything apart from 'Peanut' or 'Cat'.

*** Archie (short for 'The Archimandrite of Joppa' from the Kipling story *The United Idolaters*.

**** A character in many of the Greyfriars stories by Frank Richards. Coker, Horace James (Study No 4)– Clumsy, buffoonish, wealthy. Introduced in Magnet #143 The Head of Study 14 (5 Nov, 1910), when still in the Shell form; he was elevated to the Fifth form in Magnet #145 Coker's Catch (19 Nov, 1910). Extremely stupid, hot-headed, aggressive and overbearing; notorious for his 'short way with fags'; but when he visits the Remove passage hunting trouble, the 'fags' demonstrate a 'short way with Coker.' He is the worst speller in the School ("How many K's in 'exasperating'?" asked Horace Coker) and has a style of playing soccer and cricket that is a menace to his own teammates; yet is completely convinced that he is the best scholar and sportsman at Greyfriars. Was only promoted from the Shell after his formidable Aunt Judy pressured Dr Locke into doing so. Aunt Judy keeps Coker well in funds and hampers, and seems oblivious to his many faults. A good hearted character, dim but decent, and brave to the point of stupidity. Coker has on at least one occasion requested Dr Locke to make him a prefect, a request that was politely declined.

His reimagining of Hamlet's soliloquy is from *Billy Bunter's Benefit* (1950)

Corinna loathes the Harry Potter books and movies with a vengeance, whereas I will admit I quite like them, but I have seen the film too many times to want to see it again at this particular time, but I will admit that there is a certain mildly delicious irony in the television showing the film which introduced some concepts of the esoteric arts to a new generation of youngsters, whilst I am trying to explain the events of a Wednesday morning a couple of months ago when everything went tits up, and my world (peculiar enough at the best of times) changed beyond all recognition once again.

But what I have been wanting to explain requires the invention of a neologism. It was an unauspicious day; there were no portents of doom, and no suggestions of power and glory either. It was one of those sunny days that happen in the dog days of summer, which suggest that an Indian Summer might be just around the corner. These are the days when exotic butterflies from warmer climes occasionally turn up on British shores, and although the kids have gone back to school, ice cream sales go through the roof as doting mothers do their best to reassure their offspring that although they are 'back in the jug agane'[*] life as they know it has not completely come to an end.

---

* Nigel Molesworth, as any fule kno.

Nigel Molesworth is a fictional character, the supposed author of a series of books (actually written by Geoffrey Willans), with cartoon illustrations by Ronald Searle.

The Molesworth books were the result of an approach by Willans to the cartoonist, Searle, to illustrate a series of books based on a column he had been writing for Punch. They appeared in instalments in the children's magazine The Young Elizabethan, described by Molesworth as "the super smashing New Young Elizabethan ahem (advert.)". Searle had grown disillusioned with his (very popular) St Trinian's School series but had promised his publisher Max Parrish another Christmas best-seller. Searle was initially sceptical about another school-based project but was won over by the examples he was given to read by Willans. Between the initial publication in 1953 and Willans' death in 1958 (aged 47) three books were completed and most of a fourth (*Back in the Jug Agane*) written; the *Compleet Molesworth* anthology was also under way.

Nigel is a schoolboy at St Custard's, a fictional (and terrible) prep school located in a carefully unspecified part of England. It is ruled with an iron fist by Headmaster Grimes (BA, Stoke-on-Trent), who is constantly in search of cash to supplement his income and has a part-time business running a whelk stall. St Custard's has 62 pupils and, according to Molesworth, "was built by a madman in 1836". Pupils include Grabber, the head boy and winner of the Mrs Joyful Prize for Raffia-work, whose father owns a publishing business; Peason, Molesworth's "grate frend" [sic] and companion on his frequently imagined interplanetary adventures; Fotherington-Tomas, the school sissy; and Molesworth 2, Nigel's annoying younger brother. The school's traditional local rivals are Porridge Court, who regularly beat them at sporting events.

Nigel's spelling is consistently poor, with most words rendered phonetically, a feature found endearing by fans.

It is only as I sit typing these references that I realise what a wide level of interests I have: from 1950s spoofs on Public School literature to the real thing written forty years before, and from history to magick and rock and roll. Basically - as I have been told on many occasions - I have a grasshopper mind and hop from one subject to another at the slightest possible encouragement. I am nowhere near as clever as some people think; I merely know a bit about lots and lots of things, but there is little that I know much about.

So, as I was saying, there were no hints - one or another - that this was going to be an important day. The postman had come and gone, without either having delivered cheques or bills, I had just finished my breakfast (a bowl full of various bits of antipasti that Graham was kind enough to bring me), and was just going through my emails as I was drinking my second cup of coffee, and doing my best to ignore the fact that despite having finally quit six months before, every pore of my body was gasping for one of Messrs Benson and Hedges' finest.

My emails were roughly the same as normal - large amounts of data from the Google News Alerts service which I use each day for updating the CFZ news blogs, the occasional letter from friends and acquaintances, and the normal heavy frosting of attempted scams, adverts for viagra or soft pornography, emails from wannabe Russian mail-order brides, and Nigerian widows trying to give me a million quid. And there are the bottom of the heap (OK its not a heap, but you know what I mean) was an email from danny.m@sexgod.com.

Before I even opened it, my heart dropped. I hadn't heard from Danny for nearly a year, since I had lost my temper with him for being complicit in the abduction of one of my best friends in the village, in an attempt to promote a Festive hit single. (Don't ask)

I have known Danny for over a third of a century, and have disliked him intensely for most of that time, and I have no reason to suppose that he likes me very much either. However, it seems that his destiny and mine are inextricably interlinked, and I have begrudgingly accepted that he will probably be part of my life for the duration. But, for the first eight and a half months of the year I have been in a happily Danny-free position, and - although it was too good to last - I had gotten used to it. Now that window of security and happiness was about to be closed forever.

With trepidation I opened the email. It read.

"Yo man, soz not to have been in touch, but am very busy. cAn I borrow fifty quid? I owe it to some friends of yours"

I wrote back:

"No you can't. What friends?"

And half an hour later came a reply.

"Pleease man. Malcky and Trace".

It was then that I made my great mistake. Instead of just ignoring him, or sending him a burst of verbal abuse, my curiosity was piqued for all the wrong reasons. So I replied:

"How the hell did you get involved with those arseholes? They owe me a lot of money, and if I ever see them again there will be trouble".

By doing that I had committed the unforgiveable mistake of opening up a channel of communication with Danny. In the split second it took me to press the SEND button, the day had suddenly stopped being unauspicious. It was to be decidedly inauspicious from then on!

XII

There are people in life whom it seems that you are unable to shake off, a bit like a bad smell. They keep on coming back into your life at the most inopportune times, causing havoc and then disappearing again. I have told you all about the aetiology of my relationship with Danny bloody Miles earlier in this narrative, and - indeed - he has turned up in several of my books over the years. But Malcky and Trace are a different kettle of fish entirely.

In February 2006 my Father died. I inherited half the old family home here in North Devon, and as a result I got myself in hock up to my armpits in order to buy my brother's share of the estate. I also inherited about £20,000, and to my horror, various people who had been involved in my activities for varying lengths of time, decided that it was their duty to help me spend it, often without my knowledge or agreement. Malcky, an irritating sports instructor from Lanarkshire who had been doing various bits and bobs to do with our annual conference, was one of these, and with the benefit of hindsight I now know that he was robbing me blind. But I cannot prove it.

Things got worse when he met a fat and vindictive woman called Trai-Cee (am I the only person who dislikes alternative phonetic spellings of female names?) * on a message board for Mods **. Yes, you know, those people that Pete Townshend sang

---

* Actually I am not. Bertie Wooster intimated as much in a Jeeves short story, "The Spot of Art" (collected in *Very Good, Jeeves* by P.G.Wodehouse). Bertie is in love with the artist Gwladys Pendlebury, who has painted Bertie's portrait. However, Aunt Dahlia is confident that Jeeves will be able to split up Bertie and Gwladys, get rid of the painting, and make Bertie join Aunt Dahlia on her cruise.

** Mod is a subculture that began in London in 1958 and spread throughout Great Britain and elsewhere, eventually influencing fashions and trends in other countries, and continues today on a smaller scale. Focused on music and fashion, the subculture has its roots in a small group of stylish London-based young men in the late 1950s who were termed modernists because they listened to modern jazz.

about who trundled up the A23 from London to Brighton on Lambrettas. The idea of either the gawky, ridiculously self satisfied Malcky, or the morbidly obese woman who was soon to become his wife, on a scooter is a disturbing one, but as far as I am aware, this story is completely true. Trai-Cee soon claimed she was pregnant and a hastily convened wedding service took place at a village church just outside Barmstaple.

Corinna and I were guests of honour (probably because we were the only people that either of them knew who had a video camera that they hadn't got in hock at the local office of Cash Converters). So we found ourselves roped into filming the whole tawdry affair, and I believe that it is still up on You Tube. If you are able to find it, you will - no doubt - notice that bits of the service, and what happened afterwards, are shaking badly, giving all the indications that the cameraman was suffering from Parkinson's Disease.

The cameraman was me, and - although recently I have been sent to the specialist at North Devon District Hospital with Parkinson's-like symptoms - back in 2008, I had no such neurosurgical complications in my life. I was merely laughing uncontrollably at the freak show which unfolded beneath me, and was - despite my wife's vicious glares in my direction - unable to keep the camera still.

The service was totally excruciating.

The Bride shuffled up the aisle to the accompaniment of a song by Elvis Presley which cut off mid-line as she reached the side of the Groom resplendent in dinner jacket and purple cummerbund. I had tried to explain to him that Dinner Jackets were for evening wear, and that the appropriate wear would be Morning Dress, and that to insist that all the men wore evening wear for a daytime event was just vulgar. However, he stared at me gormlessly, and obviously had no idea what I was talking about and as I really did not care that much, I let the matter drop.

The Bride's dress looked like it was something from a touring production of *Alice in Wonderland,* and revealed far more of her rather unattractive Décolletage than anyone could possibly have thought seemly.

As is the modern fashion, both the Bride and the Bridegroom had tinkered with the vows that are in *The Book of Common Prayer,* but as the Bride was chewing gum, and the Groom had an unfortunate bout of Sinusitis one could only understand about one word in three that they said.

Then after they shuffled off into the Vestry to sign the registry, the Groom's sister, a statuesque Lesbian covered in tattoos got up to sing a tuneless version of one of the more irritating modern hymns whilst accompanied by an organist who gave every indication of not having actually played his instrument before. Then we all trooped outside where I was able to let my long held ambition to be the Devonshire equivalent of John Waters * reach some degree of fruition as I filmed the freak show that was taking place before me.

Let's start with the bridesmaids. There seemed to be dozens of them, all wearing massively skimpy outfits which ranged between inappropriate and arrestably obscene. Two of them were very obviously pregnant, but most of them were heavily made up and about eleven years old. All wore dresses so diaphanous that one could clearly see the expanses of podgy flesh that lay beneath. No sooner had the congregation trooped outside than 90% of the adults started to smoke, something to which the vicar objected. Marching over to the Bride's mother who was there with her Jamaican toy boy, he asked her politely not to smoke on consecrated ground, only to have the Jamaican shake his fist at him and mutter something belligerent of which the only word I understood was "Raasclaat" (which is why I knew he was Jamaican). **

I hope for his sake that the vicar didn't know what he meant, but he obviously got the gist of it, because he quickly went and locked the church door, disappeared into the presbytery and we didn't see him again for the rest of the day.

The Groom's family, whom I knew vaguely (except for the lesbian sister who was actively engaged in trying to press her advances upon one of the pregnant bridesmaids), looked mortified. His mother, wearing a peculiar netting hat that looked like the things old fashioned tea houses at the posher end of the spectrum used to use to keep flies off the cream buns, tried her best to look as if she was proud of her son's part in the freakshow (and yes, I know that I have used that word liberally quite a lot in this description, but for once my thesaurus has let me down) unfolding in front of him, but her husband made no effort at all. Her husband had been a minor member of staff for one of the less popular and most ineffectual British politicians of recent years, and his family was very proud of this. I wonder whether Sir Peter will be

---

* John Samuel Waters Jr. (born April 22, 1946) is an American film director, screenwriter, author, actor, stand-up comedian, journalist, visual artist, and art collector, who rose to fame in the early 1970s for his transgressive cult films. Waters' early campy movies present exaggerated characters in outrageous situations with hyperbolic dialogue. Pink Flamingos, Female Trouble, and Desperate Living, which he labeled the Trash Trilogy, pushed hard at the boundaries of conventional propriety and movie censorship. A particularly notorious scene from Pink Flamingos, added as a non sequitur to the film's end, featured—in one continuous take without special effects—a small dog defecating and Divine eating its faeces.

** Bum Cloth. your 'raas' is your bum, a 'claat' is a cloth. Toilet paper! This is the actual meaning, but it is often used as an adjective when expressing dissatisfaction

coming to the wedding, Malcky and Trace had gushed. Although I was by no means a fan of the right honourable gentleman, I so hoped that he would be there. The idea of arranging a photo opportunity for him and the Bride's mother, who by this time was smooching like a hormoned up teenager with the bad tempered Jamaican youth, was too delightful a prospect to miss.

There was a scuffle as the boyfriend of the pregnant bridesmaid objected to his girlfriend having her buttocks fondled by the Groom's lesbian sister, and out of the corner of my eye I could see the Bride's father refreshing himself out of a small bottle of brandy that he had secreted in the inside pocket of his jacket. What a good idea, I thought, and did exactly the same thing with the small bottle of brandy I had secreted in the inside pocket of mine.

Then we walked up the hill to the Church Hall where the reception was to take place. I felt that my reputation as a Cinema Vérité cinematographer was at stake, so - ignoring my dear wife's angry glances - I made sure that I was following the pregnant bridesmaid (who was, by the way, wearing an unfeasibly short purple satin dress) up the hill filming the way that her cellulite rippled in the autumn sunshine.

Not entirely to my surprise, the Church Hall door was locked, presumably by the retreating vicar. To my surprise, even the bellicose Jamaican tough balked at kicking open the door of a building which was - after all - attached to the Church. But the Father of the Bride proved his worth by refreshing himself once again from his little bottle of brandy, reaching into another pocket for a small but functional jemmy and forcing the lock. I don't think he or anyone else realised that I was filming the whole thing.

We trooped into the Church Hall, and I took my place next to the small line of Wedding Dignatories which is now *de rigeur* at even the most informal of events. There they were: The Bride (still chewing gum), The Groom (who had been sharing a suspiciously long cigarette with his new Mother-in-Law's boyfriend, and looked distinctively worse for wear), The Bride's Mother (who was scratching her ample buttocks), the Bride's Father who seemed to bear no animosity towards his ex-wife, and slouched there shiftily, and the parents of the Groom who just looked as if they wished that they could be anywhere else in the world at that moment, and wished the ground would swallow them up.

The Groom's Father saw me positioning myself to film the unlikely group preparing to welcome the assorted wedding guests. "For God's sake don't film me" he muttered, pressing twenty quid into my hand. Like so many smalltime wannabe politicians he was apparently a sexist, because the fact that Corinna was at the other end of the queue filming away merrily completely passed under his radar.

So I pocketed the twenty quid, and sloped off to share the rest of the Jamaican boyfriend's spliff.

It turned out that his name was Calvin, he had been to Eton, and the only time he put on the patois of a down at heel Yardie, was when he wanted to appear like one. He was, apparently a relative of the Jamaican High Commissioner, training to be an accountant, and with only two vices; a taste for marijuana and a penchant for fat working class women twice his age. *Tout comprendre c'est rien pardonner.* I could understand one of those vices, but the other was totally incomprehensible.

XIII

I don't consider that I am racist, sexist, classist or any of the other '-ist' thoughtcrimes that are so prevalent across the board in the canon of 21st Century thought crimea. But the Malcky-Trace nuptials involved two groups of people that I find most abhorrent in the universe; ill-bred Chavs and inbred Tories. And the idea of an alchemical wedding between two such unlovely social subgroupings was something that I found most disturbing.

I have been a journalist for long enough to be able to know how to make my excuses and leave fairly discreetly, * so as soon as we could possibly do so without completely compromising the bounds of good taste, and so as the bride and groom went off to honeymoon in a North African country that should probably remain nameless. Corinna and I went home; Corinna to play Lord of the Rings Online, and me to get drunk, both of us doing our best to expunge the unpleasant vibes of the day from our collective psyche.

We weren't to see the happy couple again for several months. And it turned out that the honeymoon in North Africa had been less than idyllic.

On the first morning Trai-Cee had come down with diarrhoea which eventually turned out to be dysentry, and two days later, as they were on their way to the free clinic (they had, of course not bothered with holiday sickness insurance) they were kidnapped by a band of Arab brigands intent on securing a handsome ransom (if I

---

* See footnote on p.23

49

may quote *Fury in the Slaughterhouse*). *The fact that one of them was a lanky streak of piss with red hair and clothes which it was pretty obvious had come from the bargain bins at Primark, whilst his companion was a grossly fat woman with the galloping trots and big purple botches all over her skin, really does cast doubt upon the perspicacity of the North African criminal fraternity. One would have thought that the fact that when the raiders searched the hotel room in which the unhappy couple had been staying, and found two hundred bucks in US Traveller's Cheques, and a stash of rather unpleasant S&M pornography that Malcky had bought from a seedy looking bloke in the Gents toilets at the airport, together with some extra large underwear complete with embarrassing stains, might have insinuated that their new captives were unlikely to make them even slightly wealthy.

Now, I shall make no attempt to drop any hints by which the more perspicacious reader could identify the crappy little resort town where this all took place, but it is located not too far from the border with a far less stable country where the rule of law has largely become non-existent, largely because there are huge swathes of country, that since the ignominious exit of the quondam Colonial Power several decades ago, nobody really knows who owns. In fact, this is not quite true. Three different countries (one of which is only recognised as a nation by a couple of its tiny neighbours, and one of which is basically the Human Resources Department of one of the nastier and less ethical oil companies) lay claim to the region, but for the last thirty years a fairly laid back guerrilla war has been going on between the three claimants, and no-one outside the region actually cares.

In the meantime (and it doesn't realistically look like the matter is going to be settled any time soon) the region is like a geographical analogue to the areas of the Internet accessible by the Onion Router; a haven for criminal activities of all sorts where - basically - anything goes.

Malcky and Trace were taken to a very grotty little house on the outskirts of a small town a few kilometres across the border, where they were locked in the cellar, and there they stayed for the next three weeks wallowing in their own feculence, and being fed one rather nasty meal of rancid couscous each day. Ironically this was probably the best thing to happen to Trai-Cee , because as a result of this she was not only cured of dysentery, but lost a considerable amount of weight and was now -

---

* Fury in the Slaughterhouse was a rock band from Hannover, Germany, founded in 1987 and disbanded in 2008. Their hits include: "Time to Wonder", "Every Generation Got Its Own Disease", "Won't Forget These Days", "Radio Orchid", "Dancing in the Sunshine of the Dark", "Milk & Honey", and "Trapped Today, Trapped Tomorrow". The name comes from the German version of Champion the Wonderhorse in which theequiid was called 'Fury'.

They toured with Steve Harley and Cockney Rebel (and me) in 1990; a tour that is immortalised in my book *Road Dreams* (1993).

although hardly sylph like - lighter than she had been since puberty.

Then on Day 21 of their ordeal Malcky had a remarkably good idea, and managed to persuade their captors that it would be in their interest to allow them to send a message to Malcky's Father (who, diligent readers will remember, was last seen bribing me with twenty quid to keep him out of his son's wedding video) entreating him to ask his employer (a shadowy one-time Tory Cabinet Minister whose friendship with Jimmy Savile [*] had precluded his elevation to the Upper House) to pay the ransom necessary to ensure the unhappy couple's safe return to Blighty.

Although the impression that I had got from the wedding was that his Father would have been unlikely to part with the coupons from the back of a packet of cornflakes to ensure their safe return, *somehow* this stratagem worked. However on the day that the ransom money arrived, so did the militia which was owned and operated by the Tourist Board of the country to which the young marrieds had gone on honeymoon, and after a spectacular shootout that left most the un-named brigands dead in a colander-like state, they were rescued.

Things were looking up for Malcky and Trace, but not for long. They travelled back to the hotel in the certain knowledge that Sir Peter's money would be waiting for them, and that they would be able to snaffle some or all of it secure in the knowledge that Sir Peter regarded Johnny Foreigner as a rum cove and wouldn't expect anything less. However, things were not going to work out so easily for them.

No sooner did they go back to their hotel room they were immediately arrested. It turned out that the authorities were not impressed with Malcky's collection of S&M pornography, which was - apparently, for I have no knowledge of such things - illegal in that particular corner of North Africa. They also found some smutty Polaroids taken (one sincerely hopes) before Trace had come down with dysentery, and these were also impounded. Bizarrely, the fine for being in possession of an offensive wife was worse than the fine for being in possession of some rather nasty locally produced pornography, and coincidentally the cumulative costs of both fines, the court administration fee and various other sundries was exactly covered by Sir Peter's largesse.

---

* Sir James Wilson Vincent Savile OBE (1926 – 2011) was an English DJ, television and radio personality, dance hall manager, and charity fundraiser. He hosted the BBC television show Jim'll Fix It, was the first and last presenter of the long-running BBC music chart show Top of the Pops, and raised an estimated £40 million for charities. At the time of his death he was widely praised for his personal qualities and as a fund-raiser. After his death, hundreds of allegations of sexual abuse were made against him, leading the police to believe that Savile had been a predatory sex offender — possibly one of Britain's most prolific.

The British Consul managed to negotiate a compromise whereby they avoided the public flogging usually meted out to those convicted of crimes of moral turpitude by the powers that be in that morally enlightened slice of the Northern Sahara, and - after several more weeks in an Arabic chokey - the two unhappy honeymooners were shipped home in disgrace.

As the British Government stopped paying for 'Distressed British Citizens' to return home many decades ago, and Sir Peter, having discovered what had happened to his first slice of largesse, via arcane diplomatic channels of his own, flatly refused to send any more money, Malcky and Trace had only one option open to them; they sold their stories to one of the grubbier British lifestyle magazines, together with some shudderingly revolting pictures of Trace topless on a North African beach whilst Malcky, dressed like Laurence of Arabia, towered over her leering disturbingly.

This paid for them to get back to North Devon, but when they got back they had a further shock awaiting them. Despite having told the reporters - in great detail - about their ordeal at the hands of the kidnappers, the scions of Her Majesty's Press chose to ignore most of it, and instead focus on the more prurient aspects of the case. So instead of returning as heroes who had been kidnapped by terrorist brigands, the newlyweds returned having been lampooned as pornographers who had been justly punished by the morally upright authorities in one of Britain's oldest allies, after trying unsuccessfully to market a lewd and depraved piece of home-made smut to the local chubby chaser community.

Poor Malcky and Trace. When I had stopped laughing, I actually felt sorry for them, and that was one of my biggest mistakes!

XIV

At the risk of sounding like Bertie Wooster in *Jeeves and the Feudal Spirit,* I, like my Father before me, have always tried to be nice to the people who work for me. Unlike my Papa, however, I don't emphasise the differences in status, and always try to make my household a sort of extended family. And on the whole it works pretty well, although on occasions this policy turns round and bites me on the bum.

Many years ago when my Uncle Chas died, my aunt came down to stay with us, and my Father bought a long lease on a small cottage in Bideford so that she would have somewhere to live. Unfortunately, however, my aunt soon had a stroke and as a result of her erratic behaviour my parents decided that she should go into a home, which is -

by the way - a decision for which I have never forgiven them. But I digress.

My Father then let a woman who had been his secretary in Hong Kong and who had since fallen on hard times, have the cottage for a peppercorn rent, and she lived there until she died a year or so after my Father. I had completely forgotten about the property, and it was only when we went through the lists of the family property for probate reasons that we found out about it. When Ms Ottecraft died, we were left with the problem of what to do with it, and so it stayed empty for a couple of years.

Then Trace and Malcky came back from North Africa in disgrace with everyone who ever read the tabloid papers believing that they were failed pornographers, and - possibly worse - that both of them (but particularly Trace) had picked up some exotic sexual tastes from her swarthy gaolers. I knew exactly what Malcky meant when he muttered about the sins of the cities of the plain, and what had happened to Laurence of Arabia in prison, and so I felt even more sorry for him. This as I intimated above, was not necessarily one of the cleverest things to do.

So I gave him a job in my garden, and allowed the odd couple to take over the tenancy of the little cottage in Bideford. Both these decisions were ones that I would soon come to regret. Malcky was a completely useless gardener, and between them, he and Trace managed to wreck the cottage. My wife, being the angel incarnate that she is, was good enough not to say "I told you so" too many times, because she had always disliked both of them, and had always wanted us to have nothing to do with them.

But I am getting completely ahead of myself. I realised that Malcky was a complete liability and was a danger to himself and everyone else when I found him climbing one of my beech trees with a chainsaw, planning to prune the tree from above the ground. I am very fond of my beech trees; they are very old, and whilst I accept (grudgingly) that they do have to be pruned each year, we are always very careful how we do it, and Corinna always goes outside to explain to the dryads why and what we are doing. This *modus operandi* leaves no space for a drunken Scotsman waving a chainsaw about willy nilly. "What the fuck are you doing?" I shouted up at him, whereby he fell out of the tree, and if there had not been a safety circuit breaker on the extension lead he would probably have been the first amputation victim in my house's long and chequered career.

The next day he managed to destroy three of my Grandmother's rose bushes (I'm really not too sure why and how) and when his efforts at digging a new flowerbed caused the corner of one of my aviaries to collapse, I decided that enough was enough, and over what the newspapers would no doubt have described as "a frank exchange of views" I told him that I had no option to let him go. But to sweeten the blow I let him off the next two months rent for the little cottage on the outskirts of Bideford, up where the zoo used to be before it went bust in the late 1970s.

I assumed that he would just go off and find alternative employment that was more suited to his talents (whatever they might be), and I put him and his morbidly obese life partner out of my mind, and got on with preparing for our (then) forthcoming trip to Texas in search of the truth behind the grotesque Texas blue dogs. These peculiar creatures have fascinated me ever since my first trip to San Antonio back in the autumn of 2004, where I had examined the skeleton of one of these animals, and interviewed a whole plethora of witnesses.

This was also the first trip I had ever taken overseas with my beloved wife Corinna, and - after a very tedious couple of years - we were both looking forward to it a lot.

It was a very interesting trip, and by the time we returned a month or so later, I had so many things on my mind, and so many things that I had to do, that I completely forgot about my two peculiar tenants. And this was not a good move on my part.

Because it turned out that Malcky had indeed found a job suited to his talents. Being in possession of a grotesquely fat wife who had picked up some tastes in the North African chokey, that were unusual to say the least, Malcky decided that if he couldn't beat them he might as well join them, and began offering 'Personal Services for the Discerning Gentleman' with his lardy lady as the main attraction. The sweet little cottage that my Father had leased for my dear Auntie Pip had now been transformed into a particularly sordid knocking shop. And with one exception, everybody in North Devon seemed to know about it; the one exception being me!

When the Police burst through the door they were greeted with a display of depravity unparalleled in a sleepy backwater like Bideford. Malcky, naked except for a huge leather jockstrap, a World War One German helmet and a Donald Duck mask, was belabouring his naked wife's ample rump with a riding crop whilst shouting "whoa there my proud beauty", as an audience consisting of a party of visiting German Social Democrat councillors, and two prominent local politicians from North Devon drunkenly cheered him on.

How do I know so much about it if I wasn't there? I wasn't even in the country at the time but a few weeks after our return to Blighty, the Crown Prosecution Service, having discovered that I not only owned the lease on the property, but was letting Malcky and Trace live there rent free, decided that I must have been a party to the depravity, and charged me with keeping a disorderly house of ill-repute. By this time, of course, the gruesome twosome had done a flit, leaving me to face the music alone, and my dear wife to once again refrain from telling me that she had told me so!

Of course I escaped Gaol. The case never actually came to court, but my Auntie's little cottage was in a terrible state, and the legal fees alone had cost me most of the money that I had inherited from my late Father, and so when Danny bloody Miles, told me that he had joined forces with my erstwhile tenants, you can - I hope - understand why I was not best pleased!

XV

I hope that you don't mind me bellyaching on at you, but if I may misquote Penny Rimbaud [*], just because they say I am paranoid (and I do, by the way, suffer from a Schizoaffective Disorder only a few steps away from the Squirrel Farm) it doesn't mean that I am not surrounded by self-serving idiots. I don't mean my wife, or Graham, or Andy the Druid, but some of the other people in my general vicinity have been bleeding me dry for decades.

And now three of these social leeches seemed to have ganged up, and I hope that you will forgive me, but I find that a very disturbing thought.

Knowing quite how devious Danny is, and indeed how devious Malcky and Trace are, I was very careful how I proceeded, and successfully overcame my initial temptation which was to send an email full of blasphemous invective back to him, and instruct my e-mail client to send all future emails from him to the Spam Filter. But I didn't, and over the course of a series of e-mails I managed to piece together what had happened.

After the case had gone to court, and Makcky and Trace had somehow managed to persuade the magistrates that the activities which had gone on in their house were not immoral in any shape or form but that it was their legitimate method of self expression. And that any monies that had changed hands had purely been birthday

---

[*] Jeremy John Ratter (born 8 June 1943), better known as Penny "Lapsang" Rimbaud, is a writer, poet, philosopher, painter, musician and activist. He was a member of the performance art groups EXIT and Ceres Confusion, and in 1972 was co-founder of the Stonehenge Free Festival, together with Phil Russell aka Wally Hope. In 1977, alongside Steve Ignorant, he co-founded the seminal anarchist punk band Crass, who disbanded in 1984. Up until 2000 he devoted himself almost entirely to writing, returning to the public platform in 2001 as a performance poet working alongside Australian saxophonist Louise Elliott and a wide variety of jazz musicians under the umbrella of Penny Rimbaud's Last Amendment.

The quote is from *A Series of Shock Slogans And Mindless Token Tantrums* (Exitstencil Press, 1982) (originally issued as a pamphlet with the LP Christ - The Album.

gifts from the visiting dignitaries to Trace, and that the fact that they had placed bundles of bank notes in the cleft of her buttocks whilst she was rampaging around the room on all fours making pig noises, was purely a local custom. Malcky had even quoted UN General Secretary Ban Ki-Moon in saying "let us recognise the mounting threat posed by those who strive to divide, and let us pledge to forge a path defined by dialogue, social cohesion and mutual understanding," and somehow they had all got away with it. I couldn't help laugh aloud at that last revelation, even though I suspected that the magistrates had probably been clients of the gruesome twosome in the post-modern knocking shop they had run in what used to be my aunt's little cottage.

So Malcky and Trace were free, and left the court without a stain on their characters. I could make a disgusting pun here, but it would be beneath me. After visiting the DSS, they went in search of somewhere new to live. They couldn't move back into my little cottage even if I had allowed them to because there was an enormous amount of work to be done before it would be habitable for my next tenants, and so with their worldly belongings stuffed into the back of their rusty old estate car, they went to the Job Centre. Not to look for a job, mind you, but to sign on and to look for somewhere to live in the small ads of the local paper.

Bizarrely, Malcky actually found a job and a new home all in one. And furthermore it was a job that was more than slightly well paid, and for which they only had to do the smallest modicum of work.

When I was a boy, as I have written elsewhere, my parents were friends with many of the scions of what were left of the nobility and gentry who were still scattered around North Devon. Most of them have now died out or moved away, but even now there are still a few left. Just over the Cornish border from where I now live is the little town of Kilkhampton, and in a valley just inland from Kilkhampton is a small network of man-made lakes, and for some reason that I have never been able to fathom, the tiny conurbation which has grown up around them has more than the average smattering from the higher echelons of society, and most of them are now in their dotage. One couple who were particular friends of my parents lived in a largeish five bedroom cottage backing onto the sprawling forest which traverses the county border. The same forest, I should add, that I have written about elsewhere, and from which I had rescued Panne nearly a year before.

He had no children, nor indeed any close relatives, but for reasons with which I can easily empathise he didn't want to sell the property, and so, newly widowed after a marriage that had lasted over sixty years, my father's friend decided that he no longer wanted to live alone in the big house and - making an error of judgement that would have seen him cashiered to the ranks had he made it whilst leading his troops into battle during the Malayan Insurgency [*] (the war as a result of which he got his knighthood) - he employed Malcky and Trace as housekeeper and groundsman.

This was not a spectacularly wise move.

The night that they moved in, he invited his new staff to have a drink with him, and Malcky got the old man so drunk, that on the way upstairs he fell and broke his hip. In what was perhaps the only decent act I ever learned about them making, Malcky telephoned for an ambulance and the injured old man was admitted to hospital. Malcky and Trace even visited him a few times, but a few days later the old man had a stroke which left him permanently paralysed and without the power of speech. He was shipped off to a local nursing home, and plays no further part in this story.

He was, however, unlike most of the local gentry who had fallen foul of decades of Capital Gains Tax [**] and Death Duties [***], extremely wealthy, and apart from the broken hip and the effects that one would have expected as a result of his monumental Cerebro-Vascular Accident [****], was as healthy as an ox, and - as the Nursing Home administrator told his solicitor on the telephone - would probably live for another decade or more. The solicitor also told that, as the estate was entailed on a distant relative who had been missing for decades, it couldn't be sold, and so needed to be kept in order. Would Malcky and Trace be prepared to stay there, with a generous stipend, for the forseeable future?

Once again, Malcky and Trace had fallen upon their unattractive feet!

---

* The Malayan Emergency (Malay: *Darurat Malaya*) was a guerrilla war fought in pre- and post-independence Federation of Malaya, from 1948 until 1960. The belligerents were the Commonwealth armed forces against the Malayan National Liberation Army (MNLA), the military arm of the Malayan Communist Party (MCP) The "Malayan Emergency" was originally the colonial government's term for the conflict. The MNLA called it the Anti-British National Liberation War. The rubber plantations and tin-mining industries had pushed for the use of the term "emergency" since their losses would not have been covered by Lloyd's insurers if it had been termed a "war".

** A capital gains tax (CGT) is a tax on capital gains, the profit realized on the sale of a non-inventory asset that was greater than the amount realized on the sale. The most common capital gains are realized from the sale of stocks, bonds, precious metals and property. One of the primary drivers to the introduction of CGT in the UK was the rapid growth in property values post World War II. This led to property developers deliberately leaving office blocks empty so that a rental income could not be established and greater capital gains made. The capital gains tax system was therefore introduced by chancellor James Callaghan in 1965.

*** A tax paid by a person who inherits money or property or a levy on the estate (money and property) of a person who has died. Tax is assessed at 40% of the net value of the estate, after application of the nil rate band. The applicable nil rate band will depend on the date of death: if the date falls at any time from 6 August to 5 April in a given tax year, the current year's band will apply; but, where the date is after 5 April but before 6 August, and application for a grant is filed before 6 August, the prior year's band will apply.

**** Stroke

XVI

My darling wife is totally correct when she says that I have a tendency to think the worst, both of people and of events. And I will admit that when it comes to certain people who have been in my life over the years I do, indeed, have that tendency. And so when it came to the question of how Malcky, Trace and Danny Miles had all managed to meet up and - apparently, at least - be under the same roof, my mind had run riot.

I had been convinced that the solution to this conundrum was going to be a spectacularly sordid one. Ever since I first met Trace she had reminded me of a girl called Sharon (with a peculiar Eastern European surname) who had been expelled from the class below me at Bideford Grammar School during my sojourn at this, my alma mater, for going off behind the cricket pavilion with a whole succession of boys for fifty pence a throw. I never found out exactly what happened there, mainly because I never had fifty pence to spare (it was quite a lot of money in those days, and my father - who had only had a shilling a week pocket money as a boy - decided that I should have the same, it would have taken me ten weeks to have saved up). But I was convinced, especially after the well attested events in my auntie's old cottage, that something of the sort had certainly taken place, when in fact it hadn't.

I had imagined that it had all taken place in an Internet chat room or a message board dealing with some spectacularly nasty sexual perversion or other. Or possibly, *mano a mano* in some peculiar nightclub where they hold fetish nights, or somewhere else that I would have been far too embarrassed to go even if I had wanted to. But I was completely wrong on all counts.

It had all taken place in a pub.

Danny, for reasons that he was to explain to me later, had decided that he preferred to have somewhere to live that was separate from the Children of the Three and their burgeoning redoubt in the deep woods. He had been commuting between the woods and his long term boyfriend Basil's hut in the middle of the Somerset Levels, and the journey was frankly getting a bit much for him. However, he wanted to keep his new domicile, when he found it, a secret from the Gods and Guerrillas in the middle of the forest, and one night he went down to a pub in the little town of Kilkhampton, which was - incidentally - the nearest hostelry both to Tamar Lakes and the haunted woodlands. He only went there for a quiet beer, but ended up falling completely in love.

Well, I have known Danny since the autumn of 1981, and he has been openly bisexual since then, and I have never had - and never will have - any problem with that. But I do have a problem with his taste. He was unaccountably coy about whether the object of his affection was an annoying lanky Scotsman with a big nose and a bush of wiry red hair, or a heavily tattooed fat woman with an incipient moustache and the sex appeal of a roadkilled rhino. "A gentleman never tells", he smirked at me via email. How he managed to smirk as if basking in the glow of another cautiously worded sexual conquest when he had actually singularly failed to win the object of his affection, I am not sure. But if I have learned anything from my thirty plus year acquaintanceship with Danny bloody Miles, it is that he will smirk uncontrollably at the slightest provocation.

However, apparently he had fallen for the charms of one or the other of my erstwhile tenants, and went back 'home' with one or the other of them (I still had no idea which). When he got 'home' (and remember that it was not his or Trace's home, but that of my Father's erstwhile mate the war hero, hence the quotation marks) he found that the object of his affection was in what he perceived as a long term and loving relationship, and that his suit was unlikely to be accepted. However, over drinks Malcky and Trace mentioned that they were looking for a lodger, and so Danny moved in.

There would, of course, they told him, be the small matter of a deposit. Considering what had happened when I had allowed them to rent my property without a deposit, I couldn't help but laugh at this. I was also not particularly surprised to find out that Malcky had used his infamous powers of extra sensory perception to divest the hapless Danny of all the money in his wallet, and then some.

The fifty quid was for the remainder of his deposit.

Well, as I think I have already made clear in this narrative, Trace was very much a woman of negotiable virtue, and I had no reason to suspect that Malcky wasn't similarly lax in his morals, so I could only suspect that the two of them were playing another more complicated game. However, it wasn't one that interested me more than momentarily, and I had no intention of lending any money to Danny. I have leant him enough over the years to realise that his wallet is a sort of fiscal black hole, so I replied to him tersely and in the negative.

"But I don't want Loxodonta and his crew to know where I am," he replied plaintively.

I wrote back telling him that he was confusing me with someone who gave a fuck, and suggested that he had always got Basil, his boyfriend, who had been funding his stupid escapades ever since I Introduced them back in a pub in Kenton, South Devon the year I got married for the first time.

I heard nothing back, so I assumed that this was now a done deal and that I probably wouldn't hear anything from any of them for a while, at least. And I was right. I didn't.

XVII

O nce again it had been one of those weeks reminiscent of the chorus of the *Grateful Dead* song 'Trucking' from the *American Beauty* album, because it truly has been a long, strange trip this week. That weekend all my more cosmic friends were massively excited because of the eclipse of what was being referred to as a 'blood moon' in the early hours of Monday morning.

Now, for some reason, astrology has never been one of those subjects that has interested me overly, and I have a sneaking suspicion that - whilst there may well be come connection between our individual body chemistries and the positions of the heavenly bodies at the time of conception, or maybe (as the astrology dudes and dudettes would have it) the time of our birth - I think that an awful lot of the stuff people talk about these things is probably nonsense.

Then again, that is what I thought about a lot of things that I have since discovered to be fascinating. For example, I invited Jaki Windmill to the Weird Weekend during the summer of 2015 to talk about Astroshamanism, because she is a friend of mine and I thought that the WW punters would be interested, which by and large they were. But I was certainly not expecting to be taken into the weirdest out of body experience that I have ever had without chemicals, so my mind is far broader as I get older.

So, surprising even myself, I found myself up at 4:00am with a small bottle of good brandy which the Gonzo *Grande Fromage* gave me the previous Christmas in my hand, leaning on my walking stick, out on the road outside my house as I gazed up into the night sky at what was undoubtedly one of the most extraordinary celestial objects that I have ever seen. The moon was not blood red, but it was a sort of grey and pink, not as in the jolly colours of the first *Caravan* album, but more like the appearance of a blood blister or a great boil just about to burst. I have read about the moon looking "liquid" but this was the first time that I had ever seen it for myself as it hung in the sky looking like an immense globule of pus-coloured frogspawn.

I could hear other people around the village - out and about - presumably watching the sky for their own arcane reasons, and I could even hear the farm labourers bringing home the last of the harvest. And I could hear what sounded suspiciously like chanting from the village green outside the church, at the top of the little lane which runs past my house. *

But I was not in the mood to join them, and preferred my own company as I stood in the moonlight, singing Daevid Allen's 'Selene' from *Camembert Electrique* under my breath and swigging from the bottle of brandy which was so much better than the usual gutrot that I get from Tesco that I was forced to treat it with a great deal of respect.

Back in my garden I could hear the occasional click of cloven hooves. Although the dogs were upstairs in bed with Corinna, Panne and several of the cats were playing a gloriously exuberant game of catch as catch can on the round lawn with the sundial in the middle.

I am not overly fond of the full moon. It effects my mental health extremely badly, and I am living proof that the etymology of the word 'lunatic' is fairly accurate as a description of certain types of mental disorder. Specifically I am bipolar, and also suffer from a schizoaffective disorder, and as I have said already in this paragraph, any full moon makes it a damn sight worse.

But this wasn't any old full moon. This was a 'blood moon' (whatever the fuck that means) and I truthfully felt like Lon Chaney Junior, or more accurately, like the bloke in *An American Werewolf in London* just before he transformed into a vulpine predator. Now, let us stop right here. I am not claiming to be a werewolf in any shape or form; I actually have a friend who self-identifies as a werewolf, but whilst I respect him enough not to shake him by the collar and tell him not to talk bollocks, I have absolutely no idea what he is talking about. **

I am not going to pretend that I was just about to turn into a ravening predator. That would (according to *my* world view, at least) be ridiculous. But I felt as if I was completely feral, and furthermore that my body was made of some fragile and brittle

---

* There are more pagans in the village than the quondam Christian majority would like to think. Whatever chanting is done by my household takes place in the garden, but other devotees do not have the privilege of a third of an acre of England to do what they wilt in, and I suspect that some use the tiny village green, or possibly even the churchyard.

** Otherkin are a subculture who socially and spiritually identify as not entirely human. Some otherkin claim that their identity is genetic, while others believe their identity derives from reincarnation, trans-species dysphoria of the soul, ancestry, or metaphor. Joseph P. Laycock considers the belief to be religious. I consider the belief to be fucking ludicrous.

substance like old china, and that I was on the verge of shattering. And if I did shatter into a million pieces, my feral, tortured spirit would emerge unfettered and looking for vengeance, and that if it came to this I would have no control whatsoever over my baser self, which - throbbing with pain and over half a century of hatred and abuse - would be free to rend and tear and hate and mutilate and kill.

"Fuck" I thought, and took another swig from the bottle of extremely good brandy in my hand.

As it trickled down my throat, there was a reassuring burning sensation as the distilled grape juice made contact with sensitive mucous membranes.

Then I heard a movement a few feet to my left, and a human shape came out of the dark before me.

Now, what happened next was something that I truly didn't expect. Realistically, you are probably expecting it to be Corinna coming out to see what I was doing. Or perhaps one of the neighbours also out moonwatching, coming over to blag a mouthful of brandy. Or Graham who has been interested in astronomy for as long as I have known him, or even Panne - having broken off her exuberant game with the cats - coming out, so I could scratch it behind the ears.

Those of you who are devotees of soap operas will probably expect it to be Danny Miles, or Trace coming out of the darkness in order to try and con me out of some more money. And devotees of horror fiction might guess that Mr Loxodonta or even his counterpart, the mysterious, but grotesque, tall blonde woman who had a skull for a face and habitually wore a silver catsuit that would not have looked out of place on Diana Rigg half a century ago.

But this isn't a comic book, or a soap opera, so it was none of them. It was actually one of the last people that I could possibly have expected.

There, shuffling out of the darkness was Lysistrata.

"Fuck me ragged!" I said.

---

* Again see *The Song of Panne*. I have done my best not to write those words too many times in the preparation of this current volume, but - truthfully - there are some times that it cannot be avoided. I probably should have done so a few pages ago when I was writing about Mr Loxodonta and the Children of the Three. . But I didn't, so you can take it as read.

XVIII

I stared at Lysistrata in shock. It was three in the morning on a Sunday in September. I hadn't been expecting to do more than stare at the moon for a few minutes, sing a few bars of *Selene* by Gong, drink a swift toast to Daevid Allen, and go back to bed. And now this had happened!

From the first moment I saw her I knew there was something very different about this weird, semi feral, subservient little servant girl that I had known - on and off - for most of my life, or at least all but the first eleven or twelve years of it. Even before she opened her mouth I could see that somehow she had acquired a self-assuredness, and a dignity that I had never known before. And bathed in the pus red light of the blood moon she looked ethereally beautiful.

"Hello Jonathan," she said in well modulated tones. It took quite a few milliseconds for me to realise that something was very different about her. And then it clicked. Ever since I had known her, she had spoken with an ill-tempered speech impediment. I had always found her strangely sexually attractive, but now the surly downtrodden little peasant girl with the hare lip, was walking and talking like a lady. And it was completely doing my head in.

She walked slowly towards me, her arms outstretched before her, ready to clasp my hands in hers. I am far too old to be having moonlit assignations with strange women, and I am also a happily and stably married man. So I stood stock still in the red moonlight like a small creature mesmerised by the lights of an oncoming car.

"What the fuck has happened to you?" I wanted to say but didn't. But she answered me anyway. "On nights like this, which occur only very rarely, Our Lady smiles on those of us who are her servants, and lets us walk free of our fetters for a time".

I stared at her uncomprehending.

"Do you remember when The Master was still alive?"

* Australian beatnik Daevid Allen was a founder member of Britain's earliest psychedelic band, Soft Machine. He departed from the band after the release of their first classic single Love Makes Sweet Music. He was then banned from Britain, he settled in Paris where he formed the psychedelic rock collective Gong in 1970. The band appeared on stage in their "pothead pixie hats", with Allen playing "glissando guitar", his partner poet Gilli Smyth on "space whisper" vocals and a combination of tape loops. Gong created a mixture of ethereal soundscapes mixed with trippy psychedelic lyrics.

'Selene' appears on their second album *Camembert Electrique*, which - coincidentally (although we all know that there's no such thing) - was the first LP I ever bought, when Virgin reissued it for 50p in 1974.

I nodded.

"And when you and your little brother came to tea?"

I had been about twelve and my brother nine. I nodded again.

And I was just a little girl. And your brother, you and I sat at The Master's feet and he read us the stories of the boy who lived with wolves?

I remembered. I had always loved those stories since my Mother had read them to me seven or eight years before.

I nodded.

"And you remember The Night that Fear Came?"

I nodded, as she began to recite:

> "Then the First of the Tigers came back, and his pride was broken in him, and, beating his head upon the ground, he tore up the earth with all his feet and said: 'Remember that I was once the Master of the Jungle. Do not forget me, O Tha! Let my children remember that I was once without shame or fear!' And Tha said: 'This much I will do, because thou and I together saw the Jungle made. For one night in each year it shall be as it was before the buck was killed—for thee and for thy children. In that one night, if ye meet the Hairless One—and his name is Man—ye shall not be afraid of him, but he shall be afraid of you, as though ye were judges of the Jungle and masters of all things. Show him mercy in that night of his fear, for thou hast known what Fear is.'"

And by the time she had finished the first sentence, I was reciting it along with her. For I, too, know the stories of the Jungle off by heart, and as I have grown older and more infirm I have revisited them more and more.

"Tonight is my night" she said, and suddenly I understood. At the top of the hill I could still hear the uneasy chanting, and on the other side of the tall hedge I could hear Panne and the cats playing riotously in the moonlight. Like the tiger in Kipling's story, on one night, the night of the blood moon, this beautiful, enigmatic, and totally frightening woman was free from her chains, and able to walk unfettered amongst the world of men.

And she had chosen to spend this night in my company! The realisation of what this entailed both humbled and terrified me, as I looked into her obsidian black eyes.

"You have been kind to the little goatfooted one, I think"...

I spluttered some attempt at an answer, but it faded away as she continued.

"So, like The Master did when we were all children, I shall tell you a story. In a way it is also about a child in a jungle. For it is my story."

Again I tried to speak. I don't know what I was trying to say because no words came out. I was desperately trying to stifle the need for a pee, and although every pore in my body wanted to take another swig from the bottle of stupidly expensive brandy that was in my pocket, I did nothing of the sort.

I gave up my faltering attempts at speech. I had only the vaguest idea of what I wanted to say, and I had no idea how to even attempt to put it into words. So I decided not even to try.

This wasn't my night. This night belonged to the girl who a long dead cleric had called Lysistrata. The long dead cleric whom everyone called a pederast, but whom I suspected was not only nothing of the kind but something brave and noble. The long dead cleric who, I realised as I stood in the pale red moonlight, had been one of the formative influences that had made me whatever I had become today.

It was Lysistrata's night, not mine, and if she wanted to tell me her story, then I was going to listen.

XIX

Y ou don't remember me when I was a little girl...before I became Lysistrata?" She paused.

I shook my head.

"My name was Hazel Wingford, and I was in the same year at school as your brother, and we used to go on the same school bus".

There was an embarrassed silence, mostly on my part, because I truly had no memory of her. In my defence, she was talking about events over four decades in the past, but it is always embarrassing to admit that one has forgotten all about somebody's existence, even when there is no reason on earth why one should have done.

Her surname, however, rang a lot of bells for me, none of them pleasant.

"Are you any relation to Stevie Wingford?" I asked, and she nodded. "He was my brother. Except, as you know, he wasn't my brother".

Before I continue, I think that a brief history lesson is in order. Before the M5 was built in the early 1970s, and even before the North Devon Link Road was built ten years later, North Devon was far more isolated than it is today, and there were still remote rural areas which were disturbingly primitive.

These days 'disturbingly primitive' means that one hasn't got fibreoptic broadband, but forty years or more ago it was a very different state of affairs. R D Blackmore's Doones [*], and the Cannibals of Clovelly [**] may have been mere fiction, but well within living memory there were wild people in North Devon; unruly tribes of uneducated brigands who lived by poaching and other petty crimes. One of these tribes was called the Cheritons, although it is unsure whether this was actually their family name or just a reference to one of the villages (Cheriton Bishop) from whence they came. They lived north of Crediton in the late 19th Century, and were described by the Devonshire Association as:

> "Over their social life one would wish to draw a curtain, for they regarded not the holy rites prescribed by the Church, nor the authority of bishops, archdeacons, or civil laws. They had all things in common, and multiplied into a large family without marriage. Their conduct, habits, manners, and language, made them a terror and a nuisance to their immediate neighbours. Their misdeeds were the cause of their making frequent appearances before the magistrates in the local police courts. The surrounding farmers, after a time

---

[*] Lorna Doone: A Romance of Exmoor is a novel by English author Richard Doddridge Blackmore, published in 1869. It is a romance based on a group of historical characters and set in the late 17th century in Devon and Somerset, particularly around the East Lyn Valley area of Exmoor. The antagonists are the notorious Doone clan, a once noble family, now outlaws, in the isolated Doone Valley.

[**] The infamous Gregg family were supposed to have lived in a cave, a mile underground, on the North Devon coast near Clovelly. When the cave was finally stormed by men of the law they found it festooned with a multitude of "arms, legs, thighs, hands and feet, of men, women and children, hung up in rows, like dried beef and a great many lying in pickle". The horrible clan, numbering about 50 altogether, the result of incestuous union, were hauled before the magistrates in Exeter. The entire family were sent to the gallows and hanged. A stretch of Clovelly Bay was named – appropriately enough – the Devil's Kitchen.

Many believe that the story is nothing but colourful fiction though, thought up by local smugglers to keep away inconvenient nosey-parkers. So much of the story is similar to the legend of the equally fictional Scottish story of the Bean family, that it seems most likely some resourceful Devon smuggler borrowed it almost word-for-word (even down to having the King leading the vigilante party), and customised it for their own purposes.

forbore to summon them as their ricks, stacks, barns, and homesteads were fired. By whom? None could tell, though pretty shrewd guesses were levelled at the Cheritons."

No less a personage as Rev Sabine Baring-Gould [*] confirmed that they were still about at the turn of the Century, but after falling foul of the authorities in Exeter one too many times they migrated North during the years of the First World War, and took over a derelict farm in the wild country between Holsworthy and Bradworthy when the two brothers who owned it failed to return from Flanders. There they stayed for another half century until they met their match in the early 1960s when they encountered another burgeoning tribe that was beginning to make its mark on rural England; the Department of Health and Social Security.

By this time there were about thirty members of the Cheriton tribe, maybe a third of them being children, and they were all doing rather well out of their lifestyle of low level banditry. However, as soon as the powers that be realised that there were people out there who lived in incestuous glory, never sent their children to school, that the children who mostly ran around naked and filthy couldn't read or write, and WORSE didn't pay any taxes, the days of the tribe were numbered. So in 1964 as the myth of Swinging London spread across the globe, the Cheriton family were dealt with after some three hundred years of lawlessness. The adults mostly went to prison and the children mostly went into care.

All this took place nearly a decade before, and fifteen miles away from the village in which I first came to live in 1971, but the social reverberations were still echoing through the parishes.

Mr and Mrs Wingford were a well meaning, childless couple who lived in Bradworthy. They ran one of the smaller and shabbier shops in the village and went to chapel devoutly every Sunday. And so, when the opportunity arose for them to test out their untried parenting skills on a toddler who had been impounded after the raid on the Cheriton tribe, they leapt at it. And this was probably the worst decision of their life.

They fostered and then adopted the nameless little boy, and decided that he should be

---

* The Reverend Sabine Baring-Gould (28 January 1834 – 2 January 1924) of Lew Trenchard in Devon, England, was an Anglican priest, hagiographer, antiquarian, novelist, folk song collector and eclectic scholar. His bibliography consists of more than 1240 publications, though this list continues to grow. His family home, the manor house of Lew Trenchard, near Okehampton, Devon, has been preserved as he had it rebuilt and is now a hotel. He is remembered particularly as a writer of hymns, the best-known being "Onward, Christian Soldiers" and "Now the Day Is Over". He also translated the carol "Gabriel's Message" from the Basque language to English.

given a suitable name for the son of two devout Methodist shopkeepers, and had him Christened Stephen. Nobody ever called him anything but Stevie, and he grew quite quickly into the nastiest little boy in the village. Something that everyone but his doting parents knew only too well.

"Yes, I remember Stevie" I said to Lysistrata. "But I don't remember him having a sister".

I certainly remember him. From the moment that I first arrived at Bideford Grammar School in 1971 to the day that I left in 1976 he did his best to make my life a misery, and usually succeeded. He bullied me unmercifully, and left scars on my psyche which have never healed, and which I seriously doubt ever will.

"He didn't have a sister" she said, still bathed in the peculiar red silver moonlight of the blood moon, looking me straight in the eye. "But no sooner had my parents adopted the little shit, than I was born, and from the moment that he first saw me, he hated me and tried to get rid of me until he basically succeeded".

And then I remembered who she was, and that I had known her several years before she turned up as the taciturn, but ever so slightly sexy, maidservant to the Rev Cymbaline Potts and his sister Britannia.

XX

I had hated her stepbrother for five long years. And if the truth were to be known, (and I have not lied *yet* in these pages, and I am not going to start now) I hate him still. It is a cliche to say that he made my life a misery during my years at Bideford Grammar School, but for some reason of his own he tormented me on every occasion that he could.

It is tempting to lapse into Pink Floydian imagery here, and talk about Stevie Wingford being just one of the bricks in my wall of madness but he was a damn sight more than that. And anyway I have another visual and emotional simile that works better for me.

> Fasces (Italian: Fasci, Latin pronunciation: [fas.keːs], a plurale tantum, from the Latin word fascis, meaning "bundle") is a bound bundle of wooden rods, sometimes including an axe with its blade emerging. The fasces had its origin in the Etruscan civilization, and was passed on to ancient Rome, where it symbolized a magistrate's power and jurisdiction.

The image has survived in the modern world as a representation of magisterial or collective power. The fasces frequently occurs as a charge in heraldry, it is present on an older design of the United States ten cent coin and behind the podium in the United States House of Representatives, it is used as the symbol of a number of Italian syndicalist groups, including the *Unione Sindacale Italiana*, and it was the origin of the name of the National Fascist Party in Italy (from which the term fascism is derived).

The whole united we stand, divided we fall thing is a very powerful, and deceptively true social image, but it has also been perverted into social objectification which caused nothing but pain and grief. Instead of the bundle of neuroses and psychoses which envelop and threaten to define my psyche being a huge brick wall across the stage at Earl's Court *, I prefer to visualise them as a tightly bound bundle of birch twigs, malleable and even destructible individually, but an impermeable and indestructible bundle of pain and hate when bundled together. The process of psychoanalysis is supposed to help one cut the ties that bind the bundle together so through cognitive exercises, mindfulness, or whatever, one can deal with each of them separately. But it didn't work like that for me. Therapy gave me some coping strategies, and - most importantly of all - showed me the effect that my mental illness had on other people in my life. But it didn't cure me, and my bundle of pain and anger, my psychosocial birch twig bundle, is still there as prominent and agonising as ever. It is impossible to quantify such things, but I believe that Philip Larkin was right, and the greatest number of my birch twigs were given to me by my Father. But somewhere near the top of my birchtwig hit parade has to come Stevie Wingford.

I looked him up on Friends Reunited *, and then Facebook seven or eight years ago, and I was surprised to discover that he had become quite a well known fine artist. I was even more surprised to find that I actually liked some of his work.

When I am particularly angry, my darling wife has been known to quote Atticus

---

* Pink Floyd staged their classic double album The Wall in 1980 and 1981. As the band played, a 40-foot (12 m) wall of cardboard bricks was gradually built between them and the audience. Several characters were realised as giant inflatables, including a pig, replete with a crossed hammers logo. Gerald Scarfe was employed to produce a series of animations to be projected onto the wall. At his London studio, he employed a team of 40 animators to create night-marish visions of the future, including a dove of peace exploding to reveal an eagle, a schoolmaster, and Pink's mother. The bricks symbolised the building blocks of the protagonist's eventual mental health issues.

** Friends Reunited was a portfolio of social networking websites based upon the themes of reunion with research, dating and job-hunting. The first and eponymous website was created by a husband and wife team in the classic back bedroom internet start-up; it was the first online social network to achieve prominence in Britain, and was responsible for the dissolution of many shaky marriages. The main Friends Reunited site aimed to reunite people who had in common a school, university, address, workplace, sports club or armed service. It closed after 16 years in 2016. I never had much luck there, and was not able to decide whether my old schoolfriends were so happy and secure in their lives that they no longer needed to reach into their past for validation. or whether the people who had been my friends had grown up into a bunch of low-life losers who couldn't afford a computer.

Finch [*] at me, and tell me that instead of hating someone I should try and walk a mile in their shoes.

Well I tried. I honestly did. But no matter how hard I tried, I could not bring myself to feel anything but hate for the man, and my dreams each night were full of my totally unrequited plans to torture him and everyone he held dear, to death with pliers and a blowtorch.

Now I don't feel good about this. I have already told this particular story once in a song called *I know where you Live* on an album I made a few years ago [**], and - bizarrely - it was writing a song about it all which freed my psyche for a while, and relieved my night times of their terrible burden. But Lysistrata's words brought it all rushing back into my head.

And even more importantly, I remembered who she was.

In my family's early days in the village, we used to go to tea with Rev. Cymbaline Potts quite regularly. As I have written elsewhere [***] the tumbledown cottage that he shared with his sister Britannia was a treasure trove of interesting bric-a-brac, and thus paradise to a strange introverted and enthusiastic schoolboy like myself. As Lysistrata carried on talking about her childhood in Bradworthy, I slowly began to remember that as well as my parents, my brother and myself, there was often a little girl wearing the sort of pink cotton dress that little girls wore in those days when they went out to tea.

"That was me" said Lysistrata.

What happened to the Wingford family is actually quite a commonplace sociological paradigm. Once the emotional pressure to conceive has been alleviated for a childless couple by adopting or fostering a child, they quite often then conceive one naturally. I vaguely remember one of Agatha Christie's novels [****] being based around the premise of a vivacious and beautiful adopted daughter suddenly having to deal with a surly, dumpy and frowsty stepsister who happened to be her 'parents' flesh and blood offspring. In this case the parents overcompensated by treating the adopted daughter

* The father of the protagonist in Harper Lee's *To Kill a Mockingbird* (1960)

** *BiPolar* (2011)

*** *The Song of Panne*

**** And for the life of me I cannot remember which, and it doesn't really matter.

better so she wouldn't feel jealous....with tragic results.

In the case of the Wingford family, the parents managed it much better. They treated both the children equally, never showing favouritism of any kind, a stratagem that really should have worked. And it would have worked if their own daughter had not been sweetly shy, vulnerable and empathic to an almost supernatural degree, and their adopted son had not been a psychopathic scion of a tribe of savages, taking pleasure in causing pain and distress to everyone and everything...

...especially his so-called sister.

XXI

I was outside talking to Lysistrata for over an hour, but it was an hour that felt like only a few minutes. But in that hour I learned things which filled in a lot of the gaps in both my own personal story, and the stories of others whom I held dear. I don't remember the evening in an entirely linear fashion, and suspect that the communication was partly non-verbal, but I cannot be sure, and - indeed - as far as the narration of the story is concerned it truly doesn't matter.

I knew that Stevie was a vicious, manipulative, and sadistic little scrote. When I was a child at the cutting edge (quite literally in some cases) of his psychopathic gunsights I had a re-occurring dream that one day the worm (with me in the role of the vermiform revenger) would turn, and I would end up killing him. I never did, of course, but for many years throughout my adult life I had the same nightmare every month or so; that I had not only killed him, but that I had disposed of his body down a deep drain underneath a manhole cover round the back of where Woolsery Village Hall used to be before they replaced it with what I believe are bungalows for sheltered housing.

Well into my adult life I would dream that I was back in Woolsery, and feeling the immeasurable guilt which I would imagine is felt by someone who had unlawfully killed his fellow man, no matter how insurmountably great the temptation. But I think if I had realised then what depths of depravity the little bastard had sunk to, I would have been even more tempted.

Because as well as knocking me about, and - worse - applying psychological torture to me, just because I "talked posh" and wasn't the slightest bit interested in sports, he was also doing much the same to his little "sister". This was bad enough, but in addition, from about the age of nine she had been forced by him into being a sexual plaything for him and his gang of friends.

The (I'm not entirely sure that he is) completely fictional character Lazarus Long [*] is alleged to have said that one should not underestimate the power of human stupidity, and this is a maxim whose veracity I have seen over and over again during my life. But I have noticed something else. When the aforementioned stupid people are highly religious, despite being on a Veritable Crusade against sin and wrongdoing in all its forms, they are remarkably gullible and have enormous blind spots when it comes to character flaws in those whom they love.

And there is no doubt whatsoever that Mr and Mrs Wingford loved both their children very much and they loved them both equally. It could never be said that they favoured their own natural born daughter over the surly young wild man whom they had adopted. And indeed they trusted him implicitly and were so proud that, despite his unfortunate genesis as part of a tribe of semi feral savages, he had adopted so many of the behaviour traits that one would have hoped for in the scion of a family of gentlefolk.

"And his little sister loves him soooo much", they would gush to their friends at the Methodist church coffee mornings, totally mistaking terror for adoration. Because by this stage in her young life, Hazel Wingford was almost mute with terror.

Stevie took advantage of this, and claimed to his adoptive mother that the little girl had continual night terrors, which was why his guardians continually found her in his bedroom, and often in his bed. He was only being a good brother he protested, and Mr and Mrs Wingford so used to accepting all the unlikely things which are chronicled in the Old Testament, were gullible enough to believe him. Stevie went on to explain that his younger 'sibling' continually wet herself, which was why she was so often in a state of partial undress. And Mr and Mrs Wingford not only believed him, but praised and rewarded him for being such a good son.

And they were so proud of him for taking his little 'sister' out with him even when he had

---

[*] Lazarus Long is a fictional character featured in a number of science fiction novels by Robert A. Heinlein. Born in 1912 in the third generation of a selective breeding experiment run by the Ira Howard Foundation, Lazarus (birth name Woodrow Wilson Smith) becomes unusually long-lived, living well over two thousand years with the aid of occasional rejuvenation treatments.

His exact (natural) life span is never revealed. At one point, he estimates his natural life span to be around 250 years, but this figure is not expressed with certainty. He acknowledges that such a long life span should not be expected as a result of a mere three generations of selective breeding, but offers no alternative explanation except by having a character declare, "A mutation, of course——which simply says that we don't know". A rugged individualist with a distrust of authority, Lazarus drifts from world to world, settling down periodically and leaving when the situation becomes too regimented for his taste——often just before an angry mob arrives to capture him.

The Lazarus Long set of books involve time travel, parallel dimensions, free love, individualism, and a concept that Heinlein named World as Myth—the theory that universes are created by the act of imagining them, such that even fictional worlds are real.

his friends over to play. What a lovely boy he was, they told everyone, and a complete vindication of their own personal beliefs in the power of the Church in the ongoing debate of nature versus nurture.

It was the same at school. I was not the only child that was the brunt for Steve Wingford's terrifying attentions, but not only was nearly everyone scared into submission, but when someone did complain about him to someone in authority, like I did once, no action was ever taken.

Why?

Because boys like me - the ones who were the victims of bullying - were always the peculiar; the disabled, the eccentric, the artistic, the ones who wrote poetry and composed peculiar songs, whereas the bullies (I use the plural because there were a whole clique of them, although Stevie Wingford was the uber bully) were usually teacher's favourites. Many of the teachers at what was then Bideford Grammar School had a distressingly old fashioned view of school life, in which the 'manly' boys were those who were accomplished at sports, and it was they who upheld the honour of the school. Stevie Wingford, for example was Captain of the Under 14s First XV, and all the teachers liked him. So when somebody who was universally seen as a thorn in the side of the old fashioned school ethos made a complaint about him, it was not treated with any great seriousness.

I would like to think that things would be different if these events had happened today. I would like to think that we as a society know more about bullying, sexual and physical abuse, and post traumatic stress disorder than we did four decades ago when I was a boy. And I would like to think that sensitive boys with an obvious mental illness would have been dealt with differently, and I like to think that shy little girls are no longer sexually and emotionally abused by their adopted brothers and his thuggy friends.

But human nature being what it is, I wouldn't bet on it.

XXII

The world in which we live today, or at least the world in which *I* live today, is almost unrecognisable as the world in which I lived forty years ago, even though I actually find myself living in the same house as the one I lived in back then. For example, although I have put advertisements up in the village shop over the past few years, I have found it nigh on impossible to find a schoolboy who wants to earn a few extra quid working in my garden. These days, the younger generation is far more financially motivated than they ever were in my day, and the sixteen and seventeen year olds are drawn towards the fleshpots of Bideford where they can earn far more than I can afford to pay working in Asda or Macdonalds. But the younger ones are mostly not interested in part time jobs, and I am finding it increasingly hard to find assistance in my increasingly beleaguered garden. But in my day all the kids had jobs.

I started off working each summer for a farmer friend of my parents, but the summer I turned seventeen, just before I failed most of my GCE O Levels, and my parents packed me off to a boarding school that I hated with a vengeance, I got a job at the local hotel, which - peculiarly - was actually owned by members of *Pink Floyd* as some sort of failed tax scam [*]. The same summer little Hazel Wingford, three years younger than me, got her first job working as a cleaner cum housemaid cum general help for the increasingly eccentric Rev Cymbaline Potts and his sister Britannia.

She had known them for years, and - as she had been going to tea there on and off since she was a little girl, and their previous housekeeper (an elderly Scottish lady named Hattie) had died a few months earlier - she had approached them for a job.

Others in her family were less industrious.

Although he was the same age as me, and had failed his O Levels just as ignominiously, Stevie Wingford had sneered at the idea that he should get a job, opting instead to hang around the town square of Bradworthy with his coterie of yobbo friends, leering at the girls and making a nuisance of themselves. Emboldened by their experiences with Hazel, Stevie and his gang became notorious amongst the young women of the little town, very few of whom we lucky enough to have escaped their predations entirely.

Now, this is something that I am pretty sure would be a completely alien concept to young people today. In those days girls *didn't* complain about sexual and emotional abuse. Whether it was because they felt that they wouldn't be believed, or whether they felt that they would be tarred by the indelible brush of public opinion if they did so, I don't know. My personal suspicions are that it was a mixture of the two. I

---

* I will go into more details about the unsavoury saga of financial planners Norton Warburg Group (NWG) later on in this narrative, but sufficient to say that they had invested £1.3–3.3 million (up to £17.4 million in contemporary value) of the group's money in high-risk venture capital to reduce their tax liabilities. And, unsurprisingly, it all went spectacularly tits up.

I hadn't realised, until I started doing these footnotes, quite how important *Pink Floyd*, or to be more precise, the Roger Waters-led era of *Pink Floyd* has been in this narrative. Even the way that Danny Miles first became introduced to the redoubt in the woods could be described as a result of the *Pros and Cons of Hitchhiking*.

remember when one of the young women of my village was raped in the late 1980s my Mother behaved as if it was somehow the girl's fault, and insisted on referring to her as "that village wench" who was now "damaged goods".

So for all sorts of reasons Stevie and his coterie of unpleasant ruffians continued to cast a long and unpleasant stain upon the social organism of the little town of Bradworthy, and as the long hot summer of 1976 continued, they got more indolent and more threatening.

Then they discovered car theft. It started off with what was then (and may still be, for all I know) known as 'Joy Riding', but when they found that there was a tumbledown garage out on the Liskeard road that dealt in 'bent MOTs', * the gang discovered that there was actually money to be made in car theft. Stevie Wingford had found a job at last!

Hazel, however, was happier working for the Potts ménage than she had ever been before. Because unlike her parents who doted on him, the elderly gentlefolk for whom she was now working found nothing admirable in young Stevie. And one day when Hazel arrived at work with a black eye after Stevie had come home drunk and Hazel had tried to resist his boorish advances, 'Miss Britannia' had inveigled the truth out of her.

These days, of course, one would like to believe that things would be completely different. There are specialist police officers, social workers and family therapists trained to deal with cases of familial sexual abuse, but if indeed people like that existed four decades ago, they certainly didn't exist in Bradworthy. And whilst little Hazel, still only thirteen, felt better now she had someone to confide in, she refused point blank to go to the police, or even to let Miss Britannia go and talk to her mother and father.

And so things continued for another three years. I went off to boarding school and was expelled two and a half terms later. My parents were so embarrassed by all this that they tried to bully me into joining the army, and when I failed the entrance physical on the grounds that I was completely insane, procured for me a series of jobs that I couldn't possibly do, with old business associates of my Father in different parts

---

* The MOT test (Ministry of Transport, or simply MOT) is an annual test of vehicle safety, roadworthiness aspects and exhaust emissions required in the United Kingdom for most vehicles over three years old used on any way defined as a road in the Road Traffic Act 1988; it does not apply only to highways (or in Scotland a relevant road) but includes other places available for public use, which are not highways.

Until the whole process was computerised there was a brisk trade in bent or illegally issued MOT certificates for unroadworthy cars.

of the Home Counties. All of these jobs were pretty disastrous, and I ended up destitute, unable to even claim Unemployment Benefit (as it was called then). I came back to Woolsery with my tail between my legs to do another job that I was completely unable to do, working for my Father. I soon made friends with the relatively small number of arty alternative types in the vicinity, and until I passed my driving test a year or so later I was totally reliant on public transport.

But I was still away, working for a company in Reading which specialised in installing plasterboard office partitioning, when the word went around the gentlefolk of my particular sector of North Devon that the Rev Cymbaline Potts had been caught soliciting the sexual favours of a little boy in the public lavatory in the middle of Bradworthy Square.

Except (and it was nearly forty years before I found this out) it wasn't a rosy faced choirboy. It was Stevie Wingford!

XXIII

Until that evening I had no idea whatsoever that it was Stevie Wingford whom the elderly clergyman was alleged to have assaulted. By the time it had all kicked off I was living away from home in a flat in Northam just outside Bideford, and attempting to change the world via ingesting large quantities of psychoactive plants and listening to reams of cosmic bullshit from Danny Miles.

Yes him. He will come back into the story very soon, I promise you.

The story that I had got third hand from my Mother was that The Rev Potts had been caught *in flagrante delicto* with a young innocent boy, and had only escaped gaoltime by the skin of his yellowing teeth. And it wasn't until the momentous evening that I met Lysistrata - by my accident and her design - under the pus red beams of the September blood moon that I found out the truth.

In early 1977 when I was seventeen and she-who-was-to-be Lysistrata was three years younger, her parents had died in an unfortunate car accident, and their not inconsiderable worldly goods were left, divided equally to her and Stevie. But Hazel, being underage, was left in the care of her older adopted sibling, who used his new found freedoms to further torment and terrorise the hapless child. She told me the details that night as the Lady Hecate spread her arms of light across the landscape, and they brought tears to my eyes. I am not going to repeat them for you, partly because I don't want to break a confidence (although she never told me not to repeat them) but mostly because I am only too aware that there are some people who would find the prurient details of what Stevie did to his little sister arousing, and I have no intention of contributing further to such a disgusting web of depravity.

For the next five, long, years, Stevie and his coterie of thugs continued to use and abuse the girl, whilst at the same time expanding their criminal activities to include burglary. One would never have imagined that a quiet little town like Bradworthy, little more than a village really, could have had any degree of organised crime there, but what had once been the staid residence of a family of Methodist gentlefolk became the one stop shop for stolen goods across the area, as well as a shebeen and knocking shop with young Hazel as the star performer.

One thing that had been confusing me was how I could have escaped making the connection between little Hazel Wingford, the painfully shy little girl in the pink dress who used to go to tea with the elderly, and now disgraced clergyman, and the deformed but peculiarly sexy housemaid that turned up in the same household a few years later. But the next horrific twist in the story explained that anomaly only too well.

Hazel had developed the habit of furtively listening at keyholes, in order to find out her captor's plans, so she could minimise the effect of them on her own increasingly beleaguered life.

One evening, apparently, young Hazel overheard her older 'brother' and his unlikeable cronies planning their next burglary. And to her shock and shame, their target was none other than the isolated cottage where Cymbaline and Britannia lived. Stevie had remembered all the stories that Hazel had told their quondam parents about the cornucopia of antique delights with which the elderly couple had filled their tumbledown residence, and decided that here was a fruit ripe for the picking.

Hazel was horrified, and - summoning up all her reserves of bravery - burst into the room and - for the first (and only) time in her life - confronted her hated big brother. She leapt at him battering him with her tiny fists and screaming. But he was a burly young man in his late teens and she was a particularly slight child, and her assault was nigh on worthless.

"Please leave them alone" she sobbed as she collapsed to the floor like a pile of old rags. But as I knew to my cost after six years of being terrorised by the little bastard at every opportunity, he was a consummate bully. I only saw him in school hours between September 1971 and May 1976, and there were always people within some sort of shouting distance, so although the hurt and humiliation was horrible to live through and I still bear the scars to this day, it was finite. Stevie's hold over his 'sister' however, had no limits.

My Father was a complicated old sod, and had many esoteric interests, including the history of Naval signalling, Theology and - of all things - the intricacies of Devonshire dialect. My Mother died in the early spring of 2002, and after that I telephoned my father every day that I was in the UK, and found myself working with him on publishing his collection of Bible stories, translated into Devonshire dialect. We worked on it for several months, going through each passage again and again on the telephone. But having already speed read it, I knew that the account of Christ's torture and crucifixion, was going to be a particularly harrowing experience to go through with the old man. Peculiarly it was on March 12th 2003, the first anniversary of my Mother's death that we finally did the passage, and I was right. Reading and rereading it with my Father, with whom I had always had an uneasy relationship, on a day when we were both feeling emotionally labile, was a very peculiar experience.

Well I am feeling a bit like that now. OK nobody gets nailed to anything, but what happened next is still pretty horrific.

Well I know that I have to write what happened next to poor Hazel in some detail because it is germane to the story, and one needs to know far more details than I am comfortable with writing in order to understand what happened next, and - indeed - the whole complicated relationship between me, Panne, Britannia, Lysistrata, and the people of the deep woods.

But just because I have to do this thing, doesn't mean that I am going to enjoy doing it!

XXIV

And so it came to pass.

Stevie pushed his 'sister' away, and laughed unkindly in her face. "I'll do what I fucking well like. I already do everything and anything I want to with you, you worthless little cunt" he snarled.

And then Hazel had the idea which would change her life forever. She summoned up the courage and spluttered…

"If you don't leave the Reverend and his sister alone, I will never have sex with you again" sobbed the frightened little girl emboldened by grief.

"Fuck off" snarled Stevie Wingford, pushing her to the ground, and stamping on her face with—what in my day were known as his—size ten bovver boots. He continued to stamp on her face until she was unconscious, which was probably a merciful act in its own way so that she never knew what happened next.

And truthfully she would never be the same again, because when the fire brigade broke the door of the little house down two days later, she was naked in a pool of urine. There was congealed blood on her face and her body was covered in bruises and cuts, one arm had multiple fractures, and both her wrists and several ribs were broken and she was tied to the legs of the kitchen table. She had been repeatedly raped and violated by three or four different assailants, who had then urinated on her and set the house on fire. She suffered permanent brain damage, and her face was battered beyond recognition. What I always thought was a congenital hair lip was actually the result of being kicked in the face again and again by one of her 'brother's' coterie of vile friends, who also slashed her face with what had once been one of her mother's kitchen knives.

Sometime between Hazel losing consciousness and the Fire Brigade being called two days later, Stevie Wingford went into the main Police Station on Bideford's riverside, and made an official complaint against the Rev Cymbaline Potts and his sister, alleging that for years the elderly clergyman had sexually abused him, and had done so with the tacit approval of his sister.

He then went to the offices of the Bideford newspaper which in those days were still in Bideford High Street, and told the whole story (none of which was true) to their cub reporter Kevin, who coincidentally I had *also* been at school with, but that is another story. Before the newspaper had a chance to print the story, the Fire Brigade had been called to the conflagration at what had once been the Wingford family family home. The Fire Brigade rescued the battered naked child, took her to the hospital (where in another coincidence I was still living at the time) and called the police. Luckily my schoolchum at the newspaper heard the truth before he had the chance to lay his employers open to massive charges of libel, and so spiked the story.

However, it turned out (and a couple of days later, after Lysistrata told me her story, I made it my business to find out, and I have friends in low places) that at the time some work was being done in the newspaper offices by a local plumber, who again I had been at school with, and - worse - had actually bought dope from back in the day, and it was he who had overheard Stevie's spurious testimonial, and he told his mother, who told her sister, and before anyone could have said Jack Robinson (and by the way, does anyone have any idea who Jack Robinson is or was?) half of North Devon believed that the Rev Cymbaline Potts was a pederast of the foulest kind, and the local gentry (including my Mum and Dad) expunged the Potts' from their Christmas card list.

Hazel Wingford spent the next six months in hospital, but whilst the bruises and fractures and burns were treatable, the brain damage wasn't. And what was worse, as she was now suffering from incurable brain damage, which by the standards of the 1980s meant that she was never going to be anything but an inhabitant of one of the NHS residential units for such people, and had no living relatives, there was no point in carrying out expensive reconstructive surgery to her face, and so she was damned to spending the rest of the world as a shambling, massively deformed, mental patient.

But that was not the way that things worked out.

The early 1980s were turbulent ones in Britain. For about fifteen years Britain had been governed by a succession of remarkably progressive governments. We had seen the end of capital punishment, the legalisation of homosexuality, and great strides forwards in the fields of sexual and racial equality.

But then came Mrs Thatcher, and a war in the South Atlantic [*] and the opening skirmishes took place in what was eventually to be culmination of another war which had existed ever since the General Strike of 1926; the ruling Conservative Party declared war on the miners, and a long and vicious dispute took place which tore the country apart [**].

---

[*] The Falklands War (Spanish: Guerra de las Malvinas), also known as the Falklands Conflict, Falklands Crisis, Malvinas War, South Atlantic Conflict, and the Guerra del Atlántico Sur (Spanish for "South Atlantic War"), was a ten-week war between Argentina and the United Kingdom over two British dependent territories in the South Atlantic: the Falkland Islands, and its territorial dependency, the South Georgia and the South Sandwich Islands. It began on Friday, 2 April 1982, when Argentina invaded and occupied the Falkland Islands (and, the following day, South Georgia and the South Sandwich Islands) in an attempt to establish the sovereignty it had claimed over them. On 5 April, the British government dispatched a naval task force to engage the Argentine Navy and Air Force before making an amphibious assault on the islands. The conflict lasted 74 days and ended with the Argentine surrender on 14 June 1982, returning the islands to British control. In total, 649 Argentine military personnel, 255 British military personnel, and three Falkland Islanders died during the hostilities.

[**] The miners' strike of 1984–85 was a major industrial action to shut down the British coal industry in an attempt to prevent colliery closures. It was led by Arthur Scargill of the National Union of Mineworkers (NUM) against the National Coal Board (NCB), a government agency. Opposition to the strike was led by the Conservative government of Prime Minister Margaret Thatcher, who called the strikers and organisers "the enemy within." The NUM was divided over the action and many mineworkers, especially in the English Midlands, worked through the dispute. Few major trade unions supported the NUM, primarily because of the absence of a vote at national level. Violent confrontations between flying pickets and police characterised the year-long strike, which ended in a decisive victory for the Conservative government and allowed the closure of most of Britain's collieries. It was "the most bitter industrial dispute in British history." At its height, the strike involved 142,000 mineworkers. The number of person-days of work lost to the strike was over 26,000,000, making it the largest since the 1926 general strike. The journalist Seumas Milne said of the strike, "it has no real parallel – in size, duration and impact – anywhere in the world".

At the same time, the political situation in Northern Ireland was quite possibly the worst that it had ever been.

The second hunger strike in two years by IRA prisoners took place in 1981 * and was a showdown between the prisoners and the Prime Minister, Margaret Thatcher. One hunger striker, Bobby Sands, was elected as a Member of Parliament during the strike, prompting media interest from around the world. The strike was called off after ten prisoners had starved themselves to death—including Sands, whose funeral was attended by 100,000 people. The strike radicalised Irish nationalist politics, and was the driving force that enabled Sinn Féin to become a mainstream political party.

Against all this turmoil nobody really cared when one little brain damaged girl called Hazel, still only fourteen, but unable now to talk in more than the most disjointed of sentences absconded from hospital and basically disappeared. And smalltown gossip being the pernicious beast that it is, nobody who was anybody in the county was talking to The Rev Potts and his spinster sister anymore, so nobody either knew, nor cared, when a few days after her disappearance young Hazel turned up at the Potts' cottage in the middle of a thunderstorm on the night that most right thinking people in the area were toasting the surrender of Brigade General Mario Menéndez, when the British forces retook Port Stanley.

Now that her parents were both dead, and her elder 'brother' was on remand awaiting the trial that would eventually lead to his spending fifteen years in prison for a string of crimes including the multiple rapes and brutalisations of his underage 'sister', Hazel had no relatives left in the world, and nobody apart from the Potts siblings who actually cared whether she lived or died. And so she stayed in the little cottage as the two elderly gentlefolk did their best to look after her.

---

* In 1980, seven Provisional Irish Republican Army (IRA) prisoners in the Maze Prison launched a hunger strike as a protest against the revocation by the UK government of a prisoner-of-war-like Special Category Status for paramilitary prisoners in Northern Ireland. The strike, led by Brendan Hughes, was called off before any deaths, when the Government seemed to offer to concede their demands; however, the Government then reneged on the details of the agreement. The prisoners then called another hunger strike the following year. This time, instead of many prisoners striking at the same time, the hunger strikers started fasting one after the other in order to maximise publicity over the fate of each one.

Bobby Sands was the first of ten republican paramilitary prisoners to die during a hunger strike in 1981. There was widespread sympathy for the hunger strikers from Irish republicans and the broader nationalist community on both sides of the Irish border. Bobby Sands was elected as an MP to the UK's Houses of Parliament and two other hunger strikers, Paddy Agnew and Kieran Doherty, were elected to Dáil Éireann in the Republic of Ireland by electorates who wished to register their opposition to the UK Government's then policy. The ten men survived without food for 46 to 73 days,[8] taking only water and salt, before succumbing. After the deaths of the men and severe public disorder, the Government granted partial concessions to the prisoners, and the strike was called off. The hunger strikes gave a huge propaganda boost to a previously severely demoralised Provisional IRA.

The elderly couple soon realised that there was actually very little that they could do.

She was not going to recover, and with half the county believing that they were guilty of some of the most heinous crimes that a clergyman can ever be accused of, nobody was going to help them look after her. But they were decent people, and furthermore - having pieced together Hazel's pathetic story, and, most importantly, the account of her final valiant stand against her ogre of a brother - they realised that it was up to them to look after the pathetic child that they were already referring to as an orphan of the storm.

Gentlefolk of their ilk, however, were Conservatives of the old school, rather than the neoliberal Visigoths who travelled in Mrs Thatcher's wake, and they did not believe in charity. So they never applied for state assistance in looking after Hazel, but instead trained her up into the only social role that they thought that she could ever fulfil; that of a lowly housemaid (and that was - one must remember - in a world where nobody had housemaids any more).

The Potts siblings were unworldly in the extreme, especially by the standards of the decade that taste and decency forgot, but even they realised that they should probably not advertise the fact that they had a refugee from the Mental Health system living under their roof. So they decided that Hazel Wingford should change her name. Britannia suggested just changing her surname, and claiming that Hazel Potts was a long lost niece, but the Rev Potts was a student of Aristophanes, and having heard Hazel describe what happened immediately before the attack which crippled her, decided there was only one name for her.

Lysistrata is a comedy by Aristophanes. Originally performed in classical Athens in 411 BC, it is a comic account of one woman's extraordinary mission to end the Peloponnesian War. Lysistrata persuades the women of Greece to withhold sexual privileges from their husbands and lovers as a means of forcing the men to negotiate peace—a strategy, however, that inflames the battle between the sexes.

And so Hazel Wingford became Lysistrata Potts and, once again, the world was never the same again. *

---

* It is almost unbelievable to look back three and a half decades to Britain in the first half of the 1980s. Although those of us who were living through it considered ourselves to be at the cut and thrusting edge of modernism, it is a fairly shocking lesson to look back from the vantage point of the present day (2018, as I sit here typing this) when we have almost instantaneous global communication and even the four computers in my potato shed office talk to each other.

Back in the 1980s, even computers belonging to different Government departments didn't 'talk' to each other, and it was far easier for someone to simply vanish beneath society's radar, than it is today. I am certainly not looking back through rose tinted spectacles, because I was truly miserable for much of the decade, and am basically much happier and much better off now, but the social changes over the last three and a half decades have been enormous.

XXV

As I have written at length elsewhere, I am a great believer in the interconnectedness of all things. And I am not going to go all fractal on you, but it does seem to me to be a self-evident truth.

Just try to imagine the world in which we live to be a large pond. Bits of it have nice clear water with ducks swimming on top of the water and sticklebacks below, and other bits are full of rusting supermarket shopping trolleys. Others are a morass of mud, and other parts still are an evil smelling discharge from some chemical works or other. Like I said, it is a very large pond.

The weather on this pond is extremely localised; some bits are calm and others stormy. Some rain-lashed, others drought-stricken, and there are even occasional icebergs. For not only is it a very big pond, but it is a highly conceptual one, and as I am the one who conceived it I feel perfectly entitled to make my conception as singular as I like.

Now, one afternoon a horrid little boy called Stevie Wingford threw two large rocks into my conceptual pond. And the waves caused by these two Godalmighty splashes reverberated across the pond both above and below the water. They weren't boulders at all. In fact on a cosmic scale they weren't even *very big* rocks, but they were big enough to effect the currents and eddies of the water, to dislodge vegetation, and to forever change the lives of a surprisingly large number of the little creatures that lived in the pond.

One of the metaphorical rocks that hit the metaphorical surface of my metaphorical pond that spring afternoon in 1982 was the multiple rape, brutalisation and attempted murder of his 'little sister'. The other was his accusation that the Rev Cymbeline Potts was guilty of what our transatlantic chums call serial sexual battery against the person of Stevie Wingford himself. Well, as we are already aware, the accusations fell apart in the wake of Wingford's arrest for the crimes against his sister, but not before the

---

* The three-spined stickleback (*Gasterosteus aculeatus*) is a little fish native to most inland coastal waters north of 30°N. It has long been a subject of scientific study for many reasons. It shows great morphological variation throughout its range, ideal for questions about evolution and population genetics. Most populations are anadromous (they live in seawater but breed in fresh or brackish water) and very tolerant of changes in salinity, a subject of interest to physiologists. It displays elaborate breeding behavior (defending a territory, building a nest, taking care of the eggs and fry) and it can be social (living in shoals outside the breeding season) making it a popular subject of enquiry in fish ethology and behavioral ecology. Its antipredator adaptations, host-parasite interactions, sensory physiology, reproductive physiology, and endocrinology have also been much studied. Facilitating these studies is the fact that the three-spined stickleback is easy to find in nature and easy to keep in aquaria.

reverberations across the local rumour mill made it certain that the local gentry would no longer have the Potts siblings on their Christmas Card list, and that they would be basically *persona non grata* in all the local villages.

Many years later I heard that the Rev. Potts paid a visit to my Father and attempted to explain the true state of affairs, but that my Father had curtly turned him away at the gate and told him never to return. He never did, although if he had still been alive when I inherited the house in 2006 he would have been most welcome. But by then it was far too late.

In fact, as far as I am aware, the elderly couple never set foot in Woolsery or Bradworthy ever again, taking their business to Holsworthy, some fifteen miles to the south, which was a sprawling enough metropolis so that the elderly clergyman and his sister were able to go shopping in relative anonymity.

Let us deal with Stevie Wingford first. Several members of his gang turned what I believe is called 'Queen's Evidence' and did the sort of plea bargaining act which doesn't usually happen in our small corner of North Devon. Stevie Wingford was found guilty of a whole string of offences against his sister, and - when the word got out amongst the young women of the district, upon whom Wingford and his cronies had lavished their unwelcome attentions - within a matter of weeks his charge sheet was several pages long, and within days Wingford was on remand in Exeter Prison, and was not to see the world as a free man again for fifteen long years.

But I didn't know anything about this, although I would doubtless have been quite happy to have engaged in quite serious degrees of *schadenfreude* as Wingford had made most of the years of my adolescence a misery. But I knew nothing about it because on 2 April 1982, Argentine forces mounted amphibious landings of the Falkland Islands, following the civilian occupation of South Georgia on 19 March, before the Falklands War began. The invasion was met with a nominal defence organised by the Falkland Islands' Governor Sir Rex Hunt, giving command to Major Mike Norman of the Royal Marines. The events of the invasion included the landing of Lieutenant Commander Guillermo Sanchez-Sabarots' Amphibious Commandos Group, the attack on Moody Brook barracks, the engagement between the troops of

---

* A criminal turns state's evidence by admitting guilt and testifying as a witness for the state against his associate(s) or accomplice(s), often in exchange for leniency in sentencing or immunity from prosecution. The testimony of a witness who testifies against co-conspirator(s) may be important evidence. In the United Kingdom and the Commonwealth realms, the term is to turn Queen's or King's evidence, depending on the sex of the reigning monarch. The term "turning approver" or "turn king's approver" was also historically used; an approver "not only admitted his own guilt to a crime but also incriminated his accomplices both past and present" in exchange for avoiding a death sentence (and obtaining a lesser penalty, such as life imprisonment or abjuration of the realm) or improving prison conditions.

Hugo Santillan and Bill Trollope at Stanley, and the final engagement and surrender at Government House.

The whole Falklands War was basically a costly propaganda exercise on the part of two unpleasant national leaders; Margaret Hilda Thatcher of the United Kingdom and General Leopoldo Fortunato Galtieri Castelli of Argentina. Both leaders were facing faltering popularity and decided to try and keep hold of the reins of power by surfing the crest of a wave of nationalism. In Thatcher's case it worked. *

People like me who were already disturbed by the state of the nation and the cavalier way that Thatcher and her cronies were riding roughshod over civil liberties soon joined the protests. It all became mixed up with the peace camps at Greenham Common and elsewhere, and - eventually - the miner's strike, and by the end of it all I was well and truly politicised.

I was also living in South Devon by that time, embarking on three years as a Student Nurse at the now defunct Royal Western Counties Hospitals near Dawlish, and I also found my first serious girlfriend and then my first wife, and so all this stuff passed me by.

But as it turned out, although my parents refused to have anything further to do with the Potts family, (and so, the fact that it had been increased in number by fifty percent passed them by) my late Mother was pivotally involved in what happened next. Because just before Stevie Wingford effectively excised the two elderly gentlefolk

---

* Thatcher stayed in power until 1990, but Galtieri fared less well. On 14 June 1982, the Falklands' capital, Stanley, was retaken by British forces. Within days Galtieri was removed from power, and he spent the next 18 months at a well-protected country retreat while democracy was restored to Argentina. Along with other members of the former junta, he was arrested in late 1983 and charged in a military court with human rights violations during the Dirty War and with mismanaging the Falklands War. The Argentine Army's internal investigation, known as the Rattenbach report after the general who led it, recommended that those responsible for the misconduct of the war be prosecuted under the Code of Military Justice. In 1986 he was sentenced to twelve years in prison. Galtieri was cleared of the civil rights charges in December 1985, but (together with the Air Force and Navy commanders-in-chief) in May 1986 he was found guilty of mishandling the war and sentenced to prison. All three appealed in a civil court, and the prosecution appealed for heavier sentences. In November 1988 the original sentences were confirmed, and all three commanders were stripped of their rank. In 1989, Galtieri and 39 other officers of the dictatorship received President Carlos Menem's pardon.

Following his release from prison, he moved to the Villa Devoto suburb of Buenos Aires, and lived modestly with his wife Lucía. He became a recluse and refused most requests for interviews by journalists, though in a rare interview he stated he had "no regrets" over anything he had done during the Dirty War. He lived on an army pension of about $1,800 per month, and attempted to claim a Presidential pension, but a judge denied it. In her ruling, the judge stated that his presidency had been illegal due to his never having been elected, and she also ordered him to pay court costs. In July 2002, new civil charges were brought concerning the kidnapping of children and the disappearance of 18 leftist sympathizers in the late 1970s (while Galtieri was commander of the Second Army Corps), and the disappearance or death of three Spanish citizens at about the same time. Galtieri faced prosecution with 28 other officials, but due to his poor health, he was allowed to remain at home. He died several months later.

from my parent's address book, my Mother had lent Britannia Potts a couple of books by a largely discredited, and now almost forgotten academic called Margaret Murray.

Now, although not as dramatic as the two rocks which Stevie Wingford had cast into my metaphorical (or should that be allegorical? I'm not quite sure) pond, the ripples caused by my mother's innocent loan of a couple of books on speculative British history caused ripples and reverberations no less important. In fact, in one way the reverberations were even *more* important, as these books led directly to the eventual death of the Rev Cymbeline Potts.

XXVI

Now I am afraid we need to digress for a few moments. Because when Lysistrata told me what she told me next, I was already possessed of the knowledge necessary to know what the blinking flip she was talking about. But because we are talking fairly obscure and massively arcane knowledge here, I think that I have to assume that at least SOME of you people reading this could benefit from a brief history lesson.

My parents were strange people. Pillars of the Establishment and the Church (with a capital C) they were also far more involved in esoteric pursuits than anyone realised. My paternal Grandmother was - as I have already mentioned - a witch (as are two of my cousins), my maternal Grandmother came from an old and rather odd Sussex family so entrenched in the "old ways" that no sooner had she been born than the Gardener took the naked baby to the bottom of the garden and placed her on one of the beehives, so she could be introduced to the bees.

My Father could divine water and regularly had conversations with ghosts *. They had

---

* We spent nine months in 1963/4 in a little red brick cottage called 'Partridge Piece', in a hamlet called Ogdens, just outside of Fordingbridge in Hampshire. This was fifty years ago, as I write, and my memories are perforce very fragmented. So I looked it up on the internet and fairly soon found a photograph of a house which rings absolutely no bells in my memory whatsoever. According to one of the property websites, it has an estimated value of over £1million. Apparently it is a desirable residence which last sold for £750,000 in 2006. I wonder whether the new owners know about the ghost. I may not remember much about the building itself, but I *do* remember the ghost. Or rather, I *do* remember my parents talking about the ghost, because - although I was, apparently, the only person to actually *see* it, I have absolutely no memory of the fact. But, piecing together things from various memories, I *can* tell you what happened, both at the time and in the immediate aftermath.

Apparently my family had been plagued by low-level poltergeist activity. Knowing what I know now about things parapsychological, I don't think of such things as having anything to do with the spirits of the dead, and the fact that there was a teenaged girl in the house who was going through some emotional upheavals at the time, tends to explain it all to my satisfaction, at least with the benefit of hindsight. We will come back to the enigmatic figure of the emotionally disturbed teenage girl later in the narrative, because I am doing my best to keep my narrative in some sort of logical order. Father became convinced that the windows that slammed for no good reason, the warm pebbles that materialised in mid air, and the sound of footsteps that could be heard padding steadily across the floor of the upstairs /CONT rooms, were manifestations of something demonic, or at least cries for help from an unquiet spirit. Once again with hindsight I am very pleased that my father had never read anything by H.P.Lovecraft, or else his imagination would really have started working overtime. He did some digging, by talking to the neighbours and to some of the regulars at the local pub, and came back with the story of a macabre event which, allegedly, happened some thirty years before, in the years immediately leading up to WW2.

The house had then been inhabited by an elderly woman, who lived with her grown-up farm labourer son, who was - what these day's one would probably call - educationally subnormal. Please remember that I am piecing this together from memories of what happened half a century ago, tempered with what happened when I discussed the affair with my father one night many years later when he was on his deathbed and we had both been drinking. Neither of these are the best, or at least the most accepted ways, for a diligent researcher to do his homework.

It appears that this couple had a peculiar, incestuous relationship. For many years the people in the village had ignored them and let them get on with their lives in peace, but for some reason this changed. I have no idea why, how, or what, but as a result of the ensuing scandal, the farm labourer lost his job, killed his mother/lover and hung himself. It would be so easy here to insert a macabrely written Gothic horror story, but despite all my efforts, I have not been able to find out anything more about the affair, and all that I know is the bare bones of what I have told you.

My Father then tried to communicate with the ghost. He named the spectre 'Hob' which is revealing in itself.

A hob is a type of small mythological household spirit found in the north and midlands of England, but especially on the Anglo-Scottish border, according to traditional folklore of those regions. They could live inside the house or outdoors. They are said to work in farmyards and thus could be helpful, however if offended they could become nuisances. The usual way to dispose of a hob was to give them a set of new clothing, the receiving of which would make the creature leave forever. It could however be impossible to get rid of the worst hobs. Hob is the root word from which both Hobgoblin and Hobbit are derived, but it is nit the sort of thing that one would expect a middle ranking Civil Servant, part time Naval Officer, and wannabe Churchwarden to know.

Apparently his attempts to communicate with the spirit were vaguely successful. One night as my father was putting me to bed, I apparently asked him what the white thing that was following him around was. This horrified my poor father. he was quite happy to carry his own little bits of psychic research, but he was so full of guilt about my sister's death, and the series of obstetric problems that my mother had suffered that he was appalled at the idea that he could have done anything to harm his eldest son. So he turned to 'Hob, and told him to follow him out into the garden, where he threatened 'Hob' with exorcism if he ever scared me or my brother again. The fact that neither of us were scared didn't enter into the equation, but it has to be said that his threats seemed to have worked, and the psychic disturbances pretty well dried up for the rest of our stay there.

However, there is another explanation which I would like to consider. My parents had engaged a Nanny - a Scottish girl in her late teens or early twenties. She was called Judy and I totally adored her, and in return she spoiled me rotten. However, in my chequered career as an investigator of Fortean phenomena, I have found that more often than not poltergeist and allied phenomena including quite a few ghost sightings are often found in houses where there is a n emotionally disturbed girl somewhere a few years on either side of puberty. Now, fifty odd years later, I have no idea when Judy went through the menarche, but I do know that whilst she was living with us, her father - in Scotland - was taken ill suddenly, and died soon after she had returned from visiting him. This was probably the first time that I recognised that my father could be the most unreasonable old bastard on the planet. Judy was understandably distraught, and terminated her employment with the Downes family so that she could be with her family, and my father hated her for it. He let her go with the worst possible grace and ranted about the poor girl in the most vicious of terms for many years to come. I still remember the shouting, the tears and the rants with terror. For the first time, but by no means the last time in my life I found myself in the position of knowing that my father (whom I loved very much, even though I was terrified of him) hated someone that I also loved very much, and this set up the first of many irresolvable conflicts within my already fragile psyche; conflicts which would eventually threaten to tear me apar again and again and again throughout my life.

I have no way of knowing whether 'Hob' appeared, before, after or during the horrors of Judy's departure, but I would hazard a guess that they were somehow linked. After her's and Hob's departures from our lives my relationship with my parents got progressively worse.

both become interested in West African folk magic during their years in Nigeria. Both of them had seen ghosts and UFOs and experienced poltergeist phenomena. My Father was a rabid devotee of - amongst other people - Immanuel Velikovsky, and my mother was an avid reader of all sorts of strange books including those of Professor Margaret Murray.

Who hell she? I hear you shouting in my inner ear. I mentioned her briefly earlier in this book, but I think it is now time to return to her in more depth.

Well first and foremost she was an Egyptologist. But Margaret Alice Murray (13 July 1863 – 13 November 1963) did all sorts of other things as well. She was an archaeologist, anthropologist, feminist, historian, and folklorist. The first female to be appointed as a lecturer in archaeology in the United Kingdom, she worked at University College London (UCL) from 1898 to 1935. She served as President of the Folklore Society from 1953 to 1955, and published widely over the course of her career.

But the thing for which she is best known, and - indeed - the thing for which she has both become academically reviled and almost sanctified by the neopagan movements across the world is her hypothesis that the original religion of Western Europe was a fertility cult that she called 'Dianic' because she believed that the female goddess worshipped was Diana, originally the Roman Goddess of the hunt.

She believed that the Western European witch trials, which she was the first to examine from a feminist perspective, were a concerted attempt by the Christian establishment to destroy this ancient religion, and she believed that the classic image of Satan as a horned man with cloven hooves (a little bit like a larger version of the hairy little urchin who was - as I leaned on my car and heard Lysistrata's extraordinary story - playing an immensely energetic game of tag with my cats on the upper lawn next to the sundial) was a corruption of the images of the male deity worshipped by these devotees. Her second book - *The God of the Witches* - expanded on this hypothesis which had first been laid out in a book called *The Witch Cult in Western Europe*, first published a year before my mother was born.

She also believed that a race of very small people, who also practised this Dianic

---

* Diana was the goddess of the hunt, the moon, and nature in Roman mythology, associated with wild animals and woodland, and having the power to talk to and control animals. She was equated with the Greek goddess Artemis, though she had an independent origin in Italy.

Diana was known as the virgin goddess of childbirth and women. She was one of the three maiden goddesses, along with Minerva and Vesta, who swore never to marry. Oak groves and deer were especially sacred to her. Diana was born with her twin brother, Apollo, on the island of Delos, daughter of Jupiter and Latona. She made up a triad with two other Roman deities; Egeria the water nymph, her servant and assistant midwife; and Virbius, the woodland god.

religion and who had lived hidden in the wildernesses of Western Europe until the early modern era, and that these were the origin of the pan-European myths of fairies, gnomes, pixies and other assorted little people. The fact that they too practised the ancient religion explained the multitude of folkloric links between little people and witches.

And In 1954, she published *The Divine King in England*, in which she greatly extended on the theory, taking in an influence from Sir James Frazer's *The Golden Bough*, an anthropological book that made the claim that societies all over the world sacrificed their kings to the deities of nature. In her book, she claimed that this practice had continued into medieval England, and that, for instance, the death of William II was really a ritual sacrifice. She also claimed that a number of important figures who died violent deaths, such as Archbishop Thomas Becket, were killed as a replacement for the king.

Professor Ronald Hutton, who is an author and academic whom I admire very much, and whom I have met on a couple of occasions (most recently at Tintagel during Corinna's and my brief honeymoon back in 2007) is one of the contemporary academics who are less than convinced by Murray's hypotheses. In his 1999 book *The Triumph of the Moon*, Hutton asserted that Murray had treated her source material with "reckless abandon", in that she had taken "vivid details of alleged witch practices" from "sources scattered across a great extent of space and time" and then declared them to be normative of the cult as a whole. And I see no real reason to doubt him.

Sadly for those people who - like me - were brought up on this stuff, Hutton is far from being the only one.

Together with my friend and colleague Nick Refern I have researched and written about the early history of the neopagan movement, and I am convinced that Murray's writings were amongst the main texts plundered by the founding fathers of modern neopaganism, like Gerald Gardner and Cecil Williamson, when they set out to found a new religion.

And Murray's ideas - possibly because they were so empowering to women - also became immensely popular with a certain type of intelligent and well educated women in the middle of the 20th Century. Women like my mother.

My Mother swallowed Murray's hypotheses hook, line and sinker, and recommended her books far and wide. She first gave them to me when I was about thirteen, and it seems that as a result of a long conversation with Britannia Potts just before her brother's fall from grace in the early 1980s, she lent her precious copies to her... And never got them back.

And apparently Britannia Potts soon also became a neophyte follower of Murray's disputed witch cult hypothesis.

XVII

*H*istory is full of examples of religions which spring up from basically fallacious roots. People will believe any old crap as long as it is wrapped up in enough quasi-mystical bullshit. And if they can tell everyone that they are somehow tapping into the mainstream of an ancient consciousness then even better. *The Book of Mormon*, for example. As far as I am concerned there are so many logical, historical and doctrinal holes in the belief system of the Church of Latter Day Saints that it beggars belief.

But I have known many Mormons, and although I dislike their religion intensely, I would never dispute that most of them were sweet, well meaning, and Godly people.

And so was it with Britannia Potts and her new found faith. She embraced the idea of a primal Dianic religion with open arms, and - like so many neopagans before and after her - interpreted this religion of the sacred feminine to embrace the Blessed Virgin Mary, Hecate, Isis and a dozen others as well as Diana into an all encompassing female deity. The interesting thing about her newfound faith, which slowly began to influence her brother as well, is that it only had two sets of sacred texts. The works of Margaret Murray and a monumental work called *The Golden Bough*, which I mentioned *en passant* above.

For those of you who don't know, once again I am pillaging those jolly nice fellows at Wikipedia:

---

* The Book of Mormon is a sacred text of the Latter Day Saint movement, which adherents believe contains writings of ancient prophets who lived on the American continent from approximately 2200 BC to AD 421. It was first published in March 1830 by Joseph Smith as The Book of Mormon: An Account Written by the Hand of Mormon upon Plates Taken from the Plates of Nephi.

According to Smith's account and the book's narrative, the Book of Mormon was originally written in otherwise unknown characters referred to as "reformed Egyptian" engraved on golden plates. Smith said that the last prophet to contribute to the book, a man named Moroni, buried it in Cumorah Hill in present-day New York, then returned to Earth in 1827 as an angel, revealing the location of the plates to Smith, and instructing him to translate it into English for use in the restoration of Christ's true church in the latter days. Critics claim that it was fabricated by Smith, drawing on material and ideas from contemporary 19th-century works rather than translating an ancient record.

"*The Golden Bough: A Study in Comparative Religion* (retitled *The Golden Bough: A Study in Magic and Religion* in its second edition) is a wide-ranging, comparative study of mythology and religion, written by the Scottish anthropologist Sir James George Frazer (1854–1941). It was first published in two volumes in 1890; in three volumes in 1900; the third edition, published 1906–15, comprised twelve volumes. The work was aimed at a wide literate audience raised on tales as told in such publications as Thomas Bulfinch's The Age of Fable, or Stories of Gods and Heroes (1855). The influence of The Golden Bough on contemporary European literature0 and thought was substantial."

The Golden Bough was undoubtedly one of the major influences on Margaret Murray, and both sets of books were pivotal texts to a new generation of witches. However Britannia was the daughter of one Church of England parson, the granddaughter of another, and the sister of a third, and there was something about "witches" that was "not quite nice", and so whether or not she was aware of the mushrooming of neopaganism in Britain since Gerald Gardner and Cecil Williamson's early forays into the subject, she would have no more thought of reading one of the many books on the subject than she would have considered wearing a bikini or voting for the Labour Party.

But Murray and Frazer were both noted academics and gentlefolk, and Frazer had even been knighted by George V, so they were perfectly respectable sources on which Britannia was able to base her new belief system.

Both the Potts siblings were keen gardeners and amateur botanists, and had several books on herbalism and the propagation of herbs on their overflowing bookshelves, and so the pursuit of herbal alchemy and magick was a logical one for both of them. As the dear old couple and their brain damaged ward became more and more isolated, they withdrew further and further from the faith of their ancestors, as they came to realise that the established churches could well be argued to have very little to do with the teachings of the humble 1st Century rabbi. And they both realised quite quickly that within their newly found belief system they could quite happily follow the teachings of the rabbi whilst searching for enlightenment in the arms of their composite Mother goddess.

The only thing wrong with all this is that whereas Frazer's *magnum opus* is a classic of anthropology, the three books by Margaret Murray which my Mother had lent Britannia just before their estrangement were mostly bunkum. However, one should never let the truth get in the way of a good religion, and the Potts siblings heartfelt belief that there was an ancient belief across most of Europe in the divinity of the moon, is no more bizarre than the belief that an angel called Moroni gave instructions to an unsuccessful treasure hunter as to how to interpret a bunch of golden plates that nobody else would ever see. And at least the Potts siblings didn't use their religious revelations as an excuse to have loads of spouses. In fact, as far as I am aware, both of them were celibate throughout their lives. But it is none of my business anyway, and totally irrelevant to the main gist of this narrative.

And so the odd trio lived more or less happily together for the next fifteen years. I came to visit them occasionally, and I strongly suspect that I was probably the only one who did. But I couldn't help but notice that on each of my infrequent visits they were more and more withdrawn from any sort of consensus reality that I inhabited, and as my hold upon whatever can loosely be described as reality is tenuous to say the least, this isn't actually saying very much.

Then in 1997 a while string of peculiar events piled up on top of each other, and culminated in a totally unforseen and totally tragic result.

The first notable strange event of the year may have been first observed by ancient Egyptians during the reign of pharaoh Pepi I (2332–2283 BC). In Pepi's pyramid in Saqqara is a text referring to an "nhh-star" as a companion of the pharaoh in the heavens, where "nhh" is the hieroglyph for long hair. However, more recently, in 1995 the comet was discovered independently on July 23, 1995 by two observers, Alan Hale and Thomas Bopp, both in the United States. The comet became known as the Hale Bopp comet, and - despite the fact that we are all supposed to be living n the age of science - all sorts of arrant nonsense was spoken about it. There was popularly believed to be a UFO following it, and in March, Marshall Applewhite, leader of a religious group called Heaven's Gate, led his followers (all thirty eight of them) in a mass suicide. Whereas everyone else thought that the Heavens Gate posse had - at the very least - just got carried away with ill-judged cosmic enthusiasm, most people interested in esoteric disciplines believed that the advent of the comet in the night sky was an important omen for good or for ill.

Ever since reading *Comet in Moominland* [*] as a boy, I had wanted to see one, and so - evening after evening - I used to sit on the little concrete bunker outside my little house in Exeter, (I lived alone at the time) smoking a joint and looking up at the honey coloured tadpole shape in the night sky and letting my mind wander into all sorts of unexpected places. The Reverend Cymbeline Patrick Potts, however, was affected in an entirely different way.

---

[*] Comet in Moominland (Swedish: Kometjakten / Mumintrollet på kometjakt / Kometen kommer) is the second in Tove Jansson's series of Moomin books. Published in 1946, it marks the first appearance of several main characters, such as Snufkin and the Snork Maiden. In it Moomintroll and his friends journey to the Observatory on the Lonely Mountains, where the Professors would be able to tell him whether a comet will hit the Earth. It is bizarrely apocalyptic for a children's book and effected me a great deal.

XVIII

The next spanner in the proverbial works happened just after Bealtaine[*] when - after fifteen years incarceration at Her Majesty's pleasure - Stevie Wingford was released from prison, and returned to Bradworthy. These days I believe that there is a battery of organisations which proffer help to victims of crime, and indeed there were so back in 1997. However, I don't believe that they existed back in 1982 when Wingford was condemned to durance vile, and anyway, by the end of that year, Hazel Wingford, the teenaged victim of her adopted brother's vile behaviour had effectively ceased to exist.

When she absconded from the hospital she had become a statistic; just one of the thousands of people - horrifically, a large proportion of whom are teenage girls - who disappear each year. And as she had no known relatives or friends, the police investigation was short, sweet and fruitless.

(And, as I believe that I have already explained, 1982 was a year with unprecedented levels of civil disobedience, industrial action, protests against the war in the Falkland Islands, and terrorism threats following the deaths of Bobby Sands and his nine comrades in the H Block, and the police across Britain had all sorts of other things on their collective mind which could be argued as being more pressing than the disappearance of one brain damaged teenaged girl).

And by 1997 nobody would have thought that - fifteen years after her disappearance - that little Hazel Wingford, now a dumpy, taciturn and bad-tempered woman just short of thirty, would be living in the tumbledown cottage owned by the Potts siblings, who had by this time disappeared from the public consciousness just as firmly.

In a well ordered and decent (not to mention equitable and fair) society, one would like to think that a Victim Support Officer would have come a knocking on the cottage door to warn Cymbeline and Britannia and Lysistrata (whom nobody had called Hazel for a decade and a half) that Stevie had been released, and was returning to Bradworthy. But none of them were on the Electoral Roll, all their post was delivered to a conveniently obliging newsagent named Nusrat Khan in Holsworthy, and none of them had been in Bradworthy or Woolsery for fifteen years.

No.

They learned about it from a suitably alarmist story on the front page of the more

* 30thApril (see note on p.13)

resolutely downmarket of the local newspapers.

For a man whose life was apparently full of spiritual and intellectual matters, Cymbeline lived an ascetic and luxury free life. He had no television or radio, no telephone, was not on the Electoral Roll or Council Tax Register, drank only on the rare occasions that I arrived unexpectedly on his doorstep, and - although he happily puffed away on a huge and old fashioned briar pipe - had few outside interests. But he *was* a football fan. In fact, so I found out nearly two decades after his death, when he had been a curate, back in the 1930s, he had been an avid amateur player, and had even been approached by talent scouts for Charlton Athletic [*], who had not realised that the bookish youth would not allow anything to distract him from his chosen life path with the Church of England.

But even in his mid seventies, he still liked to know the football results, so each week - when on the weekly shopping trip to Holsworthy, he would collect the post, and pop in for a swift half pint in the White Hart - he would buy the newspaper, and revel in the list of statistics which had enthralled him since his childhood. Sitting with his half of musty bitter he would happily read the list of club names as if they were a litany of saints, but on this day things were horribly different.

Because on the front page of the paper was a photograph of Stevie Wingford as a schoolboy glowering out at him, with the headline BRADWORTHY MONSTER RETURNS HOME.

Apparently, although the good folks of the Victim Protection Unit had singularly failed to come and tell Wingford's adopted sister of his release from incarceration (if indeed they had actually remembered that she existed) they *had* told another one of his victims, who - despite the fact that her hurt from Wingford was far less than that suffered by she-who-was-once-known-as Lysistrata - was now the wife of a local bank manager, and thus, not only easier to locate, but far more important in the eyes of society.

Her name was Sandra, and her best friend was Jenny, a Journalist for the local TV news, and the wife of the editor of the aforementioned resolutely downmarket local newspaper, which also happened to be the one that the Rev Cymbeline Potts read each week for the football results. And between them, they were in a perfect position

---

* One has to make a judgement call as to where one stops when providing footnotes for this book, and I had drawn a line in the sand, where football was well on the other side of said line. However, when fact checking for this book I was surprised to learn that the football club dated back to the middle of the First World War. My only interest in Charlton FC is that *The Who* played there in 1974 (part of the concert was televised on BBC2) and my parents were offended by Keith Moon's rendition of 'Bell Boy'.

to make a fuss about WIngford's imminent return to the village of his youth.

The newspaper story gave the bare bones of the story of the events leading to Stevie Wingford's arrest and incarceration. It included the fact that he had been found guilty of several sexual assaults, crimes of violence, burglary, auto crime, and even the attempted arson of his family home, but completely ignored any of his attacks on his poor beleaguered sister.

It even quoted Wingford as saying that he was innocent of all the charges of which he had been accused, that they were all a pack of trumped up lies from a local clergyman, and that he was returning to Bradworthy in order to clear his name and fight for justice, and that he would "make sure that the people truly responsible would get what was coming to them".

Bizarrely, although it had all started as a brave protest by Sandra about the very real fear that the boy who had made her life so unpleasant whilst she was a schoolgirl was coming back in order to do it all again, it ended up as something completely different. Because Jenny had her own agenda, and she knew that one does not become a famous TV journalist by sitting on the sidelines. A crusading TV journalist needed at least one *cause célèbre* to her name, and ever since Sandra had snogged her husband at the Christmas Party, she had been looking for a way to get back at her.

The Rev. Cymbeline Potts was utterly aghast. This was totally unexpected. What the hell was he going to do now? His first thought was to go to the police and ask for twenty four hour protection, and then he remembered Lysistrata.

She had been only a child when she stumbled onto his doorstep that rainy night. He and his sister had done what they believed, and still believe, was the right thing. They had taken her in and welcomed her into their non-existent family. But they had never told anyone else what they had done, and there was - he realised with horror - the very real possibility that if he went to the police for protection, he would be charged with kidnapping.

And he was a retired priest that half the people who were anybody in the county already believed was a child molester. And he hadn't paid any Council Tax for the best part of two decades.

He would have no chance whatsoever. What on earth was he going to do?

XIX

It was a grey, wet day of the sort that the people who write novels about the idyllic English countryside like to pretend doesn't happen at the beginning of May when we are all supposed to be living within an Alfred Bestall [*] watercolour. It would be good at this point to point the finger at climate change, and rant on for a few paragraphs about how mankind has royally screwed the environment, and how we are all reaping what we have sown blah blah, but the truth is that the English weather has always been unpredictable, and North Devon is far more unpredictable than most.

As the dark rain clouds scudded across the sky, distinguished only by being a slightly paler shade of grey than the rainclouds, the elderly clergyman sat in the corner of the pub as if he had been poleaxed. Having turned his back in disgust upon the people that he had once called his friends, and upon the society that he had once believed to be equitable and fair, until he discovered that it was actually nothing of the sort, he found himself unexpectedly alone, and that his little family - an elderly and eccentric sister already showing the first spring shoots of senile dementia, and a brain-damaged and surly child (she would never be anything else but a child) some forty years younger - were now vulnerable to attack, and quite possibly death at the hands of someone who, as a boy, had been a violent and sadistic brute, and who had now had fifteen years of close confinement with other like-minded souls, to perfect his craft.

He sat nursing his nearly empty half pint glass until the landlord called 'time' [**], and so he shuffled outside to find that he had missed the one and only bus back home. And so, in a long raincoat that had seen better days, but bare-headed he started to walk the fifteen miles home.

If this was a story, then it would be lovely to read how he was picked up in his hour of need by a mysterious stranger who somehow made everything right and saved the day. But it isn't, and he wasn't. He stumbled along the dank and overgrown lanes, which are picturesque and beautiful in broad daylight, but in the shifty half light of what had become a full-blown rainstorm, just looked increasingly squalid and

---

* Alfred Edmeades "Fred" Bestall, MBE wrote and illustrated Rupert Bear for the London *Daily Express*, from 1935 to 1965, creating the most beautifully crafted illustrations in the Rupert Bear annual publications. Much of the landscape in Rupert is inspired by the Snowdonia landscape of North Wales, notably around Beddgelert. He had first visited Beddgelert whilst holidaying with his parents at Trefriw in the Conwy valley in 1912 and 1913, where their holiday home was called 'Penlan'. Bestall produced his last Rupert story on 22 July 1965. He retired from the *Daily Express* in July 1965, but continued creating annual publication covers until 1973.

** Traditionally "Time, Gentlemen Please"; is the way that the Landlord gives notice that the bar was about to close.

unpleasant. Even the gay (and I am using this word in its traditional terminology) wildflowers: the foxgloves and the honeysuckle, which make the Devon lanes at this time of year such a thing of wonder, peered shiftily and malevolently at the old man as he shuffled along.

Occasionally a car would come past, and he offered up a silent prayer that the driver would take pity on him, pull over and offer him a lift. But it was the early summer of 1997, Thatcher had decreed that there was no such thing as society * a decade and a half before, and so her words had come to pass. The cars didn't slow down. They just went on in their own inexorable way showering him with muddy water as they did so.

It began to get dark. Nightfall comes late in Devon of a Maytime, but the Rev Cymbeline Potts was an old man, and it takes a long time for an old man to stumble fourteen miles in the pouring rain. But slowly and unsteadily he continued, until there was hardly light enough to see. When he reached the little village of Bradworthy he knew that not only was there only a mile and a bit left to walk, but that he knew the way like the back of his hand. And so, heartened by this knowledge, he picked up his feet and tried his best to march on bravely. He even whistled *The British Grenadiers* as he did so **. But, as everyone is so proud of telling us, pride comes before a fall, and he was only about a quarter of a mile away from the safety and solace of his own front gate, when a motor bike being driven far too fast by a surly looking young man who didn't even bother to stop for more time than it took to pick himself and the machine up again, swerved round the corner, careered into the old clergyman and threw him into the muddy ditch, tearing the ligaments in the poor old

---

* "I think we have gone through a period when too many children and people have been given to understand "I have a problem, it is the Government's job to cope with it!" or "I have a problem, I will go and get a grant to cope with it!" "I am homeless, the Government must house me!" and so they are casting their problems on society and who is society? There is no such thing! There are individual men and women and there are families and no government can do anything except through people and people look to themselves first. It is our duty to look after ourselves and then also to help look after our neighbour and life is a reciprocal business and people have got the entitlements too much in mind without the obligations." She has often been misquoted about this line, but as I loathe the woman even in death, I will write no words that could even slightly make me seem like a Thatcher apologist.

** "The British Grenadiers" is a traditional marching song of British and Canadian military units whose badge of identification features a grenade, the tune of which dates from the 17th century. The following text is the most well-known version of the song. The text arguably dates back to the War of Spanish Succession (1702–1713), since it refers to the grenadiers throwing grenades (a practice that proved to be too dangerous and was ended soon afterward,) and the men wearing "caps and pouches" (i.e. the tall grenadier caps, worn by these elite troops, and the heavy satchel in which grenades were carried) and "loupèd clothes"- coats with broad bands of 'lace' across the chest that distinguished early grenadiers.

Some talk of Alexander, and some of Hercules
Of Hector and Lysander, and such great names as these.
But of all the world's brave heroes, there's none that can compare.
With a tow, row, row, row, row, row, to the British Grenadiers.

man's left leg as he did so.

"Fuck off you stupid old cunt" the lout snarled, and went upon his way, leaving the old man injured and sobbing with pain and humiliation in the ditch.

Eventually he recovered his strength enough to pull himself out of the ditch, and, stumbling, half crawling and half limping he eventually managed to reach the tumbledown cottage where his sister and ward - distraught with worry - were waiting for him.

Even in 1997 some people didn't have telephones in their houses, didn't have cars, and had no conception of what The Internet was, so the two women, with only each other for comfort, had been waiting for him since about three o'clock, and when the battered old man, clothes torn, plastered with mud, with big bruises and swollen tissue up his left leg, and with his knuckles and the palms of his hands bleeding from having made his way on his hands and knees along the rough tarmacadam road finally crawled up to their front door, they were out of their mind with worry and anguish.

They undressed him, washed and dressed his wounds as best they could, and tucked him up in his own bed, where they left him reading *The Bible* and wondering what on earth he had done to deserve all the woes that he had experienced that day.

The answer is, of course, nothing. It is one of the biggest fallacies of most organised religions that bad things never happen to good people, unless - like Job[*] - they are somehow being tested by a deity who is moving in even more mysterious ways than usual. When the stark truth is that there is no rhyme or reason or underlying morality behind the way that things work. Some people are good, some bad, and there are a couple of million ill-defined gradients in between. Good things happen to bad people, and bad things happen to good people, and so it is, and so it always has been, and so it always will be.

---

[*] Job is the central figure of the Book of Job in the Bible. In rabbinical literature, Iyov (אִיּוֹב) is called one of the prophets of the Gentiles. In Islam, Job (Arabic: أَيُّوب translit. Ayyūb) is considered a prophet. Job is presented as a good and prosperous family man who is beset by Satan with God's permission with horrendous disasters that take away all that he holds dear, including his offspring, his health, and his property. He struggles to understand his situation and begins a search for the answers to his difficulties.

Job: A Comedy of Justice is a novel by Robert A. Heinlein published in 1984. The title is a reference to the biblical Book of Job and James Branch Cabell's book *Jurgen, A Comedy of Justice*. It won the Locus Award for Best Fantasy Novel in 1985 and was nominated for the Nebula Award for Best Novel in 1984, and the Hugo Award for Best Novel in 1985. The story examines religion through the eyes of Alex, a Christian political activist who is corrupted by Margrethe, a Danish Norse cruise ship hostess — and who loves every minute of it. Enduring a shipwreck, an earthquake, and a series of world-changes brought about by Loki (with Jehovah's permission), Alex and Marga work their way from Mexico back to Kansas as dishwasher and waitress.

XX

I was once a nurse, and the remnants of my nursing training are still in the background of my mind, from whence they emerge at the most unexpected moments. So I was not at all surprised to learn that within a few days the elderly clergyman, of whom I had always been so fond, had contracted pneumonia.

Now, before I go on any more with this part of the story, I need to explain something. Remember, that on the occasion that Lysistrata told me her story, it was the middle of the night on one of the most astrologically significant full moons of the year. I was half cut, having drunk well (if not entirely wisely) on the remains of a bottle of particularly good brandy that my boss had given me for the previous Christmas. And I was out in the lane outside my house, leaning against my ageing Vauxhall Astra communing with a woman whom I had always known as the disfigured, brain damaged housemaid of some quondam friends of my parents, and who now seemed wildly and un-naturally beautiful like a dryad in some piece of annoying new age art from the sort of shop Pete Loveday always used to lampoon as "Gaias and Dollars". [*]

She was undoubtedly telling me her story as we stood bathed in the pus red moonlight, with the distant sound of chanting wafting towards me on the warm September wind. But whether it was verbally, or by some psychic or psychological connection, or a mixture of all three, I truly can't tell you. Elsewhere I have written how little Panne communicated its own story to me at great cost to its own life and limb. Then I was immersed in its experiences, experiencing them for myself as if they were my own. But this was nothing like that. I saw no visions except for the exceptionally beautiful woman who was standing with me. But her narrative seemed to be compressed into an impossibly short time. In real terms I was not out in the lane for more than twenty minutes, but the conversation - if I can call it that, although it was certainly nothing of the kind if one is to use the conventional meaning of the word - seemed to go on for many hours.

Once again I am handicapped by the fact that my writing skills are totally inefficient for the task that I have set myself. Or perhaps it is that the Queen's English just

---

[*] Pete Loveday is a British underground cartoonist. He drew many comics charting the adventures of hippie character Russell including *Big Bang Comics, Big Trip Travel Agency, Plain Rapper Comix* printed by AK Press. He draws like Robert Crumb or Gilbert Shelton with lots of cross-hatching. Big Bang Comics is Britain's most successful underground comics.Recurring themes in the comics are drugs, Rock festivals, environmentalism etc. Plain Rapper Comix #2 is Loveday's pamphlet in comic book form on a history of hemp and why it would be beneficial for the environment to replace tree paper with hemp paper and he practices what he preaches by being the first publication in modern times to be printed on such paper. The Russell comics were reprinted in book form *Russell, The Saga of a peaceful man* published by John Brown Publishing.

doesn't have the words to describe what I am trying to say. But I think that it is probably the former.

Anyway. Not to my great surprise, the Rev Cymbeline Potts, a retired clergyman in his mid seventies, had contracted pneumonia.

The Potts household possessed neither a car or a telephone, but there was a rusty old bicycle in the garden shed, and Britannia mounted it and wobbled intrepidly, if unsteadily, towards the nearest telephone box half a mile away, so she could telephone the doctor. By 1997 the brave new world that had been ushered in by the twin gorgons of Mags and Di left little room for medical house calls, but the medical practise that had cared for the Potts siblings for so long, was of a pleasantly old fashioned variety, and within an hour or two the battered old Rover belonging to the family doctor was pulling up outside the tumbledown cottage.

Cymbeline flatly refused to go to hospital, although that was the preferred course of action proposed by the doctor, and so he was given a course of strong antibiotics, and instructions to have plenty of fluids and rest, whereupon the doctor went about his business and promised to return in a few days.

The peculiar trio that made up the Potts household were therefore left to their own devices. And what happened next was really rather interesting from a theological point of view (and that is something that you don't hear me say very often).

My Aunt was a Deaconess, my Father a Lay Preacher, and my Brother is a Clergyman, but I have a problem with theology. The dictionary definition of the subject is that it is the study of the divine. But I believe that *some* things are unknowable, and this includes the nature of Almighty God. And I believe that each person individually can choose to have a relationship with God, whether or not they choose to do so through a religion. And as such, all religions are equally true, equally false, and only effective if the supplicant wishes them to be so.

And so it was with the Reverend Cymbeline Potts. I have written about his long, slow, alienation from both the society of his fellow gentry and the Church of England (which even as recently as 1997 was still basically the same thing). It was a nasty, inexorable, and pretty much unstoppable slide away from the belief in everything that he had always held dear. But now something came along to replace it.

His horrible journey back home from Holsworthy, in the mud and water of a North Devon gale, which had ended up leaving the already frail old man with a life-threatening condition, had sorely tested his faith, and his faith had - not particularly surprisingly - been found wanting.

I have explained how Britannia had borrowed three books by Margaret Murray from my Mother, swallowed the convoluted theses contained within hook, line and sinker, and - together with bits and bobs taken from *The Golden Bough* constructed a complex theology all of her own based on nothing more concrete than her own preconceptions. And I have written how Cymbeline was increasingly interested in his sister's new beliefs. But now, confined to his bedchamber except for the occasional visits to the lavatory, with nothing to do but think (his glasses had been lost somewhere on his long and tortuous journey home the day before) he became a sickbed convert. And like all sickbed and deathbed converts to any belief system throughout history, he became a confirmed zealot.

And his world, and that of his peculiar little household, was never to be the same again.

XXI

Magick is a strange thing. It is basically the process whereby somebody imposes their will upon the universe. It is often described as being a process whereupon the practitioner entreats a deity for their aid in solving some earthly problem or other. And so, in many ways, there is no difference between magic and prayer. It is just that magic is a little bit more proactive.

Anybody who has read my writings here or elsewhere, will know that I have a wide range of friends and acquaintances covering an even wider range of social, academic, and life skills. Some are Christian, many are various brands of Pagan, there are a whole slew of atheists and agnostics, a couple of Buddhists and some with much less mainstream beliefs.

Some years ago I was having a conversation with an acquaintance of mine who amongst other things is a Church of England lay preacher. She was telling me about her study towards her Masters degree in theology. Now, I have already vented my spleen about the study of theology in these pages, and so I won't do it again. However, she was trying to explain to me about how miracles differ from magic. She had done her Masters dissertation, or thesis, or whatever the bloody hell it is called, on the precise nature of the miracles attributed to Jesus Christ both within the canonical Gospels and the various apocryphal ones.

Those people reading this who believe that the Bible is the literal word of God, probably don't realise that it is more like a sort of ecclesiastical Wikipedia. This is not the time or the place to enter into a scholarly examination of biblical history, but by the time that the Emperor Constantine made Christianity - or at least *his* version of Christianity - the state religion of the Roman Empire, about 300 years after the death of Christ, there was already a fair amount of disagreement as to what should and what shouldn't be part of the Bible. And over the years a whole slew of Gospels, Epistles and whatever have been rejected by the ecclesiastical establishment for one reason or another, mostly because they don't fit into whatever the current orthodoxy is.

The best known apocrypha contains those books of the old Testament which - for some reason or other - were not included in the Jewish Scriptures by the rabbis who were the most notable authorities on the subject. But, less well-known, until the books of Dan Brown that is, are the books which purports to describe the life of Christ, and the events that happened soon after his death. And, I have to admit, that I can see no good reason why some of these have been excluded, when the more well-known gospels remain canon. And when it comes down to the reasons why various of the Epistles were chosen whilst other ones were not, I can only imagine that it all comes down to politics. Either that or money. My father always insisted that St. Paul had been a bit of a prick, and - although I have never made it my business to study the matter, what little I know has basically made me tend to agree with him. All that stuff on the road to Damascus always smacked of opportunism to me! And I have always thought that although not very elegantly put, John Lennon had a point when he told Maureen Cleave that: "Jesus was all right, but his disciples were thick and ordinary. It's them twisting it that ruins it for me". *

So I did not share my acquaintance's knee jerk reactions concerning the less well known and attested documents purporting to tell the story of our saviour. One of these books - *The Infancy Gospel of Thomas* - which purports to tell the story of Christ's childhood, and which was probably written by a Greek dude about fifty years after the crucifixion, tells a story that I remember being told as a child at Peak School in Hong

---

* Cleave interviewed Lennon on 4 March 1966. At his home, Kenwood, in Weybridge, she found a full-size crucifix, a gorilla costume, a medieval suit of armour and a well-organised library, with works by Alfred, Lord Tennyson, Jonathan Swift, Oscar Wilde, George Orwell, Aldous Huxley, and The Passover Plot by Hugh J. Schonfield, which had influenced Lennon's ideas about Christianity. Cleave's article mentioned that Lennon was "reading extensively about religion", and quoted a comment he made:

Christianity will go. It will vanish and shrink. I needn't argue about that; I'm right and I'll be proved right. We're more popular than Jesus now; I don't know which will go first – rock 'n' roll or Christianity. Jesus was all right but his disciples were thick and ordinary. It's them twisting it that ruins it for me".

His opinions drew no controversy when originally published in the United Kingdom, but angry reactions flared up in Christian communities when the comment was republished in the United States five months later.

Kong about how the child Jesus breathed life into clay models of birds.

The same story is in The Q'ran:

> "Then will Allah say: "O Jesus the son of Mary! Recount My favour to thee and to thy mother. Behold! I strengthened thee with the holy spirit, so that thou didst speak to the people in childhood and in maturity. Behold! I taught thee the Book and Wisdom, the Law and the Gospel and behold! thou makest out of clay, as it were, the figure of a bird, by My leave, and thou breathest into it and it becometh a bird by My leave, and thou healest those born blind, and the lepers, by My leave. And behold! thou bringest forth the dead by My leave. And behold! I did restrain the Children of Israel from (violence to) thee when thou didst show them the clear Signs, and the unbelievers among them said: 'This is nothing but evident magic.'"

My acquaintance wrote her *magnum opus* on the difference between the attested miracles performed by Jesus as described in the Gospels of Matthew, Mark, Luke and John and the magickal acts attributed to him as described elsewhere, and the idea that our Saviour performed magick was completely anathema to her. The Q'ran evidently makes no distinction between them and, truly, neither can I.

Miracle Shmiracle. It's all magick to me.

But the conversation took place at a dinner party thrown to celebrate the birthday of a mutual friend, and so social niceties precluded the opportunity for me to tell her that she was talking bollocks. However, even if we had been in other circumstances I probably wouldn't have done so because it would have caused a lot of upset and done no possible good.

But basically, according to what a radiant Lysistrata told me that moonlit night last September, as he slowly recovered from his ordeal, and from his subsequent bout of pneumonia, the Rev. Cymbeline Potts soon came around to my (and - apparently - Mohammed's) way of thinking.

XXII

Most of the low life people with whom I spent much of my thirties are now dead, and - I will admit totally openly that - I lost touch with the rest a long time ago. But at least one of them is still alive, although I haven't spoken to him in the last fifteen years, and very much doubt whether I shall ever do so again. I have received the occasional friend suggestion on Facebook proposing that I rekindle our friendship, but this is a can of worms that I truly do not want to investigate, and whilst I wish him no harm at all, I decided long ago that I would prefer to leave our friendship well and truly in the past.

He owned, and - so I discovered from Lysistrata, during the blood moon last September - still owns, a junk shop on one of the less travelled thoroughfares of Tiverton. He always insisted that what he sold were antiques and *objets d'arte*, but to most people, the disparate collection of furniture, ornaments and vintage hi fi separates that filled his grubby shop window, was nothing but rather noisome junk. I used to hang out there because we had similar tastes in music, and because I enjoyed his company, but as the years went on I realised that he was - totally without meaning to be - one of the most dangerous men in North Devon.

Because he always had a friendly face and a kind word for vagrants, troubled young people, often homeless, and usually hopeless, would gravitate there, and spend their days with him, (and I shudder to admit, often me) listening to music, smoking fragrant hashish cigarettes, and talking surreal nonsense to each other. But his shop was not just a Mecca for these young and often innocent lotus eaters. The lure of so much young and impressionable flesh was an irresistible call to a bevy of more sinister visitors and as the years progressed more and more of these impressionable (and basically harmless, though troubled) young people were sucked into sexual, criminal or chemical adventures that would otherwise never have occurred to them purely because of people that they met at this particular little shop of horrors. Over the years I came to realise that as well as the musicians, poets and dreamers who hung out there, there was a small, but ever growing coterie of pornographers, heroin dealers, Satanists and extortionists who were also regular visitors, and the place began to lose its allure for me. One day I even met a pair of grave robbers who regularly visited the local cemeteries at night to dig up the corpses interred there in search of jewellery and other personal adornments. And can you guess where they took their wares to sell?

I first discovered the sinister little shop soon after I passed my driving test in 1980, and I was a regular visitor there until I moved to south Devon a couple of years later. As I think I have intimated on occasion during these pages, my first marriage was not a happy one especially towards the end, and I am afraid that I took all sorts of excuses to absent myself from the family hearth. And often I would drift aimlessly towards Tiverton and my friend's tawdry little shop full of rubbish, where I would drift the

---

* Whether these 'Satanists' were actually members of Anton LaVey's Church of Satan, or just oiks with tattoos and a collection of heavy metal albums who picked up on the 'glamour' of the hornéd one and decided that this was a lifestyle option that they wished to pursue, I have no idea. And truly—I don't really care.

hours away doing as little as possible. And when Alison's and my relationship imploded over twenty years ago as I write this, I continued visiting, on occasion, until finally I realised that my friend was actually like an emaciated hippy spider in the middle of a web of greed, corruption, and vices that made my own insalubrious tastes seem mild in comparison. So I stopped going, and eventually had a flaming row over the telephone with my erstwhile friend, and that was - as they say - that.

In the basement of the shop was a small occult bookstore operated by one of the Satanists to whom I alluded earlier, and as Lysistrata told me how the Rev Potts, still weak from his almost fatal brush with pneumonia, sought the shop out in his search for magickal answers, I shuddered. I could almost feel the horror that this neat and tidy elderly gentleman must have felt as he negotiated the tortuous back lanes of Tiverton until he found the grubby little shop.

It had once been an undertaker's, until it went bust some time in the early 1970s. It had then been squatted by a few renegade members of an outlaw biker gang whom I shall not name because I would like to keep what remains of my kneecaps. How my erstwhile friend had managed to take it over was a mystery that had always mildly puzzled me, but eventually it turned out that one of the bikers had been his brother-in-law, and when he was incarcerated for some nameless crime against public decency, my friend had found out who actually owned it, picked up the lease, paid off the arrears owing, and set up shop.

The rest is rather unpleasant history.

How the Rev Potts heard about the tawdry little establishment history doesn't relate, and although he had turned his back upon the imperium of the Church of England, I cannot imagine that he took kindly to the rack of T Shirts emblazoned with the motto 'Jesus is a cunt' which was positioned just inside the door, or to the seven foot tall rubber skeleton with the devil mask that someone had crucified on the wall. One has to actually admire his bravery at going so far outside his comfort zone in search of arcane knowledge that was even further out. But the generation of gentlefolk born in the years between the wars were a doughty breed, and - after an hour or so spent in earnest conversation with the aforementioned Satanist, and even more earnest perusal of the grubby shelves - poor Cymbeline left the shop, having spent that week's pension on a large and unwieldy carrier bag of books on a dozen murky subjects, as he made his way to the bus stop for his long and tortuous journey back to North Devon.

XXIV

istory doesn't relate exactly what books the Rev Cymbeline Potts bought in Tiverton that fateful day in early summer, but I have a pretty good idea, considering that quite a lot of my own library of occult literature came from the same source. I *do* know that at least one of the books was either by or about Gerald Gardner, and others were by Aleister Crowley.

How do I know this? Well, basically by a series of deductions.

Cymbeline and Britannia continued their occult studies, and together with Lysistrata, the peculiar little triad began to compile their own Book of Shadows * based on Britannia's herbal folk magic, and bits and bobs of Crowley, Gardner and other such heroes of modern Italy who passed their way.

Cymbeline became quite a regular visitor to the sordid little shop in Tiverton during the long, hot, summer of 1997, and - with the benefit of hindsight - as this was the summer that my divorce came through, and I was engaged in a highly emotionally fraught affair with a female occultist from Cornwall who was in the habit of coming to visit me for weeks on end and wandering around suburban Exwick in the hours before dawn skyclad with a pair of roe deer antlers strapped to her head **, and that said female occultist had been introduced to me by the bloke who owned the occult

---

* A Book of Shadows is a book containing religious texts and instructions for magical rituals found within the Neopagan religion of Wicca, and in many pagan practices. One famous Book of Shadows was created by the pioneering Wiccan Gerald Gardner sometime in the late 1940s or early 1950s, and which he utilised first in his Bricket Wood coven and then in other covens which he founded in following decades. The Book of Shadows is also used by other Wiccan traditions, such as Alexandrianism and Mohsianism, and with the rise of books teaching people how to begin following Wicca in the 1970s onward, the idea of the Book of Shadows was then further propagated amongst solitary practitioners unconnected to earlier traditions.

Initially, when Wicca was still dominated by covens, "only one copy [of the Book] existed for an entire coven, kept by the high priestess or high priest. That rule has proved unfeasible, and it is [now] commonplace for all Witches to have their own copies."

An online guide by Patti Rigington reads: "The Book of Shadows, or BOS, is used to store information you'll need in your magical tradition, whatever it may be. Many Pagans feel a BOS should be handwritten, but as technology progresses, some use their computer to store information as well. Don't let anyone tell you there's only one way to make your BOS, because you should use what works best for you!

Bear in mind that a BOS is considered a sacred tool, which means it is an item of power that should be consecrated with all of your other magical tools. In many traditions, it is believed you should copy spells and rituals into your BOS by hand; this not only transfers energy to the writer, but it also helps you to memorize the contents. Make sure you write legibly enough that you'll be able to read your notes during a ritual!"

** See *The Rising of the Moon* by Jonathan Downes and Nigel Wright (Domra, Corby,1999)

bookshop in the basement of my mate's shop, and we spent much of that summer visiting them and smoking raw opium as we went about various pieces of magickal business, I am truly surprised that our visits, and those of the Rev Potts never seemed to coincide.

His magickal library certainly became quite extensive over the next few months, and the old man spent much of his stipendiary pension on it. Lysistrata told me how the three of them - perfectly secure in each other's company - began doing workings, mostly intended to protect the little triad from the impending predations of a Stevie Wingford, fifteen years older, and fifteen years nastier, after his time in prison.

I wondered then, and have wondered since what sort of magickal workings the three earnest neophyte occultists carried out. As both Cymbeline and Britannia were kindly old souls and fond of animals, I was certain that Crowley's more unpleasant workings involving crucifying toads and disembowelling other small denizens of the hedgerows would have turned their stomachs and have been rejected out of hand.

However, the year earlier[*], I had seen Lysistrata collecting roadkill and had wondered them what she and Britannia had been using them for. I suspect that the three magicians had reached some sort of compromise with the Goddess, and that these had been for some arcane sacrifice to Hecate. Certainly the skulls of foxes and badgers, some with half decomposed flesh still adhering to the whitening bones had been impaled on sticks and placed around the garden for some magickal purpose.

I had, in fact, seen something like this before.

One of the strangest people that I met back when I lived in Northam, the summer that I first met Danny Miles was a bloke called Derry [**] who lived in a small hut in the middle of the woods on one of the steep valleys on the edge of Exmoor six or seven miles from Barnstaple. He wrote - what I thought at the time - were extraordinary songs, but which - with the benefit of hindsight - were probably just stoned drivel. However, fuelled by the legendary exploits of such outsider artistes as Syd Barrett and Julian Cope, I was determined to have a go at making a record with him, and so when he invited my semi-girlfriend Samantha and me to visit him in his tawdry little shanty, I jumped at the chance. Samantha - who was, admittedly not too bright,

---

* Once again, see *The Song of Panne* but I am embarrassed to say so, as I I truly don't want to look as if I am one of those breadhead authors who spend their time trying to flog other books in the same series. I am not, but if you want to expend a speculative few quid, don't let me stop you.

** See *Monster Hunter* by me (CFZ, Exeter, 2004)

although she was a complete slut which was fine by me - looked askance at the idea. She liked hanging around at the *Royal Norfolk* * because she had ambitions to be a rock chick and was determined to dump me as soon as she had the chance to jump on one of the roadies from *Mötorhead* **, and was not at all impressed with the idea of sleeping in a grubby, rough, wooden shack with no electricity, her on-off boyfriend with a penchant for alfresco lovemaking and a smelly, hirsute and not very talented singer-songwriter with a silly name.

The following Saturday we drove out of Barnstaple, and with some difficulty I managed to locate the nearest bit of road to the hillside where Derry had set up his home.

Samantha complained for the entire duration of the journey. The truth is that we didn't actually like each other very much, but she was determined to get a rock-star boyfriend and, although I wasn't actually a rock-star, I had made a record, played the guitar, and had even written a song for her called *Beautiful Mutant Monkey.* *** As far as I was concerned; I just wanted a slutty girlfriend with big breasts and no morals. She was perfect.

We parked the car, locked it, and slowly climbed up the steep, heavily wooded hillside. Eventually we reached the hut where Derry lived. Not entirely to my surprise there was nobody there although the hut was unlocked. We pushed the door open and peered in. Imagine, if you will, if a family of alcoholic badgers with a penchant for football hooliganism had lived together in a pile of cardboard boxes on a diet of tinned pasta and pickled onions. Then multiply your mental image tenfold. Then pour yourself a stiff drink.

Over the years I have visited some of the most squalid places to live that one could possibly imagine. I have even lived in them myself, but this was by far the worst dwelling place that I have ever seen a human being inhabit. It was filthy dirty and full of rubbish. In the corner were a pile of pelts which had been removed from road killed animals and outside various decomposing skulls from these animals were perched on poles and left to rot.

---

* The pub where, in the early 1980s, the rock and roll aristocracy of North Devon (yes there *was* one) used to hang out

** FFS. You mean I have to tell you who *Mötorhead* were? Bloody hell. Blah blah Lemmy Kilmister ex *Hawkwind* bassist, kicked out by Brock etal and starts his own noisy trio..

*** on my 1982 album *The Mistake.* Long unavailable, like every album I recorded before 1995, there is at least one live version on YouTube.

I was feeling somewhat amorous by this time, but unfortunately even the ever-horny Samantha did not feel like making love on top of a pile of half-cured fox skins. I managed to inveigle her into the woods, and we were semi dressed by the time that Derry - stoned out of what was left of his tiny mind - wandered back up the hill towards the hut, and we rearranged our clothing hurriedly. He had, of course, forgotten that we were coming, and furthermore had left his guitar at some squat in Barnstaple, so although I had gone to the expense of hiring an expensive 4 Track Revox Tape Recorder with which to record his songs, he was in no condition to record anything, and being without a guitar, would not have been able to play them anywhere. So, we spent the rest of the afternoon sitting in the little clearing in the woods, both trying - half-heartedly - to seduce Samantha, and chatting about this and that.

Samantha was in no mood to be seduced and went off into a sulk while Derry and I chatted inconsequential nonsense and puffed away on suspiciously long cigarettes. I asked him why he had decorated the clearing in the forest with animal skulls on poles, and he told me that it was to appease the spirits of the wood.

"Eh?" I asked, wondering what on earth he was talking about. I pointed out that the spirits of the wood would - if, in fact they actually existed - be the guardians of animal life, and would therefore not be particularly impressed - or indeed appeased - by the sight of over a dozen semi-squashed dead animals impaled on sticks outside a malodorous shanty. However, he was unimpressed by my argument. He had seen the avatar of the earth spirits, he told me, and apparently she had taken on the guise of a giant black panther.

He explained that the decomposing roadkill acted in a similar manner to Tibetan prayer flags; A prayer flag is a colourful rectangular cloth, often found strung along mountain ridges and peaks high in the Himalayas. They are used to bless the surrounding countryside and for other purposes. Prayer flags are believed to have originated with Bon. In Bon, shamanistic Bonpo used primary-coloured plain flags in Tibet. Traditional prayer flags include woodblock-printed text and images. The flags do not carry prayers to gods, which is a common misconception; rather, the Tibetans believe the prayers and mantras will be blown by the wind to spread the good will and compassion into all pervading space. Therefore, prayer flags are thought to bring benefit to all.

Derry told me that the process of decomposition, when the dead creatures were placed in a certain manner, had a similar effect, and that he urged anyone to do the same. I found the idea revolting then, and I find it revolting now, but I couldn't help wondering whether Cymbeline and his family had stumbled upon this idea somewhere, and if it actually worked.

Having been in the intensely magickal garden behind the Potts family cottage just outside Bradworthy the year before, I could take my hat off and honestly attest that something had happened there. But could this revolting demi-thaumaturgical nonsense of Derry actually have made sense. And if so, did he invent it himself, or had he got it from somewhere else, and if so who?

XXV

*T*he summer of 1997 was a surprisingly peaceful one, both for me and for the peculiar little triad living in the increasingly grotty little cottage outside Bradworthy. I was getting used to my newly single status and was embroiled in an increasingly intense sexual friendships with two totally separate women, and - as my parents had finally come to terms with the idea that their eldest son had committed the ultimate social no no of becoming a divorcee - I visited North Devon several times, once with one of my paramours. On most of those occasions I made my excuses to my parents and paid the Potts menage a visit.

Eighteen years after the event, as I leaned against my dilapidated Vauxhall Astra under the pus red light of the so-called 'Blood Moon', she-who-was-once-called Hazel Wingford, whom I had known on and off for decades as a surly, deformed (and unaccountably sexy) maidservant named after the protaganotrix of a play by Aristophanes, and who now appeared more like a glistening dryad than anything even slightly human, I heard her version of the events of that fateful summer, and I felt like kicking myself. Because on the two or three times that I had visited the Potts cottage I had thought that everything was the same as normal, when in fact it was nothing of the sort.

In all the years that I had known the Rev Cymbeline Potts, I had never considered him as anything but a kindly, intelligent - if absent minded - old scholar; in many ways the sort of person I had always aspired to being. Someone surrounded with his books, with a good cellar, and a life untrammelled by the complications of the real world. And on the various occasions that I visited the little cottage during that long hot summer I blush to recall that I truly didn't notice that anything was different.

But there was something strange in the air that summer. Over large swathes of South Devon there was a wave of UFO sightings unparalleled in my experience before or since. Together with my friends and partners in crime Graham Inglis and Nigel Wright we recorded sightings, tracked witnesses, interviewed experiencers and made a hundred and one extrapolations from the data which were almost certainly wrong. The story of those strange months can be found in a book called *The Rising of the Moon* that Nigel and I wrote the following year completely without realising that we were copying the plotline of the movie *The Forbidden Planet* to an alarmingly plagiaristic degree.

On the 12th August, I even saw one of these mysterious lights for myself. The Exeter Strange Phenomena research group held a skywatch at various locations across Devonshire. Whilst Graham manned the Exeter location the rest of the core team, together with five other members of the group, and Janet Kipling, from BBC Radio Devon were on Woodbury Common.

I arrived at about quarter past nine with a friend of mine. It was in fact the first time that I had visited. Woodbury Castle for many years and I took the chance to look around. Dusk was falling as my dog and I wandered around the walls of the ancient earthwork. It was very quiet and very still. It was the sort of heavy summer night that one usually only experiences in the tropics and there was a distinct feel of thunder in the air. I climbed to the top of the ridge, and as Toby half heartedly ambled after rabbits (who paid no attention to him whatsoever), I looked over towards the great mass of Haldon Hill on the other side of the Exe Estuary and wondered what the night ahead was going to bring.

The air was rich with the scent of gorse flowers and the little chirping sounds made by grasshoppers and other small insects. For a moment I allowed myself a brief daydream, mentally substituted the sound of English grasshoppers for the strident squeaks of crickets and tree-frogs, and it was like I was back in Hong Kong as a small boy.

Just for a moment I could imagine that instead of the Exe estuary I was looking out over the myriad of tiny islands in the bay of Hong-Kong and that the lights from the town of Topsham way below me, were in fact the lights of dozens of little junks embarking on nocturnal fishing expeditions. For the first time in many months I felt happy and I drifted on a cloud of self indulgence until my reverie was shattered by the sound of approaching cars and the arrival of the other members of the team.

I called to Toby who had found something incredibly interesting to sniff at, and wandered purposefully back down to the car park. There were tiny pin-pricks of light on some of the bushes as I passed and I realised, much to my delight, that for the first time in nearly three decades I was seeing glow worms.

The intrepid investigation team unloaded their equipment, mounted telescopes and video cameras onto their tripods, opened cans of beer and waited expectantly for something to happen.

Nothing did and it started to rain.

There was almost 100% cloud cover in North and West Devon and so our Bideford, Totnes and Tavistock groups decided to call it a night but at Woodbury we still had about 40% visibility and so despite a light drizzle we struggled on. At about eleven (unfortunately just after Janet had concluded her interviews with us and gone home), all seven of us saw what seemed like a very dim blue-white star moving very erratically just within the burgeoning cloud cover. We watched it for several minutes, and then, as now, the best visual analogy that I can give is that it looked like a quasi-stellar version of the whirligig beetles that whizz around on the surface of ponds and slow moving streams during hot summers.

Half an hour after our sighting, two young men, walking on Exmouth sea front saw two red lights behaving erratically. I met one of them at the BUFORA conference at Sheffield and he told me that they were "whizzing along just above sea level". His mate works for BAe, saw it in more depth, but refused to talk to our researchers even with confidentiality ensured because he works on government defense work.

At midnight on the 12th-13th, DJ John Pierce said on Gemini Radio that there were power cuts in the Budleigh area that SWEB couldn't explain. I rang one of my contacts at Gemini the next day and they told me that one of the Torquay area transmitters had been struck by lightning. Although we can confirm that we saw thunder and lightning over Torbay on the previous night from our vantage point high up at Woodbury castle there does seem to be a minor mystery surrounding the whole affair. Graham rang SWEB on the 13th August at 19:45 and they denied that anything of the sort had happened.

The `lightning strike` had occurred at approximately the same time as we had seen the strange blue light in the sky, and at the same time another one of our group who was in the Torbay area, was trying to contact us on her mobile `phone and found that for some inexplicable reason that she was unable to get any reception.

But as all this was happening in Exeter, Exmouth and the villages in between, strange things were afoot in North Devon. I don't know if there was any connection, but at the same time as my compadres and I were chasing unidentified flying wassnames across the moorlands of the south of the county, in the little patch of woodland adjoining the Potts family's tumbledown cottage, the quondam Reverend Minister of the Church of England was experimenting with raising a cone of power, using very specific instructions that had originally come from the pen of Gerald Gardner. [*]

Because a very wise, not to say venerable, friend of mine had once insisted that there are no such things as coincidences[**], I tend to think that all these events were somehow interconnected. There had been sightings of strange objects in the skies of North Devon, and - completely contradicting the conclusions that I came to in *The Rising of the Moon* - I suspect that there were probably as many sightings in North Devon as there had been in South Devon; the only real difference being that me and my rabidly eager compadres were in the south ready to catalogue them.

A friend of my parents who at the time lived a few cottages up the street from where Corinna and I live now was driving back to the village, down Cranford Hill when she saw a basketball sized globe of deep orange coloured light hovering in the air in front of her car, and this was far from being an isolated case. Such balls of what appeared to be glowing balls of plasma appeared all over the region on the night of the 12th August 1997 [***], and not entirely to my surprise, as I was collating these sightings for this current narrative, I discovered that most of them were on the capillary-like network of tiny lanes between Woolsery and Bradworthy. And, presuming that you have been paying attention, you will realise that it is on one of these lanes that the Potts menage have lived for many decades.

XXVI

Cones of power? Perhaps I should explain.

At various points during this narrative you will have seen me mention a man called Gerald Gardner who is often referred to as the father of modern neopaganism. Indeed, in a paper I wrote with Nick Redfern nearly two decades ago [****], I opined that Gardner actually invented most of what contemporary Wiccans actually do. However this is neither the time nor the place for that argument, so - just

---

* The **cone of power** is a method of raising energy in ritual magic, especially witchcraft. The term refers to the idea that the raised energy forms a cone with the circle forming its base. As a group the cone is formed by the coveners standing in a circle, holding hands, and focusing on a single point above and in the centre of the circle. They then dance, drum, chant, and perform various other ritual gestures, in order to raise the energy. This is called "Raising the Cone of Power".

** See *The Owlman and Others*, CFZ, Exeter, 1997

*** See *UFOs over Devon* by yours truly (Bossiney, Newquay, 2000)

**** In one of the volumes of *Fortean Studies* and embarrassingly I cannot remember which, but I think that they are all well worth checking out as a high point of what theGang of Fort achieved.

for the moment - let us suppose that everything that Gardner claimed is *actually* the unvarnished truth.

In the late 1930s after having spent some years in Malaya, Gardner went to live in the New Forest where, he became involved with a number of local occult organisations. He claimed that one of them was a coven of witches led by a lady called old Dorothy Clutterbuck. Whether or not the New Forest Coven actually existed anywhere outside Gardner's imagination is a matter for discussion which still divides pagan historians to this day, but Old Dorothy certainly existed, although she was - on the surface at least - an eminently respectable woman who was (amongst other things) a pillar of the local church and the local Conservative Party.

Believing the coven to be a survival of the pre-Christian Witch-Cult discussed in the works of Margaret Murray, he decided to revive the faith, supplementing the coven's rituals with ideas borrowed from Freemasonry, ceremonial magic and the writings of Aleister Crowley to form the Gardnerian tradition of Wicca. Gardner only ever described one of their rituals in depth, and this was an event that he termed "Operation Cone of Power". According to his own account, it took place in 1940 in a part of the New Forest and was designed to ward off the Nazis from invading Britain by magical means. Gardner claimed that a "Great Circle" was erected at night, with a "great cone of power" – a form of magical energy – being raised and sent to Berlin with the command of "you cannot cross the sea, you cannot cross the sea, you cannot come, you cannot come".

From what I can gather from my long and rambling conversation with Lysistrata on that strange September night, Cymbeline Potts became very excited when he first read about Gardner and the New Forest Coven's working, and carried out a number of experiments of his own throughout the summer of 1997 - both by himself and with the aid of his sister and his ward - to try and raise a cone of power to protect his family from the vengeful wrath of Stevie Wingford.

At first it appeared that he might have succeeded, because although he had first read about Stevie's imminent return in the May, by August he still had not returned to Bradworthy, and the fragile little triad in the tumbledown cottage had still not been under threat.

But then in mid August, The Rev Potts was in Bradworthy for the first time in years. His sister had been prowling the lanes looking for herbs that she could use to make her sacred potions when she had come across a bedraggled cat that had obviously come off worse in an interaction with a motor vehicle of some description. She took it back to the cottage, but it was in need of veterinary attention, and so that very afternoon, Cymbeline took it into Bradworthy in a cat basket rudely affixed to the handlebars of his bicycle.

He was coming out of the old vet surgery in the square when he noticed Stevie and a couple of his cronies leaning against the War Memorial and guffawing loudly at some unknown witticism. They saw the elderly clergyman riding unsteadily off on his velocipede and taunted him viciously.

Their words rang in his ears, and he cycled home, with the cat - now bandaged and with antibiotics coursing through its feline circulatory system - still in its basket on his handlebars. But he now realised for certain that the threat he had agonised about for months was now here, and that if he was to do anything about it he would have to act fast.

Back in South Devon the UFO reports and other accounts of High Strangeness were reaching their climax. In many ways it was this summer that made my career, because before the summer of 1997 I was a fat bloke on the dole, whereas after that I was a fat bloke on the dole that appeared in lots of newspapers and magazines and was widely cited as an authority in what is vulgarly known as weird shit.

I appeared in a lot of newspapers that summer, but the culmination of it all was when I actually managed to sell a story about the UFO wave to the Old Thunderer itself. On 30th of August *The Times* sent down one of their photographers to get images to go alongside the story. Over the years I have been photographed a lot for newspapers, but the seven hour photo session for *The Times* was something else entirely. I had originally intended to take him out to Woodbury Common where I had had my own UFO experience six weeks before, but he had such a lot of lights and reflectors and filters and other gubbins that would only work from mains electricity that I was forced to think again.

At the time I was living in Bohemian squalor in a mid terraced house in Exwick, a suburb of Exeter, and when the photographer took one look at my sitting room and all the esoteric impedimenta therein he shook his head worriedly. This just wouldn't do he lisped.

Then Graham piped up. "What about The Vortex?"

Some months before we had been visited by one of the computer magazines who were having a special 'Paranormal Issue' and wanted to interview me for a cover mount CD. God knows why.

The bloke doing the interviews was a pleasantly sceptical bloke who looked like a rugby player in a novel by Richard Gordon *. He wore a tatty tweed jacket, and had healthy ruddy cheeks and an expense account, and before filming took us down to *The Thatched House* for a very boozy pub lunch. Over lunch he regaled us with stories of other places he had filmed including somewhere called the Oregon Vortex.

The Oregon Vortex is a roadside attraction located in Gold Hill, Oregon, in the United States. It consists of a number of interesting effects, which are gravity hill optical illusions, but which the attraction's proprietors propose are the result of paranormal properties of the area.

For some reason this struck Graham as magnificently funny, and when - after lunch - we staggered back home to film on the overgrown patch of tree bespeckled wasteland at the end of the terrace in which I lived, he indulged in one of his rare pieces of whimsy. This piece of land was meant to be a children's playground, but it had never been developed as such, and basically the only people ever to use it were us, both to allow my dog Toby to answer the calls of nature he didn't answer on the kitchen floor (he was a very old dog) and to do various film and photo opportunities. Over the year it had stood in good stead for Sumatra, Bodmin Moor, Dartmoor and Roswell New Mexico. The bloke who was interviewing me asked what the patch of wasteland was called. I was about to say that it didn't actually have a name, when Graham piped in that it was the Exwick Vortex. And it has been known (to us, if no-one else) as 'The Vortex' ever since.

The photographer from *The Times* was very pleased with the suggestion, and so we spent the next seven hours there while he got exactly the right spot. By the end of this palaver Graham, Nigel, my UFO-spotting mate Jan Scarff, and I were heartily sick of the whole thing, but were heartened when the photographer (whose name was Paulus, believe it or not) said that he was very pleased with the photographs, and that his editor would "love them".

Being a natural cynic I muttered to Jan something along the lines of "how much do you want to bet that some member of the Royal Family has a fucking car crash and the story gets bumped?"

---

* Gordon Stanley Ostlere (15 September 1921 – 11 August 2017), better known by his pen name Richard Gordon, was an English surgeon and anaesthetist. As Richard Gordon, Ostlere wrote numerous novels, screenplays for film and television and accounts of popular history, mostly dealing with the practice of medicine. He was best known for a long series of comic novels on a medical theme beginning with Doctor in the House, and the subsequent film, television, radio and stage adaptations. His The Alarming History of Medicine was published in 1993, and he followed this with The Alarming History of Sex.

At four the next morning Toby and I were fast asleep when the phone rang. it was Jan.

"Turn the fucking television on now!" he said.

XXVII

O ne of the central arguments in Margaret Murray's 1954, book *The Divine King in England*, is a theory greatly extrapolated from Sir James Frazer's *The Golden Bough*, which claimed that societies all over the world sacrificed their kings to the deities of nature. In her book, she claimed that this practice had continued into medieval England, and that, for instance, the death of William II was really a ritual sacrifice. She also claimed that a number of important figures who died violent deaths, such as Archbishop Thomas Becket, were killed as a replacement for the king.

Although, like so many books of pop academia, the theory had quite a following amongst lay people who read the book, few if any academics took the suggestions seriously, and the theory lapsed into obscurity, only to be dragged kicking and screaming into the dog days of the 21st Century when - on the last day of summer - a princess named after the Queen of the Chase, died under mysterious circumstances in a Paris underpass. Me? I think the driver was drunk, and although back in the days when I used to drive three sheets to the wind, I not only never got caught, but never got in an accident, I am perfectly aware that drink driving causes accidents, and I have not done it for a lot more than twenty years.

But Diana paranoia grabbed the collective psyche of the nation, and whilst most of the paranoiees (if I can coin another one of my half-arsed neologisms) believed that she had been assassinated by shadowy figures inside the British establishment, a significant subset took this as a sign that Margaret Murray's most bonkers theory was correct.

Bizarrely these people included my Mother.

Less bizarrely these people included the Rev Cymbeline Potts and his sister Britannia. This coincided with Cymbeline's researches into the methodology of raising a cone of power as described by Gerald Gardner.

As I have mentioned, the summer of 1997 was unparalleled in my experience for incidences of what is vulgarly called "weird shit" amongst the moorlands and sunken lanes of Devonshire, and whilst I cannot be sure whether these were caused by the Potts siblings experimentation into the left hand path, or whether said experimentation was actually enhanced by whatever eddies in the fabric of the aether had been caused by these strange occurrences, I am convinced that these things are all somehow linked.

I think I probably added to the general psychic confusion in the Westcountry because I became involved with another bit of ritual magick in the south of the county at the same time. A couple of years previously, a stable girl called Jessie Hurlstone had been battered to death in her caravan at Buckfastleigh. Probably because I was nowhere near as sane as I am now, I became convinced that the killer had been possessed by the spirit of one of the area's less salubrious historical figures.

Hawson Court was once owned by Richard Capel, one of the most notorious men ever to live in Devon. He was the Lord of the Manor at Buckfastleigh in the 17th century. Little is known about his life, or indeed about the manner of his death, but his horrific exploits have become the stuff of legend.

The Devon folklorist Theo Brown wrote:

> "We know practically nothing about him except that he rebuilt part of his house - the date 1656 is carved over the door - and enjoyed a terrible reputation as a persecutor of village maidens. Having captured one, he would keep her under lock and key across the valley at Hawson Court".

He had an unenviable reputation as a violent and powerful squire, and when he came to die in 1677 his end was unpleasant. One legend says he was chased across the moor by a pack of "whisht" hounds until he dropped dead." Brown went on to say in her 1982 book *Devon Ghosts*, that Capel was buried with a "square-shaped house with an iron grill" on top of his grave to keep away the demon Dartmoor hounds who allegedly killed him (an oft-cited inspiration for Conan Doyle's Hound of the Baskervilles).

Other self-styled experts on occult matters have claimed that the local people interred him *above* ground because he was too evil a character to be interred in consecrated ground, and he is even supposed - by some people - to have been in imminent danger of becoming a vampire, and that his "square shaped house" not only had an iron grill, but an oak door; oak and iron (forgetting the fact that there were no oaks in 1st Century Judea) were popularly supposed to be the substances used in Christ's crucifixion, and therefore efficacious in keeping away the undead.

Local children, would often come to the porch at night, walk thirteen times around it widdershins, and insert a trembling finger into the keyhole of the huge oak door, to see if the evil squire would gnaw at it.

In 1992 the church was gutted in an arson attack, and sometime between then and 1995 when I made an episode of *Mysterious West* for Westcountry TV there, the old oak door was broken in. Thus, I surmised in my paranoid state, the phantasm of the evil squire could walk again across the lands that he once owned. There were sightings of black dogs in the driveway of his old home, and then Jessie Hurlstone was murdered. I told my suspicions to a coven of equally paranoid witches, and some occult shenanigans involving naked witches, black candles and holy salt ensued. I have no idea if they were successful. I suspect not, partially because we didn't know what we were doing, partly because there is no real evidence that Stephen Webber, the farm labourer convicted of her murder was possessed by anything except for a jealous rage, and partly because in matters of magick intention is everything, and my only real intention here was to see one of the aforementioned wyrd sisters naked.

But it was a weird (ok, a wyrd) summer, and all sorts of strange shit was going down, and it was a time, the like of which I hope I will never see again. There was a mutilated roebuck (the skull of which is still in my collection), a mutilated whale, alien abductions, UFOs, poltergeists, sightings of mysterious creatures, hooded figures, and even the story of the weird warbling whatsit that turned out to be a novelty alarm clock. And then on Tuesday 16th September it all stopped.

And I have never known why. Not until now.

"And the Master continued his workings" said Lysistrata. "Sometimes with me and Miss Britannia, sometimes alone. Sometimes skyclad, sometimes clothed. And then at the Full Moon, without telling us what he was going to do, that was done which may not be done except in great emergency".

"Oh Fuck" I said. But now I understood.

XXIX

As regular readers of my ramblings may well be aware by now, I have a rich and varied collection of friends and acquaintances, some of whom are particularly peculiar, and many of whom inhabit one or the other of the sacred groves of Academe in some capacity or other. One acquaintance whom I wish that I knew better is a guy who operates under the soubriquet of 'Dr Beachcombing' and who is the head honcho of a website called 'Strange History'.

He has an entertaining habit of throwing out cerebral questions to his readership, a bit like Esther Rantzen did on her late lamented TV show *That's Life* between 1973 and 1994. One of these questions, a few years ago, was about the last human sacrifice in Europe, to which a reader using the ratite *nom de guerre* of 'Ostrich' wrote:

> "There's a persistent story that the New Forest coven of witches employed a human sacrifice in May of 1940 as part of an effort to prevent Hitler from invading England. Gerald Gardner, the mid-20th century popularizer of Wicca, is quoted by JL Bracelin as saying 'We were taken at night to a place in the Forest, where the Great Circle was erected; and that was done which may not be done except in great emergency.'The phrase "that was done which may not be done except in great emergency" is generally held to refer to human sacrifice, of course. The usual story attached to this is that the sacrifice was a willing one – the oldest member of the coven celebrated the rite nude, on an exceptionally cold May night, and took an extra portion of the fly agaric mushroom which formed part of the ritual. Within a few days, whether from exposure or poison or both, he was dead. If true, then the man's as great a war hero as any, in that he willingly gave his life to help stop Hitler, whether it had any effect or not. I'm sorry to say that I've got my doubts as to whether it actually happened. Gardner's rather coy remark seems to be the only primary source for this – lots of writers relate the details of exposure and poison (mainly over-excitable fundamentalist Christian writers expounding on the dangers of Wicca – most seem to skip over *why* the alleged sacrifice took place, as well as the exceptional nature of it), but none seem to cite a source. Wiccan Roots by Philip Heselton seems to be where the fleshed-out version originated, as best I can tell, but I make no claim to authority on this. The problem there is that Heselton admits that he's speculating on the details. It seems rational and informed speculation, but it's speculation nonetheless.'

I recognised the words immediately that Lysistrata spoke them, and knew that the kindly old clergyman had killed himself with the highest possible motives: to spare the two people he loved most from an unpleasant and painful death at the hands of a nasty bucolic psychopath.

As far as the world at large was aware, Cymbeline had committed suicide out of remorse for the deeds that he was popularly supposed to have committed nearly two decades before. Why he had waited seventeen years nobody cared, and - indeed - nobody bothered to ask. They - my parents included - just supposed that he had taken the gentleman's way out, retiring to the library with a decanter of port and a revolver.

Or in this case, into the woods naked with a shotgun.

The fact that he had been naked with a pentacle sigil painted on his forehead had been conveniently ignored by the *demi monde* of rural North Devon, if indeed they ever knew, and although I have no way of proving this, and indeed it doesn't really matter nearly twenty years later, I suspect that either Britannia or Lysistrata or both cleaned, washed and dressed the body before leaving his pitiful corpse to be found by the dogwalking daughter of a local farmer who then informed the police.

Lysistrata insisted that neither she or Britannia had known about his plans, and that by the time that they had found out it was too late. I see no reason why she would have lied to me about it, having confessed so much else that must have been terribly painful to impart.

But his death was literally a game changer, because from then on everything changed.

Some years ago John Higgs wrote an extraordinary history of the life and career of a band called the KLF aka *The Justified Ancients of Mu Mu* in which he claimed that the band's notorious bonfire on which they burned a million pounds was "a magical act that forged the 21st century". One of the cultural signposts which led him towards this conclusion was a minor plot twist in Alan Moore's *From Hell* which suggested that the conception of Adolf Hitler at the same moment as one of the Jack the Ripper Murders kickstarted the horrors of the 20th Century.

I think that it is highly unlikely that the death of Diana Princess of Wales was anything but a drunken accident, but - unless everything that I think that I know about the nature of magick and its relationship with the universe is wrong - the public outpouring of grief after a much loved public figure named after the Goddess of the Hunt was killed on the last day of summer, must have had some effect on the aether, and therefore on the years that followed.

But the thing which I find impossible to ignore is that after the death of my old friend and mentor in early September, the strange occurrences across the county of Devonshire, which had been the focus of my life all summer, suddenly came to an end. Something had happened, and I think that unlike Dylan's Mr Jones * I actually know now what had happened.

---

* If you have not heard Bob Dylan's *Ballad of a Thin Man* then go and stream the fucking thing now. It can be found on the *Gighway 61 Revisited* album from 1966. Al Kooper, who played organ on the record, has recalled that at the end of the session, when the musicians listened to the playback of the song, drummer Bobby Gregg said, "That is a nasty song, Bob." Kooper adds, "Dylan was the King of the Nasty Song at that time."

But that night in September 2015, my heart was heavy, and Lysistrata and I, standing on either side of my rusting old Vauxhall Astra, both wept as the moon stared down on us implacably.

XXX

Well, after that, I think that anything would have been an anticlimax, and we were both too lost in grief for our old friend and mentor to talk much more. Anyway the noises of chanting from the other side of the village were getting louder and nearer, as were the sounds of the farmers hastily gathering the harvest in as they worked the nearby fields by moonlight.

But before she bade me her farewell and melted into the halflight like a fish disappearing into a bank of water weeds, Lysistrata explained that not only had the Rev Potts' sacrifice appeared to have had the desired effect, but it had also had a number of other results which dear Cymbeline may or may not have forseen.

Lysistrata had been brain damaged ever since her rape and torture at the hands of her adopted brother back in 1982, and ever since then - she told me - that her understanding of events, and perception of the things that went on around her were (in her words, not mine) muddy. She had become wary of everyone except for the brother and sister who had shown themselves to be far better Christians than most of the people who would have described themselves thus, and who had shunned poor Cymbeline after the totally erroneous story of sexual battery had spread around North Devon like a viral infection. She had been particularly wary of me, because I was one of the very few people who Cymbeline and Britannia trusted enough to let into their family circle, and unlike the others (mostly very old people who came to see Cymbeline for an old fashioned 1662 * Holy Communion, or Britannia for herbal

---

* The Book of Common Prayer is the short title of a number of related prayer books used in the Anglican Communion, as well as by the Continuing Anglican, Anglican realignment and other Anglican Christian churches. The original book, published in 1549 in the reign of Edward VI, was a product of the English Reformation following the break with Rome. It was the first prayer book to include the complete forms of service for daily and Sunday worship in English. It contained Morning Prayer, Evening Prayer, the Litany, and Holy Communion and also the occasional services in full: the orders for Baptism, Confirmation, Marriage, "prayers to be said with the sick", and a funeral service. The 1549 book was soon succeeded by a more reformed revision in 1552 under the same editorial hand, that of Thomas Cranmer, Archbishop of Canterbury. It was used only for a few months, as after Edward VI's death in 1553, his half-sister Mary I restored Roman Catholic worship. Mary died in 1558 and, in 1559, Elizabeth I reintroduced the 1552 book with a few modifications to make it acceptable to more traditionally minded worshippers, notably the inclusion of the words of administration from the 1549 Communion Service alongside those of 1552.

Following the tumultuous events leading to and including the English Civil War, another major revision was published in 1662 (Church of England 1662). That edition has remained the official prayer book of the Church of England, although in the 21st century, alternative provision under the title Common Worship has largely displaced the Book of Common Prayer at the main Sunday worship service of most English parish churches, and many Anglicans resent this.

remedies) she knew that I found her sexually attractive and after her ordeals from Stevie, that was something which frightened her above all others.

But after Cymbeline's valorous death something changed. His death was made all the more noble by the fact that his Christian background generally considered suicide a terrible act. In the sixth century AD, suicide became a secular crime and began to be viewed as sinful. In 1533, those who committed suicide while accused of a crime were denied a Christian Burial. In 1562, all suicides were punished in this way. In 1693, even attempted suicide became an ecclesiastical crime, which could be punished by excommunication, with civil consequences following. In the 13th century, Thomas Aquinas denounced suicide as an act against God and as a sin for which one could not repent. But Cymbeline did it anyway to protect the two women that he loved above all the people on the earth, and - possibly as a direct result of this selfless and charitable act, or possibly because of something else that we who are not students of the occult can only wonder at - Lysistrata's life changed miraculously.

She told me how most of the time she was still in the prison that her poor abused neurones had created, but that sometimes, in the middle of the night, when the full moon was high in the night sky, the veils would drop and she would see the universe as others saw it. At first she was merely jubilant that her curse had been lifted if only for the occasional night, but then she slowly began to realise that the world, or at least *her* little world was a very different place than it had been when she had left it.

Like me she had spent much of her childhood exploring the secret places of the woods and streams, and the little forested valleys which one cannot see on Google Earth, but which one can stumble across occasionally if one knows where to look. And on her nights when Diana the huntress gave her freedom in return for her adopted father's ultimate sacrifice, she revisited these places where she had spent hours of solitary happiness when she had been but a girl. But something was very different.

Like me she had noticed that the ecosystem of the area had undergone massive damage over the years since we had been children. Streams that were once full of darting brown and silver fishes and a myriad of small invertebrates all living their interconnected lives, were now barren. Meadows where the ghost moths of the family Hepialidae once flourished were now empty. And the hunters of the forest - the foxes and the badgers - had to work harder for their dinner. But this wasn't all.

The animals that she knew as a child had been joined by others; dark, frightening and deadly creatures that were beyond her understanding. As she stood in the moonlight on the evenings that she thought if as "her nights" echoing the story from *The Jungle*

Book with which we had regaled each other at the beginning of our evening together leaning on the bonnet of my battered old Vauxhall Astra, she could see the cone of power for which Cymbeline had paid such a great price. It was like a silver dome with a pointed apex that covered the little cottage and its grounds with its protection. But she could see something else; a small stream of peculiar black shapes marching, hopping and occasionally striding out of the protected forest, through the enchanted walls and out into the world outside. Half things. Things of the shadows. Things that were not meant to be in this realm. And when Lysistrata ventured into the woods in which she had played and explored as a child, she could feel them there; lurking behind trees, in makeshift burrows, and in the long grass. They never spoke to her. She had no contact with them. But she could feel them there, watching her. And Lysistrata was afraid.

As she told me this the sound of rapidly approaching footsteps cut through our conversation like a hot knife through a block of frozen cheese. I turned to Lysistrata, but she was gone, and so - not wishing to talk to anyone else that night with the possible exception of my darling wife upstairs in our bedroom - I turned on my heels and went back through the rusty wrought iron gate, out of the lane and back into the garden that I had known and loved for nearly half a century.

Panne and the kittens were still playing a complex game of tig around the sundial on the round lawn as I went into the house, locking the door behind me before going upstairs to bed.

XXXI

*O*ne must find out for oneself, and make sure beyond doubt, who one is, what one is, why one is" wrote Aleister Crowley in his treatise in *Magick.* he continued:

" ...Being thus conscious of the proper course to pursue, the next thing is to understand the conditions necessary to following it out. After that, one must eliminate from oneself every element alien or hostile to success, and develop those parts of oneself which are specially needed to control the aforesaid conditions."

Bizarrely I never heard the most popular song of 1997 until the following year. I was in Mexico with a from crew from UK Channel 4, and we were pulled over on the verge of a lonely road leading deep into the Puebla desert. Peculiarly we were in the process of being turned over for an impromptu poll tax by some enterprising members of Mexico's police force. The radio in the police car was blaring the local pop music radio station.

"Goodbye English Rose" sang Elton John as the policeman glowered at us, submachine guns at the ready. Despite the fact that we were in very real danger, I started to laugh, and for some reason my laughter broke the spell, and the two policemen started to laugh as well. Our general factotum gave them a couple of hundred dollars and they waged us on our way.

I was not a fan of Diana, Princess of Wales, and although I would not have wished any harm to her, I did not grieve when she died. Right at the beginning when she was first in the public eye at the age of nineteen, my Mother sniffed peevishly and said that her upper lip was too narrow. I tried to push her for an explanation, and she sniffed again and muttered something about "The Perfume Counter at Woolworths", but my Mother was a strange lady with deep set ideas. I thought she (Diana not Mother) was a simpering ninny and was never impressed by what she did and said. But she had been named after the Lady Huntress, the Queen of the Night and one of the most revered of the ancient Goddesses.

In Roman mythology, Diana was the goddess of the hunt, the moon and nature being associated with wild animals and woodland, and having the power to talk to and control animals. She was eventually equated with the Greek goddess Artemis, though she had an independent origin in Italy. Diana was worshipped in ancient Roman religion and is revered in Roman Neopaganism and Stregheria. Diana was known to be the virgin goddess of childbirth and women. She was one of the three maiden goddesses — along with Minerva and Vesta — who swore never to marry.

Oak groves were especially sacred to her as were deer. According to mythology (in common with the Greek religion and their deity Artemis), Diana was born with her twin brother Apollo on the island of Delos, daughter of Jupiter and Latona .Diana made up a triad with two other Roman deities: Egeria the water nymph, her servant and assistant midwife; and Virbius, the woodland god.

Whether or not one agrees with the majority of academics who believe that Margaret Murray's theory that ancient Europe was home to a continent wide religion venerating Diana in all her forms is arrant nonsense, it is an undoubted fact that many people (including my late Mother and the Potts siblings) *did* and *do* believe just that.

Whether or not one agrees with the majority of academics who believe that Margaret Murray's other theory that there is a long tradition of sacrificing royal leaders at the height of their power as part of the veneration of The Goddess Diana, is arrant nonsense, it is an undoubted fact that many people (including my late Mother and the Potts siblings) *did* and *do* believe just that.

And it is undeniable that the death of Diana, Princess of Wales, the namesake of the huntress, in a Paris underpass on the last day of summer in 1997 had an enormous effect on the collective psyche of the United Kingdom, and indeed much of the world. Britain was engulfed in a shroud of mass grief that coincided with a mass belief that Diana had been murdered - not as a sacrifice to the ancient gods - but on the orders of her ex husband and/or other members of the Royal Family. British royalty was more unpopular than it had been for years, and - ironically - would not start to recover in the eyes of the public until another royal death five years later.

There were sightings of Herne the Hunter, ironically not in Windsor Great Park, but - appropriately enough - across the wilder parts of the Duchy of Cornwall; a land without a Duchess for the first time since 1981. There were accounts of the Wild Hunt heard roaring triumphantly across Dartmoor; a land owned by the Prince of Wales. And a little brain damaged girl who had known little but abuse in her short life, suddenly found that on certain nights she not only had her faculties restored but somehow assumed the mantle of a demigoddess.

There was wild primal magick in the Westcountry air at that time, and although some things remained the same, other things found themselves changed forever.

I don't really believe in conspiracy theories surrounding celebrity deaths.

"James Dean was just a careless driver/and Marilyn Monroe was just a slag" sang *Half Man Half Biscuit* * and that just about sums it up. I am not saying that the British establishment was (and is) not capable of having murdered Princess Diana, but if they were going to do it, why do it then? I would have thought that they would have done it before Mishcon De Reya made all the embarrassing revelations in the divorce court.

---

* Half Man Half Biscuit are an English rock band, formed in 1984 in Birkenhead, Merseyside. They are known for their satirical, sardonic and sometimes surreal songs, the band comprises lead singer and guitarist Nigel Blackwell, bassist and singer Neil Crossley, drummer Carl Henry and guitarist Karl Benson. The lyrics quoted are from a song called "99% of Gargoyles Look Like Bob Todd" from their debut album, 1985's Back in the DHSS, which topped the UK Indie Chart and reached number 60 in the UK Album Chart. Its title was a play on The Beatles' "Back in the U.S.S.R." and also a reference to the DHSS, the government department that dealt with the unemployed, Nigel Blackwell having been on unemployment benefits since 1979.

Bob Todd, by the way, was an English comedy actor, mostly known for appearing as a straight man in the sketch shows of Benny Hill and Spike Milligan.

I would have thought that they would have done it as soon as Diana started collaborating with Andrew Morton on a book *which he openly admitted was written with the aim of damaging the Royal Family enough that Britain would become a republic. I would have thought they would have done it as soon as Diana's extramarital activities threatened to become public. The idea that it was done after all that makes no sense at all. But then again much of the way that the world works makes no sense at all, at least from where I am sitting.

Neither do I believe that Diana was sacrificed on the altar of her namesake. In 2002 former royal butler Paul Burrell claimed that the Queen warned him that his close relationship with Princess Diana had put him in danger from shadowy "powers at work in this country". But he was paid by one of the tabloid newspapers just after being on trial, accused of stealing over three hundred items that had belonged to the late Princess. He claimed that the Queen told him: "There are powers at work in this country, which we have no knowledge about". This may or may not be true, but we do not live in the pages of a Dan Brown novel **, and I find it hard to believe that the country is ruled by a secret Pagan cabal with the power to sacrifice prominent members of the ruling elite for their mystickal ends.

Crowley wrote:

> "As St. Paul says, "Without shedding of blood there is no remission"; and who are we to argue with St. Paul? But, after all that, it is open to any one to have any opinion that he likes upon the subject, or any other subject, thank God!" ***

---

* Andrew David Morton is an English journalist and writer who has published biographies of royal figures such as Diana, Princess of Wales, and celebrity subjects including Tom Cruise, Madonna, Angelina Jolie and Monica Lewinsky; several of his books have been unauthorised and contain contested assertions.

Andrew Morton wrote a biography of Diana, Princess of Wales called Diana: Her True Story. Following Diana's death in August 1997, Morton issued an edition entitled Diana: Her True Story, Commemorative Edition in October. Basically an underhand little shit (I guess I should shove the word 'allegedly' in there somewhere so that I don't get sued.

** Or do we? Daniel Gerhard Brown is an American author of thriller novels, most notably the Robert Langdon stories: Angels & Demons (2000), The Da Vinci Code (2003), The Lost Symbol (2009), Inferno (2013) and Origin (2017). His novels are treasure hunts set in a 24-hour period, and feature the recurring themes of cryptography, keys, symbols, codes, art, and conspiracy theories. I find them enjoyable hokum, and have rarely read any more than once.

*** Magick, Liber ABA, Book 4 is widely considered to be the magnum opus of 20th-century occultist Aleister Crowley, the founder of Thelema. It is a lengthy treatise on Magick, his system of Western occult practice, synthesised from many sources, including Eastern Yoga, Hermeticism, medieval grimoires, contemporary magical theories from writers like Eliphas Levi and Helena Blavatsky, and his own original contributions. It consists of four parts: Mysticism, Magick (Elementary Theory), Magick in Theory and Practice, and ΘΕΛΗΜΑ—the Law (The Equinox of The Gods). It also includes numerous appendices presenting many rituals and explicatory papers.

And continued:

> "Those magicians who object to the use of blood have endeavoured to replace it with incense. For such a purpose the incense of Abramelin may be burnt in large quantities. Dittany of Crete is also a valuable medium. Both these incenses are very catholic in their nature, and suitable for almost any materialization. But the bloody sacrifice, though more dangerous, is more efficacious; and for nearly all purposes human sacrifice is the best."

I am no student of magick, high or otherwise. I have merely learned a little about it tangentially whilst about my studies on other matters. But unless I am terribly mistaken, the mass outpouring of odylic life force energy [*] in the form of National Grief will have had a massive effect on the aether. But was this accidental sacrifice and its aftermath enough to partially heal a battered woman with the mind of a child?

Or was it caused by another sacrifice. A deliberate sacrifice carried out with great care. The willing auto-sacrificial act of an elderly clergyman who had spent his life following the teachings of a great man, who - if we are to believe what we are told - sacrificed himself for the love of others. An elderly clergyman who had taken the young fugitive Hazel into his care when nobody else would. An elderly clergyman who - having embraced the teachings of what he believed was an even older religion, sacrificed himself to protect the two women that he loved above all others?

I know what I think.

XXXII

A couple of Christmases ago I gave the people I love most in the world, a copy of Russell Hoban's 1967 children's novel *The Mouse and His Child.* It is one of those books that is very dear to me.

It is the story of the eponymous central character's search for self actualisation via the metaphor of dog food cans.

Honest.

Their travels will take them through the air and down to the bottom of the pond, as

---

[*] The Odic force (also called Od [ŏd], Odyle, Önd, Odes, Odylic, Odyllic, or Odems) is the name given in the mid-19th century to a hypothetical vital energy or life force by Baron Carl von Reichenbach. Von Reichenbach coined the name from that of the Norse god Odin in 1845. The study of Odic force is called odology.

they search for the elephant, the seal, and the doll house, assembling a ragtag family to help them fight for their lives and their chance at happiness. Along the way they encounter a travelling theatre company called The Caws of Art (it consists of two crows and a parrot). The Caws of Art are performing an experimental play called *The Last Visible Dog*, written by C Serpentina, * inspired by the image on the label of Bonzo Dog Food cans. The dog on the label is holding a can of dog food, on the label of which there is a smaller dog, holding a smaller can on which there is an even smaller dog, and on and on as far as the eye can see.

When the mouse and his child finally reach their goal they erect a banner consisting of the dog food label and a sign reading "transients welcome", and I gave this book to the people I love most of all because it seems like an analogy for the way we live our life, even down to searching for what lies beyond the last visible dog.

Panne had been living with us for the best part of a year, and Corinna and I had basically accepted it as part of the family. The more time we spent with Panne, the less human it appeared to be. When I had first met Panne, when it had been brought to my house by my egregious 'friend' Danny Miles it had spoken a few words to me, in the voice of a young teenage girl. But we had not heard Panne speak in all the months since it took up residence with us.

At first, back when I had considered Panne to be a goatfooted little girl, the idea that she would join the motley collection of people and animals that live with us would have seemed to be fraught with all sorts of issues. But just as in everything else that we do, it just sort of happened, and before we knew what was happening Panne was part of our family. In the colder months of the year we are kept warm at night by various dogs and cats who jostle for position beneath the duvet, and when Prudence, Archie, and the cats were joined by a little sylvan wood godling, who - it transpired - liked being scratched behind the ears just as much as Archie the Jack Russell does, it seemed the most natural thing in the world.

Panne not only remained mute except for grunts and squeaks of delight when playing with the other animals, but also showed no sign of any of the magickal powers that it had demonstrated on various occasions the previous year. Until, however, the day after I had spent a peculiar long night of the soul with Lysistrata under the blood red moon.

---

* The common snapping turtle (*Chelydra serpentina*) is a large freshwater turtle of the family Chelydridae. Its natural range extends from southeastern Canada, southwest to the edge of the Rocky Mountains, as far east as Nova Scotia and Florida. The three species of Chelydra and the larger alligator snapping turtles (genus Macrochelys) are the only extant chelydrids, a family now restricted to the Americas. The common snapping turtle, as its name implies, is the most widespread.

It had been a warm, wet summer, and the breeding season for all of the garden birds had been extended well into what would normally have been the season of mists and mellow fruitfulness. There are at least three pairs of blackbirds which normally nest in the garden, and one - in particular - has nested in the overgrown yew tree outside my office window. Yew trees are forever associated with graveyards in English lore. The website 'Trees for Life' notes:

> "The yew tree is another of our native trees which was held sacred by the Druids in pre-Christian times. They no doubt observed the tree's qualities of longevity and regeneration (drooping branches of old yew trees can root and form new trunks where they touch the ground), and the yew came to symbolise death and resurrection in Celtic culture. They will also have been familiar with the toxicity of the tree's needles in particular, which can prove fatal, and which may have further contributed to its connections with death. Shakespeare too was familiar with these qualities when he had Macbeth concoct a poisonous brew which included "slips of yew, silvered in the moon's eclipse".

The themes of death and resurrection continued into the Christian era, with the custom of yew shoots being buried with the deceased, and boughs of yew being used as 'Palms' in church at Easter. Yew trees have in fact established a popular association with old churches in Britain, to the extent that very old specimens of yew trees are now relatively rare outside of church grounds. According to Richard Mabey in his Flora Britannica "... no other type of ancient tree occurs so frequently inside church grounds ..." and he goes on to say that he does not know of any similarly exclusive relationship between places of worship and a single tree species existing anywhere else in the Western world. In some cases yew trees have been traditionally planted beside churches. In other cases it seems that very old yew trees may have already been growing on a site before the earliest church building was erected there; some, "such as the one beside Fortingall's church may even predate Christianity itself".

I have noted elsewhere that considering the fact he was a churchwarden and pious member of the Church of England, my father had many pagan leanings, and so - although I don't remember him doing it - I am sure that it was him who planted the yew tree in the garden, and I have no idea why. Unlike me, he always had logically thought out reasons for everything he did, and so I am sure there was a very good reason for him planting the emblem of a churchyard outside what was then his study window. However, he had always fancied his hand at topiary, and had kept the yew tree neatly pruned. Graham and I prefer a more natural look, and so we have let the tree grow wild, so the birds can nest there, and nest there they have done for years.

However, in the spring of 2015 we acquired two kittens - Dotty Periwinkle and Squeaky Biscuit (I added the confectionary suffix after realising that I had haplessly named the elder after one of the core members of the Manson Family) [*] - and by September they were going out for the first time. Dotty, despite being a sweet little thing indoors came into her own as a fierce predator, and had presented us with an endless procession of dead and fatally injured rodents which we fed quickly to the semi tame crow who lives in the big iron cage in the kitchen.

However, on this particular occasion she surpassed herself.

I was in the office typing away in my constant efforts to produce deathless prose, when I heard a cacophony of screeching, growling and spitting. Assuming that a couple of the cats were having a frank exchange of views I ignored it, but the noises got louder and more anguished until I felt compelled to go and see what the bloody hell was happening.

Just round the corner from my office door, on the surprisingly neat gravel path along which the ghost of a grey lady wearing a long dress is sometimes seen to glide, was what I believe is known as a Mexican standoff between Dotty Periwinkle, standing guard with arched back and bottlebrush tail, over a freshly killed and (as my Mother would have said *"very* dead" newly fledged blackbird, oozing blood and entrails). Facing him, looking like the famous sepia photograph that Joseph Singh took of the alleged wolf girl Amala in the early 1920s, [**] was Panne, its back arched, its teeth bared and snarling like a wolverine.

My appearance on the scene startled Dotty Periwinkle who ran away, abandoning her prey. But what happened next will stay with me until my dying day. Panne leapt forward - almost in slow motion - and scooped the mangled fledgling up in its hands. It stood up and raised the pathetic little corpse to its mouth. I thought Panne was going

---

* Lynette Alice "Squeaky" Fromme (born October 22, 1948) is an American would-be assassin best known for attempting to assassinate U.S. President Gerald Ford in 1975. A member of the infamous "Manson family", she was sentenced to life imprisonment for the assassination attempt and released on parole on August 14, 2009, after serving nearly 34 years. She turns up more in *The Song of Panne* (not being a breadhead, blah blah blah) and I truly didn't name our semi feral litlle black and white cat after her. I called her 'Squeaky' partly because she squeaks, and partly after a minor character in Robert Heinlein's *Number of the Beast* which I constantly re-read, because I keep a very battered copy on the bathroom windowsill.

** Amala (c.1918 – 21 September 1921 and Kamala (died 14 November 1929) were two "feral girls" from Bengal, India, who were alleged to have been raised by a wolf family. Their story attracted substantial mainstream attention and debate. However the account was reported and promoted by only one source, the clergyman who claimed to have discovered the girls. Because of this, there is some controversy as to the authenticity of the story with some researchers arguing that the girls were autistic. French surgeon Serge Aroles concluded in his book *L'Enigme des enfants-loup* (Enigma of the Wolf-Children, 2007) that the story was a hoax.

to eat it, even though I had never seen it eat anything but chocolate and glutinous bowls of bread and milk which Mother which would make it for a treat, but instead it breathed on the small bird, which somehow became whole again and flew away.

XXXIII

So the funny little forest creature that lived in the airing cupboard in what used to be my Father's dressing room was a God after all. I had always known this, but had pushed it to the back of my mind together with all sorts of other inconvenient truths that I do my best to ignore. The incident with Panne, Dotty Periwinkle and the dead fledgling was uncomfortably close to the story of the Christ Child "breathing life" into the clay bird that appears - as I have mentioned earlier - in both the allegedly apocryphal Gospel of St Thomas and parts of the Muslim scripture.

Ever since my parting of the ways with my ex-girlfriend Lydia, some sixteen years before, my relationship with Mother Church has been crumbling, and by now I have reached the point that I call myself a Christian Anarchist, and am not a practising member of any church apart from the one in my heart. As I get older I find myself leading more towards a sort of broad Paganism, but I truly find no incompatibility between my various belief systems. Pagans, however, are merely the people who live in the fields, as Heathens are those who live on the heath, and I live in a tumbledown cottage on the edge of a village that most people have never heard of. And my religion and politics are a peculiar mixture of Paley's Natural Theology [*, **], the Sermon on the Mount [***] and the liner notes to the second *Crass* album [****].

* William Paley (July 1743 – 25 May 1805) was an English clergyman, Christian apologist, philosopher, and utilitarian. He is best known for his natural theology exposition of the teleological argument for the existence of God in his work *Natural Theology or Evidences of the Existence and Attributes of the Deity*, which made use of the watchmaker analogy.

** Natural theology, once also termed physico-theology, is a type of theology that provides arguments for the existence of God based on reason and ordinary experience of nature. This distinguishes it from revealed theology, which is based on scripture and/or religious experiences, and also from transcendental theology, which is based on a priori reasoning.

*** The Sermon on the Mount (anglicized from the Matthean Vulgate Latin section title: Sermo in monte) is a collection of sayings and teachings of Jesus, which emphasizes his moral teaching found in the Gospel of Matthew (chapters 5, 6, and 7).It takes place relatively early in the Ministry of Jesus after he has been baptized by John the Baptist and preached in Galilee. The Sermon is the longest continuous section of Jesus speaking found in the New Testament, and is one of the most widely quoted elements of the Canonical Gospels including some of the best known teachings of Jesus, such as the Beatitudes, and the widely recited Lord's Prayer. The Sermon on the Mount is generally considered to contain the central tenets of Christian discipleship.

**** *Stations of the Crass* is the second album by Crass, released in 1979. The record, originally released as a double 12", includes live tracks from a gig recorded at the Pied Bull pub in Islington, London, on August 7, 1979. The first three sides contain the studio tracks and play at 45 rpm, while the final side comprises the live material and plays at 33 rpm. The album's title is not only a pun on the Catholic rite of the Stations of the Cross (such jibes against the religious establishment were typical of Crass), but is also a reference to the graffiti campaign that the band had been conducting around London's underground railway system, the cover artwork depicting a wall at Bond Street tube station that had allegedly been 'decorated' by them.

Peculiarly, the fact that Panne had demonstrated its powers openly, didn't appear to make a jot of difference to the complex hierarchy of the Downes household. Archie still gazed at Panne adoringly like one of the dogs in a sentimental Victorian engraving, whilst Panne - despite its divine nature - still demurred to Prudence as alpha female and Captain Frunobulax the Magnificent aka Peanut as alpha male, and Panne and the two kittens (even the one who had been robbed of what she must have considered to be her lawful prey) still played games of rough and tumble tig around my Great Grandmother's sundial on the round lawn.

But I was concerned. What did the advent of Panne's new powers mean for me and my peculiar little family? In the year it had been living with us, I'd had no contact whatsoever with the sinister commune living deep in Meddon Woods, no contact whatsoever with the elephant headed Mr Loxodonta, or the enigmatic pop group he fronted *. And despite the fact that as far as I was aware, my old 'friend' (and I use the term very loosely) Danny Miles was still living with my erstwhile tenants in fraudulent luxury near Tamar Lakes, I'd had practically no contact with him, either. And, to be quite honest all these states of affairs were a *status quo* that I was perfectly happy with. I have always had a firm policy of letting sleeping fucktards lie, and I didn't see that I wanted to change that policy now.

But I felt that I really should try and find out more about Panne's newly demonstrated powers, and so - realising that I was quite possibly opening a can of very nasty, and very wriggly little worms - I fired off an email to Danny. Having known the bloody man for over thirty years now, I knew that when dealing with him, one had to tread very carefully. So, rather than writing in my true voice and revealing more of my anxieties than I was prepared to, I write to him in a forcedly light hearted tone, saying that I hadn't heard from him for a while, and that I wondered when I was going to hear some more music from *Xtul*. Lying through my teeth, I hinted that some unnamed major figures within the music business were anxious to find out more about the band, and I suggested that if we all played our figurative cards right we could be looking at a major record contract for the band, and furthermore, one that would make both him and me rich men.

This was exactly the right bait with which to tempt the bloody man, but - even though I knew perfectly well that there are occasions that the end justifies the means - I felt mildly guilty when I pressed the send button on Windows Live Mail. I don't like lying to people, even though Danny Miles is quite possibly the biggest liar and bullshit artist that I have ever met.

---

* Blah blah blah *The Sing of Panne* not a breadhead, blah blah blah.

But he is also immensely greedy and self serving, and so I was sure that if anything was going to prompt him to get in touch with me, even the slightest whiff of the chance of money and fame was going to do it. So I was confident that I was going to hear from him soon.

But I didn't.

Hours passed, and then a day.

Twenty four hours after I had sent the email I was beginning to get worried. Not for Danny's wellbeing; I was sure that he would be alright. People like him are always best at looking after number one. But because I was increasingly concerned about the situation with Panne. Although I am very fond of the little creature, I felt that for its sake, as well as for the sake of my motley family of animals and people that I needed to find out more information.

Two days passed, and then three, and still nothing.

On the late evening of the fourth day I was sitting in my study typing. Although it had been a very hot summer and autumn, I knew that the good weather was not likely to last much longer, and that this was possibly one of the last chances that I would have to be able to sit after dark with the front door open, (one of my favourite pleasures), and I was happily working whilst the new album by *Belle and Sebastian* blared out of my hifi which is connected to one of my PCs.

I didn't hear the gate open, or the footsteps on the raked gravel path outside the office window. But I did hear the knock on the door. Expecting it to be Danny, I clicked 'pause' on Windows Media Player, before raising my head and swivelling the office chair around to face the door.

It wasn't Danny.

"Christ on a fucking bike!!" I burst out, in shock and surprise.

"Ever the blasphemer, I see" spat Lydia as she scowled at me with an expression of distaste on her face.

XXXIV

The annals of English literature, and indeed less impressive bodies of work, are full of descriptions of what happens when old lovers meet many years after they had ceased being lovers, and how they fall into each other's arms and rekindle the flames of their passion. However, I cannot recall reading a description of what happens when two people who had once been lovers, and who had heartily hoped that they would never see each other again, bump into each other by accident. Two people who had seen each other naked, done all sorts of things with each other that would make a pornographer blush (she had some fairly singular tastes in that department), had plumbed the depths of each other's lives, only for it all to go tits up in a melange of debts, recrimination and general beastliness. Two people who had every reason to dislike each other intensely, and had come to do so, and who had never thought they would ever see each other again.

That was me and Lydia.

I gestured her to come in.

Just about to issue forth my opening gambit and ask what the blinking flip she was doing wandering into my office, and indeed my life, after sixteen years absence, she pre-empted me, (which I then remembered was one of her more annoying habits when we were together).

It turned out that she had moved to one of the new housing estates on the outskirts of the village. These had been woodland when I was a boy, and I have always resented them, but that is another story. When faced with the problem that had confronted her, she discussed the issue with the local vicar, who - much to my surprise - had recommended that she come and talk to me. However, although she had given Lydia my address, she had neglected to mention my name, and she had no idea that she was coming to see me until we were face to face.

As the vicar knows perfectly well what my name is, and has been a guest at a Weird Weekend cocktail party in my garden, I find this all rather hard to believe, and I suspect that Lydia knew perfectly well who she was coming to visit, and decided to just make up a cover story with which she felt more comfortable. But I can't prove it, and I don't actually care one way or the other. She was always a complicated and peculiar woman, and I have no intention of wasting too much energy trying to understand her motivation.

My feelings when confronted with this ghost from my past were almost overwhelmingly negative. I had not only been (in my opinion) treated extremely badly by her and her loathsome family, but (as alluded to elsewhere) I had resorted to witchcraft to sever the emotional ties which we once had. And so I felt nothing but mild distaste for this mad-looking lady of a certain age who was now sitting only a few feet away.

"So what can I do for you?" I asked as formally as I could manage. But as her story unfolded, I became fascinated despite myself.

Now, I am aware of my limitations as a writer, and one of them is that I am not terribly good at writing dialogue, especially complicated dialogue, and as the story that Lydia told me is an intensely complicated one, and furthermore one with a whole slew of cultural references and nuances which flashed across my cerebral cortex, much of what she said will have been paraphrased, and put into my own words, simply because I am not a good enough master of my art to be able to communicate what happened in any other form.

Her first question, however, was so completely unexpected that I can't resist the temptation to quote it:

"Have you ever heard of a group of girls called The Maenads?"

Well yes, as it happens I had.

Over, once again, to those jolly nice people at Wikipedia:

> "In Greek mythology, maenads (/ˈmiːnædz/; Ancient Greek: μαινάδες [m]) were the female followers of Dionysus and the most significant members of the Thiasus, the god's retinue. Their name literally translates as "raving ones." Maenads were known as Bassarids, Bacchae /ˈbækiː/ or Bacchantes /ˈbækənts, bəˈkænts, -ˈkɑːnts/ in Roman mythology after the penchant of the equivalent Roman god, Bacchus, to wear a bassaris or fox-skin.
>
> Often the maenads were portrayed as inspired by Dionysus into a state of ecstatic frenzy through a combination of dancing and intoxication. During these rites, the maenads would dress in fawn skins and carry a thyrsus, a long stick wrapped in ivy or vine leaves and tipped with a pine cone. They would weave ivy-wreaths around their heads or wear a bull helmet in honor of their god, and often handle or wear snakes. These women were mythologized as the 'mad women' who were nurses of Dionysus in Nysa: Lycurgus "chased the Nurses of

the frenzied Dionysus through the holy hills of Nysa, and the sacred implements dropped to the ground from the hands of one and all, as the murderous Lycurgus struck them down with his ox-goad." They went into the mountains at night and practiced strange rites."

I knew most of that anyway, and imparted same (including bits of Ancient Greek which I quoted because it is always good to show your ex-girlfriends what a clever bugger you are). What I didn't tell her is that I had first heard of the rite of sparagmos (a sacrificial rite whereby the living victim, human or animal, was torn apart by the maenads) from Albert Goldman's biography of Elvis Presley, and my first knowledge of the maenads themselves came from *Prince Caspian* by C S Lewis where they, and the two Greek gods Bacchus and Silenus are portrayed in a manner suitable for Middle Class English children of the 1950s.

So I told her all this, and probably sounded a bit smug and know-it-all as I did so, because she cut in on me, pointing out that she had a degree in Classics and certainly had forgotten more about Greek Mythology than I had ever known.

"No", she said. "I mean, *modern* Maenads. More particularly *modern* Maenads in North Devon. Because my grand-daughter Dorcas has become one".

"Fuck!" I said. And this time Lydia did not remonstrate with me.

XXXV

Children have far more freedom nowadays than they did when I was a boy. And they take these freedoms for granted rather than having to snatch them furtively like my generation did. They also have access to communication media that I would never have dreamed of. The telephone in my family home was situated on the sitting room windowsill, behind the place now occupied by a large and comfortable sofa on which the dogs and my Mother-in-Law now jostle for the most comfortable position.

I was only allowed to use the telephone on special occasions, or if I had managed to persuade one or both of my parents that my reason was both genuine and appropriate. The idea that most children from about the age of eight seem to have mobile phones and a generous amount of call credit would have seemed to the teenaged me to be a concept out of science fiction. And the fact that these telephones give their owners access to a wide range of social media would have been completely incomprehensible to me.

I dislike social media, although I seem to spend an unconscionable amount of my life on Facebook, buying things, selling things, and chatting to friends, enemies, colleagues and family. And I know from Jamie Bartlett's *The Dark Net* [*] that there are all sorts of disturbing and downright horrific communities only just below the surface of the Internet, and that you don't have to look very far to find them.

But it was ever thus.

Once upon a time in a universe far away (ok, London in the 'Swinging Sixties') lived a couple called Mary Ann and Robert de Grimston (originally Mary Ann MacLean and Robert Moor). They were, or at least had been members of the exceedingly dodgy Church of Scientology which decades later was to provoke the wrath of Anonymous. They formed a splinter group called The Process Church of the Final Judgement, which pissed off the elders of Scientology so much they were declared "suppressive persons" by L. Ron Hubbard in December 1965.

In 1966, members of the group underwent a social implosion and moved to Xtul on Mexico's Yucatan peninsula, (any of this beginning to ring any bells somewhere in your cerebral cortex, guys?) where they developed "processean" theology (which differs from, and is unrelated to process theology). They later established a base of operations in the United States in New Orleans. [**]

They were often viewed as Satanic on the grounds that they worshipped both Christ and Satan. Their belief was that Satan would become reconciled to Christ, and they would come together at the end of the world to judge humanity, Christ to judge and Satan to execute judgment. Vincent Bugliosi, the prosecutor of the Charles Manson family trial, comments in his book *Helter Skelter* [***] that Manson may have borrowed philosophically from the Process Church, and that representatives of the Church visited him in jail after his arrest. According to one of those representatives, the purpose of the visit was to question Manson about whether he had ever had any contact with Church members or ever received any literature about the Church. The

---

[*] *The Dark Net: Inside the Digital Underworld* is a 2014 nonfiction book by Jamie Bartlett, and is a book that I heartily recommend that you read. Bartlett discusses online communities away from the mainstream, including those on Tor and the Deep Web. It discusses the darknet and dark web in broad terms, describing a range of underground and emergent subcultures, including social media racists, cam girls, self harm communities, darknet drug markets, cryptoanarchists and transhumanists. P.D Smith of *The Guardian* described it as "An intelligent and revealing introduction to the denizens of the web's underworld.

[**] Most of what I know about this group comes from *Love, Fear, Sex, Death* by Timothy Wylie (2009) but I would also steer potential readers towards *Xtul: An experience of The Process* by Sabrina Verney (daughter of my favourite children's author) which is a book on which I worked, but didn't publish due to a series of disagreements with the author.

[**] The best known book on the Manson murders.

group published an article about Manson and the jail visit in the The Process magazine's special "Death" edition.

Their basic tenet of belief seems to have been:

> *Christ said: Love thine enemy. Christ's Enemy was Satan and Satan's Enemy was Christ. Through love, enmity is destroyed. Through love, saint and sinner destroy the enmity between them. Through love, Christ and Satan have destroyed their enmity and come together for the End. Christ to judge, Satan to execute the judgment.*

I have always been fascinated by this group, ever since I read about them in Ed Sanders book on Charles Manson *, and became even more fascinated by them when I actually met one of its erstwhile members. Sabrina Verney is the daughter of Sir John Verney, one of my favourite authors and painters who died in 1993. I had a brief acquaintance with her father, and ran into her through the good offices of my mate Andy Roberts, an avid chronicler of psychedelic culture and the weirder parts of the 1960s. Sabrina (the original for February Callender in the series of childrens novels written by Sir John) was one of the girls who went to Xtul, and I very nearly published her book on the subject (the original manuscript and other supporting documents being somewhere in my archives).

I have always been interested in the trajectory of the group. Judge Smith, another friend of mine who was one of the founder members of *Van der Graff Generator* remembers the Process turning up at various countercultural events dressed in black and with fierce looking Alsatians. Mick Farren, another mate of mine, told me before he died that the group were "absolutely fucking terrifying", when he encountered them at various events during the mid 1960s. But it is what happened to them that is most interesting.

Mary Anne kicked Robert out in a quasi-Stalinist move in 1974. He tried to continue with a similarly named organisation, but it was a failure and he disappeared into obscurity, defying the best efforts of me and Andy Roberts to locate him, although some claim that he is living under his birth name in Staten Island. The group moved to Utah, and eventually morphed into the Best Friends Animal Sanctuary, where Mary Anne died some years later, according to some reports having been torn apart by a pack of wild dogs.

There is still a Process Church today, active on Social Media, but as far as I am able to understand, none of the original members are involved, and the Best Friends

* My favourite book on the subject.

Animal Sanctuary, with a slightly changed name, is still going strong. So, an established (though dodgy as fuck) church threw off an even dodgier mind control cult, that self identified as a Satanic cult, and eventually became an animal welfare group. But could something like this have happened in reverse?

Well, yes, if my ex-girlfriend Lydia was to be believed. IT most certainly could.

XXXVI

2008 was a strange year by anybody's standards. The world was hit by the biggest financial crisis since the Great Depression of the late 1920s, and global markets were in chaos leading to the collapse of major financial institutions which had not managed to find a government to bail them out, and even entire countries, like Iceland, found themselves insolvent.

On top of that, my own family had undergone a series of crises including the death of my Father-in-law, a financial crisis of our own when those jolly nice people at the National Westminster Bank decided to cancel all my accounts without a by-your-leave, and the situation hinted at earlier in this narrative when we were conned out of fifty grand of my wife's savings by people we had considered as friends. There was all sorts of other shit as well, but that will be enough to be going on with.

I usually keep an eye on animal welfare events on the global, national, and local stage, but I hope - in the light of all the crapulence described above - that I can be forgiven for not having paid as much attention to the activities of the group that was later to become 'The Maenads' as I probably should have done. But I didn't, and as my dear departed Mama would have said, "if iffs and ans were pots and pans, we'd all be travelling tinkers", and I truly think that the life of a travelling tinker wouldn't suit me very well.

It all started with a fried chicken restaurant in one of the seaside towns along the North Devon coast. You will, I hope, forgive me for being coy as to the details, but some of the people involved were not very nice and - even now - have a longer reach than makes me feel comfortable. It was an open secret that the proprietors of the restaurant, a pair of brothers - half Greek Cypriot, half Devonian - were an unpleasant bunch. I had been at school with the younger of the two, and even after four decades I remember that he was a nasty, sadistic little shit. Their chicken meat was sourced from a local farm owned by one of their relatives (whether on the Greek or the Devonian side I do not know, and it doesn't really matter) and when the local newspaper did an expose on their unethical, not to say downright cruel, farming practises, it made uncomfortable reading.

I remember being as pleased as anyone else when the backlash started. Their windows were broken, their shopfront daubed with graffiti, and - most amusing of all - a series of what can only be described as eco-friendly letter bombs were donated in the restaurant itself.

I cannot think of any better way of describing them, and - even now - I wish that it had been I who had thought of them, because they were most ingenious. The people responsible had made boxes, about the size of shoeboxes, using the cheapest 2x1 as the frames, with the bottom and sides made from hardboard and the top made from quarter inch thick balsa wood. It was covered with decorative wrapping paper, and a powerful spring was placed in a plastic sandwich bag, together with the bomb's payload, inside. The whole thing was held in place with a coloured ribbon complete with decorative bow, and thus, as soon as the bow was undone, the spring would tear through the sandwich bag, break open and deposit the payload far and wide.

The payload? Didn't I mention that? Sometimes it was maggots from a fishing bait shop, sometimes putrefying liver that had been left in the sun, sometimes liquified animal faeces. I could go on, but I won't. Sufficient to say it was always the sort of stuff that even the most lenient Health and Safety Nazi would never allow within half a mile of a place where human food was prepared and eaten, let alone smeared all over the walls of it.

"Hooray for them" I thought at the time, but was too much overwhelmed by my own and my family's issues to pay much attention. But even if I had, I have never been in the habit of hanging out in the sort of online locations aimed at teenage and preteen girls, and so I missed a seriously proactive Facebook campaign that urged young women within these two target groups to join a new Facebook group dedicated to animal welfare. It was called the "Kewl Chix" and was apparently loaded with all the buzzwords ("self empowerment", for example) which seem to have been created, fully formed, in order to attract young women who feel there is something missing in their lives, and was liberally dotted with cute pictures of cats.

I was vaguely aware when the campaign against the chicken restaurant reached its climax. A slurry tanker leaving one of the larger local farms, one morning, stopped to see if they could be of assistance to two scantily clad young women, who were standing tearfully at the side of the road next to their car which had obviously and messily broken down. Persons unknown did their business with chloroform [*] and black hoods, and when the driver awoke, he was alone by the side of the road without even the broken down car for

---

[*] Believe it or not, chloroform is easier to obtain than you might think. And no, I am not going to tell you how.

---

company. The slurry tanker, however, was next heard of late that night when a circular hole was made in the window of the poor beleagured chicken restaurant and 86 gallons of liquid slurry were pumped into the premises.

Nobody ever claimed responsibility, but as the restaurant closed its doors for good, and the two unpleasant brothers left the area never to be seen again, there was no real need to, and if there was any link between the completely successful (if mildly revolting) campaign against the restaurant and the Kewl Chix on Facebook, nobody ever made the connection. However, that very same night, the Facebook group changed its status from "open" to "secret" and everybody soon forgot that either the Kewl Chix or the chicken restaurant had ever existed.

XXXVIII

The ecoterrorist attacks continued, and - I have to admit - that I cheered them on from my safe place in the sidelines. A North Devon petshop found itself in court following allegations of animal cruelty in the local paper. I cannot remember the details, but it was something to do with live guinea pigs being fed to a python, which is all very natural if you want to get all Jack London * about it, but is both unethical and illegal under successive pieces of legislation that deal with Animal Welfare. They were acquitted on a technicality, but within days they had been raided by persons unknown one moonlit night.

The animals in the shop were all taken, and the shop itself was vandalised to such an extent that it never reopened. The words "No Sense Makes Sense" were daubed on the walls in white pain, and the windows and all the shop fittings were broken, and the stock was either stolen or broken beyond repair. The till, however, was not touched.

The *Call of the Wild* is a short adventure novel by Jack London published in 1903 and set in Yukon, Canada during the 1890s Klondike Gold Rush, when strong sled dogs were in high demand. The central character of the novel is a dog named Buck. The story opens at a ranch in Santa Clara Valley, California, when Buck is stolen from his home and sold into service as a sled dog in Alaska. He becomes progressively feral in the harsh environment, where he is forced to fight to survive and dominate other dogs. By the end, he sheds the veneer of civilization, and relies on primordial instinct and learned experience to emerge as a leader in the wild.

There is a phrase in the third line of canto 56 from Alfred Lord Tennyson's In Memoriam A. H. H., 1850 which has often been linked to the animal stories of Jack London, and which seems appropriate when considering these circumstances:

Who trusted God was love indeed
And love Creation's final law
Tho' Nature, red in tooth and claw
With ravine, shriek'd against his creed

I am not being overly poetic here when I describe it happening one moonlit night. As you know, if you have been following the narrative so far, me and full moons do not really go that way together, and I had been undergoing a pretty bad full moon when I was contacted by the local paper who had me on their books as an animal welfare advocate, and I told them that whilst I did not advocate criminal acts, to my mind people who abused animals, whether wild or domestic, got what they deserved. I pointed out that the words painted on the wall were a quote from Charles Manson, and I may also have muttered something about karma. Truly I should not be allowed to give interviews over the period of the full moon.

A few days later I had a visit from a female police officer, concerned that I had appeared to show sympathy for the wrongdoers. For some reason the newspaper had bigged up who I am and what I stand for, describing me as the Director of a major animal research organisation. The Policewoman was, I strongly suspect, expecting to find laboratories, animals in cages and men in white coats doing arcane things. As it was, everyone was out that day except for me, and what she *actually* found was a fat hippy eating diabetic chocolates and reading a dogeared copy of *Psychic Self Defence* by Dion Fortune.

I showed her around the CFZ, explaining that all the animals we have are rescues, except for a breeding colony of Rio Cauca caecilans; small worm-like creatures from South America, which we were (as far as I am aware) the only people in the UK who had managed to breed for at least half a century. We then settled down for a cup of tea and a chat, and instead of spending a difficult few hours discussing the animal rights attacks along the North Devon coast, and trying to convince her that I had nothing to do with them (which I hadn't, although as noted above, I had probably expressed too much enthusiasm for them to a journalist, whilst in a moon-crazed state) we found ourselves discussing Dion Fortune.

Although Dion is a man's name, probably most well known these days for being the name of a flash in the pan singer from the late fifties and early sixties who had an international hit with a song called *Runaway* Dion Fortune (born Violet Mary Firth, 6 December 1890 – 6 January 1946) was actually a woman. She was a British occultist, Christian Qabalist, ceremonial magician, novelist and author. She was a co-founder of the Fraternity of the Inner Light, an occult organisation that promoted her own philosophies which she claimed had been taught to her by spiritual entities known as the Ascended Masters. A prolific writer, she produced a large number of articles and books on her occult ideas and also authored a number of novels, several of which expound occult themes.

She was a remarkable woman, and rather than paraphrase it, I have lifted the next few paragraphs directly from Wikipedia:

"Fortune was born in Llandudno, North Wales, to a wealthy upper middle-class English family, although little is known of her early life. By her teenage years she was living in England's West Country, where she wrote two books of poetry. After time spent at a horticultural college she began studying psychology and psychoanalysis at the University of London before working as a counsellor in a psychotherapy clinic. During the First World War she joined the Women's Land Army and established a company selling soy milk products. She became interested in esotericism through the teachings of the Theosophical Society, before joining an occult lodge led by Theodore Moriarty and then the Alpha et Omega occult organisation. She came to believe that she was being contacted by the Ascended Masters, one of whom was "the Master Jesus", and underwent trance mediumship to channel the Masters' messages.

Fortune and Charles Loveday claimed that in 1922, while undergoing trance mediumship in Glastonbury, they were contact by Masters who provided them with a text, The Cosmic Doctrine. She became the president of the Christian Mystic Lodge of the Theosophical Society, but believing the society to be uninterested in Christianity, she split from it to form the Community of Inner Light, a group later renamed the Fraternity of Inner Light. With Loveday she established bases in both Glastonbury and Bayswater, London, began issuing a magazine, gave public lectures, and promoted the growth of their society. Fortune also wrote prolifically, publishing both non-fiction works and novels, through which she sought to promote esoteric ideas in a fictional format. During the Second World War she organised a project of meditations and visualisations designed to protect Britain. She began planning for what she believed was a coming post-war Age of Aquarius, although she died of leukemia shortly after the war's end.

Fortune is recognised as one of the most significant occultists and ceremonial magicians of the early 20th century. The Fraternity she founded survived her and in later decades spawned a variety of related groups based upon her teachings. Her novels in particular proved an influence on later occult and modern Pagan groups such as Wicca."

Psychic Self Defence is probably her best known book. After finding herself the subject of a powerful psychic attack in the 1930's, she put together a detailed instruction manual on protecting oneself from paranormal attack. This classic psychic self-defence guide explains how to understand the signs of a psychic attack, vampirism, hauntings, and methods of defence. Everything you need to know about the methods, motives, and physical aspects of a psychic attack and how to overcome it is here, along with a subject which I find particularly interesting; a look at the role psychic elements play in mental illness and how to recognise them.

I don't necessarily agree with everything that she wrote, and said as much to my guest from the Devon and Cornwall Constabulary, but it is a fascinating book, and one which I revisit every few years, especially when I feel particularly paranoid in the wake of one of my own mental health episodes.

I was impressed to find out that my visiting policewoman (I am not sure whether I am allowed to call them that any more) was also a devotee of Ms Fortune, and that while she had (in her words) "kept her birth name for her job", had dubbed herself 'Dion-Isis' for the persona who carried out various intense occult activities.

It is amazing how the nuances of a name can change in such a short time. Nowadays the name "Isis" is regarded with horror because it is of the names by which The Islamic State, whose vile predations across the Middle East have shocked the world over the past few years. But the original Isis was, after all an Egyptian Goddess. Isis was worshipped as the ideal mother and wife as well as the patroness of nature and magic. She was the friend of slaves, sinners, artisans and the downtrodden, but she also listened to the prayers of the wealthy, maidens, aristocrats and rulers. Isis is often depicted as the mother of Horus, the falcon-headed deity associated with king and kingship (although in some traditions Horus's mother was Hathor). Isis is also known as protector of the dead and goddess of children. She was first worshiped in ancient Egyptian religion, and later her worship spread throughout the Roman Empire and the greater Greco-Roman world. Isis is still widely worshiped by many pagans today in diverse religious contexts; including a number of distinct pagan religions, the modern Goddess movement, and interfaith organisations such as the Fellowship of Isis.

Isis is also the name of a song by Bob Dylan which is why my friend Richard Dawe (who died by his own hand shortly before I finished writing this book) in Teignmouth named his daughter after her (a decision which, in these post-Daesh days, I suspect he might have been regretting. Isis is such an emotionally charged name these days that a dog of that name had to be "written out" of a currently popular period TV drama rather than offend the sponsors or advertisers, and a quick Google search will turn up lots of stories about how the windows, or cars of people with that name have been vandalised by the unthinking cohorts of morondom, convinced they are striking a blow for Christian values.

She (the Goddess, not the *Downton Abbey* dog, or my mate Richard's daughter) is often seen by modern occultists, especially those who believe Margaret Murray's theories of a pan-European Dianic religion, as being conspecific with Diana, and the original European Mother Goddess. So for my visiting policewoman to have named herself after one of the aspects of the Mother Goddess, and her favourite author in subjects from the rod less travelled, was an eminently sensible, not to say logical, thing to do.

Our conversation was brought to an untimely end, however, by the arrival home of what Star Trekkies would not doubt have dubbed 'the away team'. There was shopping to unload, dogs to restrain, and all sorts of other items of domestic complicationitude far too dull to enumerate. So I bade a swift farewell to my visitor, assured her that she would always be a welcome visitor under my roof, and dealt with what I had to deal with as she walked out the gate and up the hill.

And you know what? I never saw her again.

XXXIX

Generations of legislators believe that they have made the United Kingdom a safer place, but to be brutally honest they have done nothing of the sort. Chloroform, (trichloromethane) for example, as used by the ecoterrorists that I was beginning to feel sure were at least partly something to do with the Kewl Chix, is popularly seen as being something straight out of the pages of a Sax Romer novel. But it still has modern applications, most notably in the production of teflon and also - as we become more Americanised - in the mortician industry. Both chloroform and ether are used to euthanise animals in laboratories, and can be obtained from laboratory supply companies as long as one is able to pass the reasonably stringent security tests.

However, doing what I am best at, and putting two and two together to make 666, I am fairly sure that if one of the Kewl Chix had purloined the necessary paperwork from the educational establishment that they attended during the hours that they were not waging war upon animal abusers, and people that they perceived to be animal abusers along the Atlantic Highway, then they would quite easily be able to persuade some witless employee of a laboratory supply company to let them have a bottle fairly easily.

On the other hand, as I was to find out, the Kewl Chix, like so many teenage girls of all ages, were not above exploiting their feminine pulchritudinous charms for their own ends, and it is amazing what lengths of dishonesty a young fellow employed by this (completely hypothetical) laboratory supplies company will go on the promises of a blowjob.

But the equally hypothetical Kewl Chix might not even have had to resort to promising, or indeed *delivering* sexual favours to a laboratory assistant. Because chloroform is not particularly difficult to make, even without a sophisticated laboratory of ones own. And remember that as teenaged pupils at a well appointed school or college in North Devon, they *would* have had access to the aforementioned sophisticated laboratory at the taxpayer's because sodium hypochlorite solution (chlorine bleach) mixed with common household liquids such as acetone, butanone, ethanol, or isopropyl alcohol can produce some chloroform, in addition to other compounds such as chloroacetone or dichloroacetone.

The real mystery is why there is not more ether and chloroform out on the streets, especially after the popularity of Johnny Depp's interpretation of the good doctor's *Fear and Loathing in Las Vegas* which specifically outlines the recreational uses of the former of those substances. Here I have to note that whereas I have read the book on many occasions, I only saw the movie once, and I was stoned when I did so, so I do not know whether the following quote was actually immortalised on celluloid.

> "The only thing that really worried me was the ether. There is nothing in the world more helpless and irresponsible and depraved than a man in the depths of an ether binge. And I knew we'd get into that rotten stuff pretty soon. Probably at the next gas station."

Whichever of the methods outlined above the Kewl Chix used to get hold of trichloromethane, they - or *someone* connected with them - certainly *did*, because their predations upon the unwary animal abusing fraternity of North Devon continued. In the middle of June of 2008 when all right thinking people were at Glastonbury complaining about Jay-Z headlining on the main stage, *somebody* (and one can only imagine that it was the Kewl Chix) raided the region's largest battery chicken plant.

They broke in at midnight on the longest day of the year, chloroformed the three humans that they found, stripped them naked and wrote obscene and politically charged slogans all over their bodies. The next day they were found - still naked and covered with graffiti, with their heads shaved, and lashed to the barred metal fronts of the cages - but all the fowl had been taken, and were never seen again. When something similar happened at Lughnasadh, various people including yours truly noted that there seemed to be a pagan connection with the attacks, but as we were broadly sympathetic to them, nobody (or at least I didn't) did anything about it.

At Samhain the attacks stepped up a notch, with the science laboratories at three separate local schools being torched, and elaborate postering and leafleting campaigns being carried out to inform the pupils at these various establishments what would happen to anyone found guilty of overstepping the boundaries of decency (as the unknown authors described it) as and when the attacks escalated. And at Yule a laboratory assistant at one of these establishments was attacked, beaten insensible, stripped naked and painted blue *pour encourager les autres*.

Although I still felt broadly in sympathy with what these persons unknown (remember I had never actually *heard* of the Kewl Chix back at that stage of my life, and innocence was bliss) were doing, the mood of the general populace was very negative, and I had enough common sense to keep my own counsel as far as these things we concerned.

Bideford has always been a farming town, and although the stuffing had been knocked out of it by the horrific events of the Foot and Mouth epidemic of 2001 and its brutal aftermath, to come out publically on the side of people who were openly at war with the farming industries was not, and probably still is not a wise thing to do, although I have never been particularly known for my wisdom.

At Imbolc came the first death. A local abattoir was torched, and the night watchman on duty died of smoke inhalation, although there is some doubt as to whether this was actually intentional as a statement was telephoned in to a local newspaper claiming that it had been a tragic accident. "We do not wish to kill dumb animals, even nightwatchmen" it read, but another statement delivered in exactly the same way a few days later denounced the first one as a fake.

But both statements had something in common, despite having contradicted each other. They were both signed "The Daughters of Dionysus".

Truly something spectacularly peculiar was afoot.

XXXX

Robert Heinlein's novel *The Moon is a Harsh Mistress* which was published in the early 1960s gives complex instructions to any would be revolutionary who would want to start a revolutionary organisation. Heinlein's fictional lunar revolutionaries used the same system of clandestine cells as the French Resistance, the Viet Cong and the Provisional IRA amongst others. For those readers not familiar with the concept, a clandestine cell structure is a method for organising a group of people like resistance fighters or terrorists in such a way that it can more effectively resist penetration by an opposing organisation (such as a law enforcement organisation). In a cell structure, each small group of people in the cell know the identities of only the people in their cell. Thus, a cell member who is apprehended and interrogated will not know the identities of the higher-ranking individuals in the organisation. Depending on the group's philosophy, its operational area, the communications technologies available and the nature of the mission, it can range from a strict hierarchy to an extremely distributed organisation.

Whoever 'Dionysus' was, he or she obviously knew what they were doing, because right from the beginning (s)he utilised this tried and tested system. But (s)he gave it a twenty first century twist. They used Facebook.

Now, before I go any further I had better explain. I wouldn't personally spy on my children; I consider it a gross breach of trust, and having grown up with parents who abused my privacy, I wouldn't do it to anyone else. But in view of what happened to Lydia's daughter, one can – I think – pardon her for being what is, I believe, in the current vernacular called a 'helicopter parent', or in her case a 'helicopter grandparent' but who is counting? Those jolly nice folk at Wikipedia provide this definition:

> A helicopter parent (also called a cosseting parent or simply a cosseter) is a parent who pays extremely close attention to a child's or children's experiences and problems, particularly at educational institutions. Helicopter parents are so named because, like helicopters, they hover overhead, overseeing their child's life.

Lydia, it transpires, became worried about the amount of time that her granddaughter was spending talking to people on this Facebook page (rightly, as it turned out) and so – rather than confronting her – did something very dubious and opened a Facebook account of her own under the name Little Miss Bossyboots and she joined the Kewl Chix page, and – utilising a talent for subterfuge that I would never have guessed at during the year or so that we were an item, all those years ago, she wormed her way into her Granddaughter's peer group.

The Kewl Chix page which had lasted a few months, and which had attracted my ex girlfriend's granddaughter, was only one of a series of transitory Facebook pages, all aimed at attracting the disaffected young teenage girls of North Devon, and all only lasting a few months before disappearing into the digital primordial soup from whence it had come. 'Dionysus' was remarkably adept at recognising girls on the cusp of womanhood who could be bent to his will.

Nobody actually knew who 'Dionysus' was, but his profile picture was of a remarkably handsome young man, stripped to the waist, and with a garland of flowering ivy in his immaculately groomed shoulder-length hair. Perfect dream fodder for the disaffected adolescent kewl chick.

Every few months, when he started a new Facebook page he would invite a whole selection of girls to join, and cleverly moulded them into a seemingly harmless, and mutually supportive community of animal lovers who would raise money for animal charities, have sleepovers where they would braid each other's hair and talk about the things that young teenage girls talk about. But all of the time he was carefully cherry picking the ones that he felt would be most suitable for his long term project. Then, without warning, he would close the page, and open another, with the same *modus operandi*. But he would take the chosen few with him and they would become the core members of the next group. And for over a year this chosen few included both 'Little Miss Bossyboots' and her Granddaughter Dorcas.

But if you are thinking that this was a state of affairs which couldn't possibly last, you are perfectly correct. It couldn't and it didn't. Although neither of them recognised it, Dionysus was running quite a complex organisation, and both Lydia and her Granddaughter rose through its ranks quite rapidly, Dorcas, because she fell hook, line and sinker for Dionysus' boyband good looks, and her Grandmother because life as the daughter of a preacher in a nonconformist sect had made her remarkably good at subterfuge. Slowly, as the months passed, 'Dionysus' started to drop hints that these social pages were just the front end of something far bigger and something far more noble. Something called The Maenads.

One day, however, the whole house of cards came crashing down. Both Dorcas and Lydia received messages from 'Dionysus'. "Why are you both writing and posting from the same IP address?" he wrote. Dorcas immediately realised what must have happened.

Dorcas, went screaming to her Grandmother. "How fucking *dare* you interfere in my life like that?" she yelled impassionedly. "Who the fuck gave you the right to spy on me?"

Lydia did what her family had always done in circumstances of social stress, and hid behind some well chosen lines from the Old Testament. But Dorcas wasn't having it. "Fuck the Old Testament and Fuck You!" she screamed, and ran off to barricade herself in her bedroom.

It was the last that Lydia ever saw of her, because that night she climbed out of her bedroom window, with her favourite belongings crammed into a voluminous knapsack, and ran away.

But that isn't the end of the story.

You may remember that earlier in this narrative I touched upon a grisly triple murder at a local zoo. And you may remember me saying that the CCTV cameras had picked up images of what appeared to be naked girls with soil streaked skin, brandishing weapons. One of the seamier of the national newspapers eventually picked up on the story, and had somehow got hold of stills from the CCTV tapes. They published them, making sure that the nether regions of the young women were obscured by typesetting, but that the tits and bums on which such newspapers thrived were clearly visible.

What Lydia, a committed Christian and social prude, was doing reading such a downmarket publication I do not know. But read it she did, and she immediately recognised one of the girls. For there, scowling at the camera, brandishing a hatchet like the one we keep by the fireplace for last minute log paring, naked as the day she was born, but with mud streaked over what parts of her body were visible to the newspaper readership, was Dorcas.

"Fuck me ragged" I said.

XXXXI

o what the bloody hell was I going to do?

I have been in some peculiar situations during my long and peculiar career. And it *has* been a long and peculiar one. I never set out to set myself up as an expert in the more arcane areas of modern life. Indeed I had originally meant to be a publisher dealing specifically with cryptozoology, animal folklore, and various allied disciplines. However, soon after my first wife sued me for divorce, a whole plethora of magazines dealing with Unidentified Flying Objects, sprung up in the wake of the popularity of the *X Files*, and the fiftieth anniversary of the incidents at Roswell in July 1947.

And as I discovered that I was actually quite a good writer, and that I could burble on in a way that some people found entertaining about subjects in which some people are interested. So I amassed a large library of books on esoteric subjects, and I was quite a well-known writer on what is vulgarly called 'weird shit' by the time I first met

Lydia and fell deeply into bed with her.

However, sixteen years later, and my books on magick, occultsm, and things that go bump in the night, are relatively neatly on the shelves of my library upstairs, and I haven't touched, or even thought about them in years. And so, despite the fact that my dear, long-suffering wife and I have a hairy Godling living in my airing cupboard, and we regularly have interactions with the ghosts and poltergeists who appear to share our living space with us, I was totally unprepared for this tumultuous visit from my ex-girlfriend. And I truly didn't know what the fuck I was supposed to say to her. Our relationship had ended badly, and I think that the resulting explosion pushed Lydia and I in opposite directions, and it was obvious that the accident in social synergy that had pushed us into the same place at the same time, was never going to happen ever again.

And whilst Lydia had become an embittered single Grandparent, I had remarried, and - completely surprising everyone, even myself - had become a happily married family man with Stepdaughters and Granddaughters, an elderly mother-in-law and a plethora of dogs and cats. So we were completely different people, living completely different lives, with nothing in common except for the fact that we had once spent about ten months mostly naked together. But despite the fact that we cordially disliked each other, and that whatever fond memories we could possibly have come up with were shrouded in embarrassment, (because it had been a very torrid ten months) I did feel a great deal of sympathy for the poor woman.

But what the bloody hell was I supposed to tell her? I couldn't think of a single constructive or positive thing to say. She had done an admirable piece of detective work, and furthermore it wasn't one that I felt that I could continue, or expand upon. It seemed to me that whoever 'Dionysus' was, he had come up with an admirable way of recruiting disaffected young women to his cause. But what exactly *was* his cause.

My mate Steve Jones, who was the first known practising pagan to become a JP once told me that there were three main reasons that people did magick: to get rich, get laid, or get even. I have written elsewhere of my suspicion that a big slice of Gerald Gardner's original Book of Shadows and other writings upon much of which modern Wicca is based, were indicative of his own sexual predilections, and from what I have read of many different cults throughout the ages, sex, money and power were an important part of the rationale of those people who had started them. The Daughters of Dionysus, The Maenads, the Kewl Chix or whatever you want to call them were almost undoubtedly a cult by anyone's definition, and it seemed that they were under the control of this 'Dionysus' person. And call me perverse, but the sexual allure of naked teenage girls streaked with mud and brandishing weapons would seem to be an obvious one. At least it was a logical place to start.

But what the hell was I going to do about it? I was already involved in monitoring the activities of one group of psychopatholigically charged runaway schoolgirls. But the *modus operandi* of the Children of the Three, who were hiding in the depths of the forest between Meddon and Hartland and seemed to be grouped around three supernatural characters, one of whom had the head of an elephant, and the other of whom was living in my airing cupboard, seemed to be completely different than this new group. For one thing they kept their clothes on, and apart from using the pulchritude of two of their members to lure poor stupid Danny Miles into their clutches, had kept their sexuality strictly under wraps. In fact, even during the sordid affair which had taken place in the previous year when Danny was accosted by two sultry looking temptresses at *The Westcountry Inn* on the A39 between Hartland and Kilkhampton, the sexuality had been no more than hinted at, and no clothing of any sort had been removed. *

But I was left with the impossible question of what the bloody hell was I going to do next. And then the last thing that I wanted to happen took place.

Corinna came into the study.

Do you remember back when you were at school and the teacher asked the class who was responsible for some transgression of the rules or other, and everyone blushed and looked guilty. Or at least I did. Even on the rare occasions when I *wasn't* guilty.

It was like that then.

I had no wish to extend my relationship with Lydia for any longer than I needed to. I certainly didn't want to revisit the months of our intimacy. But when Corinna came in, I have no idea why, but I felt horribly guilty. The fact that the two of us were poring over a newspaper pictorial featuring naked teenage girls didn't help.

Corinna smiled at the two of us sweetly. "Hello. I didn't know we had visitors", she said. Lydia scowled at her, and I felt even more unreasonably guilty, and there was an uncomfortable silence.

"Um this is Lydia, darling", I said hesitantly. "You may remember me talking about her. She has come to us with a problem. Her granddaughter has joined some sort of Internet Death Cult"…

* I am getting tiredof writing this bit, so check out what I say in the footnote at the bottom of .133

XXXXII

I do not understand women, I have never understood women, and I doubt if I shall ever understand women between this point of writing and the day that I shall die.

I have been accused of being sexist, but this has been by people who do not understand what the term means. I have a scatological, and vulgar sense of humour, akin to that of a schoolboy just entering puberty. I find many bodily functions irresistibly amusing, in particular those which are not discussed in polite company. I am childish, and sometimes vulgar, but not in the slightest bit sexist.

I tend to agree with Robert Heinlein who wrote:

> "Whenever women have insisted on absolute equality with men, they have invariably wound up with the dirty end of the stick. What they are and what they can do makes them superior to men, and their proper tactic is to demand special privileges, all the traffic will bear. They should never settle merely for equality. For women, "equality" is a disaster." [*]

And I agree wholeheartedly with Simone de Beauvoir who wrote (in a book that was banned by The Vatican until 1966) that "to carry off this supreme victory, men and women must, among other things and beyond their natural differentiations, unequivocally affirm their brotherhood".

Women are superior to men in every way that I can think of. They are better designed, live longer, and have a far more important social function within society. Ever since the human race was a bunch of hairy geezers living in caves and mud huts (and as my house is made primarily of cob [***], it is *still* basically a mud hut) it is women who have held the social groups together, women who have nurtured, women who have borne, cared for and reared the next generation, and women who have done all the important stuff, while the males of the species rampaged about spreading their

---

[*] Originally in *Time Enough for Love* (1973)

[**] The Second Sex (1949)

[***] Cob, cobb or clom (in Wales) is a natural building material made from subsoil, water, fibrous organic material (typically straw), and sometimes lime. The contents of subsoil naturally vary, and if it does not contain the right *mixture it can be modified with sand or clay. Cob is fireproof, resistant to seismic activity, and inexpensive. It can be used to create artistic, sculptural forms, and its use has been revived in recent years by the natural building and sustainability movements.*

DNA willy nilly, and then tended to get themselves killed in nasty ways by the bunch of hairy geezers living in the next valley.

Radical feminist acquaintances of mine have poo poohed my position and claimed that by stating that what I have written in the above paragraph is merely a way of objectifying women, and forcing them into a specific gender role, but in my opinion such people are determined to disagree with me, whatever I say, because I have that little y chromosome which they don't. My statement is a matter of biology rather than everything else, because when it comes down to it, our nasty little species is not the pinnacle of creation, but a monkey that got lucky.

So no, as far as I am concerned, I am not sexist in any way, shape or form. But I shall never understand women until the day I die.

Why? Why do I say this at this point in my narrative? Because far from spitting feathers and hissing at each other like angry cats (which is what I was expecting) the two women - my wife of the last decade or so, and my erstwhile girlfriend of a decade and two thirds ago - immediately bonded, and before I knew what was happening, Lydia was sitting down in my Grandmother's old nursing chair, next to the hearth on which a log fire grumbled. Sitting in her armchair on the other side of the fireplace was Corinna, and Mother bumbled and bustled (and if you think those are two different things, you have never met my Mother-in-Law) about, muttering about young people today, whilst Lydia told them both the sad story that she had related to me earlier in the evening.

Me? I was relegated to the corner of the room, where I sat in my favourite armchair like a good little man, and marvelled at this great female mystery that was unfolding before my eyes.

How and why Lydia and Corinna apparently became friends, I still do not understand, but it happened, and even if I had wanted to, there would have been nothing that I could have done to prevent it. But I didn't, and truly felt sorry for my ex-girlfriend, although - at this stage, at least - I couldn't imagine what I could possibly do to assist her.

However, I did learn more about The Maenads.

After Dorcas had run away from home, never to return, Lydia - quite logically - went through her room with a fine toothcomb, and was understandably shocked at what she found there. Dorcas had amassed quite an impressive collection of weaponry. There were butcher's knives, sheath knives, a crossbow, and even a water pistol that was full of ammonia. And, as Lydia said to Corinna and Mother, if Dorcas had left these things behind, one shuddered to think what she had taken with her.

There were also some impressively academic books on Ancient Greece, including Michael B. Cosmopoulos (ed), *Greek Mysteries: the archaeology and ritual of ancient Greek secret cults* (London, Routledge, 2003) which has been on my wants list to buy for several years, and a folder full of photocopies and print outs including the following passage:

> "The first large-scale religious worship of Dionysus in Greece seems to have begun in Thebes about 1500 BC, around a thousand years before the development of the Athenian Mysteries. Cultic worship of Dionysus (and his mother Semele, a moon goddess) was performed in the earliest Dionysian temples (usually located beyond the city walls, on the edges of swamps and marshes). Its first rituals probably originated in the Mycenaean period, but were probably similar (even in classical times) to rites still held on Greek islands such as Keos and Tenedos. Here the first wine was offered to Dionysus and the now-growing vine; a bull was sacrificed with a double axe, and its blood mixed with the wine.
>
> There are indications that at one time the sacrificer of the sacred bull was himself then stoned to death, although this became a symbolic act quite early. The more-economical practise of goat sacrifice was later added to the rites. The goat (like the bull) was regarded as a manifestation of Dionysus. However, it was also seen as the "killer of the vine" by eating it—welcome in times of pruning, less so in times of growth. The death of the goat could thus be interpreted as a combined sacrifice of Dionysus and the sacrificer. The goat was usually torn apart, as the vine had been at harvest."

And, more worryingly:

> "Maenads, possessed by the spirit of Dionysus, traveled with him from Thrace to mainland Greece in his quest for the recognition of his divinity. Dionysus was said to have danced down from Parnassos accompanied by Delphic virgins, and it is known that even as young girls the women in Boeotia practiced not only the closed rites but also the bearing of the thyrsos and the dances.
>
> The foundation myth is believed to have been reenacted every other year during the Agronia. Here the women of Thebes were organized into three dance groups and rushed off to Mount Cithaeron with ritual cries of "to the mountain!" As "mad women," they pursued and killed, perhaps by

dismemberment (sparagmos), the 'king', possibly represented by a goat. The maenads may have eaten the meat of the goat raw (omophagia) or sacrificed it to Dionysus. Eventually the women would be freed from the madness and return to Thebes and their usual lives, but for the time of the festival they would have had an intense ecstatic experience. The Agrionia was celebrated in several Greek cities, but especially in Boeotia. Each Boeotian city had its own distinct foundation myth for it, but the pattern was much the same: the arrival of Dionysus, resistance to him, flight of the women to a mountain, the killing of Dionysus' persecutor, and eventual reconciliation with the god."

Lydia passed the photocopies around. Corinna gasped, Mother tutted, and I began to get seriously worried.

XXXXIV

I am a cynical old bugger, and although I *do* try and see the best in people, sometimes my innate cynicism wins out. Although Lydia was being charming and generally likeable to Corinna and Mother, I didn't trust her further than I could throw her, and I was determined not to let her have any more information than I had to. When she disappeared off upstairs to "powder her nose" (one of those petit-bourgeois phrases of hers which had always irritated me) I whispered to Corinna not to mention anything at all about Panne, and Corinna glared at me.

Graham must have met Lydia on the stairs, because he came blustering into the sitting room. "What's that mad bitch doing here? I though we got rid of her years ago!"

Grasping the nettle while the iron was hot and mixing my metaphors madly as I did so, and remembering that Graham had always disliked Lydia, and would have trusted her even less than I did, I explained to Corinna that the woman had always been a peculiar, manipulative person, and truly was not to be trusted to any extent at all, and I think that I just about managed to persuade her that Graham and I were not being nasty to a woman in need, but that we were just trying an exercise in damage limitation.

Lydia sailed back into the room with an ingratiating smile, saw that Graham was in with us and glowered at him. I remembered then that she had always liked Graham just about as much as he had liked her, and I think that this obvious quick switch of emotions had impressed upon Corinna that our visitor was not necessarily to be trusted as much as she might have first appeared.

Graham muttered something and left the room. A few minutes later we could hear the dulcet tones of *Hawkwind* playing 'Brainstorm' billowing down the stairs, and Lydia continued to lecture us on the difficulties of rearing a teenaged granddaughter who had joined an Internet death cult.

There have been several occasions in the past decade or so that I have found myself to be the only man at a female gathering at which I felt that my gender was truly excluded. The best example of this was on the morning of my eldest stepdaughter's wedding [**], whereupon she, her sister, two bridesmaids, Corinna and Mother were all bustling around Mother's tiny flat in Oakham, while I sat ensconced in a tiny box room feeling that I was truly present at a female only gathering which had its roots in prehistory, and after an hour and a half of this I felt that I wouldn't actually be surprised to see that they had erected a wicker man for me outside the window.

This was not as extreme an experience as that, but as Lydia held forth, Corinna nodded, and Mother tutted, I felt not only excluded from the conversation but completely and utterly irrelevant to it. So I reached for the box file full of photocopies, some of which I had looked at earlier, and lost myself in the rites and practises of Ancient Greece.

Sure there was a hell of a lot of circumstantial evidence to suggest that Dorcas had been recruited to a nameless organisation of violent ecoterrorists using the Kewl Chix Facebook page as a front. And there was even more circumstantial evidence to suggest that Dorcas had developed a keen interest in the Dionysian rites of Ancient Greece (unless of course, Lydia had made that part up and just spent a happy afternoon at Barnstaple reference library with a fiver's worth of change for the photocopier) but I do claim to be some sort of a scientist, and I have spent much of my professional life since the beginning of the 1990s trying to solve puzzles in a methodical and rational manner. And, sad to say, there was no empirical evidence actually linking these two suppositions. And there was no evidence whatsoever that Dorcas had become a modern day Maenad, or - indeed - that such a cult existed. And,

---

* Hawkwind are an English rock band and one of the earliest space rock groups. Their lyrics favour urban and science fiction themes. Formed in November 1969, Hawkwind have gone through many incarnations and they have incorporated different styles into their music, including hard rock, progressive rock and psychedelic rock. They are also regarded as an influential proto-punk band. Brainstorm is the opening track on their third album - Doremi Fasol Latido - released in 1972. It is also Graham's favourite of their songs, and one that he plays when in moments of emotional extremis.

** The autumn of 2010

although I shudder to admit this because I don't like going back over unpleasant memories, I had a hell of a lot of personal evidence to show that Lydia was perfectly capable of putting two and two together to make six. Or even six hundred and sixty-six.

For, probably of all the people I have known, and certainly of all the people with whom I have been emotionally involved, Lydia's tangled belief system was the most complex and the least logical. She believed in the literal truth of The Bible, but hated all Christian churches apart from her own (which had only been founded in the late 1960s). She believed that alcohol was evil (despite what St Paul had written to St Timothy[*]) but intermittently had drug binges either of hashish, opiates or both, scourging herself until she bled as a punishment after each occasion. And she truly believed that she had been chosen by God to fight a war against the Antichrist, something that if my understanding of the Revelation of St John is correct would make her the second coming of Jesus Christ. Well I know that the Lord moves in mysterious ways, but to arrange the second coming of his only begotten son as a middle aged druggie woman with at least two personality disorders and an anger management problem would be just ridiculous. In short, therefore, Lydia was not what I would consider an altogether reliable witness.

And so as the three ladies by the fire talked on and on into the night, I went through the photocopies and booklets in the file box over again, trying to find the missing link that I had missed. And then I found something that *everyone* had missed. Tucked in the seam between two pages of a pamphlet called *Feminism in Ancient Greece* was a memory card of the sort that is commonly found in mobile phones.

"Look here Girls! Here is a digital storage medium which could contain up to 32gb of encoded material which might help us in our quest for the truth! Super!" I didn't say.

In fact I didn't say anything. I palmed the memory card, and slipped it into the cigarette packet that lay in the ashtray by my chair. Lydia glared at me:

"I hope that you are not going to smoke in here" she spat at me, totally disregarding the fact that she was a guest in my house, and it is an Englishman's inalienable right to do whatever the fuck he pleases in his own house. "No, I grunted. I am going outside for a smoke, and then I am going upstairs to bed. Goodnight!" [**]

---

[*] "Drink no longer water, but use a little wine for thy stomach's sake and thine often infirmities" (1 Tim 5:23). I have a large stomach, and so therefore it is obvious that if I drink more than a little wine (or brandy or gin) I am doing a holy thing. Right?

[**] I finally quit for the final time, in January 2017

And I left, the golden Benson and Hedges cigarette packet containing four cigarettes and a mobile phone memory card clutched in my right hand.

XXXXV

I have never had any pretensions to being a hairy chested man of action. I am a thinker and a theorist and a writer rather than a doer, and even as far as the adventures of Sherlock Holmes are concerned, the bits that most appealed to me were the bits involving a languorous divan and a bolt of raw opium. And I certainly never had any desire to be James Bond; even his kind of womanising was too energetic for me.

So jiggery pokery with half inched memory cards is truly not my style. And, no matter how much I disliked her, neither is stealing said memory card from my God Bothering * ex-girlfriend. But circumstances alter cases, and I truly could not see any other viable course of action.

Now, I am sure that some of you here reading this story will be of the opinion that I am not being fair to Lydia. I am certain that my darling wife thinks so. But the truth is that Lydia and I have a shared past that I thought was over a decade and a past behind me. The Jonathan Downes that she knew doesn't exist anymore and will never exist again at any time in the future, nor would I wish him to. The relationship that we had went very nastily wrong, and I dare say that I was just as much to blame as she was, but the truth is that I don't care. On the whole I like my new life and I don't want ghosts from my past coming back to fuck it up, and if Lydia was ever good at anything apart from sanctimoniousness and horizontal gymnastics, it was fucking things up. This may not be truly the action of a *pukka sahib* but although I like to think that I am an English Gentleman, I am a pragmatic one, and I wanted to get Lydia back out of my life as quickly as I possibly could.

So, I found myself in the peculiar position of doing cloak and dagger stuff in my own house.

In fact it wasn't actually *that* cloak and dagger! I did exactly what I said I was going to do. Well, sort of. I went out the back door, along the overgrown gravel path where - for at least half a century - people have been seeing the ghost of a "grey lady" walk, and in through the front door into my office, which - as I believe that I have

---

* That phrase has often intrigued me. Does it mean that the person in question keeps on bothering one with religious prattle, or that they keep on annoying the Creator with the same. Does The Lord say to St Peter, "now *HIM* again"

mentioned from time to time - is a badly converted potato shed with cob walls and a concrete floor, which doubles as study, recording studio, editing suite and the nerve centre for all the peculiar and oddly disparate things that I do with my life.

There, as I said I was going to do, I lit a cigarette. Once I had taken three delicious lungfuls of smoke that had seldom tasted so sweet, I took the memory card, reached for an adaptor from the plastic ice cream box on my desk which holds all sorts of useful electronic impedimenta, inserted the memory card into it, and once I had made sure it fitted correctly I inserted it into my computer.

Time was of the essence, because I truly didn't want anyone, certainly not Lydia, and not even my darling wife to know what I was doing. So, once I had ascertained that the card contained just over 20gb of media, mostly jpg picture files, but a few proprietary video files and some txt files, I set the whole caboodle to copy to my hard drive. As this was going to take quite a few minutes to do, I switched over to the other computer and tried to write some deathless prose about *The Pink Fairies.*

I was half way through this delightful task (and I should, I think, point out that the *Pink Fairies* are a legendary psychedelic rock band rather than wee folk with gossamer whatsits) when my dear (and long suffering) wife came in to join me. She, too, lit a cigarette and took a deep drag before letting out a long sigh. And I realised with relief that Corinna found Lydia as irritating as I did.

"We can't just turn her out into the night", she said, adopting the Dickensian mode of language which both of us tend to adopt when saying something particularly portentous. I started to argue, pointing out that she owed me three grand, and had been responsible for me having been stalked around Exeter by a whole posse of self appointed elders of her peculiar church, and that she had sat on my autographed copy of *Led Zeppelin III.*

But Corinna had the moral high ground, and both of us knew it. So, I reluctantly agreed that she should offer to make a bed up for Lydia on the sitting room sofa, and sulkily went back to writing about *The Pink Fairies'* forthcoming album [*]. I did, however, ask Corinna to come upstairs as soon as she was able, because I "had stuff to show her", and as soon as she had disappeared out into the night, I switched back to the other computer, and set the newly copied version of the data folder from the memory card to upload to Dropbox. As it was doing so, I carefully removed the memory card, and put it into one of the filing drawers in the cabinet above my desk, where it lay safely together with some samples of scat from Tasmania which had

---

[*] *Naked Radio.* Check it out. It is very good.

singularly failed to be from a Thylacine *.

I think that we sometimes do not realise how fast technology develops. Only two years ago we had pitifully slow broadband in the village where I live, and we often attained upload and download speeds of only a fraction of a megabyte per second. That was - like so much else that is crap in modern Britain - the fault of that egregious little arse Tony Blair. Following his party policy of providing style over content, he had promised in 2004 or thereabouts that broadband would be provided the any rural community where enough of its residents signed a petition. So, together with a whole bunch of other folk, I signed the petition, and within a few weeks Woolsery, the old Anglo Saxon settlement of Wulfheard's Homestead ** which had existed in one form or another since five hundred and something AD, got broadband.

And guess what? Just like the New Labour *** government that had provided it, it was bollocks.

They had provided broadband OK, but had not replaced the crappy old telephone lines that I remember having been put into place in 1973, and which were barely adequate then.

Nearly a decade later high speed broadband came to the village, and me and my mate Martin (who has stuck his nose into this narrative at intervals, and will no doubt do so again) were amongst the first householders to sign up to it. And bloody hell it revolutionised everything. With speeds (in the wee small hours) of up to 46mb per second, it finally meant that we at the CFZ could do the automatic cloud drive back ups that everybody else in the known universe (OK I am indulging in worse hyperbole than usual, but it's my party and I'll exaggerate if I want to) had been able to do for aeons. And so it was on that misty autumn evening in 2015 that I was able to

---

* The scat sample had been collected by Richard Freeman and Mike Williams, and turned out to have been from a Tasmanian Devil.

** See my late father's booklet *Woolsery: The Village with Two Names*

*** New Labour refers to a period in the history of the British Labour Party from the late-1990s until 2010 under the leadership of Tony Blair and Gordon Brown. The name dates from a conference slogan first used by the party in 1994, later seen in a draft manifesto published in 1996, New Labour, New Life for Britain. It was presented as the brand of a newly reformed party that had altered Clause IV and endorsed market economics. The branding was extensively used while the party was in government between 1997 and 2010. New Labour was influenced by the political thinking of Anthony Crosland, the leadership of Blair and Brown, as well as Peter Mandelson and Alastair Campbell's media campaigning. The political philosophy of New Labour was influenced by the party's development of Anthony Giddens' "Third Way", which attempted to provide a synthesis between capitalism and socialism. The party emphasised the importance of social justice, rather than equality, emphasising the need for equality of opportunity and believed in the use of free markets to deliver economic efficiency and social justice.

And it was horrid. Did neither, and fucked this poor country worse than ever.

go to bed with the dogs, Panne and at least one of the kittens, secure in the knowledge that when Corinna came up (which would surely be soon) the two of us could explore the contents of the memory card together.

But though the spirit is strong and steadfast, the flesh is weak. I took my medicine, and soon, snuggled up with the dogs, the demigod and the kitten, I found myself deep in the arms of Morpheus.

XLVI

Corinna came to bed about an hour later, and - because me and my furry friends were sprawled somnolently across the entire width of the bed - woke us all up. There was the usual snappy growliness between the two dogs who like being woken up even less than I do, and the grumpy grunts from yours truly, who likes being woken up only slightly more than the dogs do. The cats joined in the general melange of mardiness with a bit of hissing and back arching, but Panne awoke langorously and elegantly and fixed all the animals with a stern stare whereupon they all shut up and began to behave.

Corinna got into bed and immediately asked me what I had been up to. Wives seem to have a sixth sense wherever husband's jiggery pokery is concerned, and whereas I am not the kind of husband who plays the field, and the things that I have tried to hide from her have always been fairly insignificant, I have never been able to keep a secret from her.

However, I am happy to say that I had never had any intention of keeping this *particular* slice of jiggery pokery from her, and I swiftly explained how I had found the memory card hidden inside the bundle of Dorcas' documentation, and - rather than have to involve myself with the regrettable spectre from my even more regrettable past - I had made myself scarce. Much to my relief, it turned out that Corinna had taken an almost instant dislike to Lydia, and although she had proffered hospitality like the dear girl she is, she was under no illusions that my ex-girlfriend was - in her terms - ' a piece of work'.

Now, don't get me wrong. I am not one of those people who takes delight in slagging off erstwhile partners. I am on perfectly cordial terms with several of my ex-girlfriends, and - as far as my ex-wife is concerned - I am quite happy to admit that whilst there were faults on both sides, the vast majority of the events that led to the dissolution of our eleven year marriage were down to me. But I knew from bitter experience that Lydia's chaotic life was like the black hole caused by the collapse of a red giant star; a vortex of unparalleled cosmic magnetism that sucked in anyone and anything unfortunate enough to be within spitting distance.

But enough of that. I hope that I have made my point clear in this narrative, and certainly - back in the closing months of 2015 - Corinna had already seen enough of our unexpected and unwelcome visitor to see what was what.

But neither of us knew what was on the memory card, so - sitting up in bed - I fired up my trusty iPad (on which I am typing this, a year or so later) and within a minute or so I logged into Dropbox. The folder which I had uploaded contained two small avi files, which were presumably video clips, a couple of txt files, and sixty-five jpg picture files. As there were so many of them, I started on the picture files first. Because of the vagaries of our internet connection (which works well downstairs, less well upstairs) it took several minutes to open the first picture file, which - not entirely unsurprisingly - showed a number of naked young women streaked with mud, and brandishing butchers knives. Equally, not surprisingly (as she was presumably taking the photograph) Dorcas was not amongst them.

The next dozen or so of the photographs were more of the same, and I have to admit that Corinna and I were getting bored. Corinna and I are not the sort of couple who spend hours looking at pictures of total strangers *dishabille* and the novelty soon wore off. After about picture #15, however the tone of the pictures became darker, and also more sexual, as the mud-streaked girls began to kiss and paw each other apparently enthusiastically.

I am not going to describe what I saw on the pictures, and later on the video clips, not because I am a prude, but because - and I need to make an embarrassing admission here - I can't write sex scenes. I have tried on a number of occasions over the years, and they either end up coming out all Mills and Boonish or they end up dryly scientific. I realised years ago that writing erotica is a specialised art, and furthermore a specialised art that I was never going to grasp.

So you are just going to have to take my word for it, that the next twenty or thirty pictures just showed an indeterminate number of young women indulging in various aspects of what the Blessed Oscar described as "the love that dare not speak its name"!* I suppose it would have been erotic if you are into that sort of thing, but the

---

* In fact it wasn't one of Oscar's at all. 'The love that dare not speak its name' is a phrase from the poem "Two Loves" by Lord Alfred Douglas, published in 1894. It was mentioned at Oscar Wilde's gross indecency trial and is usually interpreted as a euphemism for homosexuality (although Wilde denied that it was).

almost certain knowledge that I was watching the antics of a cult of young murderesses put paid to any prurient thoughts that I might under other circumstances have had.

Then at about #40 the tone of the pictures changed again. A bound naked male figure, appearing to be a few years older than the girls was frogmarched into centre stage. The moment I saw him, I gasped. Because he had little horns on his forehead which appeared to be exactly the same as those which Panne had on its forehead, although - unlike Panne - he had prominent human organs of reproduction. He was held roughly by two young women, and his wrists appeared to be bound tightly with vines.

Synchronistically there was an upheaval under the quilt at the foot of our bed as Pan, jostling for position with the two dogs, made her way up to join us. This was (and is) not particularly unusual: Panne is an inquisitive little thing, and quite often sits on its haunches looking over my shoulder when I am watching films or series of pictures on my iPad.

Corinna and I made room for Panne to take up its usual viewing position, but there was obviously something very wrong indeed. Panne was not just shivering. It was shaking as badly as my late father was wont to do during the final stages of Parkinson's disease.

Panne took one look at the photographs, and spoke first time in over a year. "Sparagmos" it screamed, and with a terrified shriek it dove back under the bedclothes to the safety of the warm huddle of dogs and kittens by our feet.

XLVII

What happened next is exactly what you are all thinking happened next. The girls surrounded the naked man (he was certainly a man not any kin of Panne because early in the proceedings one of his - purely decorative - horns fell off leaving no sign of injury) beat him to the ground, kicked him unconscious, and then tore him apart with their bare hands.

When Corinna and I watched the video file we found, not entirely to our surprise that it showed the same thing, but filmed from a different angle. How or why the media from two different phones ended up on the same memory card I have no idea, and don't really care, but I suspect that there was no shortage of source material: both the pictures and the video showed some of the girls retreating, giggling from their bloody task, in order to record the events for posterity on *their* mobile 'phones. The video was superfluous anyway. The sheer horror of watching such a barbaric event recorded in such hi-tech digital splendour in a series of crystal sharp images which would have been unthinkable only a few years ago, will stick in my mind forever. Its not that the images were particularly graphic; the videography was exactly what one would expect from an over expected teenage girl hooped up on hormones and bloodlust, and far less explicit than many horror films that I have seen (and I am far from being a devotee of such things).

I am trying very hard to avoid using the oft quoted remark first made about Adolf Eichmann [*] at his trial in Israel in the early 1960s about "the banality of evil", but it was the sheer ordinariness of this film that made it so shocking. During the first Gulf War there was a piece of BBC news footage showing a small Japanese car speeding along a stretch of Iraqui motorway. I remember thinking - when I watched it for the first time - how in all the newsreel footage I had seen of other warzones, it appeared so far away and removed from my own experience.

But here was a car, of the same make and model as the one which I had been driving only a few months earlier, speeding along a stretch of motorway which could have been the M11 heading nor out of London, but with cruise missiles flying overhead.

And here, again, I was watching that weird cusp when normal and abnormal meet. Perfectly normal looking teenage girls, laughing and giggling with each other as if they were clustered together at the bus stop in our little village. Only naked, bloody, and with the twitching body of their dismembered victim lying twitching on the ground before them.

I turned round to Corinna.

"What the fuck am I going to do with this?" I asked her rhetorically.

She glared back at me.

"You mean, what the fuck are WE going to do with this" she spluttered. "Neither of us are going to be able to unsee what we have seen tonight. This is both of our

---

* Otto Adolf Eichmann (19 March 1906 – 1 June 1962) was a German Nazi SS-Obersturmbannführer (lieutenant colonel) and one of the major organizers of the Holocaust. He was tasked by SS-Obergruppenführer (general/ lieutenant general) Reinhard Heydrich with facilitating and managing the logistics involved in the mass deportation of Jews to ghettos and extermination camps in Nazi-occupied Eastern Europe during World War II. In 1960, he was captured in Argentina by the Mossad, Israel's intelligence service. He was found guilty of war crimes in a widely publicised trial in Israel, and was hanged in 1962.

problems now".

Well, I know that the proper course of action for a normal citizen would have been to take the memory card and all it contained to the nearest Police Station, but - although I am quite happy to admit that I am paranoid, both clinically and socially - I was not convinced that this would be the safest thing to do. I have not made myself particularly popular in certain quarters locally by my opposition to the badger cull [*], those who would have the government repeal the fox hunting laws [**], and those who ignored them altogether. There are a lot of people in both high and low places who would be happy to see me up before the beak, and the unfortunate truth is that in these days of image manipulation software, and clever video editing, there was nothing on the pictures or in the video which could not have been fabricated without anyone or anything being maimed, tortured or killed. Nothing, that is, except for a large number of explicit pictures of naked girls, some of whom were almost certainly below the age of consent.

Was I, sorry were *we*, prepared to go to the local cop shop, and present them with a perfect excuse to have me banged up with Gary Glitter *et al*, and become the "bitch of D Wing" for the next fifteen years? Quite possibly not. And there was also the fact that - much as we both disliked her, and found her constant moralising irritating - Lydia had come to us for help, and here we were blithely discussing the desirability of turning her and her granddaughter over to the police for them to deal with. In my experience of such things, the Police, especially in rural areas, usually run a mile when presented with a case involving what is vulgarly called 'weird shit'. Indeed, in the years before I retired from public life in order to quietly drink myself to death in a rural backwater, my team and I had often been called in to assist the police in cases of animal mutilation and other crimes with an occult angle.

And what would happen if the constabulary *did* decide that we were not exactly on the side of the angels? Not only were there dozens of questionable images in my dropbox account, but my library contains quite a few volumes appertaining to the left

* Badger culling in the United Kingdom is permitted under licence, within a set area and timescale, as a way to reduce badger numbers in the hope of controlling the spread of bovine tuberculosis (bTB). Humans can catch bTB, but
public health control measures, including milk pasteurisation and the BCG vaccine, mean it is not a significant risk to
human health. The disease affects cattle and other farm animals (including pigs, goats, deer, sheep, alpacas and lla-
mas), and some species of wildlife including badgers, deer and a few domestic pets. Geographically, bTB has spread
from isolated pockets in the late 1980s to cover large areas of the west and south-west of England and Wales in the
2010s. Some people believe this correlates with the lack of badger control.

In October 2013, culling in England was controversially trialled in two pilot areas in west Gloucestershire and west
Somerset. The main aim of these trials was to assess the humaneness of culling using "free shooting" (previous methods trapped the badgers in cages before shooting them). The trials were repeated in 2014 and 2015, and expanded to a
larger area in 2016 and 2017. As of July 2017, there is no UK-wide policy of badger culling.

hand path. Nothing even slightly illegal, but enough books on radical politics, and the nastier side of ritual magick to provide interesting listening for the jury if read out in court.

And if the constabulary *did* decide to be unpleasant about this, it was very likely that all our computers would be impounded for the duration of the enquiry, which would mean that we could quite possibly be without the means of making a living for many months. And would the police actually do anything to find the real perpetrators of a crime for which there was no *real* evidence? I could hear the voice of one of my wiser old Irish friends whispering the words "Birmingham" and "Six" [*] in my mind's ear.

And what would happen to Panne? How could we possibly explain a hairy, horned godling living in our airing cupboard if the house was searched?

What the fuck were we going to do?

There was nothing we could do, so we decided to go to sleep.

XLVIII

*I*actually woke up early and surprisingly refreshed the next morning. It would be easy - in order to create some sort of dramatic tension - to pretend that my sleep was wracked with horrific dreams about human sacrifices, but actually I had a very pleasant night snuggled up with Corinna, Panne and the animals, and woke with my arms round Archie, and with Prudence snuggled beneath my head like a hairy and slightly smelly pillow.

---

[*] The Birmingham Six were six men: Hugh Callaghan, Patrick Joseph Hill, Gerard Hunter, Richard McIlkenny, William Power and John Walker, who, in 1975, were each sentenced to life imprisonment following their false convictions for the Birmingham pub bombings. Their convictions were declared unjust and unsatisfactory and quashed by the Court of Appeal on 14 March 1991. The six men were later awarded compensation ranging from £840,000 to £1.2 million.

There were six men in Birmingham
In Guildford, there's four
That were picked up and tortured
And framed by the law

And the filth got promotion
But they're still doing time
For being Irish in the wrong place
And at the wrong time

Shane McGowan

I actually prefer to get up early and go downstairs with my iPad, so I can read the morning news, drink coffee (and if it is one of those times when I have lapsed from having given up smoking) indulge in a visit from my friends Mr Benson and Mr Hedges. It is about the only time of the day when the house is quiet, and I truly enjoy the solitude.

I had completely forgotten that Corinna had begrudgingly invited Lydia to stay the night, and that she had made up a makeshift bed for her on the sitting room sofa. However, to my great relief she had already risen and - or so it appeared - vacated my house. There was an untidy bundle of bedding on the floor, and she did not appear to have made any attempt to tidy up after herself. "That's fucking typical" I muttered to the two spur thighed tortoises * in the vivarium on the floor, and sat down to muster my resources.

I really do not know what I would do without my iPad: I use it to listen to music, write deathless prose and worthless doggerel, play games, and most mornings - if I have time - I use it as my eye on the world as I sit down to read the day's news.

There is an old Chinese proverb (or maybe curse) which says something about living in interesting times. I have always suspected that it is neither ancient, nor Oriental, as the earliest usage of it that I have been able to find was from Robert Kennedy ** in the early 1960s, but that is besides the point. Whether it is ancient or modern, eastern or western, it is made for the second decade in the 21st Century, because the times we are living in are terrifying, and peculiar.....but undeniably interesting.

I navigated my way to bbc.co.uk. For some reason I always look at the world news

---

* The common Tortoise (*Testudo graeca*) or also known as Greek tortoise, or spur-thighed tortoise, is one of the 5 species of Mediterranean tortoise (genus Testudo and Agrionemys, family Testudinidae). The other four species are the Hermann's tortoise (*Testudo hermanni*), Russian tortoise (*Agrionemys horsfieldii*), Egyptian tortoise (*Testudo kleinmanni*), and marginated tortoise (*Testudo marginata*). The common tortoise is a very long lived animal, achieving a lifespan of upwards of 125 years, with some unverified reports of up to 200 years.

** Robert Francis Kennedy (November 20, 1925 – June 6, 1968) - younger brother of JFK - was an American politician and lawyer who served as the 64th United States Attorney General from January 1961 to September 1964, and as a U.S. Senator from New York from January 1965 until his assassination in June 1968. Kennedy was a member of the Democratic Party and is often seen as an icon of modern American liberalism.

Robert F. Kennedy's Day of Affirmation Address (also known as the "Ripple of Hope" Speech[1]) is a speech given to National Union of South African Students members at the University of Cape Town, South Africa, on June 6, 1966, on the University's "Day of Reaffirmation of Academic and Human Freedom". Kennedy was at the time the junior U.S. Senator from New York. His overall trip brought much attention to Africa as a whole.

"There is a Chinese curse which says "May he live in interesting times." Like it or not, we live in interesting times. They are times of danger and uncertainty; but they are also the most creative of any time in the history of mankind."

first, but - as always seems to be the way these days - apart from the novelty items about people who taught their pet guinea pigs how to rollerskate, or the family who did a remake of one of the nastier spaghetti westerns with a cast consisting entirely of children under the age of six, the news was unremittingly grim. The usual round of medieval style atrocities committed by various sides in the internecine conflicts in the Middle East, was now leavened by shocking acts of violence carried out by suicide bombers and urban terrorists in the urbanised west.

Wherever I looked, religious fanaticism seemed to be the order of the day. ISIS [*], The Westboro Baptist Church [**], Al Quaeda [***], and a dozen other examples of what dear old Roy Harper [****] described as "The Nutters of God" [*****] were spreading their

AUTHOR'S NOTE: It amuses me to think that there is someone reading this in the second half of the 21st Century, long after I am dead, and who probably bought the book for a couple of pennies at a car boot sale. Hopefully they will not be au fait with the subjects of the first three of these footnotes.

[*] The Islamic State of Iraq and the Levant, also known as the Islamic State of Iraq and Syria, the Islamic State of Iraq and al-Sham, ISIS, officially known as the Islamic State (IS) and by its Arabic language acronym Daesh (Arabic: داعش) is a Salafi jihadist terrorist organisation and former unrecognised proto-state that follows a fundamentalist, Salafi doctrine of Sunni Islam. ISIL gained global prominence in early 2014 when it drove Iraqi government forces out of key cities in its Western Iraq offensive, followed by its capture of Mosul and the Sinjar massacre.

The group has been designated a terrorist organisation by the United Nations and many individual countries. ISIL is widely known for its videos of beheadings and other types of executions of both soldiers and civilians, including journalists and aid workers, and its destruction of cultural heritage sites. The United Nations holds ISIL responsible for human rights abuses and war crimes. ISIL also committed ethnic cleansing on an historic scale in northern Iraq.

[**] Westboro Baptist Church (WBC) is an American church known for its use of inflammatory hate speech, especially against LGBT+ people (homophobia and transphobia), Catholics (anti-Catholicism), Orthodox Christians (anti-Orthodoxy), Muslims (Islamophobia), Jews (antisemitism), Romani people (antiziganism), and U.S. soldiers and politicians (anti-Americanism). It is widely known as a hate group and is monitored as such by the Anti-Defamation League and the Southern Poverty Law Center. The church has been involved in actions against gay people since at least 1991, when it sought a crackdown on homosexual activity at Gage Park six blocks northwest of the church. In addition to conducting anti-gay protests at military funerals, the organization pickets celebrity funerals and public events. Protests have also been held against Jews and Catholics, and some protests have included WBC members stomping on the American flag or flying the flag upside down on a flagpole. The church also has made statements such as "thank God for dead soldiers," "God blew up the troops," "thank God for 9/11," and "God hates America."

[***] Al-Qaeda (Arabic: القاعدة) is a militant Sunni Islamist multi-national organization founded in 1988 by Osama bin Laden, Abdullah Azzam, and several other Arab volunteers who fought against the Soviet invasion of Afghanistan in the 1980s.

[****] Roy Harper (born 12 June 1941) is an English folk rock singer, songwriter and guitarist who has been a professional musician since 1964. Harper has released 32 albums (including 10 live albums) across his 50-year career. As a musician, Harper is known for his distinctive fingerstyle playing and lengthy, lyrical, complex compositions, reflecting his love of jazz and the poet John Keats.

His influence upon other musicians has been acknowledged by Jimmy Page, Robert Plant, Pete Townshend, Kate Bush, Pink Floyd, and Ian Anderson of Jethro Tull, who said Harper was his "...primary influence as an acoustic guitarist and songwriter." Neil McCormick of The Daily Telegraph described him as "one of Britain's most complex and eloquent lyricists and genuinely original songwriters... much admired by his peers"

[****] *The Black Cloud of Islam* from the album *Once* (1990)

Gospel of Hatred, while at home in dear old Blighty, rich condemned poor, black condemned white, right condemned left, and the British Government had announced that they would be killing another 100,000 badgers in the public interest.

So, with a heavy heart, I moved to the local news section.

One of the reasons that I relocated to rural North Devon just over a decade ago was so that I could avoid the increasing levels of unpleasantness that were beginning to surround me on a daily basis in rural Exeter, but now it seemed that pointless violence, racial tension and general unpleasantness were becoming *de rigeur* in my own little rural backwater as well. There were no less than three gruesome murders in the North Devon news that morning, and so I gave up, and sat back in my chair, and proceeded to immerse myself in the strategy game that I had - by then - been playing for more than a year.

I have always been fond of strategy games, ever since I used to play with toy soldiers as a child, and despite the fact that I am a dodgy old hippy who somewhere has a T Shirt emblazoned with the motto "Fuck the War Machine" I derive great pleasure from them. And on this particular morning a good bout of virtual militarism, and a long chat with people whom I consider friends, but whom I shall probably never meet in real life, did much to restore my good spirits.

After about an hour, I ambled into my office as if I didn't have a care in the world, and sat down to read my morning crop of emails. Before I did so, however, the events of the previous evening came to mind, and I opened my dropbox account. I am nowhere near as paranoid about internet security as some of the people I know, but I do make sure that anything even slightly sensitive has been encrypted, and the material I had taken off the mobile phone memory card the previous night was far *more* than slightly sensitive. There is a handy little piece of freeware that is basically a virtual hard disk that encrypts files on the fly using 256-bit AES encryption. Unlike TrueCrypt, another popular on-the-fly encryption tool, it encrypts individual files, not an entire volume or container. Consequently, encrypted files sync with your cloud storage service immediately after you save them, whereas TrueCrypt syncing occurs only after you finish encrypting an entire volume.

Good stuff, eh?

I then removed any remaining traces of my activities from my desktop, and was getting back to my normal day's routine, when there was a rap on the door. Assuming that it was the postman, I shouted for whoever it was to come in, without raising my head.

When I looked up I saw two sinister looking hooded figures looming above me, and with them was Danny Miles.

XLIX

We are here, Jonathan, to communicate the wishes of our Master" Danny boomed in a voice straight out of *Ben Hur* that I had never - in our thirty-four year relationship - heard him use before.

"What the fuck are you talking about?" I spat back. "And don't come out with all this histrionic bollocks while you are on my property!"

Out of the corner of my eye I could see a terrified Panne, having gathered up a struggling kitten under each arm, scuttling for the shelter of our overgrown shrubbery, where I knew it had built a secretive little den. Whatever happened, my unwanted and unwelcome visitors must *never* see Panne. They might suspect that I had rescued the little woodland Godling, and taken it into my protection, but suspicion was not proof.

I would never claim to be a Magician, but I had carried out the strongest rites of protection that I knew how to do (two parts Dorien Valiente and a smidgeon of Crowley's *Magick in Theory and Practise*) but the fact that my three unwanted visitors had simply breezed into my garden without a by-your-leave, would suggest that my craftwork was sorely inadequate.

I stared at Danny and his companions bad temperedly. They stared back at me implacably, and I knew that we were destined for some sort of Mexican Standoff of staring. So I stared back at them, and they stared back at me.

Just then there was a flurry of barking, and a little brown and white whirlwind came rushing down the garden path. Someone had - despite all my strictures of what should not be done under any circumstances before the postman has been - left the back door open, and Archie (in full attack mode) was running down the garden path to investigate, with extreme prejudice. Whether this was just him being an aggressive little bugger, or whether he was finally a manifestation of my magickal protections.

Being a terrier, he grabbed hold of the tails of the black robe of the nearest hooded figure and started to "worry" it. This being, by the way, the technical term for a terrier shaking something from side to side in an attempt to break its neck, or otherwise damage it. And it wasn't long before he had pulled the cloak to the ground revealing what was underneath.

Now, if this had been a Harry Potter story, or Dr Who script, the cloak would have fallen away to reveal a wisp of elemental smoke, or - more likely - a hideous primeval monster that would have just emerged from some drowned corpse city or other. But this as real life, or at least as 'real' as mine gets (whatever that means) and when Archie pulled down the black cloak he revealed......nothing at all. And in all the flurry of excitement, the other hooded figure had vanished, never to be seen again. Danny was without his bodyguards, and when I looked up at his face he was grinning like an idiot.

"Thank Fuck they've gone" he said in his usual voice. "Now we can talk".

He sat himself down on the chair in the corner of my office, and - much to my surprise, as he really doesn't like strangers that much - Archie scampered towards him, leaping onto his lap for a cuddle.

"Let's get the business out of the way first", he said, reaching into his pocket and extracting (with no little difficulty) a huge bundle of bank notes, and a computer keydrive. He passed them both to me.

"The money is from Malcky and Trace. There is seventeen grand in there, which is - I believe - what they owe you" he said, as I stared at him mutely. "The keydrive is from our mutual friend Mr Loxodonta. He wants you to make it into a record".

I still stared at him mutely. There were so many things going through my head that I didn't know what to say first. I thought for about thirty seconds, still staring at Danny like a goldfish with my mouth opened, and still couldn't think of what to say. There were so many issues here. Why had Loxodonta waited ten months to get hold of me? Why had my two erstwhile tenants who had never in their lives, as far as I was aware, done anything decent to *anyone* suddenly decided to stump up the money that they owed me (actually about eighteen hundred quid more, but I wasn't going to complain)? And from where had they *got* the money? Was I going to have the outraged owner of said banknotes turn up on my doorstep with a police escort? And most of all, how come Danny was suddenly behaving like a decent, normal human being for the first time since I had known him? In the 34 years since I met him he had always talked like a slightly retarded mid-Atlantic teenager, using whatever cant phrase or patois was currently in vogue. It had always irritated me, especially as he and I got older, but here he was - for the first time since I first met him back in 1981 - using The Queen's English in a reasoned and sensible manner, with surprisingly well-modulated tones. It was as much of a shock as if I had heard Her Majesty The Queen Herself jive talking, or using the phraseology of a Jamaican Yardie.

And then he *really* shocked me. He reached into his breast pocket, got out a packet of Benson and Hedges Gold, and offered me a cigarette. This was something unprecedented; Danny was well known for never having his own cigarettes. Something extraordinary must have happened to him to have brought on this extreme sea change. *

I took the cigarette, and thanked him politely (trying to hide my incredulity). We sat there in silence, smoking. And then the office door opened, and my beloved Mother-in-law walked in. "Would you and your friend like a cup of coffee?" she asked, and disappeared, reappearing a few minutes later with a cup of tea *sans* milk, and a bottle of diet tonic water.

This broke the ice, and Danny began to tell his story.

L

hadn't seen Danny for ten months - since just before Christmas the year before, and had only had a couple of brief and irritating emails. Although I have never actually *liked* him, he has been part of my life for over thirty five years now, man and boy, on and off, and I had become quite worried about him. And I was very surprise at the level of my relief when I discovered that he was okay, and that nothing nasty had happened to him. I even began musing whether one had to actually *like* someone for them to be your friend.

For those who do not remember **, the last time I had seen him was the day he had presented me with a finished master of a song called 'Winter', by *Xtul*, the band

---

* Sea-change or seachange, an English idiomatic expression which denotes a substantial change in perspective, especially one which affects a group or society at large, on a particular issue.

The term originally appears in William Shakespeare's The Tempest in a song sung by a supernatural spirit, Ariel, to Ferdinand, a prince of Naples, after Ferdinand's father's apparent death by drowning:

Full fathom five thy father lies,
Of his bones are coral made,
Those are pearls that were his eyes,
Nothing of him that doth fade,
But doth suffer a sea-change,
into something rich and strange,
Sea-nymphs hourly ring his knell,
Ding-dong.
Hark! now I hear them, ding-dong, bell.

** I think we can take it as read that large chunks of what happens here can be explained better if you read *The Song of Panne*. But I am not a breadhead blah blah blah.

which - allegedly, at least - consisted of a bevy of supernatural entities living in the woods on the North Devon border with Cornwall, together with an ever shifting number of their followers, who all appeared to be aggressive and scary young women, whom the authorities - no doubt - would have much rather been in school, where they could learn to be good little consumers.

My last words to Danny had been angry ones, because - the night before - a muso friend of mine, who works as a freelance record producer, had been co-opted at knife point into mixing and mastering the track. I had been absolutely furious, and - at the time - I had refused to have anything mire to do with Danny or *Xtul*. But here it was, ten months later, and Danny was sitting in my office looking surprisingly pleased with himself, and proffering a key drive which - he said - contained *Xtul's* new record.

I took it gingerly, and inserted it into my computer. There were five songs. I had heard them before, and indeed had even played lead guitar and banjo on one of them, but they had been tightened up considerably in the intervening months, and I felt sure that I could discern my mate Martin's hand at the controls.

"Yeah, we went to see him a couple of weeks back, but this time there were no knives, no hoods, and we even paid him" said Danny.

Obviously something dramatic had changed in the deep woods, but what the hell could it be?

I had so many questions I wanted answering, and like a teenager in love, or a middle aged hippie with a hangover (okay, far more like the latter than the former) I was confused and tongue tied and the words wouldn't come out properly, at least not the way that my brain wanted them to. But I tried my best.

"Ummmm. Thank you for the money. I can't believe those arseholes sent it to me".

Danny had the good grace to look mildly embarrassed, which as it was the first time in all the three and a half decades that I had known him, that the words 'good grace' could be applied to anything concerning the bloody man, was enough to confuse both of us.

"Okay. I will admit that I knew all the time that they were scum", he said bashfully, "but I have mixed with scum most of my life, and at first I didn't care. But then I slowly came to realise that Malcky and Trace had plumbed new depths of scummitude that I had never imagined could have existed".

The 1960s saw a rise in domestic terrorism across the western world. In the United Kingdom, the most widely known examples of these were the Irish republican groups, the Irish Republican Army, the Provisional IRA, and the Irish National Liberation Army, to name the three most well known. However there were also paramilitary terrorist organisations in Scotland, Wales, and even Cornwall.

In December 1980, a group calling itself An Gof 1980 exploded a bomb at the courthouse in St Austell. An Gof is pronounced 'Angove' and was apparently named after the trade of Michael Joseph (Cornish name Myghal Josef), An Gof being Cornish for 'The Smith', a leader of the Cornish Rebellion of 1497. In January 1981, they claimed responsibility for a fire at a Penzance hairdressers (the business was mistaken for the Bristol and West Building Society). Later in the decade, An Gof claimed responsibility for a number of fires, including one at the Zodiac Bingo Hall in Redruth. They also claimed responsibility for an attempted explosion at Beacon Village Hall in Camborne and placing broken glass under the sand at Portreath Beach in 1984.

Over the years there have been other such organisations, and it turns out that one of them was most likely responsible for a sizeable arms cache in the woods behind Tamar Lakes. This doesn't impact directly on the events in this narrative, not yet at least, but its indirect ramifications are very important.

There is a particularly nasty family - the Billingsgates - who live in Kilkhampton. The locals refer to them as "Bloody Gyppos" but I have no idea whatsoever of they were originally of the Roma people * or not. My Maternal Grandfather was part Roma, and so I have always been vaguely positive about them. However that is besides the point. This family, who shall remain nameless are apparently responsible for the vast majority of petty crime that happens in the town, and in recent years their crimes have got nastier. Basically this is because sometime in the late 1990s, Tyler Billingsgate, one of the younger members of the tribe, was out poaching when he came across the aforementioned arms dump. Being what my friends in the north call "a canny lad" he didn't divulge this to anyone, but over the next decade, he trickled out a variety of firearms and ammunition, and sold them to anyone who was interested. This included some very dodgy people from Newquay who were engaged on a bloody but low key gang war, now in its third generation, and - not particularly surprisingly - to some of the less scrupulous members of his own family!

Thus, the low life of that particular part of North Devon and Cornwall found itself

---

* The Romani (also spelled Romany, colloquially known as Gypsies or Roma, are a traditionally itinerant ethnic group living mostly in Europe and the Americas and originating from the northern Indian subcontinent, from the Rajasthan, Haryana, Punjab and Sindh regions of modern-day India and Pakistan.

tooled up and ready to ruck. There was nothing that most of the local residents could (or would) do about it. But, if you have been following this narrative closely enough you will remember that my late Father's old friend who owned the house near Tamar Lakes where Malcky, Trace and Danny were now living, (rent free, and in the case of the first two, and with a generous stipend) was a resourceful old chap from a military background. So it should not come as too much of a surprise to learn that he, too, was tooled up.

The Enfield No.2 was a British top-break revolver using the .38/200 round manufactured from 1932 to 1957. It was the standard British/Commonwealth sidearm in the Second World War, alongside the Webley Mk VI and Smith & Wesson Victory Model revolvers chambered in the same calibre. My Father's friend was presumably issued with one during the hostilities, but it turns out that after the war, when the revolvers and other weapons were supposed to have been decommissioned, he managed to keep hold of a couple of them, which he buried in his vegetable garden in a Tiger Tim lunchbox filled with grease, in case the day dawned when the 'balloon would go up again'.

When the Billingsgate family started their armed predations in the district, the old boy decided that the balloon had well and truly 'gone up' again and got his guns out of hiding and made them ready for action. And although he never had a chance to use them, his actions meant that Malcky and Trace were now in possession of working firearms, which is a frightening enough thought for anyone.

LI

D on't want to learn about etiquette from glossy magazines" [*] sang Brian Ferry in 1973 (or possibly 1974) but I did, and so did every other bloke I know.

Like most men of my age in Western Europe (and I suspect many other cultures) the first naked women I saw were glossy and had a pair of staples down the middle. But in those halcyon days of the 1970s, the girls that were pictured in the magazines upon which I spent so much money during my young adulthood, didn't look too much different from the real flesh and blood girls that I saw unclothed for the first time in the early 1980s. But then as Thatcherism took hold, and the world became sculpted by the dictates of market forces, so did the chicks who got their kit off for the discerning purchasers of jazz mags, and so they became willing victims of

---

[*] "All I Want is You" is a single by English rock band Roxy Music taken from their 1974 album Country Life. The single is also notable for its B-side, an instrumental track called "Your Application's Failed", which is the only track to date written by drummer Paul Thompson. The track was re-released on The Thrill of It All boxset.

---

the plastic surgeon's knife, and the bikini wax, and all looked basically the same, and I lost interest in commercial pornography for ever.

But whereas I went off to pastures new like mortgagees, employment, and real women who didn't have staples in the middle of their tummy button, others railed against the pornographie nouveaux and demanded photographs of real women, like the ones that they would have dated had they not been too busy queuing up outside newsagents wearing grubby raincoats. Others were particularly interested in the woman of the fuller figure, and formed a subset of the pornography end-users with the unlovely sobriquet of 'chubby chasers', and also demand specialist smut of their own. And Malcky saw a gap in the market, and - like any good capitalist - decided that this was a gap in the market that he and his BBW missus could fill.

Here I think I should interject with what would be an Editor's Note, if I was not also the author. The acronym BBW stands for 'Big Beautiful Woman', and would certainly be a contravention of the Trades Descriptions Act if I used it to describe Trace, who was basically (to use the words of a friend of mine who should probably remain nameless) "as rough as a badger's arse" but as BWARATREOALM ('Big Woman as rough as the rear end of a large Mustelid') is a rather clumsy acronym, and B does not just stand for 'Beautiful' but could also (with a slight paradigm leap in one's imagination) stand for 'Badger's arse-like' I shall let it stand. Anyway, as I know how the story arc of this narrative develops, and know that the description of 'Big Beautiful Women' is not one that is likely to be used many more times herein, it doesn't really matter.

So Malcky and Trace continued their career path as pornographers, providing graphic pictures of fat and ugly women (actually, thank goodness, only one fat and ugly woman, but wearing an assortment of wigs, masks, and accoutrements) for the discerning consumer. And it does, I think, say a lot for the state of play in society during the second decade of the 21st Century, that they were soon doing a roaring trade.

But, ever the shrewd businessfolk, they were soon providing live performances and (what they coyly described as) 'personal services', and just as they had to my late aunt's pretty little cottage on the outskirts of Bideford, not content with getting paid an unfeasibly large sum for acting as caretakers (a role which they had completely redefined) they turned my Father's old friend's old Georgian house into a particularly sleazy burlesque theatre cum knocking shop.

And soon the money was rolling in. But with a capitalistic zeal which would have delighted Mrs Thatcher (who's face, by the way, adorned one of the masks that

Trace was wont to wear during her performances) they wanted more. And soon they worked out how to do it.

In fact it didn't take much working out. My parents used to describe prostitution as "the world's oldest profession". I don't know where this expression came from, but it makes a lot of sense, and one can easily imagine an orderly queue of male *Homo heidelburgensis* * outside a cave where a female of their species was busily engaged in providing the prehuman equivalent of 'Executive Relief', and this grand tradition has continued around the world to the present day.

An estranged old mate of mine was once making a documentary in West Africa, and he was filming a row of picturesque local fellows queuing up to get into what he assumed was some kind of temple. However, the aforementioned queue of picturesque local fellows objected to being filmed, and set about my erstwhile friend, smashing his camera. Later, in the hotel bar, he asked his trusty guide whether the aforementioned queue of picturesque local fellows were afraid that if someone filmed them that this action would somehow take away their souls, and turn them into some West African analogue of zombies, or some other manifestation of the undead. In fact he was already planning a short article for *Fortean Times* about his experience.

"No Sah" his guide said with a broad grin, and explained that the building that my erstwhile friend had assumed was some sort of temple from its ornate and relatively well managed exterior, was actually the local knocking shop and VD Clinic, and that the aforementioned queue of picturesque local gentlemen actually objected to being filmed just in case their wives would subsequently see the documentary on the Discovery Channel.

And so it is the whole world over. Whether married or not, patrons of such establishments prefer to insist on anonymity, and get both frightened and pissed off when that anonymity is threatened. And so it was in North Cornwall where - about six months previous to the conversation which I am recounting here - Malcky and Trace - secure in the knowledge that they were in possession of a small but serviceable ex-Army revolver, decided to open up yet another new cash in hand revenue stream by indulging in a spot of armed blackmail.

"Christ on a bike!" I said.

---

* *Homo heidelbergensis* is an extinct species or subspecies of archaic humans in the genus Homo of the Middle Pleistocene (between about 700,000 and 200,000-300,000 years ago), known from fossils found in Southern Africa, East Africa and Europe. African *H. heidelbergensis* is also known as *Homo rhodesiensis* (possibly an African subspecies, *Homo heidelbergensis* ssp., with an extended definition of *Homo heidelbergensis* understood as a polymorphic species dispersed throughout Africa and western Eurasia with a range spanning the Middle Pleistocene, c. 0.8–0.12 Mya).

LII

I first attended Bideford Grammar School in September 1971, a few weeks later than everyone else, because I had undergone some particularly nasty corrective surgery at Princess Elizabeth Orthopaedic Hospital in Exeter. Eighteen months or so before, whilst in Hong Kong I was diagnosed as having a particularly complicated version of knock knees, the treatment for which involved me having a number of steel staples hammered into my patella, and removed a year later. Both operations seemed to me to be some sort of exquisite Roman torture, akin to the things which our Latin teacher was so fond of reading us, and I was in serious pain for a long time.

So, I arrived at a school which one of the few people I have kept in touch with from those days described to me as a "brutal place", looking and sounding different to everyone else there, and with none of the shared cultural experiences. I had been taught by my parents that pop music was 'moronic' and played by long haired twits, and I had no idea who or what Leeds United was, and I think that it would not take a Cassandra amongst you then or now to realise that my five years there were - on occasion - pretty horrid.

The aforementioned Latin teacher was a particularly egregious example of his type. I believe that he is dead now, and even if he isn't, he will be well into his dotage and is extremely unlikely to be reading this book. He was one of the "dark sarcasm in the classroom" brigade as written about by our Rog *, and:

> *"By pouring their derision*
> *Upon anything we did*
> *Exposing every weakness*
> *However carefully hidden by the kids"*

As well as reading the class excerpts from a book about the Coliseum at the end of each lesson, which could well have been a misguided attempt to interest his unruly class in the mores of ancient Rome, but which for me - at least - only introduced me to such concepts as bestiality, child rape, and the mechanics of crucifixion, ** which scared and scarred me beyond all recognition, and blighted my psyche for many years to come, he also flaunted his heterosexuality by encouraging the more testosterone-

---

* Roger Waters of *Pink Floyd,* the lyrics quoted coming from *The Wall* (1979).

** *Those about to Die* by Daniel Mannix

filled chaos in the class to bring in girlie magazines which he would read in front of the class, and - allegedly - keep in the locked top drawer of his desk.

A few years ago I made contact with an old schoolmate via Facebook (the bloke I alluded to above) and he told me, much to my amusement (but not altogether to my surprise) that my old Lain master (whom I sincerely hope is dead, because one cannot libel a corpse, and although every word I am writing here is true, I don't really want to have to stand up and justify having written about it in court, mainly because I am a card carrying coward) was actually gay, and shacked up with a recent alumnus from the very school in which he taught. "Methinks he did protest too much" * I said with a glass of merlot in my hand and an amused look on my face. And I laughed like a motherfucking drain when I found out who his inamorata was alleged to be.

In my first year at the school there was a young man whom I shall call Victor Ludorum, because that was basically what he was. He was Captain of this Team, Captain of that, President of several societies, and I cannot remember whether he was Head Boy or not. I do know that most of the school looked up to him (including yours truly), and that despite that, this 'golden boy' was a nasty sort of bully in a sort of detached, Olympian way. I was the object of some of his more vicious desires, and I remember being slapped and punched, and made to stand on a desk, tears streaming down my face, with my trousers round my ankles, reciting "I must be a homosexual because I don't like football".

Luckily for me, he left at the end of my first year, and I heard nothing more of him for nearly half a century. Allegedly at least, he was my quondam Latin Teacher's inamorata. Over the years, one of the school staff of whom I *was* fond, would tell me of his progress, and I heard how he had gone to Canada and made a name for himself as a sporting and academic hero. But if the *on dits* are true, he actually had spent at least some of the intervening years shacked up in a Bideford lovenest with my Latin Master learning the craft of a catamite.

I asked my friend for news of my nemesis, not because I was actually interested, but because I wanted to make sure he was still as far away from me as possible. Until my old friend had told me all the decades-old gossip, I had almost forgotten about him, but I am afraid that sadistic schoolboy with the Talbot Baines-Reed ** good looks, had stayed lurking in the darkest interstices of my psyche ready to jump out and bite me

---

* Like so many other eminently quotable quotes in the English language this is from Robbie Williams. No, of course it isn't. It is Shakespeare, *Hamlet* to be precise.

** Talbot Baines Reed (3 April 1852 – 28 November 1893) was an English writer of boys' fiction who established a genre of school stories that endured into the mid-20th century. Among his best-known work is *The Fifth Form at St. Dominic's*. He was a regular and prolific contributor to *The Boy's Own Paper* (B.O.P.), in which most of his fiction first appeared.

in the ankles at the most inopportune and/or embarrassing moments.

After my friend told me all this, I did a small amount of online sleuthing of my own, and found that he had, indeed, gone to Canada where he went to university, but sometime during the years when Tony Blair had made style over substance an essential business skill, he had returned to Britain, and now lived in the outskirts of Kilkhampton where he was a "businessman" (whatever that means; it is a designation which can cover a multitude of sins, often of the venial variety). I made a mental note to avoid Kilkhampton (which, although it is less than ten miles away, is a place that I hardly ever go to, for some reason) and pretty much forgot about the matter.

However, as Danny Miles sat opposite me in my office, chattering away in the most open and healthy way I have ever known (sorry to bring Talbot Baines Reed into the equation for the second time in as many paragraphs, but it was a transformation truly akin to that of the 'bad prefect' in *The Fifth Form at St Dominics*) my schoolboy tormentor came back into my life again. Because it was he who was the victim of Malcky and Trace's first blackmail attempt, and it was largely *his* seventeen thousand quid in non-sequential used notes that was now nestling in my office safe.

LIII

I don't understand the S&M lifestyle, and I don't understand prostitution. I am not being prudish about other; I have close friends that have indulged (and continue to indulge) in both, but neither has ever appealed to me. I will admit freely that there were times between the end of my first marriage and the advent of my second, the best part of a decade later, that I was more promiscuous than perhaps I should have been. But I never indulged in power games, and no money ever changed hands, and I like to think that every sexual partner that I have ever had was with me because *at that time* I could fulfil her needs better than anyone else in the universe. And that need was not for a bundle of used tenners.

But I am perfectly aware that there are people for whom this is not the case, and - much to my bemusement, because I do not understand it at all - there are associations and clubs (for want of a better word) for people who like to re-enact *Satyricon* [*] in privacy and *en masse*. It is something that I find completely incomprehensible

---

[*] The *Satyricon,* or *Satyricon liber* (The Book of Satyrlike Adventures), is a Latin work of fiction believed to have been written by Gaius Petronius, though the manuscript tradition identifies the author as Titus Petronius. The Satyricon is an example of Menippean satire, which is different from the formal verse satire of Juvenal or Horace. The work contains a mixture of prose and verse (commonly known as prosimetrum); serious and comic elements; and erotic and decadent passages. It was filmed in 1969 by Fellini.

(although, I stress that I am not condemning it) but it is something of which I have been aware for many years. And so, I was not at all surprised to find that there was such a group operating a few miles up the road from my little corner of North Devon.

And - although I had managed to put him out of my mind, and had not thought about him for years - it made perfect sense that Victor Ludorum, once the blue eyed boy of my *almer mater,* was one of its leading lights. He had, apparently, returned from Canada just in time to make an offensively large sum of money during the dot.com boom and had the low cunning to realise that it was time to pull out before the aforementioned economic boom went tits up. He then, apparently, set himself up as a 'Financial Consultant' (whatever that means) and spent the next ten years advising a succession of little old ladies (to whom the faded remnants of his once boyish good looks were an irresistible inducement) how to invest their meagre pensions.

But behind his flawless Patrician image lay - as lies, one suspects, behind many flawless Patrician images - a sordid reality. Unlike many men who become more conventional as they get older, Victor's sexual proclivities got nastier and more unsavoury with age. And the eighteen year old who enjoyed his power trip so much as he tormented the eleven (in fact, I might have been twelve) year old me, grew into the maven of a large and powerful community of sadomasochists who either enjoyed beating, or being beaten, and various degrees of humiliation or being humiliated, as well as sex with persons of both genders. And as The Ludorum household, where he lived with his wife and a 'paid companion', and singularly failed to pay any income tax despite having enough of an income to pay for the upkeep of a sizeable house and gardens, was only a matter of miles from where Malcky and Trace were doing much the same, it was only a matter of time before they met. And, as any fule kno[*], or at least as any fule can hazard a remarkably educated guess, when they did eventually meet, both fur and sparks were bound to fly.

I know very little about the S&M subculture, mainly because it has never been something which interested me. But I understand from what I have read, and what I have been told by people who *are* into that kind of thing, that there are a complex set of rules in place to safeguard participants from both physical and social harm. I have been told by one friend, for example, that membership of any organised S&M group is only by invitation, and that any prospective new member has to be vouched for by at least two current members.

It is also practically impossible for a single man to join. Membership is restricted to single women, couples, or triads, and at each of their organised soirees (and I truly

---

[*] Attributed to Nigel Molesworth, and if you don't know who he is you jolly well should.

cannot think of a better way to describe them, and if there is a proper word for them, I have never been told it) there are marshalls to enforce the rules as well as first aiders and even paramedics resent just in case something *does* get out of hand.

It all sounds very civilised, in so far as an organised house party where rich people pay a lot of money to beat (or be beaten by) other people, and where the sideshows can include anything from mock crucifixion to the ritualised voiding of bodily wastes over those who wish to be humiliated, can be. But, I am sure that people who have been following this narrative so far will have guessed at least four things.

- Firstly, that Victor Ludorum, my nemesis from my unhappy first year at Grammar School, was the sort of person who - despite being a respected member of this shadowy community - had hankerings to delights far beyond and above what was sanctioned by his community.

- Secondly, that such forbidden delights would be expensive, and beyond either the pocket or desires of yer ordinary pervert.

- Thirdly, that Victor Ludorum was far from being yer ordinary pervert, and was well equipped financially and morally to indulge in his deepest and darkest desires.

- And finally that Malcky and his unlovely wife, were not only pretty well bereft of any of the normal moral checks and balances which keep 'normal' (whatever that means) people in order, but would also do pretty well anything for money.

The combination of the unlovely twosome and the quondam sixth former who had made my life so unpleasant during the final weeks of the spring term of 1972 at Bideford Grammar School is not a pleasant thought. And as I prophesied a few paragraphs ago, when they met, both fur and sparks were bound to fly, and as events were to show, they certainly did.

LIV

*T*out comprendre c'est tout pardonner' seems an extraordinary idea whichever way one looks at it, and it is certainly nit a concept to which I subscribe. I understand all sorts of things that I would never even begin to forgive, and so mote it be. The maxim is attributed to Anne Louise Germaine de Staël-Holstein, commonly known as Madame de Staël, a French-speaking Swiss author living in Paris and abroad who influenced literary tastes in Europe at the turn of the

19th century. As the quote is found in a book whose title is very close to the name of my dear wife, it makes perfect sense to me even if the sentiments quoted are - to me - the epitome of liberal bollocks.

A slogan which makes far more sense to me is one I saw on a tee shirt the other day whilst I was wandering about Morrisons in Bideford, trying to buy saffron buns. It read 'yes, of course everything happens for a reason: and the reason is that you are stupid and make idiotic choices'.

Because the very people who are intent on pardoning people just because they understand their motivation are just the sort of people who think that everything that happens is the result of some sort of psychic intervention by an ur-divine omniverse, and - of course - nothing to do with the fuckwitted way that they lead their lives.

Now, I understand - tota-fucking-lly exactly - why the events that happened that night in Kilkhampton during the final weeks of November 2015 happened. But it doesn't mean that I even slightly forgive any of them, even though I ended up seventeen grand the richer because of them.

It doesn't take a genius (and, although by some criteria I could be judged a genius even though I don't like talking about it) to understand why any if the three main protagonists (or groups of protagonists) did what they did.

FIRSTLY. Victor Ludorum, is, was (and I suspect always will be) an unloveable pervert whose only motivations in life have always been money, sexual gratification, and the pursuit of power over his fellow men and women. The people who follow Madame de Staël's maxim would probably say that he was just as much of a victim as any of the people upon whom he prayed. Bollocks! He came from a rich and influential family, was cursed from boyhood with almost offensive good looks, and even if he had been abused as a child (which I doubt) we as a species are gifted with the power of free will. And in every occasion of which I am aware, the egregious little pillock did nothing but fulfil (or attempt to fulfil) his own venial lusts. Surely a more perfect example of Thatcherism made flesh has never walked the Green Hills of Earth [*].

SECONDLY. Malcky and Trai-Cee (aka Trace). I actually know a bit about both of their backgrounds, which is why I felt sorry for them at first. Malcky came from a family that my late mother would have, no doubt, described as 'Social Climbers'. Except for the fact that they weren't good at it. Both Malcky and his Father had

---

[*] Heinlein. Yay!!

entered local politics with the avowed aim of bring their own brand of Social Democracy into play. But both of them appear only to have been interested in feathering their own nests, and were both accused of fraud on several occasions. I know nothing about the actual mechanism of local government, and care less, so I cannot tell you whether they were officially "impeached", but what I do know is that both Father and Son were quietly deselected from their posts, that their ridiculously ambiguous expenses claims were disallowed, and that neither of them stood for public office again. It was, I believe, one of the reasons that the family relocated *en masse* to North Devon. Malcky soon discovered that having a slutty new wife whose tastes were even more depraved than his, was an excellent moneyspinner, and - as we have seen - showed no hesitation in a wholehearted commercial exploitation of her.

THIRDLY. The punters. This is where things become a little more problematical. There were about thirty of them, and - presumably - each and every one of them had their own motivations for indulging in the sexual excesses that they enjoyed so wholeheartedly. It is not my place to point any fingers. My sexual life in the ten or so years between the end of my first marriage and the beginning of my second, was not exactly conventional, but neither was it anything like as depraved as that to be found at the soirees laid on by Victor Ludorum and his colleagues, at which Trace was the *femme fatale* and sexual *prima ballerina*. If people want to spend out five hundred quid a time for an evening of events that made *120 Days of Sodom*[*] seem like a Women's Institute charabanc trip to Weston Super Mare, then I suppose that it is their business. But don't expect me to feel sorry for them.

Now, before we go any further. Although I know a fuck sight more than I am letting on, I am not going to go into graphic descriptions of what went on at this unpleasant little soiree. Partly because I am unsure of the legality of some of the more dubious things that went on, partly because if I did so, I would probably turn my own stomach, but *mostly* because I am not in the business of writing pornography. As I wrote earlier in this narrative when describing the horrific abuses of little Hazel Wingford by her stepbrother Stevie, I would hate to think that anyone reading this - either now, or at any time in the future - found any of it even the slightest bit titillating. OK, what took place that autumn night in 2015, was somewhat less reprehensible than what happened to Lysistrata in the days before she was who she became, but only because - as far as I am aware - everything that took place (except

---

[*] *The 120 Days of Sodom*, or the *School of Libertinage* (Les 120 Journées de Sodome ou l'école du libertinage) is a novel by the French writer and nobleman Donatien Alphonse François, Marquis de Sade. Described as both pornographic and erotic, it was written in 1785. It tells the story of four wealthy male libertines who resolve to experience the ultimate sexual gratification in orgies. To do this, they seal themselves away for four months in an inaccessible castle in the heart of the Black Forest, with a harem of 36 victims, mostly male and female teenagers, and engage four female brothel keepers to tell the stories of their lives and adventures. The women's narratives form an inspiration for the sexual abuse and torture of the victims, which gradually mounts in intensity and ends in their slaughter.

for the bits involving the goat) were consensual, and even the Billy Goat might have given his informed consent had he been possessed of the cognitive ability to do so.

But I am not in the business of writing titillating prose, even if I were possessed of the ability so to do, which I am not. As I explained earlier in this book, although I have attempted to write erotica on a few occasions, I am just no good at it. And so, even if I wanted to, I wouldn't be able to inject any erotic facets into what is basically an unpleasant tale of class, power, magick and religion. So, if you have read so far in a vain attempt to find the dirty bits. Give up. There aren't any!

LV

My dear wife once told me that I was unkind to describe Malcky as "a lanky, red haired streak of piss" who was "about as much use as tits on a bull", but it seemed apposite then, as it seems apposite now. But it does seem that the bloody man learned *something* from me during the years that he hung about my household. Because from what Danny told me, the opening scenes of Victor Ludorum's perverted *soirée*, lit and stage managed by the lanky red saies streak of piss himself, were nothing short of magnificent.

Once upon a time there was a woman who went under the soubriquet of 'Dirty Gertie'. She was apparently my age (give or take a few years) and even went to the same school as me, apparently. This is not as significant as one might have thought, because until the fifth year what was to be known as Bideford School (later, Bideford College) was actually two different schools, Bideford Grammar School (which I attended) and Bideford Secondary Modern School, known to everyone as 'Geneva' because the huge, red brick edifice that held it was sited on Geneva Place, just around the corner from the Grammar School on Abbotsham Road. 'Dirty Gertie' must have attended 'Geneva', which is why I never knew her.

I say this not from any reasons of snobbery, but because - whereas Bideford Grammar School *did* start admitting girls in the autumn of 1972 - it was a year after I had started, and we only ever had a handful of girls in our class, and none of them were called 'Gertie'. In fact, to the best of my knowledge, none of them were 'Dirty' either, and I am sure that I would have remembered someone who had the reputation that 'Dirty Girtie' had even as a twelve year old. Her unlovely soubriquet apparently came not only from the fact that she was an extremely grubby young woman whose family lived in one of the more insalubrious post-war housing estates round where the industrial estate in East-the-Water is now, but because from an early age, she would do sexual favours for her male classmates in return for relatively small amounts of money.

But, as I said, I had never heard of her during my schooldays, and it was only many years later that I heard of her. In a last ditch attempt to save the family honour, my parents sent me to a fairly crappy boarding school on Exmoor after I had failed most of my O Levels. After I was expelled from there, I lived in Exeter, Bracknell and Plymouth for short periods of time, before moving back with my parents, and then living in Canada for a while. I didn't find myself back in Bideford until 1981, five years after I had left, and by this time the myth of 'Dirty Gertie' was in full swing.

Apparently she lived in one of the terraced houses above the Pannier Market, in the narrow street which had once held a pub called *The Lamb*. And it was from here that she carried out her business as a very low class prostitute, who would do *anything* for under a tenner. But I never went there, I never met her, and to the best of my knowledge I never even saw her. And to be quite honest I had forgotten all about her until that peculiar afternoon in the late autumn of 2015, when Danny Miles jogged my memory.

Although I had never met her (nor had I had any particular desire to) it did not come as any great surprise to find that she was a social and professional intimate of Malcky and Trace, or that the gruesome twosome had co-opted her to join them in their business venture. Victor Ludorum had made it clear that money was not a problem, and had given Malcky *carte blanche* to spend whatever he needed in order to make the evening a success.

So, using a fair amount of presentational nous which I am not particularly proud to say that he probably got from me, Malcky hired (or bought - I neither know, nor care) a small but useful lighting rig, a PA system and used an old trick I had told him about to make a mist machine as impressive as anything used by a Goth band in the mid 1980s.

Back in 1982 when I was a first year Student Nurse in South Devon, I became friends with a bloke called Kevin, who was one of the Charge Nurses at (the now long demolished) Royal Western Counties Hospital at Starcross. Kevin was a multi-instrumentalist who had his fingers in a whole slew of musical pies (including some that involved me) and taught me all sorts of useful tricks, including a (these days) massively illegal but very useful way of making the sort of ghostly mists on stage, so beloved of bands like *The Mission.*

It was simple. All you need is a tin bucket of dry ice, an electric kettle, an electric fan, and some water. Whereas, even back then, dry ice was not an easy thing to get hold of in most of the country, if you lived in the vicinity of a shipping port, (in our case, Teignmouth) it was pretty widely used by commercial fishmongers, and was thus reasonably easy to get hold of. Nowadays it is even easier, with several websites boasting of their ability to provide Carbon Dioxide in its solid state in a variety of easy to use shapes and sizes, to anyone with a credit card and a legal mailing address.

Cushti.

Then, you put the dry ice in the tin bucket, and pour small amounts of boiling water onto it, using the electric fan to direct the resulting white, semi-opaque vapour across the stage or other area that you wish to cover in mist. Carbon Dioxide vapour, being heavier than air, drifts spookily across the stage to greatly theatrical effect. If you then illuminate the stage area with coloured stage lighting it is even more impressive, and has provided generations of rock bands who hold the Health and Safety Executive in disdain, with a cheap and massively impressive piece of stagecraft!

LVI

According to Robert Greenfield, during *The Rolling Stones'* notorious tour of North America in 1971 [*], Truman Capote (who had been sent along on the tour by the magazine named after the band) described Mick Jagger as "about as sexy as a pissing toad"' which is an insult that I have always found highly amusing. And it is also a wonderful example of how one person's global sex symbol is another's micturating lissamphibian.

And so.....

Just because I find the whole thing mildly nauseating, and I disliked all the people involved that I knew, and feel sure that I would dislike the others if I were unfortunate enough to meet them, doesn't mean that I can't feel a smidgin of grudging admiration for a piece of 'erotic' theatre well executed. The word 'erotic' is in quotation marks, by the way, because I would like to stress once again, that not only do I find the whole concept of the events that went down that night in Kilk distasteful in the extreme, I would also find it highly disturbing, if I were to hear of anybody who was actually titillated by my description of them.

I am not trying to do a Lemony Snickett, here and implore you to "turn away" from

---

[*] *S.T.P.: A Journey Through America With the Rolling Stones* (1974)

my narrative as some sort of post-modern plot device *, but I am trying to describe the events that ended up with me getting seventeen grand that I was not expecting ever to see again, rather than write pornography.

But enough of these authorly asides. I have been putting it off long enough, and I think that I really need to explain the events, revolting though they are.

There was an Easter weekend some years ago, when Malcky and his unlovely bride were in the salad days of their relationship. (An unfortunate simile, considering the events I will be relating in a paragraph or two). Trace had behaved so obnoxiously that Malcky's father, the Dishonourable Donald, who at the time was the Mayor of one of the smaller seaside towns in the district, had thrown the young couple and all their chattels out of the family home, and - as a result - they were living in my garden shed, which doubles (at times) as my personal museum. I had boxes of unpacked books and DVDs stacked up in the corner, and I know that the unpleasant young lovers spent several evenings watching my various movies, one of which was Todd Browning's 1932 film *Freaks*, and I suspect (but cannot prove) that this was the cultural inspiration for the revolting piece of theatre that Malcky *et al* perpetrated upon Victor Ludorum and his guests.

Just in case, however, you are one of the culturally bereft people who has not seen this masterpiece of *grand guignol*, here (courtesy of those jolly nice people of Wikipedia) is the synopsis of this remarkable film, which was both genre-breaking and history-making because eponymous characters were played by people who worked as carnival sideshow performers and had real deformities.

> "The film opens with a sideshow barker drawing customers to visit the sideshow. A woman looks into a box to view a hidden occupant and screams. The barker explains that the horror in the box was once a beautiful and talented trapeze artist. The central story is of this conniving trapeze artist

---

* Lemony Snicket is the pen name of American novelist Daniel Handler (born February 28, 1970). Snicket is the author of several children's books, also serving as the narrator of *A Series of Unfortunate Events* (his best-known work) and a character within it and All the Wrong Questions. Because of this, the name "Lemony Snicket" may refer to either the fictional character or Handler.

As a character, Snicket is a harried, troubled writer and photographer falsely accused of felonies, and is continuously hunted by the police and his enemies, the fire-starting side of the secret organization Volunteer Fire Department (V.F.D.). As a child, he was kidnapped and inducted as a "neophyte" into V.F.D., where he was trained in rhetoric and sent on seemingly pointless missions, while all connections were severed from his former life, apart from his siblings Jacques and Kit (who were also kidnapped and inducted).

In the theme music for the TV show of "A series of..." he continually exhorts viewers to "look away" rather than allow their senses to be polluted by the horrors of the plot.

Cleopatra, who seduces and marries sideshow midget Hans after learning of his large inheritance. Cleopatra conspires with circus strongman Hercules to kill Hans and inherit his wealth. At their wedding reception, Cleopatra begins poisoning Hans' wine. Oblivious, the other "freaks" announce that they accept Cleopatra in spite of her being a "normal" outsider: they hold an initiation ceremony in which they pass a massive goblet of wine around the table while chanting, "We accept her, we accept her. One of us, one of us. Gooba-gobble, gooba-gobble".

The ceremony frightens the drunken Cleopatra, who accidentally reveals that she has been having an affair with Hercules. She mocks the freaks, tosses the wine in their faces and drives them away. The humiliated Hans realizes that he has been played for a fool and rejects Cleopatra's attempts to apologize, but then he falls ill from the poison.

While bedridden, Hans pretends to apologize to Cleopatra and also pretends to take the poisoned medicine that she is giving him, but he secretly plots with the other freaks to strike back at Cleopatra and Hercules. In the film's climax, the freaks attack the evil pair during a storm, wielding guns, knives and other sharp-edged weapons. Hercules is not seen again (the film's original ending had the freaks castrating him: the audience sees him later singing in falsetto). As for Cleopatra, she has become a grotesque, squawking "human duck". The flesh of her hands has been melted and deformed to look like duck feet, her legs have been cut off and what is left of her torso has been permanently tarred and feathered. She is the opening scene's cause for alarm."

A number of contemporary reviews were not only highly critical of the film, but expressed outrage and revulsion. *Harrison's Reports* wrote that

"Any one who considers this entertainment should be placed in the pathological ward in some hospital."

In The *Kansas City Star*, John C. Moffitt wrote,

"There is no excuse for this picture. It took a weak mind to produce it and it takes a strong stomach to look at it."

The *Hollywood Reporter* called it an:

"..outrageous onslaught upon the feelings, the senses, the brains and the stomachs of an audience."

I have always been rather fond of the movie, although would be the first to admit that it is possibly not to *everybody's* taste.

But enough of Hollywood in the 1930s; we need to grit our teeth and return to Kilkhampton in 2015.

On the night in question, as I have said, Victor had about thirty guests sitting around his huge refectory table. They had each paid about five hundred quid for the privilege of attending an evening of stomach turning entertainment, and were each dressed in costumes referencing their own particular fetishes and tastes. Although most of the women appeared to be wearing formal black cocktail dresses, for example, if one were to look closer they would see that most of these 'cocktail dresses' were made of rubber, and had little holes in the bodice for their nipples to poke through, and other parts of the body usually left covered were sometimes also on display.

The men were also formally dressed, but their definition of formality was more loosely defined. Their costumes too, were often (but not always) made of rubber or leather, but amongst the formal 21st century dinnerwear were several Hitlers and a Caligula, and - once again - there were more wardrobe modifications designed to exhibit reproductive organs than one would normally have seen at a semi-formal dinner party.

Upon arrival Chez Ludorum, the guests handed over their five hundred quid in cash, and were handed a glass of champagne by a butler resplendent in a pink suede codpiece and very little else. A housemaid wearing the sort of French Maid's outfit never usually seen outside one of the crappier sex comedies that the British film industry seemed to spend so much of the 1970s making, took their coats and submitted to having her bottom pinched with a resigned air.

The assembled company stood around Victor's drawing room making polite small talk. "Once a bourgeois Estate Agent, always a bourgeois Estate Agent" laughed Danny who was there in a professional capacity, and - as he told me later - marvelled at the fact that most of the guests were engaged in talking about their dull careers and lives, and their holidays in Marbella, and how their children were doing at one of the local private schools, and that there wasn't even the slightest frisson of sexual excitement in the air.

An hour or so later, they all went in to dinner, two by two, having paired off in some informal fashion that Danny didn't grok, although he noted to himself that the couples who had arrived together all paired off with other people. They all sat, uncomfortably around the huge refectory table, as Victor said a few stilted words of welcome.

Then there was an expectant silence, and at one end of the room a door opened and in came the man I have already described in this narrative as "a lanky, red haired streak of piss", stark naked except for an elaborate feather head-dress which I recognised from the description as coming from one of Tintin's adventures with Incas in Peru *. His body glistened with slippery oil, and he brandished a huge beater which he used to beat an impressive gong on a frame like a homoerotic J Arthur Rank logo.

The lights (operated by Danny) dimmed and the music from one of Borodin's orchestral invocations of the steppes of Central Asia blared out impressively from the PA System (also operated by Danny).

The main events of the evening were about to take place.

LVII

*T*he music swelled to a crescendo, the mist rolled in, and a followspot (operated by Danny) illuminated a particularly revolting sight; Malcky pushed in a trolley upon which there reposed two huge chafing dishes on wheels. On the first chafing dish was Trace, stark naked, in the pose commonly seen portrayed by a roast sucking pig. She had an apple in her mouth and other food items were distastefully arrayed across other salient parts of her flabby and unattractive body. I have never wanted to imagine this particularly unpleasant young woman naked under any circumstances whatsoever, but if there was a list of the circumstances under which I would least like to imagine her naked, her being the centrepiece for some sort of gastrosexual smorgasbord would probably be at the top of that hypothetical litany.

---

* *The Seven Crystal Balls* (French: *Les Sept Boules de Cristal*) is the thirteenth volume of The Adventures of Tintin, the comics series by Belgian cartoonist Hergé. The story was serialised daily in *Le Soir*, Belgium's leading franco-phone newspaper, from December 1943 amidst the German occupation of Belgium during World War II. The story was cancelled abruptly following the Allied liberation in September 1944, when Hergé was accused of collaborating with the occupying Germans and banned from working. After he was cleared two years later, the story was then seri-alised weekly in the new *Tintin* magazine from September 1946 to April 1948. The story revolves around the investi-gations of a young reporter Tintin and his friend Captain Haddock into the abduction of their friend Professor Calcu-lus and its connection to a mysterious illness which has afflicted the members of an archaeological expedition to Peru.

The Seven Crystal Balls was a commercial success and was published in book form by Casterman shortly after its conclusion. Hergé concluded the arc begun in this story with *Prisoners of the Sun*, while the series itself became a defining part of the Franco-Belgian comics tradition. Critics have ranked *The Seven Crystal Balls* as one of the best Adventures of Tintin, describing it as the most frightening installment in the series. The story was adapted for the 1969 Belvision film, *Tintin and the Temple of the Sun* and for the 1991 animated series *The Adventures of Tintin* by Ellipse and Nelvana.

But if Danny's description of Trace's entry into the feast was revolting, his description of how Dirtie Gertie was displayed was positively stomach-churning. This is why I have a vague suspicion that Malcky had paid attention when he had watched my DVD of Todd Browning's *Freaks*. Because Dirtie Gertie (and I still neither know, nor care her real name) was trussed like a cooked fowl, in the manner which Browning presented his anti-heroine Cleopatra when she got her comeuppance.

It appears that Dirtie Gertie is (because as far as I am aware, her abasement that night did not actually stretch to having been murdered) what I believe is called a "pain slut", (which means exactly what you think it means). And although whilst Cleopatra in the movie had her legs cut off and her flesh melted until she attained anseriform appearance, I somehow doubt whether Dirtie Gertie had to go through quite such a harrowing ordeal. However it must have been a painful and degrading process to get into character as it were.

According to the New Testament, early in the first Century, Saul of Tarsus was dedicated to the persecution of the early disciples of Jesus in the area of Jerusalem. In the narrative of the Acts of the Apostles (often referred to simply as Acts), Paul was travelling on the road from Jerusalem to Damascus on a mission to "bring them which were there bound unto Jerusalem" when the resurrected Jesus appeared to him in a great light.

The account says that "he fell to the earth, and heard a voice saying unto him, Saul, Saul, why persecutest thou me?" Saul replied, "Who art thou, Lord? And the Lord said, I am Jesus whom thou persecutest: [it is] hard for thee to kick against the pricks."

According to the account in Acts 9:1–22, he was blinded for three days and had to be led into Damascus by the hand. During these three days, Saul took no food or water and spent his time in prayer to God. When Ananias of Damascus arrived, he laid his hands on him and said: "Brother Saul, the Lord, [even] Jesus, that appeared unto thee in the way as thou camest, hath sent me, that thou mightest receive thy sight, and be filled with the Holy Ghost. His sight was restored, he got up and was baptised.

From thence on he stopped kicking against the pricks, and became the Apostle St Paul, who was a bit of a prick himself, but whether or not you are a Christian the story of Paul's conversion on the road to Damascus has entered the shared cultural heritage of much of the human race as an analogy to explain the way that some people *do* suddenly change life paths and go off on a hitherto totally unexpected tangent.

Now, I am not going to claim any similarities between Danny Miles and St Paul, excepting the fact that Danny, too was a bit of a prick, but somehow the revolting events of that night in Kilkhampton brought about a sea change in Danny, and he seemed to have truly changed.

Now, I have already described the effects on my young psyche of being read gruesome accounts of the activities in the Coliseum by my Latin master, who was Victor Ludorum's quondam sugar daddy, and so I am only too aware of how unwanted images can pollute one's mind and come back unbidden for many years to come. I also want to reiterate that I have no intention of writing anything that could even be slightly construed as being deliberately pornographic, and so because - believe it or not - I have some vague principles, and believe that the moral duty of a writer is neither to pollute the minds of one's readership, or lead them by the nose into a disgusting series of lifestyle choices, I am going to be very circumspect in how I relay Danny's description of what happened next.

Without giving away too many prurient details, it transpired that although the impression of Malcky's *danse macabre* was to give the impression of some sort of ritualised erotic cannibalism, neither Trace nor Dirty Gertie were actually going to be killed and eaten. They were not the main course of the evening's repast, merely the two vectors by which the food were to be presented to the assembled company. As is always the case at formal banquets, the Master of the Table, ate first, and then the rest of the guests piled in eating their food off, and out of Trace and Dirty Gertie. And then off each other, whilst Malcky donned his trusty Donald Duck mask and capered around the table squealing joyously as he took his sexual and gastronomic pleasure where he could find it.

And that is truly all that I am going to say on the subject.

Danny, obviously traumatised, told me a good deal more, and I have no intention of bringing it back into my forebrain by repeating any of it.

Once the orgy was well and truly underway, and the whole room was a mass of writhing naked bodies liberally smeared with food, there was no need for any more *son et lumiere*. So Danny slipped off to explore the house and to carry out the most important part of the mission on which he had been entrusted by his revolting co-conspirators.

Quietly and stealthily he reached into his pocket for a small digital camera and took enough pictures of the revolting events that were unfolding before him to act as 'insurance' should it ever be needed. He then checked his other pocket and made sure that he had the keys to his car and the Enfield No 2. 38 revolver that had been issued to my Father's old friend at some point during the Second World War.

He then slunk off to explore the house.

LVIII

Danny had not just been brought along to the sordid soiree in order to act as Stage Manager. He had a secondary, and - depending on your opinion - much more important role in the scheme of things. Although Malcky and his tag team had been remarkably well paid for setting up a vista of mock cannibalism and general depravity for Victor's coterie of disgusting dinner guests, like so many others of their ilk, they decided that they deserved more.

So Danny had been entrusted with what Malcky so charmingly described as "our fackin' shootah" and had been told to collect - what Malcky again, so charmingly described as - "our fackin' subsidiary benefits".

Now, as I believe that I have intimated at various points during this narrative, Malcky was Caledonian in origin, and so where his recently acquired Mockney accent came from, neither I, Danny, or anyone else can fathom out, and it doesn't really matter. Possibly he had seen one too many Guy Ritchie movies (but as I haven't seen *any*, I cannot really comment).

Anyway, back in the orgy room (and again I am sure there is probably a correct technical term for such a place, but I cannot be bothered to search the Internet or even my battered copy of Suetonius [*] to find out what it is, and it really isn't relevant) mine host Victor Ludorum was emulating a truffle hound, upon the writhing bodies of the trussed floorshow, whilst his guests - by now almost all completely disrobed - wriggled together disgustingly, and Malcky, naked except for his peculiar feather headdress capered around the room cackling wildly about cannibalism, and taking his pleasure intermittently and indiscriminately from the carnal smorgasbord laid out before him. Having made sure that his presence would not be missed, Danny had

---

* Gaius Suetonius Tranquillus commonly known as Suetonius (c. 69 – after 122 AD), was a Roman historian belonging to the equestrian order who wrote during the early Imperial era of the Roman Empire. His most important surviving work is a set of biographies of twelve successive Roman rulers, from Julius Caesar to Domitian, entitled De Vita Caesarum, and it includes some stomach-churning stuff to which I am not going to refer in these pages, although I am amazed (with hindsight) that I was given a copy to read aged 12 by the Latin teacher referred to occasionally in this narrative.

made his way down the corridor to the reception room in which the assembled company had been served cocktails only an hour or so previously.

Apart from the revolting state of affairs in the orgy room, the house was as still as the proverbial millpond, and Danny made his way from room to room, looking for Mr Ludorum's *sanctum sanctorum* [*]. And eventually, in a small room off the kitchen, which had probably once been the Butler's Pantry [**], he found it. He had expected to find a safe of some description, and his plans had not gone any further than that, but he needn't have worried. On the desk was a tin cashbox full of banknotes, and it wasn't even locked.

Not unsurprisingly, even though the things that were going on elsewhere in the house weren't actually *illegal,* they were not the sort of thing that anybody was likely to want to admit to. And as the dinner guests were all drawn from the upper echelons of Northern Cornwall society, it was reasonable to expect that they were loath to leave a paper trail. And as all the guests had paid in cash Danny was able to pocket something in the region of fifteen grand. But then he had another idea.

When the guests had arrived, he had seen the bored looking Butler and Housemaid take possession of their coats and bags, and from that he surmised that there was probably a cloakroom of some description somewhere on the ground floor of the house. Indeed there was, and it was a matter of no more than ten minutes to go through the pockets and bags he found there, divesting them of all the cash, credit cards, cocaine and other things beginning with c that he found there.

On describing this he flashed me an apologetic grin and offered me some of the aforementioned Bolivian Marching Powder. I declined politely. Not only was the sun still not by anybody's terms of reference over the yardarm, but I have never liked cocaine in any shape or form, and found that all it did for me was give me a headache and a self-opinionated bad temper, which is something that I can have at the best of times without the need for chemical intervention.

Danny continued his narrative, and described how - vintage revolver in hand - he

---

[*] The Latin phrase *sanctum sanctorum* is a translation of the Hebrew term Qŏḏeš HaQŏḏāšîm (Holy of Holies) which generally refers in Latin texts to the holiest place of the Tabernacle of the Israelites and later the Temples in Jerusalem, but also has some derivative use in application to imitations of the Tabernacle in church architecture.

[**] A butler's pantry or serving pantry is a utility room in a large house, primarily used to store serving items, rather than food. Traditionally, a butler's pantry was used for cleaning, counting, and storage of silver; European butlers often slept in the pantry, as their job was to keep the silver under lock and key. The merchant's account books and wine log may also have been kept in there. The room would be used by the butler and other domestic staff; it is often called a butler's pantry even in households where there is no butler.

stealthily began to explore the rest of the house to see if there was anything else worth nicking. It was while he did so that he began to have what I can only describe as his 'Road to Damascus' moment. The house was full of the sort of vulgar opulence to which he had always aspired, but once he saw it all laid out before him like the riches of the Cities of the Plain * , he found it all rather disgusting, and decided then and there that he was not going to carry out the rest of his plan, and return to the big house near Tamar Lakes with his booty, and share it all with his unpleasant landlords.

He didn't know exactly *what* he was going to do next, but he knew that he wasn't going to do *that*.

So he made his way stealthily down the great staircase, which he described as being far too ornate even for a house the size of Chez Ludorum (I discovered later, that it had originally been part of the set of an ITV costume drama, and had been bought by Victor in order to posh up his already vulgarly opulent dwelling). Just as he found himself at the bottom of the stairs, he heard a sudden and unexpected noise, and he ran back into the cloakroom that he had divested of all its valuables about twenty minutes before. Luckily for Danny, the coats had been hung one one of the freestanding coatrails that one can find in charity shops, and that I used back in the day when on tour with *Steve Harley and Cockney Rebel* to flog tour t shirts.

Danny is considerably shorter and wirier than I am, which - on this occasion at least - proved to be a good thing, as he flung himself behind the coatrack, and found a very effective hiding place from which he had a perfect vantage point to see what happened next.

"And you are not gonna fucking believe this", he said. "In marched four or five naked girls. None of them looked over the age of eighteen. They were smeared in mud, and had swastikas painted on their faces, and they were all brandishing meat cleavers".

"And they were chanting something that I couldn't quite catch.."

* Sodom and Gomorrah were cities mentioned in the Book of Genesis and throughout the Hebrew Bible, the New Testament, and in the deuterocanonical books, as well as in the Quran and the hadith. According to the Torah, the kingdoms of Sodom and Gomorrah were allied with the cities of Admah, Zeboim, and Bela. These five cities, also known as the "cities of the plain" (from Genesis in the Authorized Version), were situated on the Jordan River plain in the southern region of the land of Canaan.

Divine judgment by God was passed upon Sodom and Gomorrah and two neighboring cities, which were completely consumed by fire and brimstone. Neighboring Zoar (Bela) was the only city to be spared. In Abrahamic religions, Sodom and Gomorrah have become synonymous with impenitent sin, and their fall with a proverbial manifestation of divine retribution.[Jude 1:7] Sodom and Gomorrah have been used historically and today as metaphors for vice and homosexuality, although a close reading of the text and other Ancient Near Eastern sources suggest that this association may be incorrect.

I looked straight in his eyes. "Was it something like '*Io io Bromios, Lo Lo Dendrites, Eleutherios, Enorches, Bacchus.*'?" I asked with a sinking feeling in my stomach.

He nodded.

"Fucking hell" I said.

And Danny looked back at me in astonishment.

LVIX

Danny looked at me with a startled, rabbit in the headlight, expression on his pockmarked and unusually ashen face.

"What the fuck are you talking about?" he gasped in astonishment. "Don't tell me that you know those girls? Who the fuck are they?"

"I don't exactly *know* them", I muttered. "I don't know exactly *what* they are, but I know more about them than I would like to.."

I didn't mean to be enigmatic, but despite his apparent *volte face,* I trusted Danny just about as far as I could throw him, and had no intention of sharing any more information with him than I had to do.

Danny has always hated it when I am enigmatic. In fact, I have always hated it when I am enigmatic, and have frequently wanted to punch other people when they do it. But as you know from reading this narrative so far, there wasn't much I could tell him, so I promised that I would share what little information I had with him, but in the meantime I implored him…

TO FINISH HIS FUCKING STORY

So reluctantly, he did.

Luckily for Danny the girls marched right past where he had been hiding, and disappeared down the corridor towards the orgy room, and Danny grabbed the money, and stealthily crept towards the front door and freedom.

---

* Very badly translated as "Loud God, Tree God! The Liberator, The Dancer, The Frenzy Inducer!" https://foolsthatmenadore.wordpress.com/2014/09/03/lolo-bromios/

For reasons that remain obscure, but which probably made some sort of sense at the time that Malcky was planning his big heist, Danny had left his car in a pub carpark at the other end of the town. He understandably wanted to put as much distance as he could between him, and Victor's house, and so was at a loss as to what to do next.

Then he heard screaming coming from inside the house.

Despite the fact that my late Father always treated me as if I was some sort of teenage tearaway, in the mould of Johnny Strabler *, I was truly nothing of the sort, and I never got up to the sort of teenage shenanigans that so many of my peers did. Unlike me, however, Danny Miles *did* know how to hotwire a car (something involving connecting the two wires which complete the circuit when the key is in the "on" position (turning on the fuel pump and other necessary components), then touching the wire that connects to the starter) and he used a plantpot to break the window of Victor's Daimler, and within a couple of minutes was in the driver's seat and away down the drive.

The screaming continued.

Rather than drive straight to his own car, Danny decided to take a circuitous route in order to lay a false trail for anybody in pursuit. So he drove down the drive in a reckless manner and got the fuck out of there.

As Danny pointed out, once upon a time, it would have been no problem to collect his own vehicle and (to use his own charming, though oddly poetic, expression) fuck off into the night.

But we live in a digital age, and surveillance cameras are everywhere. And although I am sure that there are not as many surveillance cameras along the main drag of Kilkhampton, as there would be - for example - in London, Manchester, or some other seething metropolis, I am equally certain (as was Danny) that there would be enough bits of digital security equipment scattered around the aforementioned main drag of Kilk, to make it difficult to do what he needed to do.

Add to that the fact that Victor's car was undoubtedly stolen, was one of the more recognisable vehicles in the little town, and that the terrified screams that he had heard coming forth from the house, whilst Danny was in the process of hotwiring the

---

* *The Wild One* is a 1953 American film directed by László Benedek and produced by Stanley Kramer. It is most noted for the character of Johnny Strabler (Marlon Brando), whose persona became a cultural icon of the 1950s. The Wild One is considered to be the original outlaw biker film, and the first to examine American outlaw motorcycle gang violence.

Daimler, made it appear not unlikely that the good potwallopers * of Kilkhampton, (and their trusty plods) would be faced with the aftermath of a Cielo Drivesque massacre ** once they had finished their breakfast, and the news had spread across this usually sleepy backwater of north Cornwall.

So what the fuck was he gonna do?

For a moment he was beginning to wish that he hadn't stolen such an ostentatious vehicle. But Danny was an ostentatious sort of cove, and furthermore he was suffering from an unusually kind impulse, and wanted to give Malcky and Trace a chance to escape in their own car in the (admittedly unlikely) scenario that they would be able to escape the carnage which was presumably taking place inside Victor's mansion.

As I have intimated on many occasions during the course of this narrative (and other things that I have written about him over the years) Danny Miles is not unintelligent, but above all he has a sort of low cunning that mere mortals like I shall never achieve. For example, even if I had ever been in the position of stealing somebody else's car and hightailing it away from a crime scene where acts of violence were presumably taking place against a coterie of upper middle class perverts, and assorted low lives (something that I have never done, and feel certain that I shall never do) I would never have thought of doing it as efficiently as Danny. He drove to the house where he had been living with Malcky and his unlovely spouse by a circuitous route. When he got there, he quickly gathered up all of his property, bunging it into the boot of the stolen Daimler. He then went through the house, snaffling up all of his host's money reserves (another couple of grand) and their firearms (another service revolver and a pump action shotgun) and drove away.

But did he drive back to Kilkhampton to collect his car?

Nope.

---

* A potwalloper (sometimes potwalloner or potwaller) or householder borough was a parliamentary borough in which the franchise was extended to the male head of any household with a hearth large enough to boil a cauldron (or "wallop a pot"). Potwallopers existed in the Unreformed House of Commons prior to the Reform Act 1832, and in its predecessors the Irish House of Commons and House of Commons of Great Britain (until 1800) and the House of Commons of England (to 1707). The potwalloper was one of the widest variants of the borough franchise and the tendency over the centuries was for the franchise to be limited, reducing the number of electors.

** 10050 Cielo Drive is the street address of a former luxury home in Benedict Canyon, a part of Beverly Crest, north of Beverly Hills, California, where the Charles Manson "family" committed the Tate murders in 1969. The residence had been occupied by various famous Hollywood and music industry figures. In 1994, the house was demolished, a new house was constructed on the site and the street address was changed to 10066 Cielo Drive.

By this time it was well past two in the morning, and he was feeling weary after a long, and emotionally wearing, day. He drove back to the A39, and up towards the Devon border, and after a few miles he took a small side road that led into the deep forestry plantations around Meddon. He then found a convenient layby (actually the partitioned off entry to a disused ride in the forest, parked up and went to sleep).

LVX

He slept until Noon, which is something that I assume is quite easy to do in a Daimler, as I once owned a Jaguar XJ6, and on a CFZ expedition to a monster-haunted lake in the North of England, slept in her for a week, and have seldom had such a luxuriantly comfortable night [*]. Deciding that discretion was the better part of valour, he then walked the mile or so back to the A39 and hitched a lift into Kilkhampton, where he collected his own car, and drove back to the layby deep in the woods where he transferred his belongings to his own car, and made a brief telephone call to an unlisted number.

Within twenty minutes a saturnine looking bloke who had once been called Jeremy, and to whom I had given the unlovely soubriquet of 'Skullfuck' when stoned many years before, arrived on the scene. As he was dressed in the traditional biker garb of greasy jeans and black leather, it would be easy for my to write something about how the roar of a high powered motorbike came slowly up through the misty woodlands. Or something like that. But the sinister looking bikerdude actually rode up on a rusty old pushbike, which he summarily picked up and shoved into the boot of Danny's car, after a bit of rearranging had taken place. He then took his place behind the wheel of the Daimler, and drove deeper into the woods, with Danny driving a few yards behind.

Once upon a time during the 1970s when the highest rate of income tax was something astronomical like 92% the job of a pop star was little more than sitting around taking drugs and having far more sex than most people, and then writing songs about it. At that time real estate prices in the Westcountry were relatively low compared with the rest of the country, and as a result various members of the rock and roll *nouveau riche* were enticed into investing into various more or less pie in the sky projects in the region.

In the late 1980s Roger Waters, once of *Pink Floyd* was a guest on an Australian

---

* Blah blah blah not being a breadhead blah, see my book *The Monster of the Mere* (2002)

radio show, and explained how Floyd had - a decade or so before - been involved with:

> "...a company called Norton Warburg, run by a guy called Andrew Warburg. The idea was to take gross income and run it through a finance company to protect it from the immediate payment of tax on the grounds that it was being used to finance venture capital situation. It was all legal. But what Norton Warburg did was to move money from account to account and take huge management fees each time they moved it. We were going bankrupt. We lost a couple of million quid - nearly everything we'd made from *Dark Side Of The Moon*. Then we discovered the Inland Revenue might come and ask for us 83 per cent of the money we had lost. Which we didn't have. So we had gone from fourteen-years-olds with ten quid guitars and fantasies of being rich and famous, and made the dream come true with *Dark Side Of The Moon*, and then, being greedy and trying to protect it, we'd lost it all. So on those grounds we decided to go abroad to make the next record, *The Wall*, and try and get some cash to pay this potential tax bill."

One of Norton/Warburg's investments was a newly built hotel called 'Moorhead' just outside the village where I lived at the time (and still live now). As far as I am aware, the band only visited the hotel once, and much to my chagrin, it was a year or so before I got my first holiday job there during the summer of 1976. What I *do know*, is that another well known rock band for whom I worked a decade or so later, and with whom I am still on nodding terms, so I shall have to keep schtum about their identity were socially friendly with several members of *Pink Floyd*, and their management were very impressed with the ideas of Norton/Warburg and persuaded their clients to buy a five acre plot of land in the middle of the pine forests that straddle the North Devon/North Cornwall border, and which have been the prime location for most of this narrative, and its predecessor. They intended to turn it into a trout farm, and dug a number of deep ponds (I am not sure at which point a pond becomes a lake, and don't really care) which they would have stocked with trout had Norton/Warburg not gone into the high profile crisis described above by Roger Waters right in the middle of the operation.

As a result of this, the band's management immediately cancelled the project, and - as there was no great market value in a number of deep holes filled with muddy water, the whole affair was soon forgotten about, and the holes remain there until this very day. But as the semi-unofficial 'Quartermaster' of the peculiar little community that called themselves 'The Children of the Three', and who lived deep in the very same woods, 'Skullfuck' had made it his business to discover as much as he could about these woods as he possibly could. And so, when Danny telephoned him, that early winter morning, asking whether he could help Danny dispose of an opulent Daimler which was likely to have the police of two counties on its trail before the day was out, 'Skullfuck' remembered the abortive trout farm, and it was to it, that the solemn little convoy of two drove.

Once they were there it was a matter of minutes to dispose of the evidence. I have never done so, nor do I think that it is likely that I ever shall, but Danny informs me that sinking a stolen Daimler into the muddy depths of a derelict trout pool in the middle of a forest was actually a matter of only a few minutes work, whereupon the two men got back into Danny's car and drove off.

LVXI

*I*n the couple of years that had transpired between Danny's first visit to the redoubt in the deep woods, and his visit subsequent to the ignominious dumping of Victor's Daimler, the security measures had been relaxed slightly. Danny was no longer dumped in the boot of his car (which - considering that on this occasion the aforementioned boot was crammed full of those of his worldly goods that had been salvaged from the house by Tamar Lakes - was probably quite convenient for Danny. However, Skullfuck (and despite the fact that I am guilty of having bestowed his unlovely *nom de guerre* upon him, I always think of him as 'Jeremy') was sat behind the wheel of Danny's car, and Danny was in the passenger seat with a black hood over his head.

Here I should probably point out that the 'black hood' which sounds so sinister, with cultural connotations of falconry, executioners, or at the very least one of the nastier end of S&M roleplayers, was actually a pillowcase that Danny had brought with him for the purpose. As he said to me, he had been going to the redoubt in the woods for a couple of years by this time, and he could *probably* have worked out the route had he tried hard enough' but what would have been the point? He and the 'Children of the Three' were ostensibly at least on the same side, and he could go there at any time he wanted just by phoning Jeremy.

The Children of the Three were still scary as hell, and he saw nothing to be gained in provoking their wrath, so he was quite content to play it by their rules.

Once they had arrived at their destination, he was allowed to take his makeshift hood off, and he saw that things were slightly different this time around. For all the world, rather than looking like a makeshift camping area at a delightfully hippy rock festival, it was looking more like a WW2 airdrome in an old war movie, except *sans* the aeroplanes. There were a number of neat little prefabricated wooden huts, in a neat open ended square. Each of the huts had a big black sign positioned outside the door, but instead of saying '233 Squadron' or 'Quartermaster's Stores', each of the signs was emblazoned with an arcane symbol that was totally unfamiliar to Danny.

In the middle of the open ended square, in what would notionally have been the parade ground was a huge depiction of a symbol that Danny *did* recognise: a pentacle, laid out in large whitewashed stones. As a child in Hong Kong I visited enough small military or police encampments in different parts of the New Territories, that this was all very familiar sounding to me. Danny may have interpreted it by utilising the 1969 Harry Saltzman movie *The Battle of Britain* as his cultural reference points, but I saw it as a surprisingly faithful analogue to one of the smaller outposts of Empire back in the days when the Empire was committing ritualised seppuku [*].

Something had obviously changed in the couple of months since Danny had been there last. And Danny was shocked by the changes. There was a new sense of order and purpose, and the whole place felt uncomfortably militarised. But the most unsettling facet of this new order was that not everybody he saw marching purposefully about the place even *pretended* to be human.

From his first visit to the redoubt, when he had met Mr Loxodonta, the elephant headed, wheelchair bound leader of this disparate and unsettling little tribe, and Panne, the hairy, goat-footed, naked, hornéd little forest godling who had run away from the redoubt and now lived (unknownst to anyone but me and my wife) in the airing cupboard in what used to be my Father's Dressing Room) he had been aware that this group of social refugees were not all runaway kids and their quartermaster outlaw biker, but - somehow - Panne and Loxodonta had made some degree of sense to his synapses, addled after a lifetime of chemical abuse, but what he saw before him now made no sense at all.

The Slender Man (also known as Slenderman) is a fictional supernatural character

---

* Seppuku (切腹, "cutting [the] belly"), sometimes referred to as harakiri (腹切り, "abdomen/belly cutting", a native Japanese kun reading), is a form of Japanese ritual suicide by disembowelment. It was originally reserved for samurai, but was also practiced by other Japanese people later on to restore honor for themselves or for their family. A samurai practice, seppuku was used either voluntarily by samurai to die with honor rather than fall into the hands of their enemies (and likely suffer torture) or as a form of capital punishment for samurai who had committed serious offenses, or performed because they had brought shame to themselves. The ceremonial disembowelment, which is usually part of a more elaborate ritual and performed in front of spectators, consists of plunging a short blade, traditionally a tantō, into the abdomen and drawing the blade from left to right, slicing the abdomen open.

If the cut is performed deeply enough it can sever the descending aorta, causing massive blood loss inside the abdomen, which results in a rapid death by exsanguination.

originally created by Something Awful forums user Eric Knudsen (also known as "Victor Surge") in 2009. It is depicted as resembling a thin, unnaturally tall man with a blank and usually featureless face, wearing a black suit. Stories of the Slender Man commonly feature him stalking, abducting or traumatising people, particularly children. Beginning in 2014, a minor moral panic occurred over the Slender Man after readers of his fiction were connected to several violent acts, particularly a near-fatal stabbing of a 12-year-old girl in Waukesha, Wisconsin. But one thing that everybody over the age of fifteen (and most people under that age) agreed on, was that the Slender Man is a fictional character. Why then was he sitting in a deckchair outside one of the neat little hunts, smoking a cigarette and reading *Leave it to Psmith?* *

But the appearance of this fictional character was not the only thing that Danny had to come to terms with. Because wandering, apparently randomly around the campsite were about half a dozen tall, bulky, humanoid figures about half as high again as Danny or Skullfuck (which would make them eight or nine feet tall). And they appeared to be made of greasy black smoke, because he could almost see through them, as they were something just short of being transparent.

The path that led deep into the woods was now a quite well ordered little road cutting a severe and starched swathe through the trees, and from that direction he could hear a peculiar coughing, rasping, grunting sound which seemed familiar but which he couldn't place.

I had a pretty good idea what it was, but - rather than interrupt Danny in mid-flow - I decided to keep my own council for a while. Danny continued: "and standing motionless next to the furthest hut was that stupid bird headed man you have in the garden, only this one was alive and not made from a shop dummy and a Hallowe'en mask from eBay".

Ummm. Why I have a six foot model of surrealist artist Max Ernst's bird headed alter ego Loplop in my garden is a totally different story which would probably take *une semaine de bonte* to relate *.

---

* *Leave it to Psmith* is a comic novel by English author P. G. Wodehouse, first published in the United Kingdom on 30 November 1923 by Herbert Jenkins, London, England and in the United States on 14 March 1924 by George H. Doran, New York. It had previously been serialised, in the *Saturday Evening Post* in the US between 3 February and 24 March 1923, and in the *Grand Magazine* in the UK between April and December that year; the ending of this magazine version was rewritten for the book form. It was the fourth and final novel featuring Psmith, the others being *Mike* (1909) (later republished in two parts, with Psmith appearing in the second, *Mike and Psmith* (1953)), *Psmith in the City* (1910), and *Psmith, Journalist* (1915) – in his introduction to the omnibus *The World of Psmith*, Wodehouse said that he had stopped writing about the character because he couldn't think of any more stories.

It was also the second novel set at Blandings Castle, the first being *Something Fresh* (1915). The Blandings saga would be continued in many more novels and shorts.

"What are all these things?" Danny hissed at Jeremy. There was no reply. Danny tried again. "What the fuck is happening here?" He hissed again. The tired, pockmarked middle-aged biker whom I had known a lifetime away, gave a sad smile.

"They are raising and cultivating trolls", he muttered.

"Eh?" Said Danny.

LVXII

Being a diabetic, when I feel the need to answer a call of nature, I have to go fast. And as a cripple I cannot go fast, so I made my excuses and left Danny for a few minutes. So I waddled off upstairs, and as I did so, my mind was working overtime.

What is a troll? And how are we to interpret this new claim that the redoubt in the deep woods was engaged in "raising and cultivating trolls"?

Without taking too much mental energy about it, I can think of three different meanings for the word 'troll'. The first of these is only relevant to those of us of a certain age who remember when little girls had collections of little troll dolls with furry up-combed hair. These were also known as a Dam doll after their creator Danish woodcutter Thomas Dam, and gonk trolls in the United Kingdom. The dolls were originally created in 1959 and became one of the United States' biggest toy fads in the early 1960s. They became fads again in brief periods from the 1970s through the 1990s and were copied by several manufacturers under different names. Most recently they were re-launched as Trollz and failed magnificently.

Apart from the fact that they had always irritated me, it seems highly unlikely that these eminently tacky tween toys had anything to do with the sinister machinations going on in the deep woods.

So we move on to the second option. Over to those jolly nice fellows at Wikipedia:
> "A troll is a class of being in Norse mythology and Scandinavian folklore. In Old Norse sources, beings described as trolls dwell in isolated rocks, mountains, or

---

* Loplop is the name of a birdlike character featured in prints, collages and paintings by artist Max Ernst. Loplop was an alter ego which Ernst developed and functioned as a familiar animal.

Loplop first appeared in Ernst's collage novels La Femme 100 Têtes and Une Semaine de Bonté in the role of a narrator and commentator.

caves, live together in small family units, and are rarely helpful to human beings. Later, in Scandinavian folklore, trolls became beings in their own right, where they live far from human habitation, are not Christianized, and are considered dangerous to human beings. Depending on the source, their appearance varies greatly; trolls may be ugly and slow-witted, or look and behave exactly like human beings, with no particularly grotesque characteristic about them."

Like most children of my generation, I first heard the term used for the supernatural entities which lived under a bridge and did their best to terrorise the three Billy Goats Gruff. [*] I assume that today's children are likely to have first been introduced to the concept of trolldom by the first of the Harry Potter books and the subsequent movie.

However, as I grew to man's estate and started to make a living writing about things wot go bump in the night, I realised that these were not just storybook creatures, but peculiar paranormal entities which are still reported on occasion by those living in the far north of Europe. The more fundamentalist cryptozoologists ("there is no god but Heuvelmans and Coleman is his prophet") even attest that trolls are a bigfoot or yeti type creature that can reach enormous sizes, and whilst I am not prepared to nail my colours to that particular mast, there seems little doubt, that occasionally people in the wilder parts of Scandinavia *do* still encounter trolls, whatever the fuck they may actually be.

I was only too aware that there were entities living in those deep woods which would normally be found nowhere outside the pages of storybooks. I had a fugitive little forest godling living in my airing cupboard as living proof of that. But could there be trills there as well? Could the amorphous giants that appeared to be made from animate greasy black smoke be trolls? They were unlike any other troll about which I had ever heard, but then again I was no expert. In fact, that's wrong. Apart from my mate Lars in Copenhagen, or my mate Richard in Exeter, I am most probably the best expert on the matter anyone was likely to find. But are they trolls? Fuck alone knows.

And then the was the third definition.

For those of you who are not aware of Internet Trolls, I am pinching a short description from those jolly nice people at Wikipedia:

---

[*] "Three Billy Goats Gruff" (Norwegian: De tre bukkene Bruse) is a Norwegian fairy tale. The fairy tale was collected by Peter Christen Asbjørnsen and Jørgen Moe in their Norske Folkeeventyr, first published between 1841 and 1844. It has an "eat-me-when-I'm-fatter" plot (Aarne-Thompson type 122E). The first version of the story in English appeared in George Webbe Dasent's translation of some of the Norske Folkeeventyr, published as Popular Tales from the Norse in 1859.

"In Internet slang, a troll (/ˈtroʊl/, /ˈtrɒl/) is a person who sows discord on the Internet by starting arguments or upsetting people, by posting inflammatory, extraneous, or off-topic messages in an online community (such as a newsgroup, forum, chat room, or blog) with the intent of provoking readers into an emotional response or of otherwise disrupting normal, on-topic discussion, often for the troll's amusement.

This sense of both the noun and the verb "troll" is associated with Internet discourse, but also has been used more widely. Media attention in recent years has equated trolling with online harassment. For example, the mass media have used "troll" to mean "a person who defaces Internet tribute sites with the aim of causing grief to families." In addition, depictions of trolling have been included in popular fictional works, such as the HBO television program The Newsroom, in which a main character encounters harassing persons online and tries to infiltrate their circles by posting negative sexual comments."

After reading several books on the phenomenon I realise that the above description is a bit like describing Nazis as a bunch of people who "didn't like the Jews very much".

I had problems with being trolled about seven years ago: I am sure, but I cannot prove, that it was a business associate of someone with whom we had had unsatisfactory business dealings, who set up a blog accusing me and my organisation of the most appalling crimes and transgressions in a calculated attempt to destroy my career. The clever thing about what he did was that many of his allegations were almost true, and that the inferences drawn were very far from what was actually the truth.

The effect on me personally was unbelievable. It catapulted my already fragile psyche into places that it had never been before, and I truly hope will never be again. The fact that someone had that much HATE for me upset me deeply, and I don't think that I have ever completely recovered.

The fact that, as I said earlier in this narrative, someone - presumably a band of maenads - had bound his hands, squirted ammonia in his face, and shot him in the back of the head with a crossbow, actually didn't comfort me as much as one would have thought.

But what happened to me is as nothing compared to how some people have suffered at the hands of trolls. Oisin Sweeney's book *Hackers on Steroids* is full of true (or at least I have no reason to suppose that they are not true, and every bit of cross checking that I have done appears to bear the assertions in this book out) accounts of the sadistic activities of 'trolls' who get their jollies by tormenting the families of the recently bereaved. They target Facebook memorial pages for recently dead children, posting sexual slurs and photoshopped images of the deceased.

This book describes, in horrible detail, how one particular Troll - Colm Cross - was responsible for astring of atrocities including:

> "On a page operated by the friends of a 15-year-old girl who was stabbed to death:
>
> Colm Coss This crackwhore is sitting on my cock now in hell. When I have finished with her every other denizen of the place will play with her corpse for all eternity.
>
> On an RIP page operated by the family of a dead four-year-old boy: Colin Upson I ripped his eyeballs out and fucked the bloody dripping sockets. He never saw it coming."

And these were some of the milder comments. The author also describes how faked youtube videos showing the deceased child with swastikas for eyes, and photoshopped into sexual situations were splashed across the internet to general hilarity. I truly cannot bring myself to repeat the worst of these stories.

Then in the middle of the book, just as the reader is beginning to deal with the cavalcade of diabolical filth that has been laid before them, comes a chapter about Child Pornography rings on social media, including Facebook. Again, I knew such things existed, but the utter ubiquity of them horrified me.

I could carry on. But it would upset me too much.

Oisin Sweeney describes why and how he/she (I don't know their gender, and it doesn't really matter) became an Internet Vigilante, why they stopped, and why they believe that no-one else should follow in their footsteps. And they finish the book with this horrifically dystopian passage:

> "It won't end. The names of dead children will continue to be fed into the Internet machine for the sadists and the professional mourners to claim ownership of. The Internet machine will itself continue to help generate dead children for its own self to feed on. Children will die, incidents of trolling will happen, the media will ask some more questions, the PR robots will be turned on in response and the clean corporate machine will continue to glisten as brightly as the smiles

that go along with it. And then as the world turns in its orbit more girls going to meet 'boys' they found online ending up being found dead in fields or in deserts, and all as the workings of the child pornography factory continue to hum away quite silently under the much louder noise of billions of dollars' worth of social networking stock being bought and sold. I was so naïve at one early stage in all of this that I believed that all which had to be done was to get the media to report on RIP trolling and change in social networks would be forced. I was as innocent as a child in that belief. Nothing is really going to change at all, except maybe that it all is just going to get worse and worse. To look into the horribly schizophrenic mind of the Internet is to perceive in the most modern and awe-inspiring of technologies the still-primitive race which built it. Technology is helping to bring the psyche of mankind back closer to the nightmare of the cave rather than awakening us further from it".

I was in a sombre mood as I limped back downstairs. And I was no closer to finding out the truth of the conundrum with which I had been faced before my Islets of Langerhans and bladder had let me down.

To which of these different types of troll had Skullfuck been referring? There was supporting, or at least circumstantial evidence to support both the digital and the paranormal scenarios, but until I talked more to Danny I would no be able to determine which of them it was, or even if it was something else entirely. I was concentrating so hard on this conundrum that I didn't look where I was going. I nearly tripped over one of the cats, and fell arse over tit down the stairs, but luckily, my failing reflexes had not failed quite that much and I managed to right myself.

I was half expecting Danny to have done a runner, but my suspicions were unjustified. When I entered the little office I found Danny sitting there deep in conversation with my mother-in-law who was trying to persuade him to have some breakfast. I realised at this point that I was feeling far more hungry than I should do at this time of the morning, and smiled sweetly at Mama and made noises like a marmalade sandwich.

LVXIII

Now, if it had been me, I would not have been able to keep my inquisitive nature under control, and I would have spent all the rest of the time that I was in the redoubt in the woods, trying to find out the background to Skullfuck's terse comment. But I am not Danny, and Danny is not me. In all the decades that I have known him, I have always been surprised at how little intellectual curiosity he has, and so - I suppose - I should not now be surprised, that he took Skullfuck's brief comment about trolls at face value, dusted himself down, and went off with the tired and battered looking biker in search of breakfast.

The little encampment was far better organised than it had ever been, at least in Danny's experience, and continued to give the impression of a small army camp, redolent of some sort of military discipline and purpose, although there were no clues as to what that purpose actually *was*, and Danny continued nit to actually *ask*.

The two men walked into the woods where Danny was not particularly surprised to find a large green army tent containing a small field kitchen, manned by beautiful girls and serving bacon and eggs. Danny ate his full, whilst Skullfuck talked. He talked mostly about the music that was being produced by a band called *Xtul* which was based in the strange little community, and much to my surprise, and a certain amount of consternation on my behalf, he talked about me.

He admitted that the shadowy organisation had misplayed their hand quite considerably as far as I was concerned, and that burglarising my house and threatening my friends and colleagues with violence was no way to get anything out of me. "I've known Jon a long time" Skullfuck admitted, and continued," he is a stubborn old bastard, and doesn't like to be pissed around".

This came as an enormous surprise to Danny. It was the first time that he had head even an inkling of an idea that Skullfuck and I knew each other. I had been careful to keep my own counsel, and even though I had been pretty sure that Skullfuck was the young biker lad whom I knew from back when I was a student, I had decided that it would be a sensible idea to keep that information firmly under my conceptual hat.

Danny looked at me accusingly. "You never told me that you knew that bloody man", he whined.

"You never asked", I said. And in a spirit of reconciliation I explained how back when I was a student, I lived in a house called Staplake in Starcross, and drank in a boozer called *The Dolphin* in Kenton. And how I had been friendly with a bunch of lowlives who drank there, including a young man called Jeremy whom I had named 'Skullfuck' after a *Grateful Dead* album. You already know this, if you have been following the saga of mine and Danny's involvement with 'The Children of the Three' from the beginning. But it was Danny's first inkling of all of this, and I think that it shook him.

"So when did you last see him?" He asked accusingly, and I told him how, in the last year or so of my student years I had met and fallen in love with a girl called Alison.

How, in the year or so before we got married I curtailed my drinking and drugging and stopped hanging out with the lowlives in the bar, but how one evening - when we were sitting in the TV lounge at Staplake drinking tea, and I was doing my best not to want a pint or six, I was completely taken aback to see Skullfuck shambling into the room, hand in hand with one of the younger, prettier, and more airheaded girls who also lived in the huge Edwardian house. It transpired that I was not the only one of the Kenton lowlives to have been seduced by the trappings of respectable society.

"Hey Skullf...umm Jeremy" I said with more enthusiasm than I felt. "What brings you here?"

That was a spectacularly stupid question, as it was perfectly obvious what had brought him here. He had somehow become ensnared by an eighteen year old siren called Cynthia Prosser who had reached new heights of vacuousness even for girls of my experience back then, and who - if I have to be honest - always reminded me of P G Wodehouse's creation, Madeleine Bassett. (Bizarrely, it is only whilst sitting here frantically typing this in order to meet a self-imposed deadline, that I realise that 'Cynthia Prosser' is actually quite a Wodehousian name).

For those of you who are not intimate with the Wodehouse canon, and shame on you, Bertie Wooster describes her as "a pretty enough girl in a droopy, blonde, saucer-eyed way, but not the sort of breath-taker that takes the breath", though elsewhere he describes her as "physically in the pin-up class", with blonde hair, attractive curves, and "all the fixings". These charms must be considered in balance with her personality, which is that of "the soppiest, mushiest, most childish and whimsical, sentimentalest young gawd-help-us that ever was". For example, she remarks in casual conversation, on different occasions, that she believes that "every time a fairy sheds a tear, a new star appears in the Milky Way", and that "the stars are God's daisy chain" (Bertie muses to himself that these two comments, besides being inane drivel, are mutually contradictory; "I mean, you can't have it both ways").

Such comments would be in keeping with her general conversational style, which is all too apt to revolve around elves, gnomes, flowers, and small furry animals. This excessive soppiness is wedded to an impressive degree of self-centred idealism which she tries to impose on others, for instance by insisting that one of her fiances take up vegetarianism.

Cynthia had not quite reached those levels of inanity, but was certainly have been described by Bertram Wooster as being well within the "sentamentalist gawd-help-us" category of young womanhood, and here she was hand in hand with a relatively hard headed young biker, clad head to foot in greasy leather, with shoulder length locks somewhat in need of shampoo, and whom I guessed that I was not going to be able to refer to as 'Skullfuck' for the foreseeable future.

LVXIV

I had more than a few misgivings about this new development. To start off with, over the previous year or so I had gone through a number of mildly sordid chemical and alchemical adventures of which young Skullfuck had been a part.

On a personal level I wasn't even slightly ashamed of any of them, but I had decided from the start that the less that my new fiancée knew about my druggy adventures of the recent past the better. For when I had made the pledge to settle down to married bliss in suburbia, I had also made a pledge to myself to leave drugs and wanton promiscuity behind for good.

The wanton promiscuity stayed in limbo for the duration of my twelve year relationship with Alison, although my drugless state lasted only about four years, ending when - at a Record Fair in Taunton in 1988 - my mate Paul from Bristol passed me a spliff, and I took a big toke on it without thinking, and looked around guiltily to see Alison laughing at me.

But back to Staplake four years earlier. I was not only afraid that my sordid past would come back to bite me on the bum, but I was also concerned for young Skullfuck.

Because, apart from his unfortunate soubriquet which was, after all, nearly completely down to me, he was an oddly sweet young fellow, and surprisingly innocent of the ways of the world, and particularly of the machinations of mad chicks.

His family were surprisingly wealthy and influential tenant farmers, who had farmed their particular portion of the Powderham Estate of the Earls of Devon for centuries, and they were (and always had been) stalwarts of the Parish Council, the PCC and all the other things that families of that sort had always been, and will probably always do.

As someone who had come from a comparable background myself, I could understand the layers of what is now called "shaming" that must have been ladled down upon the poor young biker from his family, who were appalled that instead of wearing tweeds and a flat cap, their son was now dressed head to foot in leather, had long and greasy hair, and sported various tattoos including one of an image that

Stanley Mouse * had nicked from an old edition of the Rubaiyat of Omar Khayyam ** (which a downy old bird *** once told Beetle **** was 'a poem not yet come into its own'.

Now, a brief sidestep. I hope that the reader will forgive me when I pepper this narrative with literary allusions. I am not showing off, although I am quite aware that it might seem like it at times. But this whole story is broadly about magick high and low, and geomancy often in particular. As I get older I realise more and more that words have a high magickal power of their own, and as the written language is one of the greatest inventions of the human race, word magick may actually be one of the most important facets of the esoteric crafts. J K Rowling wrote about something that she called legilimency, but I cannot determine whether that has any real substance outside the world of Harry Potter. But there is a Japanese discipline about which I have been finding out more and more in recent years. Kotodama or kototama (言霊?, lit. "word spirit/soul") refers to the Japanese belief that mystical powers dwell in words and names. English translations include "soul of language", "spirit of language", "power of language", "power word", "magic word", and "sacred sound". The notion of kotodama presupposes that sounds can magically affect objects, and that ritual word usages can influence our environment, body, mind, and soul.

So, as the *genius loci* of Rudyard Kipling is magickally deployed across North Devon, and as the visual representation of his mentor's favourite poetry is now irresistibly linked with the magickal culture of the 'Children of the Three' (albeit because of a bit of stoned japery by yours truly back when he was a student) it should, I think, be noted upon.

So, before I end this slight literary anabasis, let me reiterate.

1. I am not being pretentious (not much, anyway)

---

* Stanley George Miller (born October 10, 1940), better known as Mouse and Stanley Mouse, is an American artist, notable for his 1960s psychedelic rock concert poster designs for the Grateful Dead and Journey albums cover art as well as many others.

** Rubáiyát of Omar Khayyám is the title that Edward FitzGerald gave to his 1859 translation from Farsi to English of a selection of quatrains (rubāīyāt) attributed to Omar Khayyam (1048–1131), dubbed "the Astronomer-Poet of Persia".

*** A fictionalised version of Cornell Price

**** Rudyard Kipling

EDITOR'S NOTE: Am I being deliberately obtuse here? Yes, probably.

3. I believe in all sorts of weird things that most people don't
4. Whether I am barking mad or not is basically irrelevant
5. All of the above

Back to the story.

Young Skullfuck may have looked like one of the four Bikemen of th' Apocawassname but he was at heart an upper middle class farmer's son, and so - when it came to searching for a mate - his target group were basically not going to be sexy biker chicks from the Planet Freakout.

Nope, he went after a dull girl just like the one that had married dear old Dad.

The difference was, however, that the dull young lady who had married his dear old Dad was not as big a bundle of neuroses and delusions as Cynthia (who went under the nom de guerre of 'Cindy' would turn out to be.

By this time in my nurse training I was only too aware that I was stuck on a career path that I didn't want to do, alongside a bunch of people that I mostly didn't want to be with, who had aspirations that I neither cared or wanted to care about, and who disliked me nearly as much as I was disinterested in them.

There were, of course, some of my fellow students of whom I was very fond, and I am still friends with them to a greater or lesser degree three and a half decades later. And one of them was a young man a year or two younger than me, who was both interested in and involved with the promotion of the burgeoning indie music scene.

It was he who first told me about the music of *The Smiths* for example, (and I will admit shamefacedly that I thought they were complete bollocks then, and until about seven years ago) and several other jangly guitar indiemeisters. I last saw him in about 1991 at a gig by *Carter the Unstoppable Sex Machine* at Exeter University, and like me he had grown his hair and left the dust of the Royal Western Counties a long way behind him (although, I suspect, that like me, the scars would be with him for ever).

Like me, he had also left nursing under a cloud, but the cloud that he had left under was called Cindy Prosser.

LVXV

N ow, I hope that you will forgive me here, but although it would be hyperbole to describe myself as an old man, I am definitely ageing at a rate for which I was totally unprepared! And my memory is failing at an alarming rate. The events which I am describing took place over thirty years ago, and *Anno Domini* exacerbated by years of alcohol abuse have taken their toll upon my poor beleaguered synapses. And the truth is that after all this time I am not 100% sure of my facts. But the gist of the story is that Cindy took a shine to my friend the indie kid, and followed him around with a soppy look on her face, a bit like that worn by an ailing sheep.

It was peculiar, I remember thinking then, that I had seen no end of my male friends and colleagues suffering from sick sheep syndrome, as they obsessed over an unattainable female. Hell, I had even done it myself on many occasions.

If I may quote the divine Neil Hannon:

> *"Out or in - this is not a sin, it's not even original*
> *and hey we're all individuals - so let the games begin*
> *I fall in love with someone new practically every day but that's okay*
> *It's just the price I pay for being a man (if that's really what I am)*
> *And I refuse to take it all too seriously*
> *It's such a strange activity far too peculiar to be taken any other way"* [*]

But this was, I think, the first - and probably the only - time I had seen a reasonably attractive young woman, mooning about the place, making unrequited sheep's eyes at a member of the male gender. Or at least doing it in such a blatantly 'teenage boy' manner. Of course I have seen members of the fairer sex sad because of unrequited love, but the was something peculiarly masculine about the way she did it. And I am afraid that I do not know how I can describe it any better. There was something peculiarly disturbing about seeing a girl of nineteen behaving like a boy of fifteen, and - with hindsight at least - it was always going to end with something going tits up.

Then, all of a sudden, Cindy was swaggering around the old red brick house in which we all lived, claiming that she had finally "got her man", but it was only a matter of days later, that one of the other residents and I found her curled up in a foetal position on the big black leather sofa in the common room, sobbing her eyes out.

---

[*] *A Short Album About Love* is the fifth album by The Divine Comedy, released in 1997.

Overwhelmed by a flood of compassion, we did our best to comfort her, and she leapt upon me, clutching me like a security blanket, and weeping uncontrollably. Slowly we managed to piece together what had happened.

She told us that she had been visiting my mate the indie kid, and that they had got into some sort of ambiently romantic situation, when my mate suddenly channelled his inner Gilles de Rais [*], and forced her into committing a string of acts with which she was not comfortable. Like Meatloaf she would do anything for love [**], but she wouldn't do that…or that… or THAT!

It has to be said that this all seemed mildly convincing. Despite the fact that Indie Kid was a polite, laid back, and eminently pleasant individual, I think that any young man who has played the field will attest that for a young woman to suddenly change her mind during a romantic encounter was (and I assume still is) far from being unheard of. And that on such occasions the gentlemanly thing to do is to ignore the hormonal demands being made upon one's cerebellum, and retreat or withdraw gracefully.

Well, apparently Indie Kid didn't do anything of the sort, and had continued to press his suit, and had ended up "forcing" her into doing a whole string of things that revolted her. I was as gentlemanly as I could be, and did not ask for details, but merely did my best to comfort the crying girl, who still clung to my shirtfront like a baby three toed sloth does to its mother.

It is testament, I think, to the way that things have changed that, whereas these days one would certainly have telephoned the police straight off, and awaited the arrival of a specialist police officer with training in women's issues and trauma counselling, all we did was hug her and make her a nice cup of tea.

As she calmed down, her vitriolic rants against my mate continued unabated, and - shocked to hear such allegations against someone whom I had always thought of as a harmless sort of cove - I offered to call the police on her behalf.

---

[*] Gilles de Rais (c. September 1405 – 26 October 1440), Baron de Rais was a knight and lord from Brittany, Anjou and Poitou, a leader in the French army, and a companion-in-arms of Joan of Arc. He is best known for his reputation and later conviction as a confessed serial killer of children.

[**] I am not the only fat rock singer in the omniverse…

But I'll never forget the way you feel right now,
Oh no, no way.
And I would do anything for love,
Oh I would do anything for love,
I would do anything for love,
But I won't do that
No I won't do that

Her demeanour suddenly changed. I mean changed in an instant, and she stopped crying and started to gush about how much she loved him, and how - despite his bestial behaviour - she couldn't bear to think of anything nasty happening to him. She then made us promise not to take any further action, and disappeared off into her bedroom. We kept our promise as far as the police were concerned. Even at such a young age I had discovered that getting the constabulary involved was a simple way of making sure everything got far too complicated, and would ensure that matters would get completely out of hand. However, raised on the pulp fiction of an earlier generation which told of the adventures of Hugh Drummond [*] and Simon Templar [**], not to mention Lord Peter W. [***], I resolved to take the matter into my own hands and have a word with the errant indy kid myself.

So, later that day, I got in my battered blue sports car, and drove a few miles down the road towards Exeter, and made my way towards the imposing gothic (and in this context I don't know whether this should have a capital G or not) edifice of Exminster psychiatric hospital.

LVXVI

I have always been rather fond of the architecture of the old red brick asylums that oh so recently peppered the English countryside. For some reason in the vicinity of Exeter, there was Wonford House, Digby Hospital, and Exminster Hospital, all within a few miles of each other. Wonford House - a gothic edifice next to the RD&E hospital in Exeter City is the only one that remains. DIgny has been razed to the ground, and Exminster Hospital has been converted into luxury flats.

---

* Hugh "Bulldog" Drummond is a British fictional character, created by H. C. McNeile and published under his pen name "Sapper". Following McNeile's death in 1937, the novels were continued by Gerard Fairlie. Drummond is a World War I veteran who, fed up with his sedate lifestyle, advertises looking for excitement, and becomes a gentleman adventurer. The character has appeared in novels, short stories, on the stage, in films, on radio and television, and in graphic novels.

** Simon Templar is a fictional character known as The Saint. He is featured in a series of books by Leslie Charteris published between 1928 and 1963. After that date, other authors collaborated with Charteris on books until 1983; two additional works produced without Charteris's participation were published in 1997. The character has also been portrayed in motion pictures, radio dramas, comic strips, comic books and three television series.

*** Lord Peter Death Bredon Wimsey DSO is the fictional protagonist in a series of detective novels and short stories by Dorothy L. Sayers (and their continuation by Jill Paton Walsh). A dilettante who solves mysteries for his own amusement, Wimsey is an archetype for the British gentleman detective. Lord Peter is often assisted by his valet and former batman, Mervyn Bunter; his good friend and later brother-in-law, police detective Charles Parker; and in a few books by Harriet Vane, who becomes his wife.

It was my mother who introduced me to these most British heroes of early 20th Century British pulp fiction. Luckily she did not live long enough for me to tell her that, only a few years ago, I discovered that Leslie Charteris was half Chinese. Strange but true!

Now, I don't know about you, but no matter how much I admired the grim but undeniably beautiful architecture of what is now known as Devington Park, I very much doubt whether I would actually want to *live* there. The Devon County Lunatic Asylum was designed by architect Charles Fowler, built during 1842-1845 and commenced taking in patients during mid 1845. Thus, the buildings are over 169 years old. Fowler (1792-1867) was a local Devon architect from Cullompton, who went on to become a founder member of the RIBA (Royal Institute of British Architects), later becoming vice president. In about 1842, following the winning of a competition, Fowler commenced the building of the Devon County Pauper Lunatic Asylum. His design to produce a 'model' example of a hospital for the mental care of patients was based upon the radial plan of the type pioneered at Millbank Prison, London. The design concept was for a single person to observe all of the inmates of the institution without the inmates being able to tell whether or not they were being watched. Although not of course possible it nevertheless meant that the inmates must act as though they were being watched all the time, which had the effect of controlling their behaviour at all times. The concept was known as 'Panopticon', and the design was later abandoned for such buildings. The asylum eventually had a capacity of over eight hundred beds.

By the time that I was driving hell for leather up the main drive, fuelled by righteous anger, it was 1983 and the asylum was well on its way to being decommissioned. There were only about a hundred patients left living there and these were being haemorrhaged out into community care at an alarming rate, and the whole institution was beginning to look tatty and down at heel.

I drove around to the side of the building, parked in a Nurses Only bay, and walked determinedly in through a side entrance, and climbed the stairs to the residential nurses quarters. I knocked firmly and somewhat portentously on the appropriate door, and my mate the indie kid answered with a smile. "Hey man", he said cheerfully. "What brings you here?" And with that my resolve quickly started to dissolve away.

I have never been very good at being a White Knight. On a number of occasions over the years I have ridden my steed into battle in aid of a damsel in distress, and on nearly all of these occasions I have found out that either the damsel wasn't actually in distress, or that she wasn't actually what one could call a traditional damsel. And it was the case once again on that day. I don't know actually what I had been intending to do, apart from tell my mate the indie kid that he had not behaved like a gentleman, and that he had left poor Cindy heartbroken.

But I had always found him a perfectly affable sort of cove, and about as far away from being a sexual predator as it is possible to be, and when I was actually faced with him looking cheerily out of his bedroom door at me, my righteous anger was dissolving rapidly. But in a last ditch extinction burst of said rage, I stammered out why I had come to see him, ending up "…and she is really upset, man".

He looked quite upset himself at this stage, and told me that not only had nothing ever taken place between them, but that she had been pestering him for months, and no matter what he did she would not leave him alone. He had always tried to be pleasant to her, he told me, but they truly had nothing in common, and his affections were engaged elsewhere. He told me, blushing slightly, that he had been courting a mutual friend of ours, a hippy chick called Tina, whom he had met at some gig or other, and that, whereas he was far too generous of spirit to use the words "paranoid airhead" when referring to Cindy Prosser, he had about as much interest in her as a prospective life partner as he did Ronald Reagan. (Well it was the 1980s, and the Cold War was at its height).

We shook hands, and I apologised for my well meaning, if misguided, outbreak of White Knight Syndrome. Sitting down over a cup of tea and a suspiciously long and fragrant cigarette, and some demos for what would later become the first album by *The Smiths*, we discussed the matter further, but we couldn't make our minds up whether she was a truly malicious young woman who had sort to blacken the name of the man who had politely spurned her advances, or whether she was just deluded.

Indie Kid thought the latter, but I had a sneaking suspicion that Cindy P was nowhere near as sweet and innocent as she pretended, and was the sort of person who was quite capable of causing a lot of trouble for people who did not behave in exactly the fashion that she considered was due to her. So, slightly stoned, I drove slightly unsteadily back to Starcross where I lived, completely intent on doing my best to make sure that Miss Prosser did not cause any more trouble.

But like so many of my big game plans in life, I got this one completely wring, and ended up firmly in Cindy's figurative crosshairs myself.

The wings and sparrows of outrageous fortune [*], eh?

---

* Once again see the footnote on page 42.

On the final *Pink Floyd* album released during the lifetime of the group the late Stephen Hawking appears on the song *Keep Talking* (utilising samples of his appearance on a BT advert). For some reason I have always had it in my head that the samples were of his famous quotes from Hamlet's Soliloquy (which it doesn't) making my plans to record a song featuring a vocoder reading g out Horace Coker's solililoquee (as he would most probably have said) even more pointless than many of my other ideas. However, I will still do it at some point, I expect.

Pointless art projectors are my meat and two veg.

LVXVII

The story of my run in with Cindy Prosser is far less exciting than the story of what I believed had happened between her and my mate the Indie Kid. Nobody was alleged to have taken any clothes off at all, and - to be honest - the whole affair was so uninteresting that I cannot remember any of the banal details after all this time. But basically there were about twenty of us living in Staplake House at the time. Back in those days home video recorders were nowhere near as ubiquitous as they were later to become, but I happened to own one. And I had a membership card to the local video library.

Being a nice bloke for whom TV was (as it is now) not a particularly important aspect of my life, I set my video recorder up in the main common room, and left the club card thing (I cannot even remember what the things were called after a gap of thirty four years) on the mantlepiece with a note saying that as long as they didn't abuse it, other residents were welcome to use it and my VCR. Truthfully, I was engaged in wooing the girl who was to later become my ex-wife, and between that, and serious drinking at one of Starcross's four pubs, and surreptitious drug abuse, I never wanted to watch videos until late at night when I would watch one of the arty hippy or punk things that quite often still amuse me today.

The common room had huge French Windows, and - sometime after midnight - I would open them, and wander out onto the broad green lawn where I would smoke a joint, and stagger back inside and watch *Jubilee* or *Alice's Restaurant* for the umpteenth time. I do much the same now, except *sans* the French Windows, so any thought that my life has progressed over the past three and a bit decades is fairly ephemeral.

But I am digressing once again, something which I have a habit of doing. So forgive me, while I try and tear myself away from fond memories of a house where I was actually fairly happy for one of the first times in my life, and back to the minutiae of why I fell out so badly with Cindy Prosser.

Considering the fact that it made me so angry at the time, and even more so, the fact that I got into considerable trouble because of it, it is mildly ironic that I cannot remember the details. But piecing together vague memories, Cindy had used my video club card, broken the terms of the agreement somehow by not taking a video back in time, or something like that, and brazenly informed me that the owner of the video club had confiscated the card and cancelled my membership. I telephoned the video club and was informed that not only had Ms Prosser incurred my wrath by taking the video(s) back late, but that she had somehow broken the cassette and tried to cover it up. Then came the humdinger. Because I had shared the card with my housemates, I was actually in breach of my membership arrangement, and not only was I banned for life but they wanted me to pay fifty quid compensation to avoid being taken to court. Even now I would be annoyed at losing fifty quid, but for an impecunious student in the mid 1980s, fifty quid was a small fortune.

I am afraid to say that I lost my temper, only to have Cindy channel her inner firebrand and start screaming at me. I retreated to my room, only to find when I emerged that she had made an official complaint about me to everyone else in the house. I wrote a memo about what had *actually* happened, and put it on the house notice board, only to find that the next day she had gone off sick with "stress and anxiety" and that there was a letter to me from the School of Nursing, accusing me of sexism and bullying.

I ended up being disciplined for something of which I truly felt that I was innocent, had black marks embedded on my permanent record and managed to acquire yet another hefty chip on my shoulder. I also paid the fifty quid, because I truly couldn't see that I had any other option. But I did so with the worst possible grace, and yet another chip arrived on the bit between my scapula and my clavicle (or maybe it was the same chip grown larger and more uncomfortable - I do not know enough about such things to comment).

After a few weeks Cindy came back to work, milking the sympathy cash cow for everything that she could. I couldn't even take the video recorder back to my room without being accused of sour grapeitude, and so I spent more and more time at the *Atmospheric Railway* or the *Alexandra Inn*, and less time in the house where - for a time at least - I had actually been happy.

So, as you can see from both my and my friend the Indie Kid's experiences with this girl who had turned out to be a particularly unpleasant young woman, that not only was she not at the top of my Christmas Card list, but that I became really quite concerned when I saw her flouncing into the common room in the arm of an obviously besotted Skullfuck. Because, despite his tough looking exterior (and, believe me, even I could see that he was nowhere near as tough looking as he pretended) he was a sweet and very sensitive bloke. I (believe it or not, despite the fact that I have spent a goodly chunk of this memoir bitching about things that happened decades ago) actually do try to let bygones be bygones, and so I smiled welcomingly at the odd couple. But whereas the young biker grinned disarmingly at me, his date just glowered at me and pulled him out of the room, making it perfectly clear that she was not prepared to spend any time in the same room as me.

My heart fell, and I suddenly felt very worried about Skullfuck. And my fears were very well founded, because - as I was to find out many years later - she ruined his life!

LVXVIII

But I didn't know any of that back then, and even at the time of which I am writing I was not to find out what had actually happened to Skullfuck for a little while. I had always quite liked the bloke, but we were never what one might call socially (or in any other way) intimate, and as I intensely disliked Cindy Prosser (and I hope that you will agree that I had every reason so to do) I am afraid that I made no effort to renew my relationship with the hapless biker lad. We had different friends, my fiancée did her best to keep me away from my erstwhile drink and drugging buddies down at *The Dolphin* in Kenton, and as I was in love and getting sober, I realised that my relationship with these people was basically involved with getting drunk and/or stoned whilst listening to peculiar music and swapping examples of our mutually tasteless senses of humour, the fact that I stopped seeing Skullfuck didn't really matter to me.

I honestly did my best to fit in with Alison's petit-bourgeoise ideals. I stopped taking drugs, and my drinking was under reasonable levels of control. Her friends became my friends, and the coterie of arty druggies with whom I had spent most of my life over the previous few years disappeared over the horizon before me as matrimony, home ownership and a responsible career appeared looming over the horizon before me.

A few months later there was another drama in the Nurses Home, and as a result of it, Cindy Prosser ran away, and tendered her resignation from the School of Nursing by post. there was another interminable enquiry, during which I was once again fingered as being a social and professional undesirable. But I truly can't remember the details, and don't care anyway. Cindy was never seen again, I went off and got married and moved into my little house in Exeter where I lived for the next twenty years, and I completely forgot about Skullfuck.

But Danny's narrative brought him back into the forefront of my cerebral cortex. And I remembered what an oddly sweet lad he had been; underneath the wannabe bikerfreak was a dear fellow who collected stamps and knew the names of all the flowers in the lanes around his home in Kennford.

Danny spent the next week at the redoubt in the deep woods, but - apart from

Skullfuck - he made no attempt so socialise with any other of the inhabitants. Unlike on previous occasions, he had not been summoned to partake of social communion with the elephant headed demigod in charge of the gallant little fortress, and - as he had finally realised that all the beautiful (and not so beautiful) young women there were not seduceable unless once was prepared to pay a price far above anything that he was ever going to be prepared to pay for anything - he had given up talking to any of them, unless it was to say how many dollops of baked beans he wanted on his burnt toast in the makeshift cafeteria. And so, for the next seven days, he spoke to nobody but Skullfuck.

I have already told how Danny has always been spectacularly uninterested in the world about him unless it was something that he could smoke, drink, snort or fuck. However, I still find it extraordinary that he didn't ask more questions, and even with the questions that he *did* ask, he was peculiarly unable to extrapolate any information from the data that was being presented to him each day. He realised that the whole community had suddenly been transformed to being on a war footing, for example, but seemed completely incapable of asking with whom the imminent conflict was going to be. "It just never occurred to me", he muttered shamefacedly as I berated him for his insane levels of intellectual apathy.

Likewise the newer inhabitants of the woodland ménage. Everyone he had met before (except for Panne, of course) was basically human. Even Mr Loxdonta could have passed for being human with the addition of some spectacularly expensive theatrical prosthetics. But some of the beings he was now seeing on a daily basis; the giant smoke men, the pack of talking black dogs (oh, didn't I mention them? I forgot) and the physical manifestation of the Internet meme of Slenderman, were obviously not human, nor could they ever have been portrayed as such. But although Danny was overwhelmed with awe at these things which were totally beyond the ken of practically anyone in the contemporary human race, it never actually occurred to him to find out who they were, what they wanted, what their purpose was, or - indeed - where they came from.

I had known Danny for over three and a half decades, and he had done a lot to piss me off over those years. But I don't think that I had *ever* been so pissed off with him as I was now. Every further piece of the anecdotal evidence with which he presented me, served only to make me more and more cross. How could anyone be so obtuse as to be presented with face to face evidence of the physical proof of some of the most insoluble and abiding mysteries that have ever confronted the human race, and not bother to even *ask* for an explanation?

Danny tried to explain, but I am afraid that I just took it as another one of his facile excuses and three and a half decades of dealing with his bullshit came to the surface, and I refused to listen to him. I should probably have listened to him as he tried to explain that, in the isolated little redoubt in the middle of what had once been part of Her Majesty's Forestry Reserves, but which had been sold off by one of Thatcher's more resolutely privatising governments, what would have seemed to most people as a post Marcel Duchamp * nightmare of surreality, actually became normal. "Our normal, seemed more normal than normal", he tried to explain to me. But I wouldn't listen.

Possibly I should have done.

LVXIX

I stared at him in disbelief. He had been inside what appeared to have been a veritable motherlode of high strangeness for over a week, and it had not even occurred to him to try and find out more about what had happened. It wasn't until several weeks later, with Danny long gone, and the shroud of winter's cold desert lying upon the countryside like a badly fitting, though oddly smug coverlet, that I had an epiphany. It was Danny's very lack of imagination or inquisitiveness, quite probably enhanced by the Second Foundationesque ** psychic powers of those redoubt dwellers deeper inside the woods than those that Danny had yet met, that made him a perfect candidate for the role of social conduit for which he appeared to have become chosen. If he had shown the inquisitiveness inherent in most human beings, then he wouldn't have been any use to Loxodonta and his crew, to whom he was the major ambassador to the world outside.

So how did I come to this conclusion? Well just because Danny hadn't taken it upon himself to take on the role of undercover detective didn't mean that he hadn't picked up a few clues, or - rather - things that I was able to interpret as clues. I have been one of the more conscientious Fortean investigators for the best part of three decades, and I have picked up more than a few hints on how to pick up latent clues from uninterested third party witnesses.

---

* Henri-Robert-Marcel Duchamp (1887 – 1968) was a French-American painter, sculptor, chess player and writer whose work is associated with Cubism, conceptual art, and Dada, although he was careful about his use of the term Dada and was not directly associated with Dada groups. Duchamp is commonly regarded, along with Pablo Picasso and Henri Matisse, as one of the three artists who helped to define the revolutionary developments in the plastic arts in the opening decades of the 20th century, responsible for significant developments in painting and sculpture. Duchamp has had an immense impact on twentieth-century and twenty first-century art; and he had a seminal influence on the development of conceptual art. By World War I, he had rejected the work of many of his fellow artists (such as Henri Matisse) as "retinal" art, intended only to please the eye. Instead, Duchamp wanted to use art to serve the mind.

** See a series of novels by Isaac Asimov, more of which later.

I will admit at this point that most of what I know about procedural detective work comes from old episodes of *The Bill* [*] and from the detective stories of Agatha Christie [**]. It has become quite *de rigeur* for us Fortean bods to quote Sherlock Holmes on and off during our investigations, but I have always found the slightly priggish approach of Hercule Poirot, and the homespun old lady wisdom of Miss Marple to work better for me.

I was extremely angry with Danny for his dullard attitude, but I tried not to show it. He had, after all, managed to get me the seventeen grand that I thought had been lost forever, and - furthermore - had done so without a trace of the vainglorious smugness that was a character trait that I had come to expect from him over the years. So I swallowed my anger and tried to ascertain what Danny and Skullfuck had done during the ten days or so that Danny was hiding in the woods.

"We got out deckchairs, and sat in the sun smoking hash all day"…

"But its the middle of November, man. It has been pissing down for weeks"…

And once again my bile began to rise, but as Danny - in his customary vague and disinterested manner - began to describe how the sun had been shining every day, and how it had be unseasonably hot, I remembered what had happened to me when I entered some peculiar quantum analogue of the Rev Potts' little garden a year or so before, and the idea of the redoubt in the woods being protected by some peculiar magick umbrella, did not seem as stupid as it would have done under any other circumstances. [***]

Back in the day when I was living at Staplake House in Starcross, and half heartedly

---

* The Bill is a British police procedural television series, first broadcast on ITV from 16 October 1984 until 31 August 2010. The programme originated from a one-off drama, *Woodentop*, broadcast in August 1983.

** Dame Agatha Mary Clarissa Christie, Lady Mallowan, DBE (1890 – 1976) was an English writer. She is known for her 66 detective novels and 14 short story collections, particularly those revolving around her fictional detectives Hercule Poirot and Miss Marple. Christie also wrote the world's longest-running play, a murder mystery, *The Mousetrap*, and six romances under the name Mary Westmacott. In 1971 she was appointed a Dame Commander of the Order of the British Empire (DBE) for her contribution to literature.

The footnotes in this book are - in a way - a nod to Agatha Christie, who carefully gave the reader all the information they needed to solve the mystery far before the denouement. However, I am playing Operation Mindfuckwith you all, and throwing in a bunch of information designed to obfuscate, prestidigitate and confuse. Although - as far as I am aware - I am not withholding anything that you ought to know.

Or am I just saying that?

*** See *The Song of Panne* and take the breadhead bit as read.

training to become a nurse for the mentally handicapped, I had spent several months off sick with a bad back. Well, actually, I didn't. My bad back was nowhere as bad as I had claimed, but I was in the process of the second of the major nervous breakdowns that plagued, and then shaped my adult life, and - despite the fact that I had been trained in a parallel discipline, and should have known what was happening to me - I didn't, and decided to exaggerate my lumbar distress in a vain attempt to keep the forces of law and boredom off my back, and stay off sick, whilst still living in NHS owned property.

On the days when my fiancée was at work, I spent much of my time hanging around the house with Danny, smoking suspiciously long cigarettes and watching old war movies, one of my favourites of which was the 1969 movie *The Battle of Britain*. Danny reminded me of these ill spent, though vaguely halcyon days.

"You remember the bit where they all sat around outside the hangers and Nissan huts in deckchairs? It all looked peaceful, but you knew that someone could shout 'scramble' at any moment, and some or all of them could all soon be dead?" He asked with a mildly lamentable lack of grammatical expertise.

I nodded.

"Well it was like that, only it wasn't" he said confusingly. "It was like we were all expecting something horrific to happen any moment, but while it didn't there was nothing to do but get high and chat about stuff…"

There was a long, poignant (or pregnant, I am never quite sure which is which) silence during which neither of us said anything, but Dotty, the youngest of our cats - still not quite graduated out of kittenhood - sniffed around our feet before yowling to be let unto the sitting room.

Still, neither of us said anything. Me, because I was hoping that Danny would volunteer a few more snippets of information, and Danny who looked blankly at me as if he had no idea that I was expecting to hear anything more.

After a few minutes, I gave up.

"What did you talk about?" I asked in exasperation.

"All sorts of things" he said, and there was another long and irritating silence.

This time I decided not to let it carry on as long as before.

"Such as?" I asked, trying to keep traces of annoyance out of my voice.

"Well, we talked about books one time," he mumbled.

This was like trying to get blood out of a stone, and even more frustrating because there was far more at stake.

"What books?" I spat out, rapidly losing my gentlemanly *sang froid*.

"We talked about Isaac Asimov" he said dispassionately, "and something called psychohistory".

LVXX

Although the term is also used for a relatively modern discipline investigating the psychological motivations of historical events, attempting to combine the insights of psychoanalysis with the research methodology of the social sciences, psychohistory (as most people who have heard the term understand it) is a fictional science in Isaac Asimov's Foundation universe which combines history, sociology, and mathematical statistics to make general predictions about the future behaviour of very large groups of people, such as the Galactic Empire. It was first introduced in the three short stories (1942–1944) which would later be collected as the 1951 novel *Foundation*.

The fictional Dr Hari Seldon used an analogy from physics; the kinetic theory. An observer has great difficulty in predicting the motion of a single molecule in a gas, but can predict the mass action of the gas to a high level of accuracy. Seldon (via Asimov) applied this concept to the population of his fictional Galactic Empire, which numbered a quintillion. Seldon formed two 'Foundations' - the first being physical scientists, and the second 'mentalic' scientists - to ensure that the history of the galaxy after his death would work out best for the human race. This is, of course, an immense simplification of what was eventually a series of seven books by him, and three or four by other people, and I can only wholeheartedly recommend that you go ut and read them for yourselves, because they are well worth reading.

But the general concept of the series is two groups of scientists (one hidden) working to change the path of human history. And although they are excellent books, I have always found that an absolutely terrifying concept (a stance shared by the authors of the *Second Foundation Trilogy* starting five years after Asimov's death) and it has always both amused and frightened me to find out that the literal translation of *Al*

Quaeda is 'The Foundation'

Asimov himself apparently thought differently as he is quoted as saying:

> "Well, I can't help but think it would be good, except that in my stories, I always have opposing views. In other words, people argue all possible... all possible... ways of looking at psychohistory and deciding whether it is good or bad. So you can't really tell. I happen to feel sort of on the optimistic side. I think if we can somehow get across some of the problems that face us now, humanity has a glorious future, and that if we could use the tenets of psychohistory to guide ourselves we might avoid a great many troubles. But on the other hand, it might create troubles. It's impossible to tell in advance."

All these thoughts rushed into my head at once, and I realised that I was lost in my own thoughts that had been triggered by Danny's evocation of the term FOUNDATION, and that I hadn't been actually *listening* to what Danny had to say.

"Sorry dude, can you say that again", I interrupted, and Danny was just starting to tell me how he and Skullfuck had sat in their deckchairs basking in the sun like indolent lizards, when the telephone rang. I let it ring, and then realised that both Corinna and Graham had gone out (in part because they both disliked Danny intensely, but also to carry out various chores that needed t be done). Being only too aware that the only other human being in the house was my elderly Mama in Law, who would never have answered the telephone in a thousand years, I picked it up.

It was someone from a call centre in Uttar Pradesh trying to sell me loft insulation. I said something rude and banged the telephone down in frustration. But the moment had been lost. Danny was now talking about computers, a subject about which I suspected that he knew far less than me.

While Danny wittered on about Facebook and about how he had been very successful in using social media to pick up girls, and how he and Skullfuck had spent many hours talking about how these complex virtual social networks could be manipulated for carnal ends, my mind wandered off again. And before I realised it, I was thinking about psychohistory and *Al Quaeda* again. The events in the Middle East over the previous few years had been nothing short of terrifying. The revolutions of the Arab Spring had, indeed been organised on social media. But look where they had led us; a world of dark age savagery, which was threatening to overspill to the rest of the world.

But, I thought to myself, don't we ever learn the lessons of history? The lessons of the

Second World War showed us that bestial savagery was only just below the surface of even the most so-called civilised nations. And how very few people ever seemed prepared to admit that the only reason that the Allies had one the war was because we had teamed up with Stalin, who was such a terrible tyrant that he made Hitler seem like a pussy cat.

I am in a lot of pain much of the time, and so am on a serious amount of medicine these days, and - unfortunately - it does mean that for large swathes of the day, my mind does tend to wander, and I have always found Danny's verbiage to be monumentally tedious. And so although I should have been listening to him, it was much easier to allow my mind to wander down the highways and byways of ideaspace. But I pulled myself together and did my best to bring myself back to the here and now.

But Danny had wandered off onto other subjects by now. And, bizarrely, although on one level what he was talking about was nowhere near as important, I found his description of how the little redoubt in the woods had become almost militarised, with bunkers, a commissary, and the earnest young people with laptops, who had once upon a time, been scattered about the place, now confined to portacabins and big military marquees, and forbidden to discuss what was going on with outsiders far more interesting than his ramblings on the subject of a science fiction author that he had obviously never read.

But then the telephone rang again....

---

* I believe that Alan Moore was the originator of this concept:

"...this hypothetical "space," which I have labeled Ideaspace.... Maybe our individual and private consciousness is, in Ideaspace terms, the equivalent of owning an individual private house... the space inside our homes is entirely ours, yet if we step through the front door we find ourselves in a street, in a world, that is mutually accessible to everyone.... This would explain dubious phenomena such as telepathy or knowledge-at-a-distance.... The actual ideas represent the equivalent of solid objects in terms of that space. An idea may be a pebble, a rock, a mountain or a whole continent in terms of its stature.... Distances could only be associational in Ideaspace. Lands End and John O'Groates, while famously far apart in the physical world, are usually mentioned in the same sentence and thus are right next to each other, associatively speaking.... Time, as a phenomenon, doesn't apply in the same way to the realm of the mind as it does to the time-locked material realm. We can think as easily about events ten or twenty years ago as we can about something that happened this morning, or we can think about something that might happen tomorrow.... If this were so, then this would explain, at a stroke, such phenomena as ghosts, premonitions, apparent memories of previous lives... even... de-ja-vu.

"Ideaspace, where philosophies are land masses and religions are probably whole countries, might contain flora and fauna that are native to it, creatures of this conceptual world that are made from ideas in the same way that we creatures of the material world are made from matter. This could conceivably explain phantoms, angels, demons, gods, djinns, grey aliens, elves, pixies..."

https://powerofmyth.livejournal.com/22508.html

LVXXI

t was the man from Porlock.

In fact it wasn't. It was the man from Bossington, a small village a few miles down the road. His name was Clive; a mildly irritating but occasionally useful self-styled "Paranormal Expert" who lived with his excessively ugly wife, one of his daughters and his grandson (who had been conceived in an unfortunate liaison between his other daughter and a Japanese revolutionary film maker) in a tumbledown trailer park on the outskirts of the village.

For those of you not in the know, Samuel Taylor Coleridge, the famous junkie poet, recalled that he fell asleep in his chair when he was staying at a farmhouse near Porlock in 1797. He had taken opium, to which he became addicted, and he was reading about Kubla Khan's palace. In his opium dream he imagined a poem of perhaps 200 or 300 lines. When he awoke, with the whole work clear in his mind, he began writing: "In Xanadu, did Kubla Khan/A stately pleasure dome decree...." *

But after a while, he was "called out by a person on business from Porlock, and detained by him above an hour." That made him forget the rest of the dream. And that's why "Kubla Khan" runs only 54 lines and remains, by its author's account, unfinished. My opium days are a long way in the past (mostly, I must admit, because I have no idea where on earth I would get the stuff now I am a relatively respectable member of society, and do my best to no longer consort with lowlife) and on the morning in question I wasn't tripping on anything, but I was engrossed in listening to Danny's narrative, and doing my best to get as much information as possible, and the interruption was most unwelcome.

But I am basically a polite sort of cove, and despite the fact that I have been known to scream abuse down the telephone at people trying to scam me or sell double glazing, and on one unfortunate occasion a woman from Save the Children who had telephoned the house on five separate occasions on a particular day, and finally got hold of me on a day when I was suffering agonies with piles. But, despite his irritating mannerisms, Clive Cohen was quite a nice old geezer (he was only about five years older than me, but wore his shock of white hair and his ageing wrinkles like a badge of honour, and I was quite fond of him. I have always suspected that he was about as Jewish as I am (about a sixteenth, which means that I probably wouldn't

---

* Unless you were Frankie goes to Hollywood, in which case it was "a pleasure dome erect!"

have passed the Nuremberg Laws[*]) but he always played on his ethnicity, with menorahs and stars of David prominently displayed on the walls of his caravan (and beforehand his council house) and he would gesticulate "Oy Vey my Boy" far more than was strictly necessary.

I gestured apologetically to Danny, then put my hand over the receiver and said *sotto voce* to him that he should go and see if he could get a cuppa and something to eat from Mother, and then turned back to give my full attention to Clive.

"Hey dude", I said in as welcoming a tone as I could. "I can't be long, I'm kind of in the middle of something at the moment"...

"Jon my Boy", came the reply. "How's your wife already, and your lovely Mother, and your daughters..." And I realised with a mental groan that whatever I said to him I would have to sit through his labyrinthine, not to say Levantine, courtesies before I could actually get any semblance of sense out of him.

People often complain that it takes me a long time to do things, but in my defence I would say that as well as the fact that I do a heck of a lot (a hundred page music magazine each week for starters) and run the Centre for Fortean Zoology, Wyrd Records and CFZ Press as well as doing an increasing amount of freelance work for various other people, most noticeably Rob at Gonzo Multimedia, I also have a larger than average number of peculiar friends and acquaintances who have an annoying habit of telephoning at all times of the day and night wanting to talk about things that range from the annoyingly trivial to the world-shatteringly important, and all points in between, and I could never know in advance which of the two it would be. I also have two neurotic dogs and four eccentric cats, as well as an elderly Mama in Law, any of whom are liable to invade my space for a multitude of reasons, without any apparent rhyme or reason.

And so, my train of thought is always liable to be interrupted by someone or something, and as I have a grasshopper mind to start off with I am easily distracted. But, I am sure that those of you who have followed this dialogue so far, and seen the

---

* The Nuremberg Laws (German: Nürnberger Gesetze) were antisemitic and racial laws in Nazi Germany. They were enacted by the Reichstag on 15 September 1935, at a special meeting convened during the annual Nuremberg Rally of the Nazi Party (NSDAP). The two laws were the Law for the Protection of German Blood and German Honour, which forbade marriages and extramarital intercourse between Jews and Germans and the employment of German females under 45 in Jewish households; and the Reich Citizenship Law, which declared that only those of German or related blood were eligible to be Reich citizens; the remainder were classed as state subjects, without citizenship rights. A supplementary decree outlining the definition of who was Jewish was passed on 14 November, and the Reich Citizenship Law officially came into force on that date. The laws were expanded on 26 November 1935 to include Romani people – known at the time as "Gypsies" – and Black people. This supplementary decree defined Romanis as "enemies of the race-based state", the same category as Jews.

number of tangents which I am likely to jump off upon, will not be surprised at this. Meanwhile, Clive was just about to come to the end of his long winded social preamble, and was hopefully going to get to the point of his telephone call.

I have known him for about twenty years, and have just about managed to perfect a strategy which works in dealing with him. Recognising that he had just about come to the end of asking about my family and household, and realising that unless I acted promptly I would now be inflicted with a long description of the ailments and alarums and excursions of his extended ménage, I decided that prompt measures were necessary, and so I decided to act.

"So, what can I do for you?" I asked.

"Well" he said, drawing breath and preparing himself for what would certainly be a massively enjoyable verbal salvo. "What do you know about Psychohistory?"

I gasped as quietly as I could. This was going to be a particularly peculiar day, and I had already run out of cigarettes.

LVXXII

Now, this next bit is going to make no sense at all unless I give you some of the backstory. So please forgive me if it appears that I am digressing to a ridiculous extent, but - hopefully, at least - it will all come together into some sort of logical picture in the end.

Clive's wife was called Sharleen, and was - as I think I may have already mentioned - one of the most unattractive women that I have ever met. Her heart was in the right place (I think) but that is more than could be said about any of her outward features. She was also massively mad, and her particular brand of madness showed itself most notably on Facebook where she friended and unfriended people with gay abandon, indulging in a dozen or so online feuds with people who had been guilty (in her astigmatic eyes) of real or imagined slights against her. On the plus side she ran a little *ad hoc* animal hospital, and - when she came into some money via a lucky lottery ticket - rather than using her windfall to pull her ragtag and bobtail family out of the mire, she took out a ninety nine year lease on the next-door trailer, and bought a third of an acre of waste ground next to it, and set up in business as an animal sanctuary.

This pissed off quite a few of her neighbours, who disapproved of her collection of ramshackle cages which housed an ever growing collection of disabled wildlife, most of which she had decided were not in a fit state ever to be released. Every few months it seemed that another petition or court case had been taken out against her, and on a number of occasions, the peculiar little household had been raided by police or by representatives of the local council. On other occasions, Sharleen had made herself so unpopular with the local residents that a semi permanent protest camp had been assembled outside the gates of the trailer park. As a result of that, apparently Sharleen had become so incensed that she had snuck stealthily around the village in the wee small hours delivering vicious poison pen letters that - once again - had resulted in burning coals of opprobrium being heaped upon her head and those of her husband and children.

One might ask why the proprietor of the trailer park was willing to allow such goings on which were never going to add lustre to the glorious name of his commercial enterprise, and - it had been hypothesised by people of my acquaintanceship who should have known better, but had probably known worse, that Sharleen had been treating her landlord with toothless blowjobs in order to ensure that their tenancy was unaffected. It was true that Sharleen had very few teeth, but the truth was far more prosaic and less scurrilous. The landlord of the trailer park was Sharleen's brother Dwayne, and - at least in their case - blood seems to be thicker than water.

Sharleen had been a girlfriend of Clive's back when they had been teenagers and both still had their own teeth, but the relationship had lapsed for a whole plethora of reasons (some of which I am privy too, but they are completely irrelevant to this story, and there is enough sordid sexuality already, with quite a bit more to come, and so I won't go into details). They had both gone on to marry other people, and had got back together more or less by accident in late middle age, whereupon Clive almost immediately got her pregnant. Whether or not this was intentional on either of their parts I have no idea, but he obviously adored her, and - as far as I can tell - the feelings were reciprocated, and the peculiar little family were very happy. Or almost so.

I, too, met the love of my life in middle age, and a few years before my fiftieth birthday, settled down with my new wife and I have never regretted it for a moment. As a result of this I found myself a stepfather to two beautiful young women. I have heard all sorts of horror stories from friends of mine who have found themselves in similar situations, and who have ended up in a state of open warfare with their stepsprogs.

Nothing of the sort has ever happened between me, Olivia and Shoshannah, and my two beloved girls have always treated me with love and kindness, and I them. But over the years Clive has told me a while litany of horror stories about the way that his relationship with his stepdaughter has progressed. From what I can understand, Elvira is a completely obnoxious little shit of the worst order of magnitude, and has always done his best to make Clive's life as unpleasant as possible. From her early teens she was wildly promiscuous, drank, smoked and took drugs like there was no tomorrow. In short, at thirteen she behaved like I did in my late thirties, and then did her very best to turn the blame onto her poor witless stepfather.

All children rebel against their parents, and in many cases their bad behaviour is a conscious revolt against the cultural attitudes of their parents. Mine were, or so various serried ranks of therapists did their best to tell me. I am not too sure.

But in the case of Clive/Elvira it seems that this was almost certainly the case. And the most obvious way that this manifested itself was politically. Peculiarly for someone who identified with the chosen people of Judaism, Clive had become more and more right wing in his politics as he got older. He joined UKIP and spouted more and more veiled racist bullshit on Social Media. He then joined a secret society (although *how* a society can be secret when they have a Facebook page and all the members spout on about very little else) called The Fraternal Order of the Knights Apostles, and was one of the aforementioned people who spouted on about very little else.

They were great admirers of George W Bush (well I suppose someone had to be) and when Bush's second term was over, spent much of their time claiming that President Obama was the Antichrist, mainly - as far as I can tell - because the name Obama vaguely rhymed with Osama (as in Bin Laden) and they claimed that he was indirectly responsible for the 9-11 attacks, as well as all sorts of other things. Their claims became so nonsensical that - on the whole - I ignored them all, and only spoke to Clive on progressively infrequent occasions.

But sometimes, like today, the trainwreck that was his life became too much to ignore, and I found myself being drawn in despite myself.

LVXXIII

A few years ago, when the British media were cheerfully celebrating the 40th anniversary of the *Sex Pistols'* anthem "Anarchy in the UK", Joe Corre, millionaire offspring of Malcom McLaren and Vivienne Westwood, decided to stage a huge bonfire at a "secret location" – destroying his mum and dad's clothes and assorted artefacts worth over £5m". "Everyone has problems with their Dads" said Bill Drummond, who is someone that anyone who knows me, or who has read anything much that I have written, will know that I have never met but whom I hold in very high esteem.

Well I certainly had problems with *my* Dad, but I think that it would be a over simplification to say that my political and cultural journey over the past half century is purely down to that set of problems. However, I think that some of my sexual and chemical anabases over the years may well have been. And so it was with Elvira. When you have a Father who has openly re-identified himself as a right wing Jew, the best thing that you can do to piss him off is to become a Communist, and have sex with as many revolutionary young men professing anti-semitic views, as possible.

Sadly, Elvira is nowhere near as stupid as she pretended to be, and in fact is far more intelligent than either of her parents. And she was actually interested in many of the same things as was her old man, although she would never have admitted it.

Clive - despite his eccentricities, and unfortunate political affiliations, was actually a nice guy at heart, and so, although he skirts along the surface of UFOlogy, ghost hunting and various other things, he never went very deeply into any of them. Back when one could actually make a living by writing about what is vulgarly known as weird shit, there was a whole pantheon of different magazines covering the subjects. Of these, two were particularly naive and gullible, and never let me write for them. I am not saying that there is any connection between the two statements, because I wrote widely for most of the rest. But these two magazines which were broadly "blah blah blah flying saucers are alien spacecraft, and the government knows about them", always - to my mind, at least - promulgated an irritating culture of gullible nonsense, which people like Clive (nice as he was) sucked up like Mother's milk.

The most ridiculous of the claims that these magazines printed was a series of claims that a whole string of different animals had been abducted by aliens and their bodies mutilated. Now, before we go any further, I need to give you a history lesson.

Cattle mutilation (also - according to Wikipedia, although I have never heard either term - known as bovine excision and unexplained livestock death) is the killing and mutilation of cattle under unusual, usually bloodless and anomalous circumstances. Worldwide sheep, horses, goats, pigs, rabbits, cats, dogs, bison, deer and elk have been reported mutilated with similar bloodless excisions, often an ear, eyeball, jaw flesh, tongue, lymph nodes, genitals and rectum are removed.

Since the first reports of animal mutilations, various explanations have been offered ranging from natural decomposition and normal predation, to cults and secretive governmental and military agencies, to a range of speculations including cryptid predators (like the Chupacabra), and extraterrestrials. Mutilations have been the subject of two independent federal investigations in the United States.

I have studied such things over the years in both the UK and the United States, and I believe that there is a very real phenomenon to be explored. However, the magazine article which I am describing, and (although the editor is now dead, and I believe the person who authored the study has also joined John Keel and Jim Mosley in the great UFO convention in the sky) I am not going to go any further in identifying it, presented a long series of gruesome pictures of dead small mammals, including hedgehogs and bank voles, and claimed that the damage inflicted upon the creatures had been done by little green men from the Planet Zog or whatever, when to anyone with even the slightest bit of knowledge of the natural world, it was obvious that they had been attacked by sexton beetles. For those of you not in the know, sexton beetles (genus Nicrophorus) are the best-known members of the family Silphidae (carrion beetles). Most of these beetles are black with red markings on the elytra (forewings). Burying beetles are true to their name—they bury the carcasses of small vertebrates such as birds and rodents as a food source for their larvae. They are unusual among insects in that both the male and female parents take care of the brood. They are carnivores.

No matter how many times I tried to explain this time Clive he just would not believe me. And eventually I found a dead bank vole, and put it in a glass vivarium with a group of sexton beetles, and - over the duration of a week - I showed him how these beetles had predated the dead rodent, boring out its anus, for example, in precisely the way that could be seen in the photographs of the beasts supposedly attacked by aliens. And he stared at me in silence.

However, the next time he saw me, he explained how sexton beetles had obviously been reverse engineered by NASA scientists, using alien technology in order to make these industrious little carnivorous arthropods into ideal vectors with which to gather DNA data, and eventually be used for biological warfare.

If he hadn't been such a well meaning sort of cove, I think I would have punched him at that point. But, although he would believe any old bollocks, he was essentially a kind and nice guy. However, other people within that particular branch of the UFO community were far less kind and nice. I am thinking, in particular, of a pair of "retired" police officers, who had graduated from the West Midlands Serious Crimes Squad with dishonour, and who had then set their sights on becoming paranormal superstars.

Their names were Sean and Blossom. And they led a group called The UFO Wehrwölfe Union, and unlike Clive they were neither well meaning, kind, considerate or stupid.

LVXXIV

Now, please forgive me if I give you somewhat of a history lesson, but the appalling events of the end of 1974 have - for many people - disappeared over the event horizon, and have probably been forgotten by most people under the age of fifty. But what happened is very much germane to what happened next in the main narrative of this story, and so I need to do a little bit of explaining.

In 1973 the Provisional IRA started a campaign of terrorist activity on the British mainland, and by 1974 they were attempting to stage an attack every three days. The Rotunda is a 25-storey office block that looks a bit like a huge coke can, and at the time it housed a pub called *The Mulberry Bush*. On the evening of the 21st November 1974 at 20:11 one of the Birmingham newspapers received an anonymous telephone call: "There is a bomb planted in the Rotunda and there is a bomb in New Street at the tax office. This is Double X", before terminating the call. (Double X was a then-used official IRA code word recited to authenticate any warning call).

It was then IRA policy to give a half hour warning when attacks were made on civilian targets, but it was only six minutes after the warning call had been received that the first bomb exploded, devastating the pub. The explosion blew a crater measuring 40 inches (101 cm) in the concrete floor, collapsing part of the roof and trapping many casualties beneath girders and concrete blocks. Numerous buildings near the Rotunda were also damaged and passersby in the street were struck by flying glass from shattered windows. Several of the fatalities were killed outright, including two youths who had been walking past the premises at the moment of the explosion.

The *Tavern in the Town* was a basement pub on New Street, 50 yards (46 m) from the Rotunda and directly beneath the New Street Tax Office. Patrons there had heard the explosion at the Mulberry Bush, but did not believe that the sound (described by one survivor as a "muffled thump") was an explosion. Police had begun attempting to clear the Tavern in the Town when, at 20:27, a second bomb exploded there. The blast was so powerful that several victims were blown through a brick wall. In total the explosions killed 21 people and injured 182 others.

Six Irishmen who had been residents of Birmingham since the 1960s were en route to

Ireland that evening. They were all due to attend the funeral of an IRA volunteer who had blown himself up by accident in Coventry. They may or may not have been members of the IRA, but they were certainly sympathisers, and made the terrible mistake of lying to the police when they were stopped at the Heysham ferry port in Lancashire. It was a mistake that was to cost them the next sixteen years.

On the morning of 22 November, after forensic tests and questioning at the hands of the Morecambe police, the men were transferred to the custody of West Midlands Serious Crime Squad police unit. William Power. Whilst in the custody of the West Midlands Police they were deprived of food and sleep, they were interrogated sometimes for up to 12 hours without a break; threats were made against them and the beatings started: ranging from punches, letting dogs within a foot of them and being the subjects of a mock execution. Although the resulting confessions had been obtained by coercion, and the defendants appeared in court battered, bruised and beaten, the evidence was ruled admissible on 12 May 1975 the six men were charged with murder and conspiracy to cause explosions.

It took two appeals and sixteen years of protests before their second full appeal, in 1991, was allowed. Hunter was represented by Lord Gifford QC, others by human rights solicitor Gareth. The Court of Appeal, constituted by Lord Justices Lloyd, Mustill and Farquharson, stated that "in the light of the fresh scientific evidence, which at least throws grave doubt on Dr. Skuse's evidence, if it does not destroy it altogether, these convictions are both unsafe and unsatisfactory." On 14 March 1991 the six walked free. Ten years later the six men were awarded compensation ranging from £840,000 to £1.2 million.

The really appalling thing about the whole affair is that these appeals took place two whole years after the West Midlands Serious Crimes Squad had been disbanded after "an investigation into allegations against some of its officers of incompetence and abuses of power". Depending on which source you believe between 64 and 72 people have had their convictions overturned as a result of investigations into the innate corruption of the Serious Crimes Squad.

A whole string of Police Officers were sacked, and far more were convicted than one would feel happy having been done if one was one of those people who believe that we live in a fair and equitable society, where the jolly British bobby is the epitome of proberty and the envy of the world. Other malefactors saw the writing on the wall several years before, and retired for a whole string of interesting excuses. Two of these were Sean and Blossom: he started complaining of migraines, she complained of deep depression following unexplained weight gain, and they both pocketed healthy 'golden handshakes' and were given a monthly stipend which meant that they would never actually have to sign in (or sign on) for the rest of their lives, and they essentially disappeared.

The shockwaves which followed the collapse of the West Midlands Serious Crimes Squad reverberated around the law and order industry, and the resulting enquiries and prosecutions were still going on well over a decade later. But these enquiries were all aimed at serving officers, and the retired officers named in the successful appeals by The Birmingham Six, the Guildford Four, the Maguire Seven, and various other victims of a vicious and uncaring system. And so the two wannabe UFO researchers who had been pocketing kickbacks from all and sundry for years, and were now doing something completely different, and using names which their erstwhile colleagues amongst the bent plods of Brum would never have recognised, got completely away with it.

LVXXV

As I have already explained, there were large chunks of Clive's worldview which I found worryingly right wing, but when you try and compare him with The UFO Wehrwölfe Union, he came over like a drippy bleeding heart liberal.

I first heard about The UFO Wehrwölfe Union in the first autumn of the new century, when Britain was enshrouded in palls of greasy grey smoke from the serried funeral pyres of hundreds of hooved farm animals that had been slaughtered, often in the most inhumane manner, because of an outbreak of foot and mouth disease which soon reached epidemic proportions. I have mentioned elsewhere how this epizootic plague had serious economic implications for previously prosperous little market towns like Bideford, but it is only with the benefit of hindsight, that one realises how - in a world already culturally traumatised by the events of September 11th - the cultural fallout from the Foot and Mouth plague also begat a host of conspiracy theories ranging from the sublime to the ridiculous. The most peculiar of these came from an organisation calling itself the Aryan Big Cat Society who claimed that the Foot and Mouth Disease outbreak was caused by the shadowy Alien Big Cats which have been reported from nearly every part of the United Kingdom for decades.

Forgetting the fact that the disease cannot be spread by carnivores, the interesting part of this particular farrago of nonsense was that the Aryan Big Cat Society (who propped up their claims with screeds of quotations from someone that they claimed was "Third Reich Agronomist Reinhold Shreck") were vociferous in claiming that the aforementioned Alien Big Cats had been introduced into the British countryside by illegal immigrants from Muslim countries determined to destabilise the British farming industry.

After all this preamble, it will surprise nobody to learn that the Aryan Big Cat Society were synonymous with The UFO Wehrwölfe Union,

For those amongst the readers of this narrative who are not familiar with the, more unpleasant highways and byways of 21st Century history, Wehrwölfe was a Nazi plan, which began development in 1944, to create a resistance force which would operate behind enemy lines as the Allies advanced through Germany. However Wehrwolf's propaganda value far outweighed its actual achievements. The name was chosen after the title of Hermann Löns' novel, *Der Wehrwolf*, first published in 1910.

Set in the Celle region (Lower Saxony) during the Thirty Years' War (1618–1648), the novel concerns a peasant named Harm Wulf. After marauding soldiers kill his family, Wulf organises his neighbours into a militia who pursue the soldiers mercilessly and execute any they capture, while referring to themselves as Wehrwölfe. Löns wrote that the title was a dual reference to the fact that the peasants put up a fighting defence (sich wehren, see "Bundeswehr" – Federal Defense) and to the protagonist's surname of Wulf, but it also had obvious connotations with the word Werwölfe in that Wulf's men came to enjoy killing. While Löns was not himself a Nazi (he had died in 1914), his work became popular with the German far right, and the Nazis celebrated it. Indeed, Celle's local newspaper began serialising Der Wehrwolf in January 1945.

Sean and Blossom had chosen to ally themselves with these fairly nonexistent guerilla fighters from the Twilight of the Nazi Gods, because - they claimed - western society had become far too decadent after decades of "influence from Jewish and Nigger trash" and how, as a result, the "Aryan white races" (forgetting the fact that there truly isn't actually such a thing) were now under attack from paranormal and mystickal (their spelling, not mine) "vanguards" (whatever that meant) and that it was only the spirit of the Wehrwölfe freedom fighters that would stand in the way of the ultimate defeat of the "Northwestern European Peoples".

Now, at this point I would like to make a couple of salient points (three actually).

Firstly, I am totally aware of the fact that the wording used above is considered unacceptable in today's society. However, I am quoting directly from some of the literature distributed by the self-styled "freedom fighters", and as they used deliberately shocking language in an attempt to create a deliberately shocking effect, I feel that I would not be fulfilling my self-imposed role as chronicler of these events, if I tried to pussy around their egregious racism, in an attempt to shield the sensibilities of my readers.

Secondly, no matter what spin you put on it, every single claim that these people made is absolute nonsense. The first case of Foot and Mouth disease to be detected in the 2001 outbreak was at Cheale Meats abattoir in Little Warley, Essex on 19 February 2001 on pigs from Buckinghamshire and the Isle of Wight. Over the next four days, several more cases were announced in Essex. On 23 February, a case was confirmed in Heddon-on-the-Wall, Northumberland, from where the pig in the first case had come; this farm was later confirmed as the source of the outbreak and the owner, Bobby Waugh of Pallion, an undeniably gruff, taciturn and widely disliked individual, was convicted of failing to inform the authorities of a notifiable disease, and later of feeding his pigs "untreated waste".

The theory sprung up that the pigs had become infected by eating swill containing contaminated meat imported from abroad, obtained either from Newcastle's Chinese restaurants or from the nearby Albermarle army barracks. Although the barracks did use meat from Uruguay (a country then with FMD) no proof was provided it was the source. And although various newspapers implied that Waugh had been convicted of "causing" the epizootic plague, this is just not true. No suck claims were ever made in a court of law, and now - fifteen years later - there is a burgeoning level of belief that he was made a scapegoat for widely accepted practises in the farming industry as it was.

Disturbingly it was in a wad of literature from Sean and Blossom and their followers that I first read this claim. Typically racist, their claim that Waugh was a "purebred Aryan from yeoman stock" and thus could not have been responsible for "inflicting is vile plague on his countrymen" made no sense.

Thirdly, I have been following the activities of this egregious bunch of sociopaths now for well over a decade and a half, and I have come to the conclusion that they are not even sincere in their racism. Like so many other self-styled patriots who came out with wallages of vile nonsense in the wake of the 2016 Brexit vote, they are only interested in whipping up fervour and hatred for one reason. And that reason? Money.

And these were the people with whom Clive's unpleasant daughter had decided to ally herself. No wonder, despite all the other twists and turns of the emotional rollercoaster upon which I had ridden that morning, I now had a sinking feeling in the pit of my stomach.

LVXXVI

I was confused (which is not exactly an abnormal condition when one is trying to get some semblance of sense out of Clive). This was all very complicated and unpleasant but none of it seemed to have anything to do with *me*. But within the bounds of civilised behaviour there are no protocols to allow a gentleman to say: "What the fuck are you talking about you twat? And why are you wasting my time with all this shit?"

Add to that the fact that although his family put the FUN into dysfunctional, and I dislike most of them intently, I am peculiarly fond of Clive, and I would not cause him upset for the world.

One of the things that I find increasingly annoying about the modern world in which we live, is the fact that everyone seems to self-diagnose their physical, mental and spiritual illnesses. I know various people who claim to be OCD (and I have been told that I have several of the symptoms) and the really peculiar thing is that all of them are completely different to each other. And Clive (who, as far as I know has never been diagnosed as anything) seems to find it absolutely impossible to keep his mind on any specific tangent for more than a few moments. I have been described as having a "grasshopper mind", but if my cognitive processes are those of a grasshopper, those of my peculiar friend Clive are those of a whole plague of fucking locusts, which - when one considers Clive's peculiarly Semitic pretensions - seems a particularly apposite quasi-Biblical analogy.

So is Clive OCD? Fuck knows. And it truly doesn't matter. But it does go a little way towards explaining why - all of a sudden - Clive was talking about a family wedding which had taken place in Porlock earlier in the year. Over the years I have developed a reasonably effective filter which separates Clive's verbal wheat from his voluminous levels of verbal chaff. And deep inside my psyche a little man in a grubby lab coat pulled the lever which operates said filter.

Now at the risk of being accused of some weird act of post-modern irony, I am going to make a mild explanatory sidestep and explain that for the past fifty years or so I have visualised the workings of my (and sometimes other people's) cognitive processes in terms of a classic British comic strip. The Numskulls is a comic strip in *The Beano*, and previously in *The Beezer* and *The Dandy* – UK comics owned by D.C Thomson. The strip is about a team of tiny human-like technicians who live inside the heads of various people, running and maintaining their bodies and minds. It first appeared in *The Beezer* from 1962 until 1979, drawn by Malcolm Judge.

But back to the matter at hand. Whilst Clive was waffling on about the interminably dull nuptials of someone that I had never met, and most probably never would, I was trying to make sense of all the stuff that Danny Miles (whom, I assumed, was in the next room drinking tea with my beloved Mother-in-law who can be utterly charming, whilst ever so slightly dotty, and completely confusing, all at the same time) had told me earlier.

Not only was I suddenly seventeen grand better off than I thought that I would be, but I had discovered a considerable amount more about the activities of my quondam tenants (whom I would gladly wish to be eaten alive by giant landcrabs in live TV) and about the activities of the peculiar little redoubt in the deep woods on the other side of Meddon, although his narrative had been unfortunately interrupted by Clive's waffling telephone call.

I had also heard more about the peculiar activities of a group of young women who seem to have modelled themselves on a group of bloodthirsty (and usually unclad) warriorchicks from Greek mythology. But what, why and who they were remained a complete unponderable. All I knew was that they were a bunch of naked chicks who seemed to be responsible for some horrific killings. That, and the fact that the hairy little Godling who lived in my airing cupboard appeared to be mortally frightened of them (that is, if an immortal could be mortally *anything*).

I was hard at work composing a list of questions that I needed to ask Danny as soon as I was able to finish dealing with Clive and we were able to resume our conversation, when the irrelevancy filter being operated by the numskulls in my hypothalamus flashed to Defcon 1 and I started paying attention to what Clive was saying once again…

"…and it turned out that he was a member of the Cornwall UFO Group, but had been visiting his girlfriend in Bradworthy. And being a clear night and a new moon they decided to go on a skywatch up on Bradworthy Common".

I nodded assent. Although I hadn't been there in years, back when I was a Nursing Assistant at the Kingsley Unit on Alverdiscott Road in East-the-water, I had sometimes had the unenviable job of having to drive a long wheelbase Transit Van which had been converted into a minibus in order to take various day patients who had attended an Adult Training Centre on the same campus, back to their homes. And for some reason, an inordinate number of them lived in or about Bradworthy Common, and so I knew the place well.

"And you will never believe this…"

And I was sure that I knew what was coming next. I had heard accounts of enough skywatches over the years, and had been on a few myself, and knew that what was going to come next was an inconclusive account of some vague and amorphous lights in the sky, together with a load of bollocks about U.S Government black ops projects.

But I was wrong. Terribly wrong.

"…there were three white luminescent globes high in the sky, arranged in a triangle shape, with a larger, electric blue coloured globe positioned dead in the middle of it. And this larger globe was the apex of what appeared to be a huge cone of dull green light that was somehow projected into the sky from somewhere on the ground…"

I sat upright in shock. This was not something that I had been expecting.

"Fucking hell" I said.

"But there's more", he said.

LVXXVII

And Clive went on to tell me how his friend and other contacts of his (I am not sure if he meant contacts of Clive's, or of Clive'a unnamed friend and it doesn't really matter as far as the cogency of this narrative is concerned) had reported a whole slew of different anomalous phenomena from the region; a huge amorphous black human shaped cloud of fog, a pack of spectral black dogs which rushed through the country lanes baying ferociously at the moon, sightings of what appeared to be 'Slenderman' that most 21st Century of apparitions [*], and balls of plasma-like light hovering above fields and careering in slow motion down the country lanes. There were lights in the sky, and - and as he said this, one could see him moving towards a metaphorical climax…

"You'll never guess"…

But I pre-empted him.

"A gang of naked girls, stepping out of the shadows to mutilate and attack isolated farmhouses?" I said in triumph…

But reality (as it so often does) took the wind out of my sails.

* See p.206

"No" he said, confused. "Whatever made you say that? I won't tell you if you are not going to take these things seriously". I apologised, and eventually persuaded him to continue.

"It seems that we are not the only people to be interested in these events. Unmarked black military helicopters have been seen in the sky circling the sites where these apparitions have been observed".

I was underwhelmed at this news, but didn't say so, as I had already upset Clive enough for one morning. But there are far more helicopters in the sky over our part of North Devon than one might otherwise have imagined. There is the Air Ambulance, the Naval ones from RNAS Culdrose which hosts fourteen different rotary winged squadrons and is the biggest helicopter base in Europe, the Air-Sea rescue helicopters which since April 2017 operate from 10 strategically located bases across the UK. The bases are positioned close to SAR hotspots so that Bristow's resources can be brought to bear as quickly and efficiently as possible and the nearest to us is just down the A39 at Newquay. There are helicopters which come and go from the GCHQ at Morwenstow about their own arcane business, there are scheduled passenger flights to Minehead, and even the South West Power operate five bright yellow choppers from their base in Bristol.

So there are no end of helicopters in the skies over North Devon, and - in my far from limited experience - I know that there is a whole subsection of society (most of whom are friends of Clive's) - who only have to *see* a helicopter up in the sky to start jabbering on about military black ops, when in fact the aforementioned whirlybird is only silhouetted against the sky, and not black at all.

My conversation with Clive petered out soon after that, and he rung off, still slightly indignant that I had not jumped in the air with joy at his information. And I sat down to try and process it all before resuming my conversation with Danny Miles.

I was not particularly impressed with Clive's insinuation that the woodlands outside Bradworthy were somehow some sort of temporary window area, because - in my experience - most things described as 'Window Areas' are nothing of the sort.

My mate Theo Paijmans describes how John Keel first came up with the concept of 'Window Areas':

> "In his *Strange Creatures From Time And Space*, John Keel writes about "window areas": "We have a theory. It is not very scientific but it is based upon the known facts. These creatures and strange events tend to recur in the

same areas year after year, even century after century..." but there his theorizing did not stop. If there's one important evolution in his oeuvre, it is his breaking away from the – at that time – predominant ETH explanation for the UFO phenomenon. This theory permeates his books like UFOs: Operation Trojan Horse, Our Haunted Planet, and The Eighth Tower, this last title the least known of his tremendously influential titles, but the most comprehensive in regards to his theory on the "Ultraterrestrials," and the intelligences or intelligence that inhabits the Superspectrum, all of which can be compared more or less to Charles Fort's musings on the Supersargasso Sea encircling the earth.

That Keel had a hard time to promote his theories and to voice them inside the ufological communities, is demonstrated by the following newspaper account published two years after his Strange Creatures From Time And Space was published. While never having met Keel, I only talked over the long distance telephone a couple of times with him, I can imagine that he somehow would have enjoyed the protests."

I hate to disagree either with Theo or with the eminent Mr Keel, but over the years when I have investigated so-called 'Window Areas' I have found that there is actually a background level of weirdness that occurs across the whole country, and that to slightly misquote my old friend Tony Shiels, the idea of normalness is rather over-rated. So, I have become very wary of stories about places where there is a higher level of weirdness than one would normally expect.

The story of the weird lights in the sky, however, was something else completely.

I am probably best known for a book first published back in 1997 – *The Owlman and Others.*

It tells the story of a series of sightings of a grotesque apparition of a feathered birdman seen in the vicinity of Mawnan Old Church, near Falmouth in Cornwall.

But it was only when I started researching the subject in depth over twenty years ago, that I was amazed to find something very similar from two letters published in the *Western Morning News* of the 16th and 19th February 1932:

WILL O'THE WISP?

Sir,

A few nights ago another man and I were, one dark November night at about eleven o'clock, on a hillside near the river Torridge far from any road, footpath or house. We were long netting rabbits. Between us and the river lays a stretch ofmarshy ground, perhaps one hundred yards wide. On the other side of the river the ground rose abruptly covered in timber. Suddenly we saw quite near us apparently about fifty feet above the marsh, an oblong object floating in the air. I cannot describe it better than saying that it looked like a conglomeration of very dim stars. It appeared to be about three feet by two feet in size and was clearly outlined against the dark background of the opposite hillside. It sailed about with a sort of circular motion, something like a swallow hawking over a pond.

For five minutes or so we watched it as it swept around in ever-widening circles; finally it sailed off up the river and we saw it no more. I have sent this letter, before forwarding it to you, to the man who was with me at the time, and he corroborates all that I have said.

F.W.H.
North Devon

The Headline refers to the country name for 'marsh gas', an incandescent form of methane that rises from rotting vegetation. Marsh Gas is also known as 'Jack O'Lantern', hence the opening words of the next letter which appeared four days later, and which again I quote verbatim:

ONLY A WHITE OWL?
Sir, '

'Jack' does not dance fifty feet above the ground. You will not see him on a dark November night; neither does he move with a circular motion. As a youth I was lucky to see a superb display over some bogland on our common. This land has since been reclaimed and cultivated. What 'F.W.H' and his companion saw was a white owl.

E.E.Rudd,
Torrington

Although I agree with Mr Rudd that what F.W.H saw could not have been marsh gas, it could not have been a white owl either. I have yet to meet any species of bird that is rectangular, two feet by three feet, and consists of a 'conglomeration of dim stars'. So what was it? And has it ever been seen since?

I have never been able to uncover any cases. That is, until now, because what Clive described his friend seeing seemed pretty much like it. But in a cone shape? That was pretty damn familiar as well, and the more I thought, the more disturbing I found the whole episode to be.

LVXXIX

And it was only after I put down the telephone, breathed a big sigh of relief, and tried to have a brief decompress before going back to my interrupted conversation with Danny that I realised that I had completely forgotten to ask Clive what all his perturbation about Psychohistory had all been in aid of. The fact that it had all been something to do with the appalling Sean and Blossom and their UFO Wehrwölfe Union, was disturbing enough, and I suspected that it was something to do with the UFO Community's perennial obsession with 'mind control' which has been in place ever since the first rumours about MKUltra began to proliferate in the early 1970s.

I have always thought that the whole concept of MKUltra lodged itself so deeply in the collective psyche of the UFO research community because of its similarity to the name of the (quite possibly fictional) Majestic 12, but then I am a self-confessed and card card carrying cynic.

For those of you not aware MK Ultra is the code name given to a program of experiments on human subjects, at times illegal, designed and undertaken by the United States Central Intelligence Agency, and carried out secretly over a period of nearly a quarter of a century.

These experiments were intended to identify and develop drugs and procedures to be used in interrogations and torture in order to weaken the individual to force confessions through mind control. Organized through the Scientific Intelligence Division of the CIA, the project coordinated with the Special Operations Division of the U.S. Army's Chemical Corps. The operation began in the early 1950s, was officially sanctioned in 1953, was reduced in scope in 1964, further curtailed in 1967, and officially halted in 1973, although there are - not unsurprisingly - claims that the experiments have continued to the present day, and the whole farrago of rumours, claims and counter-claims has embraced such subjects as Remote Viewing, Psychic Assassinations and all sorts of other parapsychological horseshit.

MKUltra used numerous methods to manipulate people's mental states and alter brain functions, including the surreptitious administration of drugs (especially LSD) and other chemicals, hypnosis, sensory deprivation, isolation and verbal abuse, as well as other forms of psychological torture. I extracted the bare bones of the last few paragraphs from various online sources, but although I have looked hard, I can find no evidence, or even claims, that the MKUltra team were somehow investigating psychohistory, I would not be even slightly surprised to find that they had done so. So, reading between the lines of all this, I reached the conclusion that Sean and Blossom were probably claiming that there was a tiny cadre deep inside the secret government who were performing experiments, such as those described in Asimov's *Second Foundation* in order to influence future events of history.

I wrote about them in passing earlier, and I strongly doubt whether there is anyone reading this book who is *not* aware of the 'Foundation' series of science fiction books by the late Isaac Asimov, but although still immensely popular, the books have slightly declined in popularity over the past few decades, so I suppose a brief recap may be in order. Over, once again, to those jolly nice fellows at Wikipedia:

"The premise of the series is that the mathematician Hari Seldon spent his life developing a branch of mathematics known as psychohistory, a concept of mathematical sociology. Using the laws of mass action, it can predict the future, but only on a large scale. Seldon foresees the imminent fall of the Galactic Empire, which encompasses the entire Milky Way, and a dark age lasting 30,000 years before a second great empire arises. Seldon's calculations also show there is a way to limit this interregnum to just one thousand years. To ensure the more favourable outcome and reduce human misery during the intervening period, Seldon creates a foundation of talented artisans and engineers at the extreme end of the galaxy, ostensibly to preserve and expand on humanity's collective knowledge, and thus become the foundation for a new galactic empire, but actually to place a society in a way shown by his calculations to bring around the desired outcome (the Seldon Plan). He also establishes a "second foundation" of psychohistorians to build on his work and to keep the better known "first" foundation on its intended course."

The Second Foundation is made up of psychologists and people with psychic and parapsychological powers who use their arcane abilities to make tiny adjustments to the behaviours of individual people, in order - via the butterfly effect - to effect the course of history. Although, over the years, I have met people who claim to have various psychic powers, and - indeed – one of my ex-girlfriends not only claimed to be a Remote Viewer but even claimed that she had the power to affect a long range assassination just by the use of her mind. She backed up these outrageous claims by utilising something that she called 'Binaural Beat Machine', which she claimed had been banned by most Western governments. I never did understand why she would enthusiastically demonstrate this machine, and what relevance it had to psychic anything. I was vaguely reminded of the scene near the end of Russell Hoban's *Turtle*

Diary when the protagonist went to visit a therapist, who had a machine by which his clients could regulate their "alpha and beta rhythms" and measure their progress.

A brief look on eBay shows that – far from being 'impossible to find' – there are all sorts of binaural things on the market, including a machine which appears to be a beat generator, endorsed by none other than Dr Dre [*]. But I am digressing slightly.

I have always thought that whilst the Second Foundation is a remarkable idea for a classic series of science fiction books, it was a concept purely to be found in the worlds of fiction, and that – attractive an idea as it is – it is unlikely to be found anywhere else.

So, taking a deep breath, I went into the next room to find Danny. The room was empty, save for a smattering of dogs and cats, a pair of spur thighed tortoises and my elderly mother in law. I asked Mum whether she knew where Danny was.

"Oh! He left about ten minutes ago," she said to me in tones of distress. "But he left this package for you, dear"

LVXXX

And so I took the package, which turned out to be wrapped in a Sainsbury's carrier bag held in place with an elastic band, and went out into the kitchen to see if there was any sign of Danny. I love my Mother-in-law very much, and I promise that this is not hyperbole. I was not over fond of my first Mother-in-law and I believe that the feeling was reciprocated.

But I am not naive enough to pretend that her faculties are all that they once were. And she was quite capable of telling me that Danny had left, when in fact he was sitting in the kitchen making himself a cup of tea, and having a long conversation with Corinna's pet crow. So I went into the kitchen, but not altogether to my surprise, there was nobody there. Grabbing my walking stick, I wobbled to the front gate, making sure I didn't slip up on the oilslick-like areas of slimy decayed leaves, which are the bane are anybody like me every winter. Although I have grab rails, and

[*] Andre Romelle Young: (born February 18, 1965), better known by his stage name Dr. Dre, is an American rapper, record producer and entrepreneur. He is the founder and CEO of Aftermath Entertainment and Beats Electronics, and was previously co-owner of Death Row Records. He has produced albums for and overseen the careers of many rappers, including 2Pac, The D.O.C., Snoop Dogg, Eminem, Xzibit, Knoc-turn'al, 50 Cent, The Game, and Kendrick Lamar. He is credited as a key figure in the crafting and popularization of West Coast G-funk, a rap style characterized as synthesizer-based with slow, heavy beats. As of 2017, he is the third richest figure in hip hop, with a net worth

Graham does his best to keep the paths clear, they are still a death trap for somebody who finds walking difficult.

I got to the gate, opened it and put my head around the corner. Danny has always parked his car on a bit of ground owned by one of my less amenable neighbours, and despite everything I have said to him over the years, he has never heeded my instructions one iota. But on this occasion, the car was missing, and so, I concluded – regretfully – that mother had been correct, and that he had gone. So, I negotiated the passage back into my office, wincing at the piles of literary flotsam and jetsam, which were stacked up everywhere. As I reached my chair, and lowered myself down with a sigh of relief, the sky turned steel grey, and one of the first of many hailstorms of the winter clattered down upon the tiled roof.

It was only then that I undid the parcel, and I was shocked by what I found there. Inside a plastic ice-cream box full of grease, were two WWII-era service revolvers and in another box, also packed with axle grease, was what looked like somewhere between a hundred and two hundred rounds of ammunition. There was also a bag of white crystals, and a bag of brown powder. I was sure that I already knew what the white crystals were, but I stuck my tongue out onto the brown powder and the numb feeling which spread through my mouth confirmed my worst fears. But finally, there was a letter.

"Dear Jon,

I am sorry that I couldn't wait for you to finish talking to that bloke from Minehead, but I needed to get back to Basil. I am going to spend the winter there, and I think we should be relatively safe because – as you know – Baz has a few 'friends' amongst the folk who live in the marsh.

I'm sorry if what I told you this morning worried you. It was not meant to, but something big is coming, and I only have a sketchy idea of what it's all about. You will, I think, be safe until the spring time because all the people of the forest sleep during the winter. Or at least, that is what I've been told.

You may well see me in the spring, it depends how much of a coward I am. And although I'm not as much of a coward as I used to be, I truly hope that Baz can do some hocus pocus or other, which means I never have to come back. But I think we both know that's not going to happen.

I hope the little early Christmas presents I've enclosed here will be of some use to you. I certainly think you are more likely to use them than I will.

Love, Danny."

This was a turn up for the books. What had started off as a perfectly ordinary day had turned into another bout of the sort of psychodrama that Danny Miles had left in his wake in all the decades that I had known him. There is a hymn about various saints travelling through Heaven, leaving trails of glory. Well, Danny travelled through the earthly realms, leaving trails of chaos in his wake.

Carefully wrapping up my unwanted gifts, I made my way unsteadily upstairs, and on the landing I opened the airing cupboard. Ever since Panne took up residence there, I had more than a sneaking suspicion that anything I put in there would be safe from prying eyes. And I am paranoid enough not to want guns and class A chemicals to be where anyone could find them. I had no idea what I would do with the latter, but in the light of what I had learned over the previous couple of months, and even more than what I had come to *suspect*, I was more pleased than you might suspect to finally have some ordinance of my own.

On the landing, there is a little church-like window that I have wanted to replace with stained glass any time this past half-century. The fact that it has taken so long to do anything about it means that I probably won't. However, you can look out of that window and see the full extent of the little patch of England of which I am the temporary curator.

It was cold, grey and wet. Even the youngest of the cats, who normally would be scampering around the garden with an outburst of feline glee was sat inside feeling sorry for itself. Both the dogs were there with her, and I strongly suspected that Panne (who wasn't in her cupboard) was somewhere downstairs under a blanket curled up cozily with one of the domestic animals.

Outside, the hailstorm had finished but there were still weird little patches of hail on the uneven surface of the lawn. It was shaping up to be a wet winter, and – unfortunately – there were various bits of carunculation where Prudence had run and skidded, or Archie had succumbed to his terrier nature and started digging a hole before deciding that he was too lazy. These little indentations were full of grubby white hailstones, and from my vantage point on the landing, my lovely garden looked something like the aftermath of a Christmas Card showing the Battle of the Somme. But it was my piece of England, by inheritance, by conquest and by purchase, and –

yes – I had done the Oak, Ash and thorn thing as described by Rudyard K who did write exceedingly good stories (and this particular one being found in the opening story of *Puck of Pook's Hill* [*]). Tony Shiels once told me that Kipling's mythical England had about as much substance as Yeats' Celtic Twilight, but I still believed in the former as much as I suspect Tony believes in the latter, and it had become centre stage in my own peculiarly skewed reality tunnel.

A small flock of long tailed tits landed in the wigelia bush outside the office door. My Grandmother had brought it with her when she moved in to live with us in 1975, and my Father had always kept it tightly pruned. I love the rich velvet red of the flowers which bloom from Midsummer right into the autumn, and have let it grow wild, training it over the path to make a ragged archway, alive with the humming of insects. In the winter it is naught but bare branches and twigs, but there must have been enough creepy-crawlies there to attract the attention of this jabbering band of tiny passerine hunter-gatherers.

I watched them for a few minutes, but – without a warning – they flew off for pastures new, and I decided to go downstairs and see if I could persuade Mother to make a cup of tea, while I went back to my day's writing that had been so rudely interrupted.

There was a new cloud on the horizon, but, if Danny was to be believed, and on this

---

[*] *Puck of Pook's Hill* is a fantasy book by Rudyard Kipling, published in 1906, containing a series of short stories set in different periods of English history. It can count both as historical fantasy – since some of the stories told of the past have clear magical elements, and as contemporary fantasy – since it depicts a magical being active and practising his magic in the England of the early 1900s when the book was written.

The stories are all narrated to two children living near Burwash, in the area of Kipling's own house Bateman's, by people magically plucked out of history by the elf Puck, or told by Puck himself. (Puck, who refers to himself as "the oldest Old Thing in England", is better known as a character in William Shakespeare's play *A Midsummer Night's Dream*.) The genres of particular stories range from authentic historical novella (*A Centurion of the Thirtieth, On the Great Wall*) to children's fantasy (Dymchurch Flit). Each story is bracketed by a poem which relates in some manner to the theme or subject of the story.

Donald Mackenzie, who wrote the introduction for the Oxford World's Classics edition of *Puck of Pook's Hill* in 1987, has described this book as an example of archaeological imagination that, in fragments, delivers a look at the history of England, climaxing with the signing of Magna Carta.

Of all the trees that grow so fair,
Old Engerland to adorn,
Greater are none beneath the Sun,
Than Oak and Ash and Thorn.
Sing Oak and Ash and Thorn, good Sirs
(All of a Midsummer's morn)!
Surely we sing of no little thing,
In Oak and Ash and Thorn!

occasion I thought that he could, I would have nothing to worry about until the following Spring, and – I suspected – I was probably safe until Bealtaine, when the whole cycle would begin again.

I am not a hero, I never wanted to be a hero, and I have never had any intention of being a hero. I don't like heroes and the inevitable posturing that accompanies them. All I want to do is to be left alone to get on with what remains of my life in peace and quiet. So why don't you all fuck off?

But I love my family, and I love my little slice of England, and I love the people, creatures and 'other' folk who choose to share it with me. And like Nelson, I knew that England would expect me to do my duty.

But that was going to be at least five months away, and a lot can happen in five months.

Unaccountably cheered by this thought I limped towards the office wondering if the sun was over the yardarm yet, and whether that meant I could have a little dash of milk from the Kentucky cow in my tea.

結束

Jiéshù

THE WORLD'S WEIRDEST PUBLISHING COMPANY

HOW TO START A PUBLISHING EMPIRE

Unlike most mainstream publishers, we have a non-commercial remit, and our mission statement claims that "we publish books because they deserve to be published, not because we think that we can make money out of them". Our motto is the Latin Tag *Pro bona causa facimus* (we do it for good reason), a slogan taken from a children's book *The Case of the Silver Egg* by the late Desmond Skirrow.

WIKIPEDIA: "The first book published was in 1988. *Take this Brother may it Serve you Well* was a guide to Beatles bootlegs by Jonathan Downes. It sold quite well, but was hampered by very poor production values, being photocopied, and held together by a plastic clip binder.

In 1988 A5 clip binders were hard to get hold of, so the publishers took A4 binders and cut them in half with a hacksaw. It now reaches surprisingly high prices second hand.

The production quality improved slightly over the years, and after 1999 all the books produced were ringbound with laminated colour covers. In 2004, however, they signed an agreement with Lightning Source, and all books are now produced perfect bound, with full colour covers."

Until 2010 all our books, the majority of which are/were on the subject of mystery animals and allied disciplines, were published by `CFZ Press`, the publishing arm of the Centre for Fortean Zoology (CFZ), and we urged our readers and followers to draw a discreet veil over the books that we published that were completely off topic to the CFZ.

However, in 2010 we decided that enough was enough and launched a second imprint, `Fortean Words` which aims to cover a wide range of non animal-related esoteric subjects. Other imprints will be launched as and when we feel like it, however the basic ethos of the company remains the same: Our job is to publish books and magazines that we feel are worth publishing, whether or not they are going to sell. Money is, after all - as my dear old Mama once told me - a rather vulgar subject, and she would be rolling in her grave if she thought that her eldest son was somehow in `trade`.

Luckily, so far our tastes have turned out not to be that rarified after all, and we have sold far more books than anyone ever thought that we would, so there is a moral in there somewhere...

Jon Downes,
Woolsery, North Devon
July 2010

CFZ PRESS

CFZ Press is our flagship imprint, featuring a wide range of intelligently written and lavishly illustrated books on cryptozoology and the quirkier aspects of Natural History.

CFZ Classics is a new venture for us. There are many seminal works that are either unavailable today, or not available with the production values which we would like to see. So, following the old adage that if you want to get something done do it yourself, this is exactly what we have done.

Desiderius Erasmus Roterodamus (b. October 18th 1466, d. July 2nd 1536) said: "When I have a little money, I buy books; and if I have any left, I buy food and clothes," and we are much the same. Only, we are in the lucky position of being able to share our books with the wider world. CFZ Classics is a conduit through which we cannot just re-issue titles which we feel still have much to offer the cryptozoological and Fortean research communities of the 21st Century, but we are adding footnotes, supplementary essays, and other material where we deem it appropriate.

http://www.cfzpublishing.co.uk/

Fortean Words is a new venture for us. The F in CFZ stands for "Fortean", after the pioneering researcher into anomalous phenomena, Charles Fort. Our Fortean Words imprint covers a whole spectrum of arcane subjects from UFOs and the paranormal to folklore and urban legends. Our authors include such Fortean luminaries as Nick Redfern, Andy Roberts, and Paul Screeton. . New authors tackling new subjects will always be encouraged, and we hope that our books will continue to be as ground-breaking and popular as ever.

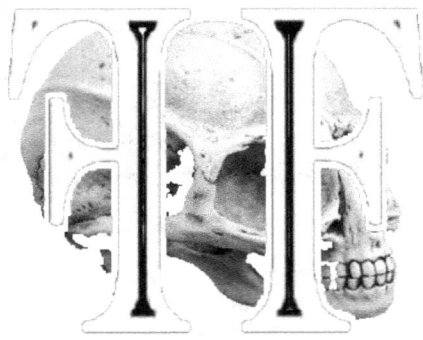

Just before Christmas 2011, we launched our third imprint, this time dedicated to - let's see if you guessed it from the title - fictional books with a Fortean or cryptozoological theme. We have published a few fictional books in the past, but now think that because of our rising reputation as publishers of quality Forteana, that a dedicated fiction imprint was the order of the day.

http://www.cfzpublishing.co.uk/

www.ingramcontent.com/pod-product-compliance
Lightning Source LLC
Chambersburg PA
CBHW071253250626
47159CB00004B/1166